FINDING THE EDGE

DEBRA WEBB

UNDERCOVER SCOUT

JENNA KERNAN

MIX
Paper from
responsible sources
FSC
FSC C007454

This book is produced from independently certified FSC™
paper to ensure responsible forest management.

For more information visit www.harpercollins.co.uk/green

Printed and bound in Spain
by CPI, Barcelona

MILLS & BOON

First Published in Great Britain 2018
by Mills & Boon, an imprint of HarperCollins*Publishers*
1 London Bridge Street, London, SE1 9GF

Finding The Edge © 2018 Debra Webb
Undercover Scout © 2018 Jeannette H. Monaco

ISBN: 978-0-263-26572-9

39-0518

FINDING THE EDGE

DEBRA WEBB

This book is dedicated to the outstanding men and women of the Chicago Police Department. Thanks for all you do!

Chapter One

"We're going to need more gurneys!" Dr. Marissa Frasier shouted.

Someone amid the fray yelled that more gurneys were coming. They had nine new victims besides the dozen already in the ER. All bleeding, some worse than others. All had been shot and all were armed. And every damned one sported white T-shirts with an odd circle inside a circle in the center and wore black beanie caps. Their shouted threats echoed like thunder, inciting fear. Thank God most of the other patients had been checked in and were either already triaged and stable or had nonlife-threatening emergencies.

Eva Bowman might have considered it just another crazy Friday night looming toward a code black if not for the three cars that had screeched into the ER entrance with those new victims. Several armed men had barged in, waving automatic guns and demanding help for their friends. The three apparently in charge had forced everyone in the waiting room onto the floor and sent the entire ER staff, including the reception-

ist and the two registration specialists, outside to help
their friends.

In all the commotion, Eva hoped someone had been
able to alert the police. One of the security guards had
been shot. He and the other guard had been restrained
and left on the floor in the waiting room, blood pooling around the injured man. One of the gunmen stood
over the small crowd, his scowl shifting from one to
the other as if daring someone to give him a reason to
start shooting. Eva wished she was more knowledgeable about the tattoos and colors worn by the different gangs in the Chicago area, though she couldn't
readily see how knowing would help at the moment.
For now, she did what she was told and prayed help
would arrive soon.

Eva pushed an occupied gurney through the double doors, leaving the lobby behind. All the treatment
rooms were full so she found a spot in the corridor
and parked. She ripped open the shirt of her patient.
Male. Mid to late twenties. Hispanic. He was sweaty
and breathing hard. He'd lost some blood from the
bullet wound on his left side. Lucky for him the bullet
appeared to have exited without much fanfare. Still,
he was no doubt in serious pain. Whatever his pain
level, he clutched his weapon and continued to bellow
arrogantly at his friends as if a shot to the gut was an
everyday occurrence. From what little she recalled of
high school Spanish, he seemed to be claiming vic-
tory over whatever battle had occurred. If the group of
wounded men who had been scattered on the asphalt
in front of the ER doors were the winners, she hated
to think what condition the losers were in. Didn't take

much of a stretch to imagine they were in all probability dead.

An experienced registered nurse, Eva performed a quick assessment of her patient's vitals. Respiration and pulse were rapid. Though his skin was warm and moist, his color remained good. From all indications he was not critical, but there could be underlying issues she could not assess. He would need an ultrasound to ensure no organs were damaged, and the wound would need to be cleaned and sutured.

"Sir, can you tell me your name?"

The man stared at her as if she'd asked him to hand over his weapon. She decided to move on to her next question. "On a scale of one to ten, ten being the worst you've ever suffered, can you tell me how much pain you're in?"

"Cero."

She sincerely doubted that was the case but if he wanted to play the tough guy, that was fine by her.

Over the next few minutes her patient as well as the others were sorted according to their needs and ushered on to the next level of care. Some were taken straight to operating rooms while others went on to imaging for additional assessment. One nurse and a doctor had been allowed to treat the patients in the lobby. Eva remained in the ER helping to attend to those who had arrived and were triaged and assigned treatment rooms before the gunmen arrived and took over. The armed patients who didn't require further care were mostly loitering around the corridor waiting for the return of their friends who'd been sent off to imaging or to the OR. What they didn't seem to realize was that those friends wouldn't be coming back to join them tonight.

One of the other nurses had whispered to Eva that Dr. Frasier had initiated the emergency assistance protocol. The police had been made aware that the ER was under siege or under duress of some sort and required law enforcement intervention.

Once before she had found herself in a similar situation. Time was necessary for the police to arrive and assess the situation, then they would send in SWAT to contain the problem. She hoped no one else was hurt during the neutralization and containment of the gunmen. So far she had hidden three weapons. Two from patients who'd been rushed to the OR and one from the guy not a dozen feet away who claimed he was in zero pain. His pain had apparently been so nonexistent that he hadn't realized his fingers had loosened on the 9 mm he'd been waving around when he first arrived.

Dr. Frasier noticed what Eva was up to and gave her a look of appreciation. No matter that she had removed and hidden three weapons—there were still six armed victims as well as the three armed and uninjured men who had taken over the ER. Thankfully, the thug who appeared to be the boss had allowed the injured guard to be treated for the bullet he'd taken. The guard's injury was not life threatening. He and his partner for the night were now both locked in the supply room.

Eva glanced at her watch. Approximately ten seemingly endless minutes had elapsed since the police were notified of their situation via the emergency protocol. SWAT would be rolling in soon. She didn't have to look outside to know that cops would have already taken crucial positions in the parking area.

All handheld radios and cell phones had been confiscated and tossed into a trash can—except for Eva's. The only reason the pat down conducted by the shortest of the three jerks who'd taken over the ER hadn't revealed her cell phone was because she didn't carry it in her pocket or in an armband. Eva kept hers in an ankle band made just for cell phones. Her last boyfriend had been an undercover cop and he'd shown her all sorts of ways to hide weapons and phones. If she'd been smart she would have carried a stun gun strapped to her other ankle the way he suggested.

They might still be together if he had been able to separate his work from his personal life. It was one thing to pretend to be someone else to catch the bad guys but entirely another to take on a separate persona for the purposes of cheating on your girlfriend.

Apparently the guys playing king of the ER weren't savvy enough to be aware that, like gun manufacturers, cell phone manufacturers thought of everything when it came to keeping phones close to users. Whatever the case, Eva was grateful her phone was still right where it was supposed to be. All she needed was an opportunity to use it. Knowing the situation inside would be incredibly useful for the police, particularly in determining how they made their grand entrance.

Her cell phone had vibrated about twenty times. Probably her sister, Lena. An investigative journalist at a local television station, Lena had no doubt heard about the trouble at the Edge. The best journalists had good contacts within Chicago PD and the Edge always had news. A Level I Trauma test unit challenging the approach to emergency medicine, the Edge was the only one of its kind in the nation.

Eva glanced toward the rear of the emergency department and the door that led into the main corridor that flowed into imaging and the surgery suite, winging off to the Behavioral Unit on the left and Administration to the right. Then she surveyed the ongoing activity between her and the double doors that opened into the lobby area. The man in charge and his cohorts were in deep conversation with the three other patients who hadn't been moved on to another level of care. Dr. Frasier was suturing the wound of one while Dr. Reagan was doing the same with another. Kim Levy, a nurse and Eva's friend, was bandaging the third patient's closed wound.

Eva eased back a step and then another. Four more steps and she would be through the door and into the corridor beyond the emergency department. Slow, deep breaths. No sudden moves. Another step, then another, and she was out the door.

Eva whirled away from the softly closing door and ran to the ladies' room. She couldn't lock the door since it didn't have one—no one wanted a patient to lock him or herself in the bathroom. Inside there were, however, two stalls with slide locks.

She slipped into the second one and snapped the stall latch into place, then sat on the closed toilet lid and pulled her knees to her chest so no one coming in would see her feet. She tugged her cell phone from its holster at her ankle and saw four missed calls and six text messages from her sister. She didn't dare make a voice call so she sent a text to her sister and asked her to update the police on the situation inside the ER.

Three uninjured gunmen. Four injured with guns, five others currently unarmed and in imaging or an OR. One injured guard. Both guards incapacitated.

A few seconds later, Lena told her to stay calm and to keep a low profile. Help was already on-site. Daring to relax the tiniest bit, Eva slid the phone back into its holster.

All she had to do was stay calm. Easy enough. She stepped off the seat.

The sound of the door opening sent fear exploding in her veins. She flushed the toilet, took a breath and exited the stall.

The man she thought to be in charge waited for her. He leaned against the door, the weapon in his hand lying flat against his chest. She decided that all the intruders were under thirty. This one looked to be early twenties. Though he appeared younger than the others, he was clearly the boss.

Eva steadied herself. "This is the ladies' room." She stared at him. "*Baño femenino.*"

He laughed. "*Si.*"

Oh crap. She squared her shoulders and took a step toward the door...toward him. "I need to be back out there helping your friends."

He shook his head. "There is plenty help already."

Eva swallowed back the scream mushrooming in her throat. There was no one to hear. This jerk was slightly taller than her five-seven. He was heavier and more muscled than her for sure, and a hell of a lot meaner. But she might be able to take him...*if not for the gun.*

As if he'd read her mind, he smiled and pointed the muzzle at her head. "On your knees, bitch."

The shaking started so deep inside her that she wondered how she remained standing, yet somehow she did. "The police are coming." The words shook, too, but she couldn't keep her voice steady if her life depended on it. Right now the ability to continue breathing might very well depend on her next word or move. "If you're smart, you'll tell your friends and you'll run. *Now*, while you still can."

He nodded, that nasty grin still stretched across his lips. "Yes," he agreed, the word sounding more like *des* with his thick accent.

Since he made no move to rush to his friends and warn them, her advice had clearly fallen on deaf ears. "So you don't care if you get caught?" She shrugged. "You want to go to prison? Then *you* can be somebody's bitch."

He charged toward her, pinned her to the counter of the row of sinks behind her. Of their own volition, her hands shot up in surrender. "Just trying to help you out. You...you don't want the police to show up and find you distracted. If you go now, they won't catch you."

She hoped like hell the guy had enough self-preservation instinct to realize she had a valid point.

"You talk a lot for a dead girl," he growled as he jammed the muzzle against her temple now. "You give me some of *that*—" he slid his free hand down her belly, forcing it between her thighs "—with no trouble and I'll be gone so fast you'll still be begging for more."

Trapped between him and the counter with his damned gun pointed at her brain, she couldn't move, didn't dare scream. Her heart flailed against her sternum. *Stay calm. Your fear makes him stronger.*

"Okay, okay." This close she smelled the whiskey on his breath, could fully comprehend just how inebriated he was. Bleary eyes. Slurred speech. No wonder he wasn't worried about the police. She drew in a shaky breath. *Play along until you come up with a better plan.* "What do you want?"

He laughed. "Suck me."

She nodded as she slowly lowered her hands. The muzzle bored into her skull a little harder as she reached for his fly. He was fully erect, bulging against his jeans. Bile rose in her throat as she unfastened the button, then lowered the zipper. She told herself over and over she had no choice as she reached into his open fly. He didn't have on any underwear so he was right there. She closed the fingers of her right hand around him while somehow managing to restrain the shudder of revulsion.

In hopes of putting off what he really wanted, her hand started to move. He made a satisfied sound, his eyes partially closing. "Oh, yeah, that's a good start."

She worked her hand back and forth faster and faster, felt his body tense. Watched his eyes drift completely shut.

Now or never.

Eva ducked her head, jammed her left shoulder into his gut and pushed with every ounce of her body weight. At the same time, she released his penis and grabbed his testicles and twisted as hard as she could.

He screamed.

The weapon discharged.

The mirror over the sinks shattered.

He grabbed at her; she twisted her upper body out of reach, spinning them both around. The muzzle stabbed at her chest; she leaned away from the gun and rammed into him even harder. Another shot exploded into the air as they both went down. His head hit the counter, making a solid *thump* as his neck twisted sharply. They crashed to the cold tile floor. The air grunted out of her lungs. Eva was still squeezing his balls when she realized he was no longer moving.

Disentangling herself from him, she scooted a few feet away. His eyes blinked, once, twice…he mumbled something she couldn't comprehend.

Eva scrambled to her feet and backed toward the door. She should reach for his weapon…she should grab it and run…

The door burst inward, almost knocking her on top of the man on the floor.

Another of the gunmen stared first at her and then at the man on the floor whose fly was flared open with his erect penis poked out.

Before Eva could speak the man grabbed her by the hair with his left hand and the gun in his right shoved into her face. "What did you do to him?"

Shaking so hard now she could hardly speak, she somehow managed to say, "He tried to rape me, so I pushed him away and he fell…he hit his head."

The man shoved her to the floor. She landed on her knees. "Help him," he snarled.

Eva moved closer to her attacker. His eyes were open but he didn't look at her. When she touched his neck to measure his pulse he mumbled but his words were unintelligible. Pulse was rapid. His body abruptly tensed. Seizure. *Damn.*

"We need to get him into the ER now." She pushed to her feet. "He may have a serious head injury."

The man grabbed her by the hair once more and jerked her face to his. "Do you know what you've done?"

A new stab of terror sank deep into her chest. "He attacked me. I was trying—"

"If he dies," he snarled, the muzzle boring into her cheek, "*you* die."

Suddenly the gun went upward. His arm twisted violently. A *pop* echoed in the room. Not a gunshot... a bone...

The man howled in agony. His body was hurled toward the floor. He landed on the unforgiving tile next to his friend.

Eva wheeled around, readied to scream but swallowed back the sound as she recognized Dr. Devon Pierce, the Edge creator and administrator.

"Check the corridor," he ordered. "If it's clear, go to my office and hide. I've got this." The man on the floor scrambled to get up and Pierce kicked him hard in the gut.

When Eva hesitated, he snarled, "Go!"

She eased the bathroom door open and checked the corridor. Clear. She slipped out of the room, the door closed behind her, cutting of the grunts and awful keening inside. Her first instinct was to return to the ER to see if her help was needed there, but Dr. Pierce had told her to hide in his office. She didn't know what he was doing here but she assumed he was aware somehow of all that had happened. Perhaps the emergency protocol automatically notified him or maybe he had been in his office working late. Bottom line, he was the boss.

She hurried along the corridor, took a right into another side hall past the storeroom and the file rooms. Fear pounded in her veins as she moved into the atrium. Pierce's office was beyond the main lobby. She held her breath as she hurried through an open area. When she reached his secretary's office and the small, private lobby she dared to breathe, then she closed herself in his office. The desk lamp was on. Apparently Pierce had been in his office working. She reached for her cell.

Before she could put through a call to her sister, she heard rustling outside the door. The roar of her own blood deafening in her ears, Eva glanced quickly around the room. She had to hide. Fast!

With no other option she ducked under his desk, squeezed as far beneath it as she could, folding her knees up to her chin and holding herself tight and small.

A soft swoosh of air warned the door of the administrator's office had opened.

She held her breath.

The intruder—maybe Pierce, maybe a cop—moved around the room. She had no intention of coming out of hiding until she knew for certain. The sound of books sliding across shelves and frames banging against the wall clarified that the intruder was neither Pierce nor a cop. Footfalls moved closer to her position. She needed to breathe. She pressed her face to her knees and dared to draw in a small breath. Black leather shoes and gray trousers appeared behind the desk. Her eyes widened with the dread spreading inside her.

Definitely male.

The man dropped into the leather executive chair and reached for the middle drawer of the desk. His rifling through the drawer contents gave her the opportunity to breathe again. He moved on to the next drawer, the one on his right. More of that rummaging. Then he reached lower, for the final drawer on that side. She prayed he wouldn't bend down any lower because he would certainly see her.

She held her breath again. He shifted to access the drawers on the other side, and his foot came within mere centimeters of her hip. He searched through the three remaining drawers. Then he stood. Sharp movement across the blotter pad told her he was writing something. Finally, he moved away from the desk.

The door opened and then closed.

Eva counted to thirty before she dared to move. She scooted from under the desk and scanned the room. She was alone. Thank God. The books and framed awards and photos on the once neatly arranged shelves lay scattered about. Her gaze instinctively dropped to the desk.

I know what you did.

The words were scrawled on the clean expanse of white blotter paper. For ten or more seconds she couldn't move. She should go…get out of this office. Whatever that—she stared at the note—was about, she didn't want to get dragged into it. The men who had stormed the ER had all been wearing jeans or cargo pants, not dress trousers and certainly not leather loafers. *Just go!*

At the door, she eased it open and checked the administrator's private lobby. Clear. She'd almost made it out of the secretary's office when she heard hurried footfalls in the corridor. Renewed panic roared through her veins.

With nowhere else to go, she ducked under the secretary's desk.

The footfalls moved across the carpeted floor. She heard the sound of Pierce's office door opening. The man was popular tonight. Had the guy who'd written the note forgotten something?

A soft curse came from the general direction of Pierce's office.

Eva hoped SWAT was ready to storm the place. She would hate to survive a bunch of crazed thugs or gangbangers or whatever they were and be murdered by a man wearing dress trousers and black leather shoes.

"Eva!"

For a moment she couldn't breathe.

"Eva!"

Dr. Pierce. She scrambled out from under the desk. "Yes, sir. I'm here."

Fury or outrage—something on that order—colored his face. "The police are here. They'll need your statement."

Thank God. "Is everyone okay? The gunmen have been contained?"

He nodded, then frowned. "I thought you were going to hide in my office."

She shrugged and in that instant something about the expression on his face made her decide to keep what happened in his office to herself. "I heard someone coming. I freaked and hid under the secretary's desk."

"Someone came in here?"

He had to know someone had. He couldn't have missed the disarray in his office or the note on his desk.

She nodded. "I couldn't see what was happening, but I definitely heard footsteps and the door to your office opening and closing."

"You didn't get a look at who it was?"

She shook her head. Was that suspicion she heard in his voice?

When he continued to stare at her without saying more, she offered, "Is everything okay?"

"Yes." He smiled, rearranging his face into the amiable expression he usually wore. "It is now. Come with me. We should get this police business squared away so we can return to the business of healing the sick."

The walk back to the emergency department was the longest of her life. She could feel his tension in every step he took. She wanted to ask him again if everything was okay but she didn't dare stir his suspicions.

Right now all she wanted was for this night to be over.

Chapter Two

Eva hurried up the sidewalk. She glanced over her shoulder repeatedly, checked the street over and over. She hated that her behavior no doubt looked entirely paranoid, but the truth was paranoia had been her constant companion for better than forty-eight hours. Since she received the first message.

Two men had swerved to the curb on her street as she walked home from the market on Saturday afternoon. She might have kept walking except the one hanging out the passenger window called her name.

Eva! Eva Bowman! He's coming for you, la perra. You killed his hermano menor.

The man who'd tried to rape her—the one who'd fractured his skull in that damned bathroom and then died—was the younger brother of one of Chicago's most notorious gang leaders.

Just her luck.

Eva walked faster. She hadn't meant to kill anyone. She'd been fighting for her life. He'd fallen...his death was an accident. An accident that wouldn't have happened had he not been trying to rape her.

The detectives on the scene had tried to make her feel better by telling her that Diego Robles—that was the dead man's name, Diego Robles—and his gang of nearly a dozen thugs had murdered six men and two women on Friday before overtaking the ER where she worked.

Except it hadn't made her feel better. Robles had been nineteen years old. *Nineteen.* He had an older brother, Miguel, who was thirty-five and the leader of the True Disciples, an extremely violent offshoot of the Latin Disciples. The brother had passed along his message to Eva on three occasions without ever leaving a single shred of evidence she could take to the police.

The first warning had come on Saturday afternoon via the two thugs in the car. Another had come when she walked out of the corner coffee shop near her apartment building on Sunday morning. Then, last night, another man had showed up at the ER asking for her. When she'd appeared at the registration desk, he'd waited until no one was looking and leaned forward to whisper for her ears only.

You will die this week.

With that he'd given her a nod and told her to enjoy her night.

She'd reported all three incidents to the police and all they could do was tell her to be careful. No one had touched her or damaged her property. She had no proof of the threats other than her word. But last night when she'd been too afraid to go to her car alone and then too terrified to go to her own apartment, she'd understood she had to do something. She worried the only evidence to back up her fears would come in the form of someone finding her body after it was too late.

Lena had demanded, to no avail, protection from the police for Eva. Kim Levy, her friend and another nurse at the Edge, had urged her to speak to Dr. Pierce. Kim had been in the ER on Friday night. She understood how terrified Eva had every right to be. But Eva couldn't stop thinking about the way Dr. Pierce had looked at her after the strange happenings in his office. She'd decided not to discuss that odd moment with Kim or anyone else. And she had no desire to discuss her personal dilemma with her boss. Still, Kim being Kim, she had gone to Dr. Pierce and told him what was going on. He had insisted on sending Eva to the Colby Agency. Eva had heard of the Colby Agency. Who hadn't? She'd certainly never expected to need a private investigations firm. Yet, here she was. She had an appointment at two thirty. Five minutes from now.

Almost there. The Magnificent Mile was always busy, even on a Tuesday afternoon with hours to go before the evening rush of commuters headed home. She looked at each face she met…wondering when one of *them* would appear.

She walked faster, pushing against the wind that seemed to want to blow her right back to where she'd parked her car.

No turning back now.

A shiver chilled her skin. It didn't feel very much like spring today. Barely sixty degrees and overcast. Just in case it started to rain again, she'd tucked her umbrella into the beige leather bag she carried. Her pepper spray was in there, too. She carried her life around in one of two bags: a well-used brown one for fall and winter and this tawny beige one her mother had given her for spring and summer. Life was complicated enough without changing the purse she carried more than twice a year. Eva went out of her way to keep life simple. She'd had enough complications her freshman year in college. She'd made a decision all those years ago never to allow those sorts of complications ever again.

Life was better when she stuck to enjoying the simpler pleasures. Like all the gorgeous tulips still in bloom and the trees that had gone from their stark winter limbs to lush and green already.

That was the ticket. Focus on the mundane...the normal.

The deep timbre of male voices was suddenly behind her. Fear crept up her spine like a cluster of spiders and her heart swelled into her throat. Her gait wavered, causing her to nearly stumble. A group of four men moved around and ahead of her. Despite the glaring facts that they paid her absolutely no notice, were dressed in business suits and kept moving at a brisk pace, her heart refused to slide back down into her chest where it belonged. The pepper spray in her bag felt wholly inadequate.

Damn, she was a mess.

It wasn't until she spotted the wide glass front bearing the address of her destination that she was able to breathe easy again. Her hands settled on the door and, despite her best efforts, she hesitated. Calm was the necessary watchword. If she went into this meeting shaken and panicky, she might very well meet with the same reception she'd received from the two Chicago PD detectives working the investigation.

Investigation. There were several aspects of the ongoing investigation. The clash between the True Disciples and another well-known gang with the resulting multiple homicides. The taking of an entire ER hostage. And the deemed justified homicide of Diego Robles. Both detectives, their captain and the DA had told her the events that happened in that bathroom were self-defense, completely justified. She had not intended to kill anyone. She'd only been trying to get away from him. The man's death was an accidental consequence of his actions.

But dead was dead.

Calm. Collected. Not your fault.

Eva squared her shoulders and pushed through the door. A wide, gleaming metal security desk curved around the center of the enormous lobby. Enough greenery to rival a small jungle softened all the glass and glossy metal.

"Afternoon, ma'am," the security guard said as she approached the counter. "You have an appointment?"

"The Colby Agency." She drew her wallet from her bag and produced her driver's license. "Eva Bowman."

The guard checked the computer screen, scanned her license into his system, then handed the license as well as a visitor's badge to her. "The elevators are to your right. Fourteenth floor is where you're headed. Your code for the elevator is on the back of the badge. Just drop the badge off here as you leave, Ms. Bowman."

"Thank you." As she moved toward the bank of elevators, she checked the back of the badge. Eight-two-six-seven. She clipped the badge onto the lapel of her sweater and tapped the call button.

The doors opened to a vacant car. Deep breath. She stepped inside and selected floor fourteen. The keypad warned that a code was required so she entered the necessary digits. When the doors closed she stared at her reflection in the mirrored walls of the elevator interior. She'd taken care to dress professionally. The soft blush color of her pants and sweater set complemented her too-pale skin. Matching leather ballet flats were easy on the feet. Her first month as an ER nurse had taught her to appreciate good shoes made for comfort. She'd swept her blond hair into a loose bun at the nape of her neck and she'd gone easy on the makeup. Just a touch of lip gloss and a swipe of mascara.

Calm. Collected.

The car bumped to a stop and the doors slid open to another lobby. A receptionist looked up from behind an opaque glass desk and smiled. "Good morning. Welcome to the Colby Agency, Ms. Bowman."

The next five or so minutes passed in a blur. After the offer of refreshments, which she declined, another receptionist appeared and escorted her to Victoria Colby-Camp's office, a large, elegant space with a wall of windows that overlooked the city from a prestigious Michigan Avenue address.

Eva had done an internet search on Victoria and her agency, but she hadn't been adequately prepared for the sophisticated woman standing behind the beautiful mahogany desk, the wall of windows a stunning backdrop. She wore her salt-and-pepper hair in a French twist. The turquoise suit fit as if it had been tailored just for her. Probably had been. Though she was no taller than Eva, her presence was commanding. The most surprising part was how incredibly youthful and fit she looked. According to Google, Victoria Colby-Camp was nearing seventy. Eva could only hope she would look that good in another forty years.

"It's a pleasure to meet you, Eva." Victoria smiled. "Please sit. Let's take a moment to get acquainted."

"Thank you." Eva settled into one of the two champagne-colored upholstered chairs in front of Victoria's desk.

"My intern, Jamie, will be joining us shortly," Victoria said. "I've reviewed your file. You're a nurse at the Edge. Dr. Pierce and I serve on Chicago's civic committee together. The Edge is an incredible step toward elevating emergency care to the highest level. We're all very proud and duly impressed by his advances in the field."

Eva nodded. "Dr. Pierce is an amazing man. His methods are changing the landscape of emergency medicine." The Edge was his brainchild. Whether it was a heart attack, a stroke or some sort of physical injury, the Edge was where everyone wanted to end up when an emergency occurred.

"You have family in the city?"

Eva smiled. Her first of the day. "An older sister, Lena. You may know her. She's an investigative journalist at Channel 7."

Victoria nodded. "I do, indeed. Lena Bowman is a household name in the city of Chicago."

Eva nodded. "She was determined to become one for as long as I can remember."

Victoria tilted her head ever so slightly, her expression turning somber. "I've also had an opportunity to review the Chicago PD's file on what happened Friday night. It's an outright miracle no hostages were killed. You and the others at the Edge handled yourselves extraordinarily well."

Eva nodded in acknowledgment of her kind words. "Since you read the file you must know about Diego Robles's death."

"Captain Cyrus explained what happened. He's very concerned that you've been approached and threatened. Dr. Pierce is immensely concerned as well. Why don't you start at the beginning and tell me what's happening."

As much as Eva had dreaded this part, somehow Victoria made her feel relaxed and comfortable—at least as comfortable as she could be under the circumstances. Eva started with what the second man who came into the bathroom on Friday night said to her. She moved on to the ones who'd shouted at her on the street on Saturday, the confrontation on Sunday, the visit at the ER last night and then to the carful of thugs who had followed her to the parking garage three blocks from here. Thankfully, they hadn't yelled more threats at her...they'd only watched her. Their hateful eyes on her had been equally threatening.

Victoria studied Eva for a moment after she finished recounting the events of the past three days. "I have full confidence the police are watching Robles's men, but they can't watch every move each of his hundreds of followers make—not with the budget cuts they've suffered recently. You haven't been assigned a protection detail for the same reason. Until a law is broken, the police can't afford to shift the resources."

"I might be dead by then." Eva hated to say the words aloud but they were true.

"Which is why we're here. We can fill that void." Victoria folded her hands atop her desk. "Since Dr. Pierce and I are well acquainted, he asked that I assign the very best to your security and he insisted that I send the bill to him."

"What?" Eva shook her head. She couldn't have heard correctly. "I'm prepared to pay for the services I need."

Victoria held up a hand. "I'm certain you are, Eva. But Dr. Pierce feels responsible. He would like to handle this and, frankly, he can easily afford to do so. Trust me, you should take him up on his generous offer."

Eva wanted to argue, but Victoria was right. She had scratched together the retainer but she would be hard-pressed to come up with more than a week's worth of the required fees. She wanted to be upset that Dr. Pierce had been brought into the financial aspect of this arrangement but she supposed it was the right thing to do. *I know what you did.* The note someone had left on his desk blotter flickered across her mind. She had no idea what the message meant or who left it. She had wanted to ask Dr. Pierce but with all that had happened that night and then the threats, she'd forgotten. In truth, she didn't feel comfortable discussing it with him after his reaction that night. She wasn't worried that he somehow felt she was involved or aware of who went into his office, but she couldn't quite dispel the idea that he'd looked at her with doubt for just a moment.

"I suppose I can do that."

Maybe when this business with Robles was behind her she would come clean and tell Dr. Pierce she'd lied about being in his office. *God, Eva, you're such an idiot.* It would have been so much easier if she'd told the truth in the first place, but it had felt so awkward in that instant. As badly as she felt about that decision, she had far more serious issues with which to deal at present.

"Good." Victoria picked up a manila folder on her desk and opened it. "When I assign one of my people to a case, I do all within my power to ensure I'm covering every possible need a client might have."

The door opened and a woman walked in. Blond hair, blue eyes. She was tall and thin. Very young. High school, maybe a college freshman. As young as she was, she held herself in a regal manner that reminded Eva of Victoria.

"I apologize for the delay." The girl smiled first at Victoria then at Eva. "I'm Jamie Colby." She offered her hand to Eva.

Eva shook Jamie's hand, noting the firm confidence in her grip.

"Eva, this is my granddaughter," Victoria said, pride brimming in her tone. "She's a sophomore at the University of Chicago and my intern two days a week."

"You look so young," Eva blurted before she could stop herself, "to have accomplished so much."

"Jamie is quite special," Victoria agreed.

Jamie smiled. "I took freshman classes my senior year of high school. It's not so unusual that I'm eighteen and a sophomore and certainly not special."

Her humility was refreshing. Eva said, "I'm certain your parents are very pleased."

"They certainly are." Victoria turned to Jamie. "All is in order?"

"It is," Jamie assured her.

"As I was saying—" Victoria turned to Eva "—I take great pride in assigning the best person for the job. Since your bodyguard—"

"Bodyguard?" Eva expected an investigator to help with the Miguel Robles situation, not a bodyguard.

Victoria and Jamie shared a look before Victoria's gaze settled on Eva once more. "We need to take this situation very seriously, Eva. Frankly, I'm surprised you're not already dead."

Eva's breath caught. She put her hand over her mouth too late to catch the sound.

"Ms. Bowman," Jamie said, turning in her chair to face Eva, "I've done extensive research on the True Disciples. Miguel Robles raised his younger brother since their parents were murdered fifteen years ago. He thought of Diego as more of a son than a brother. Typically when crossed, Miguel wields vengeance far more quickly and concisely. The idea that you're alive three days later tells us that he is planning to make some sort of example out of you. He wants you to know it's coming. He wants to watch your fear build. He wants a large audience and rumor on the street is that all eyes are on you right now."

Eva blinked repeatedly to hold back the rush of tears. "Wait, this is crazy. I didn't mean to kill his brother. He attacked me... I..."

When Eva's voice failed her, Victoria said, "I'm afraid it only gets worse. Chicago PD has a unit called

Gang Intelligence. Though they cannot provide any measure of security for you, they are watching. If you want my honest opinion, they're hoping Robles will come after you. If they can catch Miguel Robles in the act of trying to harm you, they can bring down a man who has slipped through their fingers repeatedly over the past two decades."

Oh God. "I think I see the whole picture now." Eve swallowed at the lump still lodged in her throat. "I'm bait. The police won't protect me—not because of budget cuts—but because they want to get this guy."

"In all fairness," Victoria reminded her, "no law has been broken—more or less tying their hands. At this time all anyone has are rumors and suspicions, and resources are stretched too thin already. I fully believe the police are doing all they legally can."

Jamie placed a warm hand over Eva's ice-cold one. "But we can take up that slack."

"Dr. Pierce has granted us full access to his facility," Victoria explained. "We'd like to provide around-the-clock protection until this situation is neutralized."

Round-the-clock? "Is that really necessary?" The moment the words left her lips she felt foolish for having said them.

Eva hadn't expected this insanity to consume her life. Her sister had told her it was bad. She'd spent the past two nights with Eva. If all that Victoria said was true, Lena being close put her in danger as well. Eva suddenly felt immensely grateful that Lena's boss had called about a hot-button issue in DC and wanted her there ASAP. Lena had nearly refused to go but Eva had promised she would be fine with the Colby Agency taking care of her. After considerable persuasion, her sister had reluctantly accepted the assignment. Eva now completely understood how important it was to keep Lena as far from this as possible…and to end this as quickly as possible.

"Okay," Eva heard herself say. "When do I meet this bodyguard?"

"As Victoria explained," Jamie cut in, "we take every precaution when making the selection. Your situation requires extensive training. The man we've chosen spent eight years in the military, six in the Army's Special Forces. He is an expert in all manner of defense and protection. His extensive emergency medical training will allow a smooth transition into your workplace. He's the perfect choice."

Victoria nodded her agreement. "You couldn't be in better hands."

Eva's head was still spinning. She could do this. It was necessary. Her boss understood. Lena would come unglued if Eva even thought of backing out of hiring the Colby Agency. This was the right step. *Just do this.* "All right. I'm ready to do whatever I have to."

"Before we ask him in," Victoria began.

Eva instinctively understood that something bad was coming.

"We've been made aware that there may be a stumbling block of sorts. Under normal circumstances," Victoria went on, "I never make assignments when there are personal connections. Emotions can often get in the way."

Eva shook her head. "I'm sorry. This is my first time here and I'm fairly confident I don't know anyone at your agency."

"Todd Christian."

Eva's head turned so quickly toward the woman seated next to her that her neck almost snapped. "Todd Christian?"

Impossible. Even as the word filtered through her, Eva comprehended it was not. Todd had gone straight from college into the military. She'd heard at some point later that he was in some sort of special something but she couldn't remember what. She had spent the past nine years blocking every single thing about him from her brain. Todd Christian no longer existed as far as Eva was concerned. She had worked extremely hard to make that happen.

Jamie nodded. "He is the perfect choice."

Eva shook her head. "No. Absolutely not." She could not—would not—spend one minute much less 24/7 with him. No damned way.

Another of those looks passed between Victoria and her granddaughter.

"Todd thought you might feel that way," Victoria offered. "Eva, let me just say that I've been doing this for a very long time."

"A seriously long time," Jamie echoed.

"I do not make a suggestion such as this lightly," Victoria continued. "I ask that you put your personal feelings aside for a moment before you request an alternate choice. Toward that end, Todd has asked if he might speak with you privately before you make your final decision."

"He's here?" Stupid question. He worked here. Of course he would be somewhere on the floor. Eva felt the heat rise in her face and then, just as suddenly, the color drain away, leaving her as weak as a kitten.

How could she face him? He was the last person on Earth she wanted to hear about her personal issues.

"With your permission, Jamie and I will wait in my private lobby while the two of you talk for a moment."

"There must be someone else." Eva shook her head again. This would never do. "You mentioned an alternate choice."

Victoria set her hands palms down on her desk and stood. "I pride myself in hiring only the best, Eva. Of course, there are others, but no one who would fit as seamlessly into your world. To make sure you are protected in such a way that the enemy will not simply lay low until that protection ceases, we must ensure they are taken by surprise. The last thing we want is for Robles to step back and wait out your resources. This is the only way to guarantee the outcome you desire in the quickest manner."

As crazy as it sounded, Eva had to admit that she could see her point. But could she do this? Could she allow *him* back into her life? Uncertainty and a new kind of fear coiled inside her like a snake ready to strike.

"I'll speak to him." Eva took a big breath. "I can at least do that."

Victoria nodded. "Excellent."

Jamie patted Eva on the hand and stood. "We'll give you a few moments, but we'll be right outside."

Eva tried to smile but her lips wouldn't make the transition.

When the door closed behind the two women, Eva stood and smoothed a wrinkle out of her sweater hem. Slow, deep breaths.

The door opened and she turned to face the man who had shattered her heart when she was barely old enough to understand what love was. He'd been a senior, she a freshman. She'd never lived anywhere but at home with her parents and sister until she moved into that college dormitory. Lena had gone to Europe for a year of studies abroad. And Eva had fallen madly, deeply in love with the man who taught her what a real orgasm felt like.

She might have been able to say the thirty-two-year-old man who walked into the room and closed the door behind him hadn't changed one bit except that would be utterly and completely wrong. He seemed taller somehow, his shoulders even broader. Her gaze moved down his torso, over the ridges hidden behind the crisp blue oxford she knew all too well. The long sleeves ended at his wrists where the wide hands and blunt-tipped fingers that had touched her as if she was all that mattered in this world to him didn't look as smooth as they once had. Long legs were camouflaged by navy trousers tailored to mold perfectly to the powerful muscles beneath. She blinked and shifted her gaze to the handsome face she'd dreamed of every night for years even after he left her. His face looked the slightest bit leaner, more angular, and there was a small scar on his right cheek. His lips...his pale, pale blue eyes— She shifted her gaze from his face. His brown hair was still more blond than brown and in need of a trim. So many little things had changed and yet her body reacted to his mere presence as if absolutely nothing were different. Fire licked a path along every nerve ending.

His lips—the ones that had instructed her in the true art of kissing—slid into a smile. "Eva... It's good to see you."

The hesitation after he said her name told her he was savoring it. Something else she'd yearned for night and day. The sound of his voice, the pull of every syllable he uttered. Chill bumps rose on her skin. The smile...the sound of his voice, his presence in the room even after all these years had the ability to make her nervous. Made her ache for things she couldn't name.

Eva commanded the butterflies that had come to life in her stomach to go away. She stared directly into those gorgeous eyes of his. "Is it true, what they say? That you can protect me better than anyone else employed at the Colby Agency?"

"You have my word."

Those four little words—damn him—sent another shiver racing over her too-hot skin. "I'll need more than your word, Christian." She refused to call him Todd. She could not. "You see, I learned long ago that your word is of little value."

"I hurt you, Eva," he confessed. "You haven't forgiven me and maybe I don't deserve your forgiveness, but if you'll trust me now I swear on my life that I will take care of this for you. Let me do that. Please."

The idea that she could spend the next few days making him damned miserable held some appeal. "Fine. I trust *your boss*. She says you're the man for the job. We'll see about that."

"Good."

She picked up her bag and slung it over her shoulder. "Make sure you remember that once we walk out of this building *I* am the boss."

He nodded his agreement, and just like that she jumped right out of the frying pan and into the fire.

Chapter Three

Eva didn't want him close. She'd insisted on driving separately to her building. He hadn't liked it but she'd given him no choice. He'd stayed right on her bumper on the drive from the agency to her address. Rather than warn him about the parking situation, she'd driven into the covered area for tenants and he'd had to fend for himself on the street. When he'd finally found a spot, he'd had to hurry to catch up to her before she reached the building.

Like it or not, that would not happen again. Next time they would be in the same vehicle *together*.

At the front entrance she entered the code for the door and walked in, letting go of the door as she did. The damned thing almost closed before Todd caught it. She didn't look back, obviously unconcerned as to whether he made it inside.

He hadn't really expected her to forgive him—not even after nearly ten years. Not ever, most likely. Under the circumstances he was hoping for some sort of cordiality or at least a temporary truce.

Inside, rather than going for the elevator, she headed to the door marked with the stairwell logo. No problem. He hefted his duffel onto one shoulder and followed her. His time in the service had taught him not to take his physical condition for granted. He stayed in the same shape he had when he'd been in active duty.

The climb to the third floor, however, gave him far too much time to focus on the sway of her hips. Someone else stayed in shape, he decided. He remembered her soft curves a little too well. Time had been good to her. She still looked like the nineteen-year-old he'd first met in the university library. He'd tried so damned hard to focus on the book he'd been reading for an English paper, only he couldn't stop looking at her over the top of the page. She had the blondest hair, still did. Every sweet hair on her gorgeous body was naturally blond. Her skin was the creamiest white, like porcelain. And those eyes, so green. When she smiled or got angry they shimmered like emeralds under a waterfall.

She exited the stairwell on the third floor, again without looking back or saying a word to him. He followed. This was another part they had to get straight. He went through any door first. She stayed close and behind him, preferably.

He imagined the real trouble was going to be in getting her to cooperate when he explained that she might be the boss but he was in charge.

At the door to her apartment he stepped in front of her. "I go in first." He held out his hand.

She dropped the key into his palm and stepped back. He unlocked the door and moved inside. He'd

looked at the floor plans for her building. She had a
one-bedroom. The entry door opened into a small hall.
The living and dining space along with the kitchen
were an L-shape, and then another tiny hall with doors
to a linen closet, the bedroom and the bath. No bal-
cony, but she did have two large windows. He motioned for her to come inside, but she didn't. She stared
at the door across the hall.

"Something wrong?"

She shook her head. "Guess not." She gestured to
the door she'd been staring at. "I thought my neighbor was going out of town." With a shrug she turned
to her own door and stepped inside.

Todd closed and locked it. "Stay put until I have a
look around."

She rolled her eyes and folded her arms over her
chest.

The large window overlooking the street allowed
plenty of light into the room. He was surprised there
were no blinds or curtains. The Eva he had known before had been very shy and private. Another of those
things that had attracted him. He was glad to see an
upholstered sofa rather than leather since it would
serve as his bed. A small cocktail table stood in front
of the sofa and a side table sat between two comfort-
able-looking chairs. The upholstery and the throw pillows were soft, muted shades of blues and greens and
yellows. A rug in the center of the room was scattered
with two larger pillows. Didn't take much to imagine
her on the floor curled up with a good book. Back in
college she'd enjoyed reading romance novels when
she wasn't studying. He'd often teased her about her
secret hobby.

The kitchen was tiny with an even tinier dining area. Updated three-piece bath with lots of that subway tile people went gaga over. Big mirrors that made the space look a tad larger and more of those little bursts of color that adorned the main living space. He opened the door to the bedroom and the scent of her assaulted him and made him weak. The large window in this intimate space was covered with thick curtains, ensuring the room was dark. He flipped on a light, checked the closet that overflowed with clothes and shoes and then turned to go. The unmade bed and the nightshirt tossed onto the tousled covers made him hesitate.

Selfishly, he experienced a sense of satisfaction at the untouched second pillow on the bed. He scanned the walls and other surfaces for photos or signs of a boyfriend. The only photographs were of her and her sister, Lena, and their parents. Their father had died the year before Eva started college. She had still been struggling with the loss when they were together.

"Are you finished yet?"

He pivoted toward her voice, surprised she'd gotten as far as the door without him noticing. *Distraction is dangerous.* He knew better. "The apartment is clear."

"I noticed." She executed an about-face and stormed away.

Todd heaved a disgusted breath and plowed his hand through his hair. This might not be as easy as he'd thought. He had foolishly hoped they might be able to make amends. That maybe he and Eva could be friends now that he was back in Chicago. Guess not.

He exited the bedroom and took the few short steps to the kitchen. This place was considerably smaller than it looked when he reviewed the building's floor plan. Spending a lot of time here with her would prove less than comfortable. She opened cabinet door after cabinet door, then rummaged in the refrigerator, obviously looking for something to eat.

"We could have dinner delivered," he suggested.

She looked at him over the fridge door. "Yogurt and crackers are fine with me."

He gritted his teeth and restrained any response for a moment. Her plan was obvious—make him as miserable as possible. No problem. He deserved it. "Sounds awesome."

She blinked but not fast enough to cover her surprise. A carton of yogurt and an apple in hand, she left the fridge, grabbed a box of crackers from a cabinet and carried her haul to the counter.

He tossed his duffel on the sofa and watched as she carefully sliced her apple and arranged it on a plate, then added a handful of small crackers. With yogurt spooned into the center, she sprinkled a few walnuts on top. Spoon and plate in hand, she carried both to the made-for-two dining table. She poured herself a glass of water from the pitcher in the fridge, grabbed a napkin and then took a seat.

Todd ignored her indifference and made himself at home. He grabbed a plate, rummaged for a butter knife, found peanut butter and proceeded to slather it onto as many of the small crackers as the plate would hold. He added an apple, not bothering to slice it, poured a glass of water and then joined her at the small table.

"Looks like you predicted Lena's future correctly." He stuffed a cracker into his mouth, hoping the protein in the peanut butter would satisfy him. He was starving.

Eva licked the yogurt from her spoon. He stared at his plate, then went for the apple. Anything to avoid watching her tongue slide around on that spoon.

"Channel 7 loves her. The viewers love her." Eva nibbled on a cracker. "I'm really proud of her."

Todd knocked back a long swallow of water before placing his glass back on the table. "You haven't done so bad yourself. Pierce raved about you to Victoria."

"I'm happy." She reached for an apple slice.

She didn't ask about his career or whether he was happy or if his brother Kevin was okay. The only part that surprised him was Kevin. His brother had been just a toddler when their father abandoned them. Their mother had died a few months earlier and there was no known extended family. Kevin had been adopted quickly, but Todd hadn't been so lucky. He'd spent the next twelve years of his life in foster homes. It wasn't until college that his little brother found him. They'd been damned close since. Eva was the only woman he'd ever taken to Christmas dinner with Kevin. He had loved her. She always asked about Kevin after that…at least until Todd left. Then again, he couldn't really hold that against her since he hadn't exactly been around for her when her mother died. He pushed the sensitive memory away.

The rest of the not-so-yummy and definitely not-filling meal was consumed without conversation. She rinsed her plate and placed it in the dishwasher. He pushed in his chair and followed her lead with the cleanup. "If only we had dessert."

She didn't smile. Instead she walked to the cabinets,

put the crackers away and withdrew a tub of cake frosting. She shoved it at him. "Chocolate. Enjoy."

Really? He put the frosting back in the cabinet and joined her in the living room. Since she obviously had no desire to catch up, he might as well move on to business. "How much do you know about the True Disciples?"

She curled up in one of the two chairs and started channel surfing with the sound muted. "Only what the police told me."

He took the other seat. Since she kept the volume off he viewed that as an invitation to talk. "Miguel Robles's father, Jorge, immigrated to Chicago in the '80s. He became deeply involved in the Latin Disciples. About fifteen years ago, there was a falling-out between Jorge and the leader of the Latin Disciples. Jorge walked away, starting his own band of merry men. Five years later, Jorge found himself facing cancer, so he started the transition of power to Miguel. A decade from now Miguel, since he has no children of his own, would likely have been doing the same with Diego."

With her sister's channel on the screen, Eva set the remote aside and turned her attention to Todd. "He sees me as the person who not only stole his younger brother's life but also as the person who turned his entire future upside down."

The situation was far graver than she understood. "Avenging Diego's death is a matter of honor, Eva. Whatever else happens, he has no choice but to kill you or lose face. Personally, I don't understand why the police didn't take you into protective custody."

She glared at him as if he'd offended her. "Your boss said there aren't enough resources to go around."

Victoria was right about that part, but the sheer enormity of the situation should have prompted a stronger reaction. Not that he was suggesting the police didn't want to stop Miguel, but sometimes he wondered if their priorities were in order.

"That's true," he admitted. "But some cases fall outside the parameters of the norm. Those cases should be evaluated differently. Yours, in my humble opinion, is one of those cases."

She laughed. "You've never been humble in your life." With that announcement, she pushed up from her chair and walked to the window.

Maybe there was a time when her pronouncement was true, but not anymore. He hesitated only a moment before joining her. On the street below the traffic was heavy. The neighborhood was a nice one. Towering, mature trees lined the street. Much-desired shopping and restaurants were only a few blocks away. He'd driven past her building more than once since his return to Chicago last year. Mentioning that too-telling fact would hardly be a good thing, he decided.

"I'm sure you're aware that the police see you as their first real opportunity to get this guy."

She nodded. "Your boss mentioned it."

"I can understand how much they want him and the idea that using you as bait somehow serves the greater good, but I'm not them. My job is to protect you at all costs."

She glanced at him, the worry in her eyes tugging at his gut.

"So let's not make you an easy target by standing in front of this window." He touched her arm. She stiffened but he curled his fingers around the soft limb anyway and gently tugged her back to the pair of chairs they had deserted.

Rather than sit down, she stared up at him. She searched his eyes, worry clouding hers. "Do you really believe you can stop him?" She licked her lips, drawing his attention there. He remembered her taste as vividly as if he'd only just kissed her. "That all by yourself," she said, dragging him from the forbidden memory, "you can somehow do what the police haven't been able to do in what? A decade?"

No matter the seriousness of her question, this close he almost smiled at the small sprinkling of freckles on her nose and cheeks. She had hated those tiny freckles and he had loved them. This close he noticed there was a line or two on her gorgeous face that hadn't been there before, but those fine lines only added to her beauty. He wanted her to trust him. He desperately wanted her to believe in him again. Whatever else she thought of him, he would never lie to her. He hadn't lied all those years ago and he wasn't about to start now.

"First, I don't operate by the same rules as the police. Giving them grace, their hands are tied to some degree by the very laws they've sworn to uphold. Second, I can't promise I'll be able to stop Robles, but I can promise that I'll die trying."

EVA PULLED FREE of his touch and turned away from him. She couldn't bear the way he looked at her...as if he truly cared. Of course he probably possessed some basic human compassion for her as a person but otherwise she was nothing more than an assignment and maybe a potential opportunity for sexual release. Not that finding willing women would be an issue for him—it hadn't been a decade ago and it certainly wouldn't be now. He was still incredibly handsome and far too charming.

She closed her eyes. *So not fair, Eva.* She didn't know the man standing in her apartment right now. She knew the college guy he used to be. The super hot guy who seemed to show up in the library every Tuesday and Thursday evening just like she had. The guy with the beautiful lean, muscled body and scruffy, thick hair that made her want to twine her fingers in it while she traced every line and ridge of his healthy male body with her other hand. The guy who stole her heart and ruined her for anyone else.

Not once in ten years had she been kissed the way Todd Christian kissed her. Not a single time in the last decade had another man—not that there had been very many—made love to her the way Todd Christian had.

Eva hugged her arms around herself. What kind of fool permitted *that* guy back into her life?

A desperate one.

A *splat, splat, splat* echoed in the room. The window rattled in its frame. Eva instinctively backed up, her body bumping into his. Rivulets of red rained down from a cloud of red in the center of the window.

Todd pulled her behind the chairs. "Stay down while I have a look."

He moved across the room and took a position next to the window, out of sight from whoever was out there firing something at her window. Eva peeked around the chair and studied the damage to the window. It didn't appear broken or cracked. The splats looked like the ones made by a paintball gun.

Was this just another warning from the man who wanted his revenge?

"We need something to cover this window."

Todd was suddenly standing over her, holding out his hand. She ignored it and stood. "I have extra sheets in the linen closet."

He nodded. "You round those up while I give Detective Marsh an update."

"Are you working with the police?" She didn't know why she was surprised. The Colby Agency was a prominent firm. Her internet research had indicated that Victoria was known and respected by everyone who was anyone in Chicago. She'd been voted woman of the year more than once.

"Just keeping them up to speed on what's going on. If I play nice, hopefully they'll do the same for me."

She nodded. Made sense. While he spoke to the detective she went to the bathroom. She'd tried really hard the past few days to stay strong. To keep it together. The first day, Saturday, hadn't been so bad. Her sister had kept her mind off the horror of the previous night until Eva went unconscious from sheer exhaustion.

In the bathroom, she closed the door and sagged against it. But then the threats had begun. Eva was so thankful when Lena was sent out of town. No matter that her sister had wanted to stay and had insisted that she dove into the fray of danger every time she walked onto a hot news scene, this was different. Eva was the target. She felt certain this Miguel Robles would like nothing better than to use her sister to hurt her.

At least she didn't have to worry so much about that part right now. Lena would be in Washington, DC, for several days.

With her sister safely out of reach, Eva could focus on keeping herself alive.

The memory of her neighbor's door nagged at her. Mrs. Cackowski had mentioned going to New York to visit her daughter. The plan was she would leave today and spend the upcoming Mother's Day weekend with her daughter and her family. She would fly back next Tuesday. Mrs. Cackowski said flying on Tuesdays was cheaper. Eva wasn't entirely sure that was true but the idea appeared to make the older lady happy.

The trouble was, the No Solicitors magnet was not on her door. Mrs. Cackowski and Eva had a routine. Whenever her neighbor was away from home, whether for the day or for a week, she put the magnet on her door. When she returned, it was removed. This way, even if Eva missed talking to her she knew to keep an eye on the elderly woman's apartment. She usually left a key with Eva so she could water her plants if it was an extended vacation, but not this time.

Maybe her neighbor's flight had been changed at the last minute. If Mrs. Cackowski would break down and get a cell phone, Eva could call and check with her. She should probably call the property manager and tell him about the red paint—or whatever it was—all over her window. The two windows in her apartment didn't open so it wasn't like she could clean it up herself. Since she faced the street her neighbors wouldn't be happy about the unsightly mess.

A knock on the door had her jumping away from it. "You okay in there?"

Eva put her hand to her throat. "Fine. I just need a moment."

She went to the sink and turned on the water. How was she supposed to deal with all this? Her actions had caused a man's death. Shouldn't she feel something besides empty and cold about it by now? Last night a patient had required a psychological consult. After the doctor had assessed the patient, Eva had spoken to the psychiatrist briefly about what happened to her. He'd warned that she was in the shock and denial phase right now. In time the reality would hit and she might fall apart.

Start counseling now, he'd warned.

Like every other nurse and doctor she knew, the last person she wanted to spend time fixing was herself. It was far easier to take care of everyone else's problems. Funny how she'd worked so hard and long to keep her life simple. Work, eat, sleep and repeat. Once in a great while she bothered with dating.

How had her simple existence turned so suddenly complicated?

Maybe the shrink had been right about the shock and denial. She had pretty much been attempting to pretend Friday night never happened. She might have been successful if not for the continued threats.

After splashing some water on her face, she reached for the hand towel and dabbed her skin dry. At this point she didn't know if she had enough time left to reach the reality phase.

She could be dead before then.

Chapter Four

Eva scarcely slept at all. Between worrying about what the gang leader Miguel Robles might do next and the idea that Todd Christian was on her sofa, how could she hope to sleep? At some point after two this morning, she'd finally drifted to sleep only to dream about being chased by killers. She'd jerked awake in a cold sweat to the sound of the shower.

For the next several minutes she'd battled with her errant mind and its inability to control the wellspring of images involving Todd Christian naked in her shower. When he'd finished and she was certain he'd moved to the kitchen, she reluctantly headed to the bathroom. With the water as hot as she could bear it, she still couldn't wash away the scent of him...it clung to the tile walls, to the bar of homemade soap a friend had given her, insisting that no bodywash on the planet could compete. Despite rinsing the soap thoroughly, simply smoothing the bar over her skin aroused her. Shivers tumbled over her skin with every slow stroke. Her nipples hardened with the sweet ache of need and she once again found herself fighting to keep memories of their lovemaking at bay. How could those memories still be so vivid? So intoxicating?

Todd Christian was like an addictive drug. And like the wrong kind of drug, he was bad for her.

By the time she turned off the water she felt ready to explode with tension. Taking her time, she dried her skin and then her hair. By the time she finished, she had gone from the edge of orgasm to teeth-grinding frustration.

This arrangement was not going to work. No way, no how.

Shoulders squared, purple Wednesday scrubs and her most comfortable nursing clogs on, she walked into the kitchen to tell the bane of her existence he had to sleep somewhere else. She could not have him in her apartment like this. There had to be some other arrangement. Might as well get it over with now and salvage what little sanity she had left. The sooner, the better.

"Good morning." He smiled and saluted her with his coffee mug. "I scrambled a few eggs and popped in some toast while you were showering. Hope you don't mind."

If the scent of the freshly made toast and the coffee hadn't distracted her, she might have been able to hang on to her determination. Instead, her need for fuel took over and she decided she would tell him this wasn't going to work as soon as she ate. Why let the food get cold? The least she could do was be civil. If she let her frustration show she would only look immature. She would die before she allowed him to see how easily he could still get to her.

"Morning." She poured a cup of coffee and reached for a slice of toast.

The sheets they'd tacked up over the living room window last night blocked the morning light she usually enjoyed. The lack of natural light was a stark reminder that her life was a mess. She had killed a man.

She sagged against the counter. Didn't matter that she hadn't meant to kill him; he was dead just the same. Nineteen years old. A damn kid.

"Don't go there, Eva."

She blinked, his voice pulling her from the troubling thoughts. "I… I was just thinking about work."

He shook his head. "You were thinking about what happened in that bathroom on Friday night. The pain was written all over your face."

How the hell could he still read her so well all these years later? It wasn't fair. Just another reason he had to go. Today. She absolutely could not allow him back into her life. She'd thought she could handle this situation, but she couldn't. It was impossible. Unrealistic.

"You don't know me anymore, Todd." She set her cup aside and grabbed one of the two plates he'd placed on the counter. She raked a few eggs into the plate and snagged a fork. "I'm not the same naive young girl I was ten years ago."

He stared at her with that intensity she knew all too well. "No, you definitely are not."

She bit back the urge to demand what he meant by his statement.

He pushed off the counter on the opposite side of the island and reached for the remaining plate. She told herself not to watch every damned move he made but somehow she couldn't stop herself. It was like driving past an accident—no amount of willpower would prevent her from looking. His fingers wrapped around the fork and he lifted the eggs to his mouth. His lips closed over the silver tines. Her mouth watered and she forced her attention back to her own fork. She poked a bite of eggs and stuffed them into her mouth. Butter, eggs, cheese and pepper combined into an incredible burst of flavor on her tongue. Simple but so tasty. Most mornings she grabbed a cup of yogurt or a breakfast bar and devoured it on the way to work. A groan of utter satisfaction slipped past her lips.

"Thank you." He grinned. "You still love cheesy scrambled eggs."

The bite of toast she'd taken was suddenly like cardboard on her tongue. How could she have forgotten how he made eggs with cheese and toast for her every time she stayed over at his place? More important, how could he remember something as mundane as eggs and cheese?

She finished off her coffee and glanced at her watch. "I should go."

Before he could say something else she didn't want to hear, she disappeared into the bathroom, which also prevented her from having to look at him. She brushed her teeth and put her hair up in a clip, then stared at her reflection. It didn't take a shrink to narrow down the issue in front of her right now. Todd was the only man she'd ever loved—her first love. He'd taught her how to appreciate her body and to appreciate sex. How to fall completely in love with him. He'd allowed her to believe that what they had was never going to end.

Only it had.

She might have been able to forgive him, to put it

behind her and never look back, except that she hadn't been able to fall in love again. No one had been able to lure her down that path or even near it. No matter that an entire decade had passed, she could not feel for anyone else what she had felt for Todd Christian.

Staring at her reflection, Eva realized the one thing that really mattered in all this: staying alive. All this lamenting over how he left her and ruined her for any other man was ridiculous. A man was dead. She had killed him. And now his older brother wanted vengeance. Whining and complaining about the apparent best man to protect her until the situation was sorted out was ridiculous. Worse, it was childish and petulant. She was a grown damn woman. A nurse, for God's sake.

It was time she starting acting like a mature woman rather than a heartbroken college girl. And she would be damned if she would let him see just how much power he still held over her.

Summoning the courage that allowed her to work in one of the region's most demanding ERs, she walked out of the bathroom and grabbed her bag. "I'll see you at the hospital."

He dried his hands on the rooster-embellished hand towel she'd thought matched so well with the simple decorating scheme in her kitchen—the kitchen he had cleaned up after preparing breakfast. She ignored the gesture. What else was he going to do while he waited for her? The whole breakfast and cleanup thing was probably just his way of killing time.

"We should ride together, Eva. It's far more—"

"Then I guess you'll be riding with me." She headed for the door. He was not going to be in charge of every aspect of her existence until this was over. It was bad enough he'd invaded her home and her dreams. She wasn't giving him any more power.

She walked out the door and waited until he'd done the same. Once the door was locked she turned to head for the stairwell but hesitated. Still nothing on Mrs. Cackowski's door. She'd forgotten to call and ask the property manager if he'd spoken to her. *You're a bad neighbor, Eva.*

"Give me a minute," she muttered to her shadow. Without further explanation she banged on her neighbor's door loud enough to wake the dead. No answer. No TV sounds. Eva knocked again. An entire minute passed with no answer.

"I can open the door if you'd like."

She glared at him. "You're offering to break into my neighbor's apartment?"

He shrugged those broad, broad shoulders and smiled. "If you bang any harder you're going to break the door down anyway. Trust me, my way is a lot less messy."

"I can call the property manager." She frowned. "I should have done that already."

"Why waste the time? I'll only be a couple of seconds."

For three seconds she thought about telling him to screw off, but then she thought of the men who had followed her and made all those threats—the men who had killed no telling how many people already. What if Mrs. Cackowski was in there bleeding to death? "Okay. Fine. Open the door."

He stepped toward the door in question, forcing

her to back away. Another thought occurred to her. "This can't be legal."

That grin appeared on his lips once more. "Not in any way, shape or form."

Good grief. She knew this. No more pretending. Her cognitive abilities were officially compromised. "Then why are you doing it?"

"Because you asked me to."

"Just stop!" She could not think straight with him around. Damn it! She should just go to work and hope she didn't kill any patients.

"Too late." He gave the door a push and it swung inward.

For a moment Eva couldn't move. She felt frozen to the spot. This felt wrong. No, that wasn't true. Mrs. Cackowski's absence without putting out the damned magnetic sign was wrong.

"Would you like me to go in and check on her?"

His voice snapped Eva into action. "No. I'll do it." She glanced first right then left. Thank God none of her other neighbors were in the hall to see what they were doing.

Eva took a breath and crossed the threshold. Why not add the entering to the breaking? "Mrs. Cackowski, are you home?"

The living room was tidy as always. Mrs. Cackowski had told her how when she moved in years ago she had brought with her the salmon-colored sofa her husband had purchased for their tenth anniversary some forty years back. Three hand crocheted dollies lined the camelbacked sofa. The upholstered chair that swiveled and rocked in which her neighbor spent her days, the coffee table where she served tea every time Eva visited, all looked exactly as it should.

Except there was no Mrs. Cackowski. No sign of a struggle or any other untoward activity. She called her neighbor's name again. Still no answer.

Todd abruptly moved past her and checked the kitchen. Irritation nudged Eva. "Excuse me. This is my neighbor's home. What happened to me having a look around while you wait at the door?"

He shot her a wink. "I've never been a patient man."

Well, now, that was the truth…except when it came to making love. His ability to hold out, to restrain his own needs for hers, had seemed boundless.

No more thinking about sex, Eva. She followed him to the bedroom. No Mrs. Cackowski. Bed was made. He reached for the closet door. "What are you doing?"

He shrugged. "We've come this far."

She stormed up to the door. "I'm certain Mrs. Cackowski would be more comfortable with me checking her closet."

He held up his hands and backed away. "Whatever you say. This time," he warned.

She glared at him, then opened the door. The closet was as neat and undisturbed as the rest of the apartment. Her suitcase sat on the floor of the closet next to a neatly arranged row of practical shoes. Had she bought a new suitcase? Eva shook her head. Maybe the trip had been cancelled. Maybe her neighbor was merely at an appointment. Paranoia was obviously taking full control.

Eva slammed the door. "Let's just go before we get caught."

She walked back to the living room. Todd hur-

ried around her and out the front door before she realized he was right behind her. She glanced back at
her neighbor's favorite chair once more. Maybe the
elderly woman's age was finally catching up to her
and she'd simply forgotten to tell Eva her plans had
changed. She turned the thumb lock on the knob. She
couldn't lock the deadbolt without the key but at least
she could secure the door.

Eva had the number for Mrs. Cackowski's daughter—maybe she'd give her a call today just to be sure.
This Robles business was making her second-guess
everything.

Once the door was locked again, they left. Todd
entered the stairwell ahead of her, then gave her the
all clear. Eva reminded herself that he was doing his
job. The situation was serious so she should let him.
Tamping down her frustration for now, she followed
her bodyguard down the stairs and through the lobby.

As they exited the building the burst of fresh air
helped her mood a little. The sweet smell of the aza-
leas lining the sidewalk lifted her spirits. She could
make this a better day. All she had to do was keep
the proper mindset. Focus on her work. Maybe tonight she'd go to the gym and run a few miles on the
treadmill. Running always did amazing things for her
outlook. She and her sister participated in a couple of
5k runs every year in memory of their mother and in
support of breast cancer research.

Todd suddenly stopped. His arm went out, blocking
Eva's path. "Stay behind me and call 911."

When she would have asked why, her gaze settled on her car. The windshield and the two windows
she could see had been bashed in. Red spray paint

or something on that order had been used to write a warning across the hood.

Death is coming.

Her heart started to pound.

Todd pulled her behind the nearest parked vehicle. "Stay down and make the call."

Her hand shook as she dragged her cell from her bag. Her fingers turned to ice as she stabbed the necessary digits and put through the call. She watched Todd move around the parking garage as she answered the dispatcher's questions. He carried a gun now. She hadn't even realized he was armed. She provided her location and explained the situation. No, as far as she could see the perpetrators were no longer on the scene. Yes, the police needed to come. No, there was no need for an ambulance. The dispatcher assured her the police were en route. Eva ended the call and absently shoved the phone back into her bag. She stretched her neck in an effort to get a look around.

There was no one else in the garage except the two of them. At least if there was, he or they were hiding. She doubted the bastards would hide. They liked to show off...to inspire fear. Scumbags.

Todd returned to her car. This time he looked inside, though he made no move to open the doors. Preserving the scene, she realized. If he touched any part of the car, he might disturb fingerprints left behind by the bad guys. Even as she considered his reasoning, he walked to the rear of her vehicle. He leaned down to inspect something in the area of the trunk and the lid suddenly sprang open. Todd disappeared behind it.

Eva's tension moved to a new level, sending her heart into her throat. She looked around. Still didn't see anyone. Before she could talk herself out of the move, she stood and started walking toward her car. She opened her mouth to call his name but her voice deserted her.

No shots rang out. No sound of scuffling or fighting. Yet, she instinctively understood that something was very, very wrong.

As she reached the hood, Todd stepped from behind the open trunk lid. "Let's go back inside until the police get here."

He was moving toward her as the words penetrated the uncertainty that had paralyzed her ability to reason. When his hand landed on her arm, she trembled. Why was he trying to urge her back inside now? Why was the trunk still open?

Sirens blared in the distance. The police were almost here. They should stay put. Explain what happened.

"Eva," he said, his voice frighteningly soft, "I want to take you back inside."

She stared up at him. The blue eyes she knew as well as she knew her own showed no emotion...no indication of what the trouble was. And then she understood. He was hiding something terrible from her.

Her throat went as dry as bone. "What's in the trunk?"

Two police cruisers barreled into the parking garage and skidded to a stop.

Todd gripped her elbow and urged her in the direction of the nearest cruiser "I'll explain everything in a minute. Let's just make sure you stay safe until—"

Eva broke free of his grip and ran to her car. Her

heart thudded so hard in her chest she couldn't catch a breath.

"Eva, wait!"

She'd spoken to Lena yesterday. She was safe in DC. Eva rounded the back of the vehicle. Fear constricted her chest. She stared into the open trunk. At first what she saw didn't register. Pink dress...ghostly pale legs. Plastic that looked shrink-wrapped around the pasty skin of the woman's face. Gray hair. White cheeks...purple lips encircled a mouth that was open wide as if gasping for air. Dull, unseeing eyes.

Mrs. Cackowski.

Chapter Five

Chicago Police Department, 10:30 a.m.

Lorena Cackowski's daughter had been notified of her mother's death. She was on her way to Chicago from New York now. The preliminary conclusion from the medical examiner was asphyxiation. The murder weapon appeared to be the plastic. Manner of death: homicide.

Todd paced the corridor outside the interview room. The two detectives had insisted on interviewing Eva and him separately. He hadn't been happy about the idea, but she had assured him that she was okay with it so he'd backed off.

How the hell could Robles order the murder of a helpless, elderly woman like that?

Sick bastards.

The way Eva had trembled, the tears pouring down her cheeks, had torn him apart. He would make Robles pay for hurting her. As much as the desire to go after that revenge burned inside him, his top priority had to be keeping Eva safe.

The door opened and Detective Marsh stepped into

the corridor. "Almost done." He shook his head. "This thing is getting damned hairy."

"Who's the new guy?" Todd gestured to the interview room the man had exited. Marsh was the one to take Todd's statement but another detective had shown up for Eva's official interview. "He wasn't your partner the last time we had the pleasure of your company."

Marsh hitched his head toward the closed door. "Carter is from Gang Intelligence. He's been working this one behind the scenes since the war on Friday night. Until this morning he was more focused on what happened before Diego and his friends hit the ER. Everything's changed now."

Murder had a way of changing things for sure.

"This murder will draw a lot of press to the department," Marsh confessed.

Todd nodded. "Have the evidence techs found anything in the vic's apartment that ties Robles's people to what happened?"

For whatever reason, the usual gang markings hadn't been left behind in the vic's apartment or on Eva's car. It was possible that Robles considered this personal rather than gang business. Either way, he was behind the threats and now at least one murder related to Eva.

"Not yet," Marsh said with a weary sigh. "These guys might be thugs but the ones in charge aren't stupid. They know how to cover their tracks. Even if we're lucky enough to have witnesses we know for a fact were right there watching, they rarely talk. Too afraid, and who can blame them?"

Todd understood that the I-didn't-see-anything mentality in situations like this happened all too often.

Fear was the primary motive. "I spoke with my boss. We're taking Ms. Bowman to a safe house. You have a problem with that?"

Marsh shrugged. "I think Carter is making that offer as we speak. Yours, ours, wherever she is protected works for me."

Todd was glad to hear it. "We prefer our own place. No offense."

Marsh held up his hands. "None taken. Just keep us advised."

"Will do." Todd intended to leave that part in Victoria's more-than-capable hands. She had her own high-level sources inside Chicago PD. Todd had no reason to doubt Marsh's integrity or Carter's, for that matter. Still, he wasn't willing to take the risk that there could be a leak. Frankly, CPD had its share of problems, and he didn't intend for Eva to become a casualty of the department's recent highly publicized internal issues.

The interview room door opened once more and Eva walked out, followed by Sergeant Carter. The senior detective thrust his hand toward Todd. "We appreciate your cooperation, Christian. We'll have other questions, I'm certain. So keep us apprised of your location."

Evidently Eva had already told him the Colby Agency planned to take her to a private safe house. "You got it, Sergeant."

Eva only glanced at Todd as he spoke. Her eyes were red from crying. She kept her slender arms tight around herself. The mere idea that her life was in jeopardy was a painful reminder of just how fleeting life could be. He reached for her, placed his hand at the small of her back, hoping to convey reassurance as he guided her out of this place. The sooner they were as far as possible from the streets Robles influenced, the happier he would be.

When they had reached the lobby, he waylaid her at the main exit door and leaned in close. "Ian Michaels is picking us up. He'll drop us at the safe house. A new car will be waiting for us there. I guarantee Robles won't find us where we're going. You will be safe there."

She nodded.

Outside, Michaels waited at the curb in front of the main entrance. He glanced in the rearview mirror as they settled in the back seat.

Todd made the introductions.

"I'm aware this is a terrifying situation," Michaels said to Eva with another quick glance in the rearview mirror as he eased out onto the street, "but, rest assured, we will take care of the situation."

"Thank you."

Todd resisted the urge to scoot across the seat and put his arm around her. He was fairly confident she wouldn't appreciate the gesture however well he meant it. It would be in his best interest to stay out of her personal space for now. Keeping a couple of feet between them would be the smartest thing to do. His instincts went a little haywire when they were too close for too long.

He'd thought of her often over the years. Never expected to see her again. Even after he moved back to the Windy City, he hadn't worried. Chicago was a big place. No reason they should run into each other and be forced to deal with the lingering awkwardness. Not that he hadn't looked her up. He had. He'd checked up on her from time to time over the years before he returned to Chicago. He'd felt immensely proud when she graduated nursing school. Mostly he'd watched for an engagement announcement. Not that Eva was big on social media, but her sister, Lena, was. He'd admired the birthday pics Lena had posted each year since the last time Todd had seen Eva. He closely scrutinized the occasional vacation shot or night out on the town he ferreted out on social media. He'd scoured each one looking for the man who had taken his place.

That feeling—dread—he always experienced when he thought of her with someone else filled his chest now. *Idiot.* He'd left her because he couldn't handle where he felt the relationship was headed, and yet, he still couldn't bear the idea of her with anyone else.

He was worse than an idiot. He was a jerk.

Finding Michaels watching him in the rearview mirror warned his brooding hadn't escaped the older man's scrutiny. Ian Michaels had been with Victoria at the Colby Agency since she and her first husband started the agency. A former US Marshal, Michaels was particularly good at reading people. Todd figured the man likely already had a firm handle on how he was feeling right now.

Great.

Nothing like the world knowing how badly you'd screwed up whether it was yesterday or ten years ago.

He glanced at Eva and immediately turned his attention back to the street. He'd been a selfish bastard and he'd walked away from the only woman who had ever made him want more than right now.

Nothing he could do about the past. But he could make sure her future was free of thugs like Robles.

Bastard.

"Brace yourselves," Michaels announced. "We have a tail to lose."

THE CAR ROCKETED forward and fear trapped deep in Eva's chest.

Todd's hand was suddenly against her back, ushering her down onto the seat. He used his own body like a shield, hovering over her as the car swung from lane to lane. When he pressed more firmly against her, she started to demand what the hell he was doing, but the sound of glass shattering and metal popping silenced her.

"Hang on!"

The driver shouted the words and then slammed on the brakes. The car slid sideways. For an instant Todd's body crushed against hers, every rigid muscle cradling her. Eva's stomach lurched as much from his nearness as from the wild ride. Before she could catch her breath, the car was rocketing forward once more.

Another of those crazy sliding turns was followed by a roar of the car's engine as they zoomed through the city streets. Eva was grateful she couldn't see. No doubt pedestrians and other vehicles were scattered all around them. One wrong move and the crash would be horrific.

A moment passed with no abrupt moves and her respiration leveled out to some degree. She realized then that her fingers were clutched in the fabric of Todd's shirt. One muscled thigh had burrowed between hers, his knee anchored to the seat, holding her firmly in place. His other knee was planted in the floorboard and his upper torso shielded hers. The scent of his strong body, clean and vaguely sweet, filled her lungs and made her dizzy.

Pull yourself together, girl.

Eva took a breath and ordered her fingers to unclench. She was still working on the move when Ian Michaels announced, "All clear."

Todd's face turned down toward hers, making her breath catch all over again. "You okay?"

She nodded. Her fingers finally relaxed their death grip. Todd helped her upright once more and she struggled to right her clothes and her hair. She forced herself to breathe slowly and deeply until her heart stopped racing. She kept her gaze on the street. The rear windshield was shattered but, thankfully, remained in place.

Eva closed her eyes and told herself over and over that everything would be okay. Forty-five minutes later she still wasn't completely convinced as Mr. Michaels took an exit from I-94 toward Central Avenue in Highland Park. From there he drove to Egandale Road. Eva stared out the window at nothing at all until finally the car slowed and then stopped at a keypad outside an enormous gate. A high fence was almost completely camouflaged by mature trees and shrubbery. Michaels entered the code for the gate, rolling on through as it opened.

Todd glanced at her and smiled. "Don't worry. I've been here a couple of times before. It's not as uninviting as it looks from here. The security wall only makes it look like a prison."

As they rounded a deep bend in the long drive, Eva spotted the house. It sat in the middle of thick woods.

"Beyond all those trees," Todd said as if he'd read

her mind, "is Lake Michigan. The property includes a helipad as well as a boat dock. There are plenty of ways to escape trouble if the need arises. But it would prove extremely difficult for trouble to get into the compound. The walls around the property are lined with cameras. Anyone gets close, we'll know it. A state-of-the-art security system keeps the home secure. Robles's men won't be able to get to you here."

The car came to a stop in front of an enormous house that looked more like a castle than a home. Eva stared at the stone façade that might have looked cold if not for the lush border of flowering plants, climbing vines and shrubs. "Oh my God."

Michaels looked over the seat. "Call if you need anything else."

"Will do," Todd responded as he climbed out.

He was around the vehicle and opening her door before she had the presence of mind to grab her bag and prepare to exit the car.

Ian Michaels drove away in the car with its broken glass and bullet holes. Eva turned to the massive house, clinging to her leather bag as if it was the only thing left grounding her. At the moment she was pretty sure it was. This insane situation had taken her from her home, had kept her from work, and cost her neighbor her life. On cue, her head started to spin.

Todd's steady hand was suddenly at her back, ushering her up the stone steps. "All the windows are bulletproof," he explained. "A voice command can close the steel shutters over them." At the door, he placed his hand against a large pad. As soon as the system had identified him, the locks on the door released.

He opened the door and waited for her to enter ahead of him.

Inside, the home was large but warmly decorated. The layout appeared user-friendly. The floors were a smooth, rich wood that flowed forward in a welcoming path. The walls were coated in an inviting beige bordered by gorgeous ornate trim drenched in a gloss white.

"There's a six-car garage with a nice selection of vehicles, all well equipped for speed and safety if we need to take a drive. Whenever the house is not in use, the agency investigators take turns, on a rotating basis, spending weekends here for the sole purpose of driving the vehicles. I was here two weekends ago. The solitude is incredibly relaxing."

As imposing as everything about the house was, there was no denying its infinite beauty. Someone had gone to a great deal of trouble to create a luxurious getaway. "Has anyone ever lived here?"

Todd shook his head. "Victoria had it built to replace the agency's former safe house."

Eva took her gaze from the stunning view out the towering windows. "Former safe house?"

"She and her first husband built a lake house shortly after starting the Colby Agency," Todd explained, "but their seven-year-old son was abducted from there, so Victoria couldn't bring herself to live in that house again."

Eva's hand went to her throat. "How awful. Did they find him?"

Todd shook his head. "No. Twenty years later, he found her. Her first husband had died years before. But Jim, the son, found his way home. He and his family live in the old lake house now. And Victoria and Lucas, her second husband, live in a gated community near there."

Eva was glad the story had a happy ending. It was too bad that Victoria's first husband hadn't lived to see his son return.

"The kitchen is stocked with anything you could want." He turned to Eva. "If you'd like to eat."

"I'm not really hungry." How could she eat? Poor Mrs. Cackowski was dead. She squeezed her eyes shut. Murdered. It didn't seem real...except she knew it was.

"Understandable," he said, drawing her attention back to him. He gestured to the staircase that wound around the far wall and up to the second floor. "Your room is the second on the left. Anything you might need during your stay has been provided."

Eva nodded. She needed some time to gather her composure. "I think I'll lie down for a while."

"I'll be close if you need me."

She nodded before moving to the stairs.

"Eva."

She turned back to him.

"I wish there was something I could say to make this crappy day better. You're hurting, I know. Feeling guilty. Blaming yourself for Mrs. Cackowski's death. But this isn't your fault. You just happened to be in the wrong place at the wrong time and got caught up in a gang war. But this will all get better. I promise."

Eva wanted to cry but she felt all cried out. She nodded and trudged up the stairs.

How would she ever face her neighbor's daughter? What words could she say to explain that the woman's death was her fault? No matter what Todd said, it was true. If Eva hadn't moved in across the hall from the sweet lady...if she hadn't killed a gang leader's brother...

Tears burning down her cheeks, she opened the second door on the left and walked into the room. The sheer size of the space distracted her for a moment, but it was another of those towering windows that drew her across the lush carpeting to the other side of the room. The view over the courtyard made her smile even as more of those tears spilled from her eyes. A pool with a gorgeous waterfall surrounded by lush shrubs and flowers. Rock paths bordered by dense greenery circled and cut across the rear property, creating a maze. If she were on vacation, this would be the perfect place to get lost.

But she wasn't on vacation. She was hiding from a murderer. Her bodyguard was a few steps away. If only Mrs. Cackowski had had a bodyguard.

Eva scrubbed the tears from her cheeks and turned her back to the window. She walked to the first of two doors. She couldn't think about that awful truth anymore. She had to be strong. Had to do whatever necessary to make this right.

So she focused on the mundane. Her room for the next few days had a generous walk-in closet. Several outfits—jeans, sweaters, slacks, blouses with matching shoes—had been hung at eye level. An ottoman sat in the center of the room. On top were a couple of nightshirts and a selection of lacy panties and bras.

Eva shook her head as she touched the tags on the items. She would have been certain they'd raided her closet if not for the product tags. The agency had gone to the trouble to purchase a mini wardrobe just like one she would have bought for herself based on what she had in her own closet. Why hadn't they just grabbed some of her stuff?

Didn't matter.

The next door led to a bathroom that would wow the most discriminating of tastes. From the hairbrush to the beauty products, she could be in her own bathroom except her entire space would fit into the tub of this one. This was very nice of Victoria. She hoped the arrangement wasn't costing Dr. Pierce a fortune.

Eva stared at her reflection. An elegant hiding place. And that was what she was doing. Hiding.

Unless the police caught Miguel Robles—and they hadn't been able to do so in more than a dozen years—or Robles killed her as he intended, this would never be over. More people could be hurt or murdered... like her sister.

How could she possibly hide like this?

She couldn't.

She owed it to Mrs. Cackowski and to herself to make sure Miguel Robles paid for his crimes. He shouldn't be allowed to get away with murdering a helpless elderly woman or anyone else. Since the police hadn't been able to get him, maybe she could. After all, she had the right kind of bait.

She was the woman who'd killed his little brother.

Miguel Robles wanted to kill her, too.

Sticking to her routine, staying out there where Robles could find her was the only way to lure him. The realization settled onto her like a massive stone crushing her chest. It was true. All this time the police had been unable to find enough evidence against him, but she could draw him out, make him careless—because he wanted so badly to avenge his brother.

All she had to do was convince her bodyguard to go along with her plan.

Eva trembled at the thought of Todd. That part might prove the most difficult. She had noticed the look of guilt in his eyes more than once. He felt bad for having left her all those years ago. She'd gotten that message loud and clear. If he was looking to make up and to be friends, he could forget it. She could never be friends with him.

She couldn't trust herself.

Better to stay at odds with someone so dangerous to her sanity.

A pang of hunger vied for her attention. She should eat and figure out how to convince Todd that her plan was the right one. It was the least she could do for her sweet neighbor. Dr. Pierce had ordered her not to come to work today. That was okay. The truth was she needed to pull herself back together before she dared set foot out of this safe zone.

Not to mention she had her work cut out for her right here. As much as she would love to pretend she could do what needed to be done on her own, she was smarter than that. She needed Todd's full cooperation.

She smoothed a hand over her clothes, tugged the loosening clip from her hair and finger combed it. Steadying herself, she took a big breath and exited the luxurious bedroom. Downstairs she wandered from room to room until she found Todd. To her surprise, he was scooping vanilla ice cream into a bowl.

"I seem to recall you were a chocolate man." She

moved to the massive island in the center of the room and propped herself there.

"Don't worry." He licked the scoop and set it aside. "That's coming." He reached for a jar and spooned chocolate onto the mound of creamy vanilla ice cream. "Join me."

"I think I'll see what else is available."

He moaned, drawing her attention to his lips as he withdrew the chocolate-smeared spoon from his mouth. "You should rethink that strategy. The latest philosophy on the art of eating is that having dessert first is better."

"Maybe for a guy who's solid muscle." She opened the glass door of the double fridge. "Not for a girl who has to watch every ounce of fat she eats settle on her hips and thighs."

The salad fixings in the crisper drawer would work. She gathered the bag of greens, a basket of tomatoes and the vinaigrette dressing. She pushed the door closed with her hip.

"I don't see anything wrong with your hips or your thighs."

Eva looked from him to her lower anatomy. "I've come to appreciate how scrubs can cover a multitude of sins."

"Somehow I doubt there are any sins to hide." He shoveled another spoonful of chocolate-covered ice cream into his mouth. Chocolate dripped down his chin.

Looking away, she plopped her load on the counter and searched for a plate. As hard as she tried to focus on preparing her salad and ignoring him, her gaze kept shifting over to see if he'd swiped that chocolate from his chin.

Finally, when she couldn't take it any longer, she grabbed a napkin and walked over to him, then held it out. "You have chocolate…on your chin."

Rather than take the napkin he grabbed her hand— the one clasping the napkin—and swiped at his chin. The stubble there tickled her fingers and made her breath hitch.

"Did I get it?"

She drew her hand from the clutch of his long fingers. "Yes."

Leaving the napkin on the counter in front of him, she walked back to her salad.

"I'm telling you—" she glanced back at him as he spoke "—I don't see anything that's not exactly right with those hips."

She flashed a fake smile. "Thanks."

Determined to pretend his words, his voice—his mere presence—were not turning her inside out, she placed the grape tomatoes atop the bed of Italian mixed greens and then added the dressing. As she twisted the top back on the bottle, she realized she needed something crunchy. Crackers, croutons. Something.

A bag of croutons landed on the counter next to her plate. Todd grinned. "You always liked some crunch with your salads."

"Thanks." Evidently they both remembered plenty about each other. But there was one thing she could not afford to forget. Todd Christian had stolen her heart and then he'd left it shattered on the doorstep when he walked away.

She had every confidence she could trust him completely with her life…but he could not be trusted in any capacity with her heart.

Chapter Six

Eva pushed to her limit. The grinding *whir* of the treadmill was the only sound in the room. She'd explored the entire house and decided a walk outside would do her good. Except Todd had insisted on accompanying her if she was setting one foot outside the house.

She'd wanted to shake him and inform him that her goal was to get as far away from him as possible. But that attitude wouldn't be conducive to cooperation.

A quick call to her friend Kim Levy had confirmed that they were shorthanded in the ER. Eva would use that as her first negotiating tactic. She doubted that particular tactic would carry much weight with her bodyguard, but it was a starting place. Then she had gone online and done extensive research on the True Disciples. She raised the incline on the treadmill and forced her exhausted body to comply. This well-equipped exercise room wasn't the only amenity in the Colby safe house. There was an office with three computers and the fastest internet access speed she had ever encountered, making her search all the easier.

She had discovered that Miguel Robles had been arrested no less than a dozen times but not once had the police been able to make it stick. He and his followers were thought to be involved in drug trafficking and gun smuggling across the northern border. Numerous murders were attributed to their ranks. Occasionally one or more of the followers would end up with a rap they couldn't escape. In each instance the gang member accepted his fate and never said a word. Deal after deal had been offered to lure in the "big fish" and not one of Robles's followers had accepted.

The elder Robles was more than the average thug. He was smart and he surrounded himself with above-average intelligence when it came to the highest level within or affiliated with his organization. Everyone from his CPA and his personal physician to the lawyers who represented him were from the city's most esteemed ranks. Just went to show what even an intelligent person with reasonable ethical standards would do for money.

Bottom line, she needed a better-than-average plan. An ordinary person like her couldn't hope to win a battle against Miguel Robles unless she had something extraordinary to offer.

Like the woman responsible for the death of his only brother.

She slowed the track speed and lowered the incline. Five miles was plenty to clock, particularly since she hadn't managed even a mile since last Friday. A few more minutes at a comfortable walk and her respiration was back to normal and she was ready to hit Stop. Eva grabbed her hand towel, patted her damp face and neck and headed for a shower. Maybe she would find an opening at dinner to discuss her concerns regarding her responsibilities at work. Other than her sister, her career was all she had. Though Dr. Pierce was onboard with her current dilemma, she doubted he would feel that way a month from now. He certainly wouldn't want to bankroll her situation forever.

Dragging out the inevitable wasn't going to alleviate this situation.

In the hall, she ran headlong into her bodyguard. She stumbled back in surprise, her fatigued muscles instantly reacting to the hard contours of his. "Sorry." She cleared her throat to buy time to steady herself. "I was lost in thought."

A bone-melting smile stretched across his lips. "Looks like you showed that treadmill who's boss."

"Ha, ha." She dabbed at her forehead.

His gaze slid down her body, lingering on her legs before returning to her face. The fitted running leggings were a little too well fitted, but there hadn't been anything else suitable for her workout in the provided wardrobe. The tank wasn't much better. Far tinier and tighter than she felt comfortable wearing with him around. The running shoes were high-end, and her size, and inordinately comfortable. As long as she was stuck here with him, she intended to spend as much time in the gym as possible. Alone, preferably.

Yet, deep down she understood that all the workouts in the world would not stop *this* inevitability either if she remained holed up with him for too long.

If she was lucky she would be able to talk him into going along with her plan sooner rather than later.

"Dinner's ready."

"You made dinner?" She didn't know why she was

surprised. He made dinner for her often...before. She'd assumed that was only because he had his own apartment and she lived in the dorm. Preparing dinner at home for a date was certainly cheaper than taking her to a restaurant. All that aside, he'd been a decent cook.

"Don't get excited," he warned. "It's only spaghetti."

"As long as there's a salad I'll be in heaven." At home and at work she popped more spaghetti dinners in the microwave than she would want to admit. It was the one surefire frozen entrée she could count on.

"Take your shower. I'll put together a salad and some garlic bread and track down a bottle of wine."

He flashed another of those charming smiles and goose bumps spread over her skin. She nodded and hurried to the stairs, putting distance between them as quickly as she could without breaking into a run. After finding Mrs. Cackowski murdered, the wine sounded like the best part of dinner. She could definitely use a glass to help her relax. But she had no desire to make herself even more vulnerable to Todd— especially *alone* with him.

Between the hard run and the luxuriously long shower, she felt immensely better. It never ceased to amaze her how much working out helped adjust her outlook. Hopefully, that good, confident outlook would help with what she had to do next.

Todd was heaping sauce onto a bed of noodles on a plate when she walked into the kitchen. He glanced up. "Have a seat. I'll serve."

A memory flashed through her mind, making her step falter. The image of her naked on his dining table, warm spaghetti sauce slipping down her skin, over her breasts…followed by his tongue lapping up the spicy sauce. He'd come to the living room to drag her to the kitchen to eat. She'd been waiting for him— naked and ready for more than just dinner. Together they'd removed his clothes on the way back into the kitchen. They'd had sex and eaten and had sex again… and snacked off each other's skin. He'd poured wine into her belly button and lapped it up, including the streams that slid well below her belly button.

Eva blinked away the memory and pressed onward to the table. This was not *that* table. This was not *that* house. Here and now was not who they *once* were.

He placed the loaded plate in front of her, then reached the wine bottle toward her glass and started to pour. "Say when."

She snapped out of her haze and held up a hand. "That's more than enough."

When he'd moved away, she reached for the fork and the small salad bowl he'd left by her plate. She picked at the one thing on the menu that didn't remind her of sex with Todd.

"Do you remember that time—"

"I don't know." Her gaze snapped to his.

He laughed as he filled his wine glass. "I haven't told you which time I meant."

She poked a forkful of greens into her mouth.

"We stood in line at that Italian restaurant in the pouring rain." He laughed. "It had just opened and everyone said it was the best in the country."

A laugh bubbled into her throat before she could stop it. She swallowed to prevent choking, then washed it down with a long gulp of wine. "I remember. I told you if it wasn't the best *bigoli* pasta I'd ever eaten I was going to make you regret that forty-five-minute, soaked-to-the-bone wait."

They both laughed for a minute but when their gazes locked, the laughter died. Their clothes had dripped onto the wood floor of the restaurant as they'd eaten. They'd laughed and stared directly into each other's eyes through the entire meal and then they'd hurried home to make love. Eva exiled the memories and reached for her glass again. A long gulp of wine later, she told herself to slow down. She picked at her salad a little longer before moving on to the spaghetti. It certainly did not help that images from their previous spaghetti-eating escapes kept flashing in her head.

"Did you discover anything interesting about Miguel Robles?"

Her head came up at his question. How did he know? "You monitored my online activities?"

He ducked his head. "It's my job. What kind of bodyguard would I be if I didn't pay attention to what you're doing?"

She wanted to be angry but couldn't muster up the wherewithal. "I learned more than I wanted to know," she confessed. She might as well say what was on her mind. "The police haven't been able to stop him or even come close to trapping him. Whenever they close in on some charge, someone else always takes the fall—if there's even a fall involved."

"Robles is no fool." Todd picked up his glass of water and downed a swallow.

Eva hadn't noticed until then that he had scarcely touched his wine, reaching for the water goblet more often than not. She felt a little woozy. Clearly that was what she should have done. She'd intended to keep a clear head…but those damned memories had taken her by surprise and dragged her down a too-familiar path.

"So," she set her fork aside, "what's the plan from here? If the police don't get him, and they haven't shown any sign of success so far, what do we do?"

"We've got people working on finding a weak link."

Eva wanted to believe that was good news but honestly she didn't see how. "I'm thinking he's the kind of man who either wins or he dies. No in between."

TODD STARED AT her and this time he reached for his wine. He knew better than to have even one glass when he was on duty, but he hadn't been able to help himself. She'd wanted some distance—that part had been clear. So he'd left her alone and watched over her shoulder via the sophisticated camera system in the house. He'd watched her search the web for information about Robles. He'd watched the worry on her face, the way she gnawed on her bottom lip as she read the stories that all—every damned one—ended badly.

Then she'd decided on a workout. He'd almost lost his mind watching her supple body move in that form-fitting outfit. Finding something to occupy his mind and his hands had been necessary. Somewhere in the back of his brain some neuron misfire had sent him down memory lane with an Italian menu. It wasn't until she walked into the kitchen that he'd remembered dripping that sauce on her bare skin and licking it off. Sitting at this table for the past half hour and remembering what they had done on his table had driven him out of his mind. He was so damned hard that at the moment he might not be able to stand without embarrassing himself.

He shrugged in response to her statement. "He's smart."

"We've established that he's smart," she sniped. "The question is, what are we going to do about it?" She finished off her wine. "I can't live like this forever. I have a career. I'm needed at the ER. They're short-handed today because I'm not there. And what about Lena? She'll be coming home in a few days. How do we protect her from this insane man?"

"I see where you're going with this." He stood and grabbed his plate. He'd lost his appetite as well as his raging erection.

By the time he reached the sink she was right behind him with her own plate in hand. "Then you know there's no other option. The police won't be able to stop him. You can't take down a bad guy without evidence. Their hands are tied. He'll just allow some low man in the gang hierarchy to take the fall for Mrs. Cackowski's murder—assuming his people can be tied to the scene. My sister, my friends—no one around me—will be safe until *he* is stopped. Mrs. Cackowski deserves justice."

He took her plate from her hand and put it in the sink with his own, then strode back to the table. His frustration level was way out of control. "What makes you think the Colby Agency can do anything—besides provide protection—more than the police are already doing? More important, what is it you believe you can do?"

"That's easy. The police want to charge him with one or more of his crimes. They want to prosecute him and see that he goes away for the rest of his life. We can help make that happen."

Todd's hands stilled on the bowl of sauce and the platter of pasta he'd intended to put away. His eyes fixed on hers. "You want to put yourself at risk."

She nodded, the move stilted. "Whatever it takes."

"Christ, Eva. You know we can't do that." He plopped the food back onto the table and set his hands on his hips. She was talking about sacrificing herself—sending a sheep to slaughter. "I don't ever want to hear you talk that way again."

"This is a war," she reasoned. "In wartime a soldier does whatever necessary to stop the enemy, right? This is the same thing. We have to draw him out or he'll just lay low and keep getting away with all manner of heinous crimes."

He shook his head. "Even in wartime there are rules of engagement, and protecting every single soldier in the field is priority one."

"If he isn't stopped, he'll just keep killing people. He won't stop until someone kills him. Since we can't exactly do that, we can at least help take him down." He opened his mouth to argue and she held up a hand. "I will not sit back and risk my sister's life or those of my friends. If that's what you expect—for me to do nothing and wait—then you can just take me home right now."

Rather than argue with her, he picked up the food again and headed for the counter. Maybe the wine had gone to her head. She damned sure hadn't eaten much today. He busied himself with putting the leftovers away and loading the dishwasher.

The problem was she was right. Miguel Robles would not stop until he'd accomplished his goal. That was his MO. He wasn't the sort of man to walk away.

Too much was riding on his ability to maintain a show of strength and power. The first sniff of weakness and his loyal disciples would eat him alive.

Eva watched him, her arms crossed over her chest, anger sparking in those green eyes of hers. "You know I'm right. All the police need is a decent opportunity to get to him. I can help make that happen. For Mrs. Cackowski." Tears glistened in her eyes.

"Let me think about it." The delay tactic likely wouldn't buy him much time, but it was the best he could do at the moment. He hadn't expected her to come out of the corner she found herself in wanting to dive into battle—at least not this early in the war.

Maybe she'd been right when she told him she wasn't the same naive girl she'd been ten years ago. He sighed. Which only made him want her more.

Idiot.

"You have until morning," she warned as she backed away from him. "FYI—tomorrow I'm going back to work. Hiding isn't the answer."

Chapter Seven

The Edge
Thursday, May 10, 10:00 a.m.

"Heart rate is 119. Respiration 39. BP is 90 over 60," Eva reported, her voice carrying above the sound of the gurney's wheels rolling as the EMT and paramedic pushed the patient through the emergency entry doors.

Dr. Arnold Reagan met them just inside. "Trauma room one," he ordered.

Another nurse, Kim Levy, as well as a respiratory tech joined Eva in trauma room one, taking over the patient from the two paramedics who'd delivered the young girl via ambulance. Kim checked the patient's airway and began the insertion of a trach tube.

"She's nineteen," the paramedic said as he backed toward the door. "She was walking to class. Witnesses said the vehicle carrying the shooter never slowed down."

"Alyssa Chavez," his partner added before they left to take another call.

Eva exchanged a look with Kim a split second before Reagan parted the already-torn blouse and had a look at the patient's chest. The bullet had entered center chest. Reagan swore. Their patient was in serious respiratory distress and profound hemorrhagic shock. If the internal bleeding wasn't stopped quickly, she would exsanguinate.

In the next two minutes the patient was readied and rushed to the OR. A surgeon was already standing by. Every second counted. Her life was literally slipping away in a far too rapid stream.

Eva stripped off her gloves, her adrenaline receding swiftly, leaving her weak.

The cell phone strapped to her ankle vibrated. She started to ignore it but decided it might be her sister. At this point she didn't dare ignore a call from anyone she cared about. Why hadn't she checked on her neighbor when she first noticed something was off? Maybe if she'd... *Stop, Eva.* It was too late for what-ifs. Finding justice for Mrs. Cackowski and all the others that bastard Robles had hurt was the one thing Eva could do.

A frown furrowed across her brow at the number on the caller ID. Not one she recognized. She answered with a tentative, "Hello."

"Alyssa Chavez is on you, Ms. Bowman. How many more do you want to die for you?"

The call ended.

Eva stared at the phone, her heart pounding harder and harder against her sternum. The caller had been male with a slight Hispanic accent. She stared at the blood-stained instruments on the tray...the pile of bloody gloves and sheets on the floor...the disarray in the trauma room that told the story of desperation.

A young woman was fighting for her life and that was her fault.

Eva wheeled and stormed out of the trauma room. This was enough. If that woman died…

"Eva."

She stalled and turned to the man who had spoken. *Dr. Pierce.* Her chest had grown so tight she could hardly catch a breath. "Sir?"

"When you've finished here, I'd like to see you in my office."

For a moment she wasn't sure how to respond. Flashbacks from those moments under his desk staring at the sleek leather shoes and the creased trousers joined the images of the man she had killed, her dead neighbor stuffed into her trunk and a beautiful young woman bleeding out on a gurney in front of her.

Please, God, don't let her die.

"Of course. Give me five minutes."

Dr. Pierce nodded and walked away. Eva stared after him, her head still spinning. When she'd managed to slow her thrashing heart, she washed up and headed to the station.

"You okay?" Kim glanced at her from the computer monitor she was bent over. "She might make it, you know."

Eva managed a stilted nod. "Hope so. Okay isn't something I'll be anytime soon." She heaved a big breath. "Dr. Pierce wants to see me in his office."

Kim considered her for several seconds. When Eva offered no further explanation, her friend and colleague said, "We're okay for now. See what Pierce wants and then take a break." She jerked her head toward the department exit. "Go."

"I'll be back in five."

She should let Todd know about the call. He would

need to inform the detectives on the case. Eva wasn't sure exactly where he was. He'd said he would be close, watching. There hadn't been time for her to wonder where or how he'd intended to do so. She hurried toward the corridor that led to the administrator's office. Her thoughts were rushing about in her head, a mishmash of worry and fear and desperation. The words the caller had said to her kept ringing in her ears. What she'd said to Todd last night had been right. Robles wouldn't stop unless he was behind bars—and maybe not even then.

How could she go on with her life and pretend Robles wasn't watching and waiting for the opportunity to snatch her or someone close to her off the street? If she persisted in her efforts to hide from him or to keep a stumbling block, i.e. her bodyguard, in Robles's path, he would only continue hurting innocent people like poor Mrs. Cackowski and Alyssa Chavez. Tears crowded into her throat.

Pull it together, Eva. She couldn't do what needed to be done if she fell apart.

Eva reached the lobby outside Pierce's office but his secretary was not at her desk. His door stood open so Eva walked to the opening and knocked once on the doorframe. Pierce looked up and motioned for her to come inside.

"Close the door."

Her hands shaking now despite every effort she attempted to keep them steady, she closed the door and crossed to his desk, then she waited for further instructions.

He glanced up, gestured to the chair in front of his desk. "Have a seat."

Had Pierce changed his mind about having her back at work? Had he already heard about the phone call? Impossible. She hadn't told anyone...but maybe the man who'd called her—presumably Robles—had called the administrator as well.

"Dr. Pierce, if you've changed your mind about my being here, I completely understand. Especially after what just happened." Eva squeezed her eyes shut a moment. "I am so sorry for what I've caused." More of that humiliating emotion gathered in her eyes. Where was her professional decorum?

He studied her for a moment, confusion lining his brow. "I'm not sure what you're talking about, Eva."

She met his questioning gaze. "A man called me right before you asked me to your office. He said..." She moistened her lips and wished she could swallow the lump of agony lodged in her throat. "He said Alyssa Chavez was on me." Deep breath. "It's my fault she was shot."

The tears burst onto her lashes and streamed down her cheeks before she could stop them. And she'd thought she was strong. Pierce grabbed a box of tissue and came around to sit beside her. He offered the box to her. "Have you notified Detective Marsh or spoken with Mr. Christian?"

Feeling more foolish than she had in years, she shook her head. "It just happened. I was going to after our meeting. I understand if you'd rather I didn't come back to work until this is...over."

Over? Would it ever be over as long as she was breathing?

"We need you here," he said, his voice uncharacteristically gentle.

Eva dabbed at her eyes. "My being here puts everyone in danger." She should have thought of that—she should also have realized that she was operating on emotion. Never a good thing.

"Your work here is what ultimately put you in this position, Eva. As a member of my staff I have an obligation to you. We've beefed up security. I can assure you that none of those thugs are getting in again. I'm fairly confident this Miguel Robles will keep hurting people in an attempt to get to you no matter where you are. If you'd been at home today that poor young woman may have ended up on your doorstep."

She couldn't argue with him there. Mrs. Cackowski was proof of his conclusion. The mere thought of how she'd looked stuffed into that trunk as if she were a worthless object rather than a lovely human being made her want to break down completely.

Eva took a steadying breath and gathered her scattered composure. "I appreciate your understanding. So, why did you want to speak with me?"

"I have a question about that night." The gentle tone was gone now. He sounded more like the commanding hospital administrator she had come to know.

"What would you like to know?" Her heart started that runaway galloping again. Did he somehow know she had lied to him about being in his office that night? Damn it, why hadn't she simply told him the truth in the first place?

You weren't thinking straight, Eva.

"You're certain you didn't see anyone come into or out of my office while you were in hiding?"

Damn. There it was. To reaffirm the lie was her first instinct. She hesitated. Lying to the man who was basically the only reason she had anyone watching over her in all this was simply wrong. She owed it to him to tell the truth. For what it was worth, at any rate.

"I wasn't completely forthcoming with you that night, Dr. Pierce." She shook her head and stared at her hands. "I was so shaken by what happened, I wasn't thinking clearly."

"I need you to start at the beginning and tell me exactly what happened after you left the ladies' room."

The sternness in his tone warned that he was not happy to hear her confession. Of course he wasn't happy. She had lied to the man who had given everything to designing and creating the most cutting-edge emergency department in the country. He had chosen his staff carefully and she'd just let him down. It would be a miracle if she still had a job when this meeting was over.

"I went into your office like you told me to do, but I heard someone coming so I hid in the first available space I spotted—under your desk." She braced for spilling the rest. "I hoped it was you coming to tell me everything was okay, but it wasn't."

He waited, silent, staring at her with an intensity that sent her composure fleeing once more.

"All I saw were his shoes and his trouser legs. Based on what I heard, he at first seemed to move around your office rifling through things, then he came to your desk. He opened each drawer and then I heard him scrawl something on your desk blotter." Her mouth had gone as dry as a box of fresh cotton balls.

"Did he take anything from the drawers?"

She shook her head. "Not that I saw. He pulled each

one open, rummaged through the contents and then pushed it close."

"Did it seem as though he might be photographing anything?"

Eva had to think about that one. "I don't think so. When he walked in he moved around the room without really stopping. He seemed in a hurry, maybe. At the desk... I suppose he might have photographed something during the few seconds before he started to open the drawers."

"He didn't say anything. Make a phone call?"

She shook her head again. "He just left that message."

I know what you did.

Pierce's silence added another layer of tension to the band already twisting tighter around her chest.

"Do you have any questions about that message?"

For the second time since she entered his office the urge to lie rushed to the tip of her tongue, but she resisted. "I'm certain you would tell me if there was a reason I needed to know."

"Eva." He exhaled a heavy breath. "When you create something everyone wants before anyone else can do so, you put yourself in a position to suffer extreme backlash and jealousy. Creating this unprecedented facility and launching a successful operation came at great professional and personal cost. Manufacturers of any medical product that is not used in this facility despise me. Most of the colleagues I once considered friends resent me. My efforts to do good have produced many enemies."

She'd had no idea how difficult his journey had been, though she did understand. Her sister's rising stardom as an investigative journalist had come at a high price. She'd lost lifelong friends and was as lonely as Eva. Just another confirmation that it was impossible to have it all. How sad that a man like Pierce had been forced to give up so much to create something so valuable to mankind.

"Don't waste your sympathy on me," he said, reading her face. "I executed more than my share of cutthroat maneuvers to make my success happen."

Eva felt so foolish now about the hasty decision she'd made to withhold the truth that terrifying night. "I apologize for not telling you everything. What I heard and saw didn't feel important considering the other events playing out so I dismissed the entire episode." A pretty pathetic excuse but it was the truth.

"Tell me about his shoes, Eva."

Surprised but determined to provide the best answer possible, she turned over the image in her mind. "Dark, black I think. Leather for sure. Not the off-the-shelf kind you find in a big chain department store. These were expensive shoes. The trousers, too. They were like a charcoal or dark gray color and creased as if he'd just, you know, gotten them from the cleaners."

"Tell me about his hand. You said you watched him open the drawers. Was he wearing a ring of any sort or a watch? Did you see his shirtsleeve? If so, what color shirt was he wearing? Cuff links?"

His rapid-fire questions reminded her of the interview with Detective Marsh and his partner. Had something else happened that may have been headed off if she'd told him the truth in the first place?

One more thing to feel guilty about.

Eva closed her eyes and replayed the moments in

her head. Light gray shirtsleeve to go with the darker gray trousers. She told Pierce as much. "There was a watch. No ring that I saw. No cuff links."

"What did the watch look like? Gold? Silver? An expensive brand?"

"Silver. Average size. Black face, I think. I couldn't see the brand but it looked heavy, expensive."

"Thank you, Eva. If you recall anything else, please let me know." He checked his cell. "By the way, the girl—Alyssa Chavez—is holding her own in surgery. I'll assign a security detail to her room when she comes out of surgery."

Relief swam through Eva's veins. "Thank God." She stood. "I'm not scheduled for the next two days. If you change your mind about me coming in on Sunday—"

"I won't."

"Thank you, sir."

As she exited the lobby area, Eva met his secretary, Patricia Ezell. The older woman smiled as if she understood the relief no doubt painting Eva's face. Once she reached the corridor she spotted the other possibility for the secretary's smile.

Todd Christian leaned against the wall, the nondescript tan scrubs taking not one ounce of masculinity away from him. How was it possible for any man to look that good in scrubs?

As she reached him, he pushed away from the wall. "I was hoping you'd give me a tour of the cafeteria. I hear it's the best hospital food in the city."

The tension that had held her in its ruthless grip as she entered Pierce's office eased, only to be replaced by a new kind of tension.

"It's good, yes. I just have to check in with the desk and then maybe I can take a lunch break."

He walked with her toward the ER. She tuned out the subtle scent of his soap. She should not have noticed the earthy, muted smell over the more potent odors of the hospital, and yet somehow she did.

"I received an unsettling phone call after the shooting victim, Alyssa Chavez, was taken to the OR," she told him, ready to get the painful business over. For the first time she wondered how Robles had her cell number? Who was she kidding? A scumbag like that probably had all sorts of unsavory resources.

"Robles?" He glanced at her, no surprise in his eyes. "I take it she was another message."

Eva nodded. "He said she was on me and asked how many more I wanted to die for me."

He stalled then, turned to her, one hand automatically going to her arm and squeezing reassuringly. "He wants you to feel as if this is your fault, but it's not. I'll call Marsh and let him know. Would you like me to take you back to the safe house? I'm sure Pierce will understand."

"No." She squared her shoulders and gave her head a quick shake. "I'm not going to be bullied by him. I'm here. I'm staying. Maybe before I come back on Sunday this will be behind me."

Those long fingers of his tightened on her arm once more. "We'll get him."

"Hope so."

They started walking once more and he said, "You were pretty awesome when the girl came in." He glanced at her, a big, wide smile on his face. "I liked watching you work."

"I didn't see you."

"I stayed out of the way. You were focused."

As they entered the emergency department, Eva couldn't deny a sense of pride at his words. "This is a good team. I'm lucky to be a part of it."

"I'm reasonably sure they know how lucky they are to have you as well."

She doubted Alyssa Chavez was feeling lucky. That massive cloud of doom that had disappeared for a few minutes was back. "Maybe."

Kicking aside the worry, she let Kim know she was taking an early lunch break. She and Todd could call Marsh together. Eva wanted to know what progress they had made on the case. The sooner they could tie all this to Robles, the sooner this would be over.

Except she wasn't holding her breath on that last part.

Robles wanted her and she had a bad, bad feeling nothing the police could do would change his mind.

This war was intensely private.

Eva had spent four years in college learning how and the past six working hard to save lives. For the first time in her life she contemplated the concept of taking one.

Chapter Eight

Todd did a perimeter check and then another walk-through of the house. Though it was doubtful anyone or thing could get past the security system without him knowing about it, another look never hurt.

Mainly because he needed to distract himself.

He'd spent twelve hours today watching Eva. Every move, every word…she didn't breathe without him knowing how deep. He'd kept as much distance as he dared, which was necessary on more than one level, but he'd stayed close enough to intervene if there was trouble. Other than the Chavez woman who'd served as a message from Robles, the day had been reasonably uneventful.

But watching her, listening to her voice, catching the occasional smile, had slowly but surely escalated the tension building inside him to the point of snapping. He had vivid memories of how her skin felt beneath his touch…how it smelled, tasted…but none of those memories held a candle to the real thing. Watching her was driving him out of his mind.

He shoved the last of the dinnerware into the dishwasher. When she'd announced that she was calling it a night early he'd almost hugged her in gratitude. Another few minutes and he would have undoubtedly said or done something he would regret. His self-control had long ago reached the breaking point.

Ten years was a long time to measure every woman he met, every kiss, every touch by the one he let go. He had no one else to blame for his misery...but he just hadn't been ready for the kind of commitment she deserved.

Or maybe he had been afraid he didn't deserve her.

What had a guy like him possessed to offer such an amazing woman? His parents had abandoned him and his little brother. His mother had died from the drugs she couldn't let go of and his father from a car accident—at least that was what he'd heard. He'd grown up in foster care. The last family who'd taken him in as a rebellious teenager had been good to him. He'd treated them the way he had all the others—with total indifference. Still, they hadn't given up. If he'd learned anything from those caring folks it was that his future was his to make. They'd drilled the importance of an education and a career into his head. With their encouragement, he'd made it to college. Then he'd met Eva and fallen head over heels...but how could he trust himself to do right by her when all that he'd known growing up was instability and one letdown after the other?

No matter that those last couple of years before college he'd found a good home, he could not trust himself to do the right thing. So he'd given every part of himself to her physically but he'd kept his emotional distance. Or so he'd thought at the time.

He had spent the decade since he left Chicago proving and establishing his worth. Achieving financial security. Devoted to his country at first, then back to the city that was home. As much heartache as he'd endured growing up in the Windy City, he had every right to walk away and never look back. But the truth was, Eva was still here. Not once in all this time had he admitted that part to himself. Building the life he wanted to share with someone one day had been his ultimate goal. The sad part was he hadn't found anyone else with whom he wanted to share that life. The past year he'd felt satisfied just sharing the city with Eva and waiting for her to marry some great guy who deserved her. Maybe then he could get on with his life.

Except she hadn't settled down with some other man.

When her file had been passed around at the agency's Monday morning briefing, Todd felt as if he'd been punched in the gut. He'd seen the news on Saturday about the incident at the Edge but her name hadn't been mentioned. As shocked as he'd been to learn she was involved and in danger, none of it had carried the impact of seeing her up close.

Yeah, he'd watched her a couple of times. Always from a safe distance. Educating himself on her life since he left her, keeping up with who she dated— none of it had adequately prepared him for standing in the same room with her. Watching her in the trauma room with that young woman who'd been shot had shifted something inside him. Her intense focus, capable hands and sincere care for the patient had made him fall for her all over again, only this time it was way beyond physical.

He now also fully understood he was in trouble.

He wanted to do far more than keep her safe. He wanted to touch her. He wanted to relearn every inch of her. He wanted to taste her...to hear her cry his name. He wanted her to belong to him.

Truly crazy, Christian.

An hour or so ago she had announced she needed a long hot bath and disappeared into her suite, and he had been trying to distract himself since. From time to time he checked the monitor. Looked without looking, so to speak. She was safe. In the bathroom there was no video, only audio. Just listening to her moans of satisfaction and the *drip, drip, drip* of the water had made him hard.

With the kitchen cleaned up, the perimeter and all egresses checked, he might as well hit the gym. Maybe he could burn off some of this excess adrenaline. Either that or he was going to explode. He hesitated at the door to her bedroom. His fingers fisted. She wouldn't want to hear about how badly he wanted her or how much he wished he could go back and have a do-over of the past.

He went into his own room—just across the hall—and peeled off his clothes. He tossed the scrubs on the bed and dug up a pair of running shorts and a tee. Once his sneakers were on, he hustled down the stairs. The best way to hammer down this kind of frustration was to run long and fast on an extreme incline setting. By the time he finished his body would be too physically spent for anything else.

He would defeat this need if it killed him.

EVA STARED AT her reflection as she set the hair dryer and brush aside. The ER had been hectic all after-

noon. Nothing as serious as a gunshot but more than
their fair share of automobile accidents, work-related
injuries and falls. The last patient who'd come in, an
elderly woman who'd broken an arm falling down the
stairs in her building's stairwell, had kept Eva an hour
past the end of her shift. The lady had wanted Eva at
her side every step of the way until she was released.
Eva wouldn't have left her for anything. She'd teared
up more than once thinking about how she hadn't been
there for her sweet neighbor.

Can't change that painful reality.

The best news of the day was that Alyssa Chavez
was going to make it. The surgery had been a success. Her family had arrived to be with her. Between
the newly increased security at the Edge and Chicago
PD, no one other than staff and family were getting
anywhere near her room.

Detective Marsh and his new partner from Gang Intelligence, Sergeant Carter, were less than thrilled with
the news that someone—probably Miguel Robles—
had contacted Eva and claimed responsibility for the
shooting. She suspected their plates were already more
than full. Piling on another incident, particularly a
shooting, was not helpful. For Eva it confirmed her
most troubling conclusion: Robles had no intention of
stopping until he'd gotten his revenge.

She turned away from the mirror and the weary reflection there. She'd dried her hair and pulled on a pair
of the provided PJs. These were comfortable lounge
pants with a matching tank-style tee. The pale pink
color was one of her favorites. She wished she had nail
polish and a couple of emery boards and she'd give
herself a manicure and pedicure. Not that she really

needed one or even wanted one but it would buy some time. Still too early for bed. Mostly she was too keyed up to dare lie down now. Spending a couple of hours tossing and turning was her least favorite thing to do.

Maybe she should have spent a little longer on the treadmill. No matter that her arms and legs felt like limp noodles, especially after the hot bath, the tension and frustrating anticipation hung on like a bad migraine.

Surrendering, she decided to take her towel and the day's clothes to the laundry room and then she intended to find a bottle of wine. Going for something stronger wouldn't be smart. Wine would do the trick without making her potentially do something stupid— as long as she stayed in her room and clear of any possibility of running into him. Being locked away alone in a house with Todd was asking for serious trouble.

It was silent downstairs. Images played across the television screen but the sound was muted. The main hall that cut through the center of the house was cool and quiet. No sign of Todd. The kitchen proved the same. Almost there. The laundry room was deserted, too.

She sorted her laundry into the labeled hampers. A cleaning team came in each day and took care of laundry and whatever else was needed. She imagined a clearance and a thorough background search were required of the team. Just giving them access to the property meant they were above reproach. As much as she hated doing laundry, she wouldn't want to live like this. The house and property were beautiful but far too grand for her taste. She liked simple and homey.

The security part didn't actually bother her. Dr.

Pierce was equally careful with his staff at the Edge. No one worked there without a flawless background. She found it near unbelievable that someone had managed to reach his office without being stopped. Then again, security had been focused on the events unfolding in the emergency department. There were cameras everywhere as well. Why hadn't the intruder been captured on camera? Maybe that was the reason for all the questions about what he had been wearing.

Eva had a feeling the man and his message were intensely personal to Dr. Pierce. Whatever it was, it went well beyond professional. Not that she was in the position to judge. Her life was wacked out on all levels. Her primary goal at this point was surviving—what she knew she had to do in order to stop Robles.

Without incident, she found the wine cellar that wasn't really a cellar but a climate-controlled room. Wherever Todd was he had so far stayed out of her path. She was grateful. There were hundreds of bottles on display in the wine room. Control pads showed the temperature and humidity level in the various glass-encased storage shelves. She moved through the rows of white and blush wines until she found something sweet and bubbly.

Back in the kitchen she prowled through the drawers until she found a new-model corkscrew that made opening a bottle of wine easy. When the cork popped free, she grabbed the bottle by the neck and a glass by the stem and headed back to the stairs. She'd made it all the way to the bottom of the staircase when she sensed his presence. A shiver rushed over her skin.

"Taking a friend to bed I see."

His voice held a teasing quality but there was something else she couldn't quite discern. She glanced over her shoulder to say good-night but the sight of him stopped her. He wore nothing but running shorts. The loose kind that rode high on his muscled thighs and low on his lean belly. The tee he'd been wearing was wadded in his hand and serving as a mop for his glistening chest.

The bottle in her hand felt suddenly too heavy. Her fingers tightened around it. She did the same with the glass. "Good night," she somehow managed.

Go. Now.

The words were her mantra as she climbed the stairs. The need to look back at him burned in her brain but she refused. He watched her until she disappeared beyond his view. She didn't have to look back to know he'd been watching her. She'd felt his gaze burning into her...smelled the devastatingly sexy scent of his clean sweat.

The instant she was in her room with the door closed, she poured a hefty serving of wine into her glass and downed it. She did the same with a second glass and had just poured a third when she heard the door across the hall slam.

She closed her eyes and sipped at the third glass. However hard she fought to banish the images, the events unfolding across the hall slowly unfurled in her brain. She imagined him stepping out of the shorts and peeling off his briefs—if he bothered with any these days. Then he would reach into the shower and turn on the water. Muscles would flex and contract under all that damp, smooth skin. She remembered every ridge and plane of his muscled body. The memory cut right through her, made her weak. She raised her glass and tried to drown the images.

Didn't work.

Oh, yes. She definitely should have stayed on the treadmill longer and stayed away from the wine.

"Bad decision, Eva," she said aloud.

She crossed the room, left the bottle and the glass on her bedside table and grabbed the television remote with both hands. After scanning the entire channel grid, she gave up and tossed the remote onto the bed. Flashes of her bodyguard smoothing a towel over his damp skin kept flickering in her mind. Memories from their past lovemaking whispered through her, making her tremble with need.

"Enough." She did an about-face before she could change her mind and stormed out of her room, straight across the hall and into his room without knocking or stopping or even breathing. The water still raining down in the bathroom didn't halt her either. The door was open so she walked right on in.

Her determined gaze landed on more than six feet of stunning male and then she stopped stone still.

He was still in the shower.

He stood, utterly, gloriously naked beneath the spray of hot water...steam rose around him. He was as beautiful as she remembered. Sleek skin taut over all those perfect muscles. Damp hair clinging to his neck, blue eyes closed. The heat from the shower had him semi-aroused.

As if he'd sensed her presence those pale blue eyes opened. Her heart nearly stopped as he reached to turn off the water, his gaze never leaving hers. He grabbed the towel from the hook next to the shower door and flung it around his hips. His attention focused intently on her, he stepped out of the glass cage and moved toward her like a lion tracking his prey...and she was that prey.

"Are you all right?" His gaze swept over her from head to toe and back as if he'd expected to find a bullet wound or other trauma. The fingers of one hand raked the damp hair from his face. Water trickled down his skin, disappearing into the towel draped low on his lean hips.

For a single second she couldn't move or speak.

"Eva."

The sound of her name on his lips shattered the trance she had slipped into. She closed the short distance between them and stared straight into his eyes. "We should just get this over with so we can move on. Ignoring it is wearing me out."

Those blue eyes narrowed slightly. "How much did you have to drink, Eva?"

"Really?" Her hands went to her hips. "That's all you've got?" She grabbed his face, went up on tiptoe and kissed the hell out of him.

He held absolutely still the first few seconds, his powerful arms hanging at his sides. Her fingers forked into his wet hair and she leaned her body into his damp skin. He made a sound, not quite a growl. Still he didn't give in. She drew her mouth from his, allowed her fingers to trace down his magnificent chest, over mounds of rock-hard muscle. Her gaze followed that incredible path. A smile tugged at her lips when her fingers reached his naval and the swirl of golden hair there.

"Eva, we should talk about this."

"I don't want to talk." She stepped back, peeled off her now damp top and tossed it aside, allowing her breasts to fall free against her chest. Then she shucked the lounge pants, let them hit the floor in a puddle of silky fabric around her feet. Wearing nothing but lacy pink panties, she stepped out of that soft circle and toward him once more.

His gaze roamed down her body, burning her as if he were touching her. The slight hitch in his breath had her heart pounding even harder.

"Are you going to stand there," she asked, "or are you going to man up and do this?"

His jaw hardened and the purely female muscles between her thighs reacted, pulsing with need. Oh, he was angry now.

"You don't want to do this," he growled. "It's the wine."

She laughed. Even the sound of his voice made her nipples burn. "I'm not that naive little virgin you discovered in college. I know exactly what I want and right now it's you. If you think you can handle it, that is."

She sensed the moment he broke. He charged toward her and she lost her breath all over again. He pulled her hard against his body and allowed her to feel just how ready he was beneath that terry cloth. "Don't say I didn't warn you."

"Talk, talk," she accused. He held her so tight she could barely breathe the words.

He yanked the towel from his hips, the friction of it pulling between their bodies making her gasp. He shoved the door shut and trapped her against it. Her legs went around his waist. She pressed down against him, cried out in need.

"Not so fast," he snarled.

His right hand found that place between her thighs that ached so for him. He pushed aside the lace in his way and rubbed until she thought she would die of want and then he slid a finger inside, then another. She whimpered, her eyes closing with the intensity of the pleasure.

"No," he ordered. "Look at me."

She forced her eyes open, read the fury in his. "No more foreplay. Give me what I want. Now," she demanded.

"If we're going to do this we'll do it my way." The pad of his thumb nailed that sensitive spot once more while his fingers plied her body. "I want you looking at me when I make you scream for more."

She dug her heel between the cheeks of his muscled ass and rubbed. He gasped and his eyes drifted shut. "Now who's not looking?" she accused.

His fingers explored more deeply, stretching her, readying her for what was to come. Her breath caught as a ripple of pleasure shot through her. She clamped onto his fingers with those throbbing inner muscles and squeezed. "You keep playing and I'm going to remember I don't really need you to do this," she hissed.

He snatched his fingers away, stared at her, unmoving, his jaw pulsing with more of that fury. Staring into his eyes with matching defiance, she drew one hand from his neck and reached between their bodies. She rubbed that place he refused to assuage and her body tightened with growing desire. Harder, faster, she massaged that sensitive nub until her eyes closed and she moaned with the mounting pleasure. The first waves of orgasm spiraled from the very center of her being. Her body undulated against her hand, wishing it was his wide palm and blunt-tipped fingers.

Suddenly he yanked her hand away and plowed into her. She screamed with the exquisite pain of penetration. He groaned long and loud. For endless moments they didn't move, their bodies joined so completely and yet burning and pulsing for more. He shifted ever so slightly and a full body reaction pulsed through her, taking her over the edge. He stilled, waited, letting her go without him.

Just when she thought her mind and body couldn't take anymore, he started to move. Slow, shallow thrusts, his powerful hips rocking into her. His mouth closed over hers, kissed her, savored her, tasting her lips with his teeth and his tongue and then exploring deeper. His hands tightened on her thighs, pulling her more firmly against him, forcing his thick sex farther inside her.

"Say it," he murmured against her lips.

She bit his jaw.

"Say it," he commanded, nuzzling her cheek with his nose.

"More," she argued.

He thrust harder, deeper. She gasped.

"Say it."

She closed her eyes and lost herself to the new waves building from the inside out, tearing her apart. She arched to meet his powerful thrusts. Cried out with the pleasure-pain of just how deep he was inside her. Orgasm shuddered through her a second time, making her tremble.

He pressed his forehead against the door beside her head and whispered in her ear, "Say it."

She was too weak to argue but somehow she found the strength to cry, "More!"

He pulled her against his chest, flung open the door and carried her to the bed. They came down on the mattress together. One hand went under her bottom, and he lifted her hips to him, opening her wider as he plowed over and over into her. He squeezed her bottom.

She planted her heels on the mattress and met his deep thrusts. "More," she whimpered. Sweat coated their skin, the smell of it comingling with the sweet tang of her orgasms.

With his free hand he stroked her rib cage, trailed his fingers over her, bone by bone, until he grasped her breast. He squeezed, tempted her nipple. She bit her lip to prevent calling his name. She was too weak to fight anymore…too overwhelmed to beg. Her fingers twitched, her toes curled…almost there.

He roared with the orgasm finally overtaking him.

The new waves flowed over her, dragging her into that place of pure sensation a third time while he surrendered to his own.

He groaned a frantic sound as they collapsed together.

Eva closed her eyes against the burn of tears. She should have drunk more of the wine. She should have realized that there was no getting *this* out of the way.

This part of her still belonged to him…

Chapter Nine

Friday, May 11, 8:30 a.m.

Awkward was the word of the day.

Todd opened the fridge and put away the orange juice while plates and forks rattled in the sink. Eva had said exactly six words to him. *Morning*, when she first came into the kitchen. *Yes*, when he'd asked if pancakes would be okay for breakfast. And *I'll get the dishes* when she'd finished eating.

Last night he'd wanted to talk to her about what happened but she'd rushed away so fast he'd barely had time to get his head back down to reality. She'd wriggled free of his arms and left him spent across the bed. When he'd stumbled from the tangled sheets and dragged on his jeans, he'd knocked on her door but she ignored him. He'd heard the water running in the en suite bath. Apparently she couldn't wait to wash him off her skin.

Later he'd wanted to check on her via the security system but the idea had felt completely wrong. Instead, he'd crawled back into his bed and burrowed himself into the scent of her that was all over his sheets, all over his skin. He'd dreamed of their first time together—her first time with any man.

This morning he had awakened wanting more.

She clearly had not.

Their breakfast conversation had consisted of forks scraping against stoneware and coffee mugs settling on the counter. It would be easy to blame what happened on her. She'd come to him after all. But that wouldn't be fair. He was as responsible as she was and no amount of analyzing would change that cold, hard fact.

Dissecting what happened wouldn't alter the bottom line either: he was here to protect her, not take advantage of her vulnerability. Last night she had been vulnerable and he had taken advantage of that vulnerability.

"No work today, right?" he asked, his voice sounding particularly loud after the long minutes of silence. He knew the answer but it was the only conversation opener he could come up with at the moment.

"I volunteer at a walk-in clinic once a week." She dried her hands. "Today's my day."

He leaned against the counter, keeping at least a half dozen feet between them. "I'll need the address so I can decide on the best route to take and any other relevant info to pass along to Michaels."

Ian Michaels was his backup. Todd kept him apprised of their movements. The worst thing a protective detail could do was fail to report its movements. If communications were compromised, backup would have no idea where to start the search or where to send help.

"Warren Boulevard." She wrapped her arms around

her middle and met his gaze for the first time since she clambered out of his bed last night. "It's an old church at the intersection of Warren and Western. Anyone who needs medical attention is welcome. There's no charge. Church donations pay for the needed medical supplies. Several nurses and doctors donate their time. It's important work," she tacked on as if she feared he might debate the day's agenda.

"Maybe I can help, too."

She looked away. "Maybe."

It was highly probable that Robles had made it a point to learn her routine. "Have you been to the church since last Friday?"

"No." She straightened and tugged at the hem of her blouse.

"Good. Robles might not be aware you volunteer at that location."

Staying aware was key to navigating any area and the level of risk. Anyone looking to commit a crime would always single out a distracted victim over one paying attention.

Her destination was one with which he was familiar and, hopefully, Robles hadn't connected to her. "I'm ready when you are."

"I need to grab my bag."

He watched her walk away. The jeans and gray pullover shirt hugged every sweet curve he had traced with his hands and body last night. He closed his eyes and relived the moment when she interrupted his shower. He'd been done with the shower for a few minutes but he'd stood under the spray of water in hopes it would relieve the tension vibrating in his body. The water hadn't even come close to releasing his tension when she burst in. Watching her strip off her clothes and then stand before him in offering, he'd almost lost it.

She was still as beautiful as he remembered. Every inch of her was perfectly toned yet so damned soft. The first time they were together he'd been terrified that he would hurt her. She'd seemed so tender and fragile. She'd set him straight right from the start. Eva Marie Bowman was strong and tough and damned determined. She and her sister hadn't been shuffled around to foster homes the way he had, but they had experienced their share of tragedy and hard times. Like when their father died, leaving behind a wife who'd never been anything but a homemaker and two young girls who needed a college education. Their mom had worked three minimum-wage jobs to help get them through school. She had died a few years ago while he was still overseas. One of the first things he'd done when he got back to Chicago was take flowers to her grave.

Stella Bowman had liked him. Maybe she'd changed her mind after he left, leaving her daughter's heart broken. Learning to live with that prospect had been almost as hard as leaving Eva in the first place. Even if by some stroke of luck he was able to make amends with Eva, he couldn't change how her mother had gone to her grave feeling about him. Some things couldn't be undone. Yet another of those things was Eva's sister. He wasn't looking forward to running into Lena. Like most big sisters, she preferred to kick the ass of anyone who hurt her baby sister to talking things over.

"I'm ready," she announced.

He cleared his head and led the way to the garage. At the door he grabbed the keys for the Dodge Charger. He liked that it was black with heavily tinted windows and had an engine made for speed if the need arose.

"We'll take the Charger," he said when she stood at the front of the garage surveying the line of automobiles. He hit the fob and unlocked the doors of the sleek black vehicle that sat third from the right. He'd driven it several times. He felt at home behind the wheel of the Charger more so than the other vehicles.

While she climbed in he set the safe house security system to *away* using his phone. Once he was behind the wheel and had started the engine, the proper garage door automatically opened. As soon as he'd backed out, it closed once more. Five seconds later the garage went into the same *away* lockdown as the house.

For the first few miles he deferred to her decision to keep the silent treatment going. As a soldier in Special Forces he'd learned to wait out the enemies. Hours or days…whatever it took. He'd honed his patience and his ability to remain calm and steady with years of training and operation execution.

But he was no longer a soldier. This was a different world and in this world he was in charge. And he was frustrated and annoyed—mostly at himself.

"About last night—"

"I don't want to talk about last night." She stared out the window at the luxury estates set back amid the lush trees along the road.

Okay, so maybe his strategizing skills where these sorts of things were concerned were a little rusty. Maybe a lot rusty. The past decade he'd satisfied his baser physical needs with one-night stands and no-strings-attached encounters. He hadn't been in a relationship since...

Since he left Eva.

"We should talk about last night anyway." He slowed for a turn. A couple more and they would hit Central Avenue.

"We had sex." She stared straight ahead, her jawline rigid, her hands clutching the armrest as if she feared he intended to rocket into hyper speed. "What's to talk about? It was fine. Good...enough."

"Good enough?" A jolt of outrage joined his mounting frustration. Was she kidding? The sex had been mind-blowing...fantastic. A second's hesitation nagged at him. No way. She had been thoroughly satisfied. He knew the sounds Eva made when she was enjoying herself. She had enjoyed last night as much as he had.

"That's what I said." She released her grip on the armrest to bend forward and dig around in that enormous leather bag she carried as a purse. He was fairly certain it was the same one she'd carried in college. She called it her good luck bag. It was her last gift from her mother as she entered college. She jammed sunglasses over her eyes and returned her attention forward.

He did the same. The sex had been better than good. She was yanking his chain, trying to tick him off. He got it. Fine.

The truth always came out in the end.

Good Shepherd Church, 11:00 a.m.

"YOU'LL BE AS good as new in a couple of days." Eva smiled at the elderly man whose allergies were giving him a hard time. "Nurse James will give you the meds the doctor prescribed as you leave. Remember to go to the Imaging Center for your appointment for the chest X-ray. Dr. Taggart wants to be sure there's nothing more going on with that nagging cough."

Mr. Hambrick smiled. "Thank you, Eva. You always make my day better."

She gave him a wave as he shuffled off to the checkout area. Her duty here was bittersweet. Seeing all the elderly who had no one else at home or nearby to take care of them or the incredibly poor that had no other means of medical care tugged hard at her heartstrings. On the other hand, knowing that she made a difference in their lives was a soothing balm to her soul.

Certainly made her forget all about her own problems.

As if her mind wanted to remind her that her problems were close, she glanced over at Todd. He was bandaging Rhea Gleason's ankle. She'd managed to cut herself pretty deeply puttering in her flower garden. Eva had inspected Todd's repair work and been duly impressed. With a tetanus shot and an antibiotic just to be sure, Rhea, too, would be fine in a couple of days.

Todd offered his hand to assist Rhea to her feet and she smiled up at him as if he'd whispered a secret to her that only the two of them would ever know. Eva doubted a man as handsome and charming as Todd had ever provided the woman with medical care. Not that Dr. Taggart wasn't charming and quite handsome in his own way—he was. He was also more giving than any doctor she knew besides perhaps Dr. Pierce.

Rhea glanced at Eva and smiled. Todd did the same.

Pretending she hadn't noticed the latter, Eva turned her attention to the sign-in sheet. She called the next patient's name and chatted with the older man as if all were right in her world. Last night should never have happened. She wanted to be glad she'd broken the tension mounting between her and Todd...but she wasn't. The strategy she now recognized as fatally flawed was supposed to prove that Todd Christian wasn't as amazing as she remembered. That the lovemaking skill of the man couldn't possibly be as incredible as the memories. That he would never be able to make this more experienced and mature Eva feel as if her world had tilted on its axis.

You were so wrong, Eva. So, so very wrong.

She'd hoped that at barely nineteen and with no experience that what she remembered was nothing more than blind passion driven by the sweet innocence of first love. Not the case at all. She now fully and undeniably grasped the reason no other kiss, much less any other aspect of lovemaking, ever lived up to his. He was the master. A fantastic lover.

But great sex did not a real relationship make.

Relationship?

She wasn't looking for a relationship.

"Is the old ticker still beating?"

Eva blinked away the distraction, realizing she'd had the diaphragm of her stethoscope against her patient's chest for far longer than it should have taken for her to listen to his heart and lungs.

She smiled and listened a little longer to cover her slip-up, then she removed the tips from her ears. "Sounds as strong as ever, Mr. Fry. Lungs sound clear, too."

Lawrence Fry was seventy and he'd lived in Chicago his whole life. He'd spent most of those years playing a saxophone in various clubs downtown and eventually in the street for donations. He'd told her how the basement of this very church had once been used to hide booze during Prohibition—unbeknownst to the reverend at the time, of course, he always clarified. Fry was one of the most knowledgeable people Eva had ever met when it came to Chicago history, especially the more infamous history.

Like many of their patients he had no family. This free clinic was the only medical care he received. Yet the kind older man never complained. What he did was consistently promise Eva that he intended to play his sax at her wedding. She didn't spoil the moment by informing him there were no plans for a wedding in the foreseeable future.

"That's always good news."

Eva placed the BP cuff around his right arm. "What brings you in today? Are you experiencing any symptoms I need to know about?"

"Actually, I only came so I could see you." He glanced around and leaned forward. "I heard through the grapevine that you're in trouble."

Surprise followed by a trickle of fear made its way into her veins. "You don't need to worry about me, Mr. Fry. I'm doing great, I promise. Where did you hear this?" He kept quiet while she pumped the cuff and took the reading. "One fifteen over seventy. BP looks great."

He took her hand when she reached to undo the cuff. "Word is all over the street that Miguel Robles wants to find you. You aren't safe here or anywhere else, Eva. Don't stay around here so long today. I know this man. He's the worst of the worst. I got mixed up with him and his crew years ago—before he was the big cheese he is now. He's bad, bad news. Watch your back, my friend."

Eva removed the cuff and gave him a nod. "I will. I promise."

He stood and gave her a pat on the shoulder. "I won't take up any more of your time, then. I have a gig over on Harrison Street."

"You be careful, too," she said.

"Always." Mr. Fry winked and ambled on his way.

She watched him go, worry gnawing at her. Nothing he'd said should surprise her, and yet, somehow it did. She kept thinking if she just went on with her life the whole thing would go away.

Not going to be that simple.

Not only was the problem not going away, the news was spreading. Miguel Robles had no choice. He had to save face or risk a revolution against his reign of terror.

The cell strapped to her ankle vibrated. Eva decided to take a break and answer the call in the ladies' room. She moved to the next temporary cubicle to let Betty James know she was taking a break. The exam rooms, so to speak, were made up of all sorts of donated decorative screens from sleek black Asian-inspired wooden ones to metal and fabric shabby chic creations.

Betty gave her a thumbs-up. Eva weaved her way around the makeshift exam rooms and to the entryway of the sanctuary where the restrooms were located. The small entryway was flanked on the left by the women's restroom and on the right by the men's.

A double door front entrance was monitored by two uniforms from Chicago's finest. One of the officers, Kelly O'Reilly, waved at her. Every time she worked in this neighborhood he made it a point to stop by and ask her out. Rather than merely stop by today, he and his partner were hanging around. She decided that either Detective Marsh or Todd had warned him about Eva's situation. To avoid questions about her current dilemma or that inevitable awkward moment when she would have to come up with another excuse about not going out with him, she ducked into the restroom before he could catch her.

She'd had more than enough awkwardness today already.

Eva snagged the phone from her ankle and checked the screen. *Lena.* Her heart sped into a run. She hit the screen to return the call and tried to slow the pounding in her chest. When she heard her sister's voice, her knees almost buckled. Thank God. She should have called her already. They lived in the same city and still both of them were bad to let too much time pass between calls and visits.

"Why haven't I heard from you since you moved to this secret location?"

Eva smiled, relieved to hear her sister's snarkiest tone. "Because I've been busy." Flashes of sleek skin and flexing muscles flickered in her brain. Eva pushed them away.

"So, how's it going with Dick?"

Eva laughed. Her sister always did have a way with words. The ability to summarize a situation quickly and eloquently had made her one of Chicago's most beloved reporters. "Things are fine with *Todd*. He's an excellent bodyguard." More of those sensual images and sounds from last night whispered through her mind.

"There was never anything wrong with his body," Lena retorted. "It's his heart where the trouble lies."

"I'm not having this discussion. How's it going in DC?" Why she felt any need whatsoever to defend Todd she would never understand. The idea that her sister's words inspired a glimmer of anger made her want to scream in frustration. But she wouldn't do that either.

"Oh my God."

Those three words told Eva that she was in trouble.

"You slept with him already."

Humiliation and frustration roared through her in equal measures. "I did not sleep with him." It was true. They had sex. There was no sleep involved.

"You never have been a good liar, little sister. You had sex with the man which means that when I get back I have to kick his ass."

Eva burst into full-on laughter. "Kicking his ass will not be necessary. I ended a long dry spell. No big deal. It was just sex."

"Who do you think you're kidding? You ended your dry spell with the jerk who broke your heart when you were just a baby. We need to have a long talk when I get back, sweetie. You have got to start getting out more."

"I was not a baby. I was nineteen." She ignored Lena's other comments. They had been down that "fix her up with this one and then that one" road. Her sister was a great reporter but she totally sucked at matchmaking. "Everyone gets their heart broken, Lena. It's not the end of the world."

She made a rude sound. "It's different when it's your little sister."

"Are you being extra careful?" It was time to change the subject. Eva knew Lena would not let it go unless she ignored further attempts to discuss the matter. Maybe not even then. Persistence was another of her award-winning traits.

"I am. I'm so bored I could take a cooking class. I know this political stuff is super important right now but I'd much rather be back in Chicago doing something that feels more real."

"How about I give you an exclusive when this is over?"

"That's as real as it gets," Lena said softly. "You sure you're okay? You could come stay with me. I'm sure Dick knows what he's doing but I can't help but have reservations."

"He knows what he's doing and I'm being very careful." She stared at herself in the mirror. "I'm at the church clinic today so I really should get back out there."

"I'm doing a story on that soon," Lena warned. "You guys are doing great work. I want the city's uppity-ups to hear about it more often."

"We can always use more donations," Eva admitted.

"You got it. Love you."

"Love you." Eva ended the call and tucked her phone away.

Lena reminded her more of their mother every day. There was just one place where the two had differed immensely. Lena might never forgive Todd for walking away all those years ago when their mother, Stella Bowman, had loved Todd even after he was gone. When he left she had held Eva and promised her she would be fine. She'd also made a prediction or maybe it had been nothing more than wishful thinking. Either way, her mother had been adamant about her conclusion on the matter.

He'll be back one day. You'll see. Todd Christian loves you in a way that can't be ignored.

Tears burned Eva's eyes even now and she swiped them away. "Miss you, Mom."

Eva knew her mother had meant well. She never gave up on anyone she loved. Eva hoped she hadn't spent the last decade unconsciously pushing everyone else away because of what her mother had predicted.

Stella Bowman had been right about one thing. He was back.

But it wasn't for the reason her mother had meant. It was coincidence. And when the tragic events that had aligned to create the chance reunion were no longer a threat to her, he would be gone. Just like before.

Eva drew in a deep breath and pushed out the door. She jumped when her gaze collided with the blue eyes she feared would haunt her dreams for as long as she lived.

"You ready for lunch?" Todd rubbed his lean abdomen. "I'm starving." He hitched his head toward the cop who had a crush on her. "O'Reilly tells me there's a great taco stand next to the Mickey D's across the street. He's even offered to make the food run."

Eva smiled. "Sounds good." She turned to the cop

watching Todd like a hawk. "I would love to have lunch with you, Kelly."

He looked from Todd to her and his fierce expression softened. "Text me your order and I'll be back in a snap."

Eva asked Betty and Dr. Taggart if they would like something from the taco stand, and they both declined so she sent her order to Kelly. When he returned she made it a point to chat mostly with him as the three of them ate lunch together.

As she returned to seeing patients she felt Todd watching her. She knew it wasn't right but she was enjoying ignoring her bodyguard. The idea that he seemed jealous made her far happier than it should.

Sometimes being bad just felt so damned good.

Chapter Ten

6:15 p.m.

Officer O'Reilly and his partner descended the steps at the front of the church with the final two patients of the day. The fondness in Eva's smile as she told Todd how the elderly women who came each week to have their blood pressure checked stirred an unfamiliar longing inside him. The women were sisters, twins no less, and they had lived together since their husbands passed away twelve or so years ago. Both had flirted relentlessly with Todd until he'd escorted them to the door and then they'd turned their gregarious attention to the officers.

Todd hadn't minded. In fact, he hoped he was as healthy as those two when he reached his eighties. He'd been only too happy to take care of the ladies while Eva and the other nurse packed up for the day. While he'd attended to the twins, the screens and portable tables had been stored away in a large supply closet and the remaining medical supplies had been taken away by Dr. Taggart. Eva's team had the set up and the cleanup down to a well-practiced routine.

They would be out of here in the next fifteen minutes. As he surveyed the boulevard that ran in front of the church, he noted the car parked across the street, dark, heavily tinted windows and big, shiny wheels. His warm thoughts of family and all those lifelong connections he'd missed, and suddenly found himself wanting, faded with the reality of what was no doubt about to go down.

Trouble.

Easing back into the entryway, he waited until he was out of sight of anyone in the car and then he turned and moved from window to window, checking the streets from every available angle. Thankfully only four of the windows in the main sanctuary were stained glass—the rest were clear, allowing a view of the streets that ran along two sides of the church. Eva had said that donations were slowly but surely replacing all the windows with stained glass to look like what would have originally been in the church. Today, Todd was grateful the renovation was not complete. He spotted at least one other suspicious vehicle.

Damn.

"Christian."

He turned to Rob Gates, the officer working with O'Reilly. Gates hitched his head toward the front entry as O'Reilly joined him. Todd glanced over to Eva and her friend who were finishing the cleanup before joining the two uniforms.

"You saw them, too?"

O'Reilly nodded. "My captain told me to keep an eye out for potential gang members." He nodded toward Eva. "Gates and I have monitored the streets all day. Those lowlifes showed up about two minutes ago. I've already alerted my chain of command that we may have a problem."

Relief rushed through Todd so hard and fast he almost hugged the guy. "You have an ETA for backup?"

"Six, seven minutes." O'Reilly glanced back at the front entrance. "As long as they don't make a move between now and then, we should get out of here with no problems."

But nothing was ever that easy—not when the nastiest of thugs were on the trail of their target.

As if the enemy understood they'd been made and time was short, the first hail of gunfire shattered the glass in the double front doors and burrowed into the brick walls on either side of the entry.

As O'Reilly and Gates readied to return fire, Todd rushed to Eva and her friend. "Under the pews."

The pews weren't bulletproof by any means but the thick, dense older wood would provide some level of protection, and some was better than none.

Eva grabbed Betty's hand and hurried to do as Todd asked. He took a position at a window facing Warren Boulevard. A quick look verified his worst fears. The bastards were moving in.

"We've got movement," O'Reilly shouted.

Todd kept his head down as he moved back to where the women were hiding. To Eva he said, "They're coming in. We need to find someplace else to hide the two of you."

"The basement," Eva said, fear shining in her eyes.

He shook his head. "We don't want to get pinned down where we can't get out."

"There's a tunnel," Eva explained. "Mr. Fry told me about it."

Todd hesitated again. "What if he's wrong?"

Eva shook her head. "I don't think he is. It's a risk I'm willing to take."

She turned to her friend and the other nurse nodded. "I'm with you."

Eva led the way to the storeroom that had once been a coatroom. A single door on the far side of the room opened to a narrow staircase that plunged nearly straight down. Todd pulled her back. "I go first."

She stepped aside and allowed him to take the first step down. Since he didn't spot a light switch or pull string, he used his cell's flashlight app to see where the hell he was going. "Close the door," he said over his shoulder, "and stay close behind me."

The steps continued downward for about ten feet, ending abruptly at a brick floor. He felt along the wall next to the final step. No switch. Using the flashlight app, he surveyed the small basement and spotted a pull string that led up to an old single bare bulb fixture on a rafter overhead.

He gave the string a yank and a dim glow came to life. Boxes covered in dust lined the far wall. Rows of shelves with books and literature lined another. A couple of tables and several chairs were piled in yet another corner. No windows and no doors.

"Where is this tunnel supposed to be?" Todd looked to Eva.

She shook her head. "I don't know."

"I'll start looking where the books are stored," Betty offered.

Eva headed toward the stack of tables and chairs.

Todd surveyed the bare wall beneath the staircase. No sign of an opening there so he moved on to the boxes. Some of the boxes were fairly heavy, others were so light he wondered if there was anything inside. Then he found the reason for the lighter boxes. Behind them was a small door, maybe two feet by two feet. The door was wood and reminded him of an old-fashioned crawl space door. Both the houses where he'd lived as a curious ten-year-old had doors exactly like this one that led to the area under the house. He and another foster boy had explored the space too many times to recall.

He opened the door. Sure enough, it led to a tunnel that looked to be five or six feet tall, maybe three feet wide and disappeared into the darkness well beyond where his flashlight app would reach. If the exit was sealed off, the find wasn't going to help much. In fact, they could end up trapped like rats.

If there's no exit, you already are.

A deep whoosh resonated overhead. Todd stilled and evaluated the sound. Not gunfire. Not a bomb.

Fire.

"Here!" Todd called, keeping his voice low despite the worry pounding inside him.

Eva and Betty hurried over to his position. "The two of you go first." He pulled the string to extinguish the light. "I'll pull some of the boxes back to the opening to conceal it and then I'll be right behind you."

Footsteps pounded on the stairs. Todd shoved his cell in his back pocket and drew his weapon with one hand and ushered the women into the tunnel with the other. A flashlight beam roved over the room.

"Christian? Eva? You guys down here?"

O'Reilly.

Todd straightened, allowing the officer's flashlight's beam to land on him. "What's going on up there?"

"Molotov cocktails," Gates said. "The old wooden pews are burning like kindling."

"We have to get out of here," O'Reilly urged. "Where're Eva and Betty?"

"This way." Todd ducked into the tunnel. They might die from smoke inhalation if they were trapped in this tunnel, but, hopefully, if it was long enough they could stay away from the danger until help arrived and put out the fire.

Eva and Betty were already at the farthest end of the tunnel.

"There's a ladder," Eva said. She tilted her cell phone flashlight app toward the old wooden ladder. "I don't know if it'll hold us or if the door at the top will open."

Where the ladies stood, the tunnel did a ninety-degree turn, moving upward. The opening was still only three or four feet in circumference but soared upward maybe ten feet.

"Only one way to find out." Todd put his weapon away and grabbed onto the ladder.

He measured the soundness of each rung before putting his full weight onto it. When he reached the door it was much like the one in the basement that had accessed the tunnel, about two feet square. It took some doing to force it open. When he did musty air hit his nostrils. He moved up a couple of rungs and looked around with his cell. The stone piers, the plumbing and ventilation ductwork that snaked around told him it was a crawl space. He climbed out of the hole and looked around a little more. Definitely a crawl space.

"Come on up," he called down to the others.

Eva climbed up the ladder first. Todd helped her out of the tunnel. "Watch your head."

Betty came next, then the two officers.

"This must be the crawl space under the old parsonage," O'Reilly suggested.

"There should be a way out somewhere along the foundation," Todd said, already scanning the outer perimeter. He spotted the small door in the beam of one of the flashlights roving the darkness. "There." He pointed to the north end of the crawl space. "We just have to watch out for the plumbing and the ductwork as we move in that direction."

"And spiders," Betty said.

Eva groaned. "I hate spiders."

"Spiders don't bother me," O'Reilly said. "Snakes, that's what I hate."

Eva and Betty insisted on staying behind the men as they made their way across the cool, musty space. As they crawled toward the exit, the blare of sirens grew closer and closer. Two minutes later they were crawling out into a fenced backyard. What had once been the church parsonage had been turned into apartments. Todd was grateful for the six-foot wood privacy fence that ran between the yard and the church parking lot. The instant he stood he spotted the smoke from the fire at the church.

He swore and shook his head.

O'Reilly took a call as they dusted themselves off. When he put his phone away, he said, "My sergeant says it's all clear. We can head back to the church."

Todd hitched a thumb in the other direction. "I

think Eva and I will take another route, just in case they're watching my car."

O'Reilly nodded. "Good idea. They might be laying low, waiting to see if the two of you make it out and planning to follow you away from the commotion at the church if you did. I can have a cruiser pick you up."

Todd shook his head. "One of my colleagues is already en route." He thrust out his hand to the other man. "Thanks for your help."

O'Reilly gave his hand a shake as he glanced at Eva. "Keep her safe. We count on her around here."

Eva and Betty shared a quick hug. Both swiped their eyes. Those bastards had destroyed an important part of this neighborhood—a part all those people who came through the makeshift clinic today depended on. Todd hoped he got the chance to make Miguel Robles pay.

Gates followed his partner's lead and shook Todd's hand next. "Keep your head down, Christian."

"Count on it."

The two officers and Nurse Betty James slipped through the gate next to the house and disappeared. Todd took Eva's hand in his and gestured to the gate at the rear of the yard. "Let's go this way."

EVA WOULD HAVE preferred to go back to the church and assess the damage but she conceded to Todd's judgment. She would find out how badly the church was damaged later. Right now, staying out of sight of those thugs was top priority. Anger roiled inside her at the idea that they had damaged the church to get to her. Now they'd have to find a new place willing to allow them to treat patients from the neighborhood.

Every day it was as if her troubles swallowed up more innocent victims. She had to find a way to end this.

As if he sensed her tension, Todd tightened his grip on her hand and urged her forward a little faster. Apparently being lost in thought wasn't conducive to moving quickly. She wondered if he had contacted Ian Michaels again for a ride. She had to give him credit. He was smart not to go back to the car in which they had arrived. Those thugs would be watching. When they'd attacked the church they had known the people inside would have no choice but to find a way out. Made sense that they would eventually end up back at their cars.

But Todd was a step ahead of them.

His strong grip infused her with confidence and warmth, keeping the cold worry and fear at bay. Who would ever have imagined all those years ago when he'd left her brokenhearted that he would one day come back to save her life?

Fate really did have a twisted sense of humor.

They moved along the alleyway between the rows of duplexes and old buildings that reminded her that this part of Chicago represented a century or more of the city's history. The traffic sounds of evening commuters hummed in the air. In another hour it would be dark. Several blocks stood between them and the trouble they'd barely escaped. Eventually they rounded the corner and slowed, walking along Washington Boulevard. Eva recognized the old Fahrney & Sons building. She had an antique medicine bottle from the late nineteenth century with the company name stamped into the glass that had belonged to her grandmother. Her mother had used it as a bud vase. Eva did the same.

Judging by the signs and the scaffolding around the historic building, the piece of Chicago history was finally being renovated. Eva squinted, staring ahead. How much farther did he intend to go on foot? It wasn't that she minded the walk/run pace but she'd been on her feet all day and she was exhausted. Not to mention, she couldn't help but worry that Robles's people would find them somehow.

She tugged on his hand, drawing his determined forward advancement to a halt. "Is your friend coming to pick us up?"

"Yes. We need to keep moving until he gets here."

The sooner they were off the street the happier she would be. The adrenaline had started to recede, leaving her limbs weak. She worked hard not to tremble. No need to show him her fear even if they could have been killed back there.

Betty could have been killed. Their final patients... the two officers Eva had come to consider friends. Her neighbor was dead because of her. A young girl was fighting for her life in the hospital at this very moment because of her.

How foolish she'd been to think that putting herself out in the open and going on with her usual daily activities would somehow make a difference. All she had managed to do was bring the danger to the place she loved most—her work.

"I should go back." She shook her head. "They're never going to stop until they have what they want. Running is doing nothing more than putting off the inevitable."

Todd grabbed her by the shoulders and gently shook her. "So you think giving up is the answer?"

The thought of Mr. Fry or any of the other people she had come to care about being hurt because of her—the way Mrs. Cackowski had been—was more than she could bear. "This can't be fixed by doing nothing but protecting me. Miguel Robles has to be stopped."

"And you believe you can do that?"

The fury in his eyes and in his voice warned that he had lost patience with her on the subject. He'd acquiesced to her demand of going on with her life as usual in an attempt to draw out Robles so the police could catch him. In her defense, she had hoped by baiting him that she would lure him into a mistake. She should have known better. He would simply send more of his minions. He would never risk his own safety.

"I don't know." She closed her eyes and shook her head. "I have to do something."

"You don't let him win," Todd said, his voice softer now. "That's what you do."

Eva steadied herself. "How do I do that without putting everyone I care about in the line of fire?"

And there it was, the million-dollar question no one seemed able to answer.

"We'll talk about this back at the safe house. Our ride is almost here."

She relented, allowed him to usher her forward. He put off answering her question because he couldn't.

The roar of a car engine followed immediately by gunshots jerked Eva's attention to the street. A dark car rocketed toward them.

Todd yanked her toward an old building on their right. He shoved her behind the plywood barrier that blocked off the entrance. Bullets splintered the plywood.

"Keep your head down!" he ordered.

She hunkered down and raced after him. He slammed his body into the sheet of plywood that had been nailed up over the original entrance to the building. More bullets punctured the outer wall of plywood and bit into the brick of the building. She made herself as small as possible and scooted nearer to Todd.

Another slam into the wood and it burst inward. He grabbed her by the hand and ran, clambering over the downed plywood.

With a quick survey of the gutted space, he spotted the staircase and headed that way. The staircase actually looked as if it were standing from memory since not much else appeared to be supporting it. The building had been erected on this piece of property more than a century and a half ago. Hopefully it wouldn't go down so easy. The next staircase looked no better. They rushed up it so fast Eva wondered if their feet even touched the treads.

No sooner than they reached the second floor, the sound of running footfalls echoed from the first floor.

With no police around, the thugs had apparently decided to give chase beyond the protection of their cars.

Just her luck.

Todd stalled.

Eva plowed into his back. Rather than ask why he'd stopped moving she stared at the place where the next staircase should have been.

It was gone.

They were trapped.

Todd checked his cell. He surveyed their situation once more as he shoved the phone into his back pocket.

Then his hand tightened on hers once more and he said, "This way."

Shouting downstairs warned that the men were closing in on the second staircase.

She and Todd reached the backside of the building. He moved toward a large hole that might have once been a couple of windows. It wasn't until they skidded to a stop at that hole that she saw the slide-like setup going from this floor down to the huge construction Dumpster on the ground.

"I'm going down first," he said as he slung one leg onto the slide. "Grab on to my waist and stay tight against me so I can cushion your landing."

There was no time to question the proposed exit. She grabbed on to his lean waist and held on tight.

Her stomach shot into her throat as they whooshed downward. They landed on a pile of construction debris.

Todd grunted.

Before she could ask him if he was okay, he forced her up and over the side of the Dumpster. He was right behind her.

A dark sedan rolled toward them.

Eva stalled, her heart dropping to her feet in a sharp free-fall.

Todd pulled her against him and sprinted the last few yards—toward the car. He yanked the rear door open and they landed on the back seat with the car still rolling.

"Go! Go! Go!" Todd shouted.

The car spun forward. Todd jerked the door shut and ushered Eva onto the floorboard.

Bullets pinged against the metal exterior.

Todd was suddenly on top of her and they were speeding away.

Chapter Eleven

Colby Safe House, 9:30 p.m.

Eva set the hair dryer aside and reached for the hairbrush. She dragged it through her hair, her thoughts far from the task. The fire gutted the church. She felt sick at the news. Dr. Taggart had sent her a text assuring her he'd spoken to the reverend and there was insurance which would eventually do the repairs, but there was no way to know how long that would take.

At least no one else had died.

Ian Michaels had explained that two other Colby Agency investigators were working on the case. Their efforts were being coordinated with Chicago PD. Eva appreciated the lengths to which they were willing to go. She hoped they were more successful than the local police had been so far.

Not fair, Eva. The police couldn't stop Robles if they had no evidence against him.

She braced her hands on the counter and stared at her reflection in the mirror. Her resolve was faltering, her determination running on empty. The past two days had been some of the hardest of her life. As exhausted and keyed up as she was, she wouldn't be going anywhere near the wine tonight. Not after how she'd allowed herself to go completely over the edge last night.

She turned away from the sad, uncertain woman in the mirror and padded back into the bedroom. A single functional brain cell reminded her that she should eat, but food was the furthest thought from her mind. Her mood fluctuated between defeated and furious. In her whole life she had never felt more helpless...more uncertain of the future. To make matters worse, she had lost her cell phone in the fray of today's frantic escape. Tomorrow she'd have to pick up a new phone and deal with transferring her contacts and other content. Eva sighed. Sometimes it felt like more of her life was available as data rather than as a real life. When had her existence become so dependent on notifications and alerts coming from a tiny object scarcely larger than a credit card?

She wandered to the door. Todd had promised they would talk about her concerns later. It was later and he'd avoided a face-to-face with her since they'd agreed that showers would do them both a world of good. He'd headed to his room and she'd headed to hers. Scarcely five feet of carpeted hallway stood between the two doors. She should just go over there, knock on the door and demand to know if he was ready to talk, or simply tell him she was heading downstairs and would be waiting for him so they could have the promised discussion.

Dredging up her battered wherewithal, she opened her door and took the three strides to his door. She curled her fingers into a fist and reached up to knock and his door abruptly opened.

He blinked, stared at her and then his lips parted as if he intended to speak, but no words made it past the tip of his tongue.

She took a breath and prepared to launch the first question but her attention stalled on his bare chest. It wasn't like she hadn't seen his chest hundreds of times. Well, maybe not hundreds but at least one hundred. His skin was damp as if he'd hastily scrubbed the towel over that sleek terrain. A drop of water slipped down his lean, rippled abdomen. She jerked her gaze upward as his torso widened into the broad shoulders where she'd lain her head dozens of times, moving on to the strong, muscled arms that had held her close on so many occasions.

Her attention whipped back to his right shoulder. A wad of gauze stained with crimson was stuck there. "What happened?"

He grinned, the expression a little lopsided. "I guess a nail or something from the construction heap snagged me. I can't reach it with both hands to do the repair."

Eva frowned. She remembered his shirt being torn in a couple of places. Hers had been as well but she'd walked away with nothing but a few sore places that would likely turn into bruises. "Let me have a look."

He moved into the hall, stepping away from her as he did. "I'll get the first aid kit then you can take care of it. I'll be right back."

He hurried down the stairs before she could do the smart thing and suggest they take care of his wound in the kitchen—far away from sheets still perfumed with their lovemaking. Instead, Eva stared after him for a few moments, then she hugged her arms around herself and entered his room. She felt somehow cold and too warm at the same time. No one had been seriously injured or killed today, she was grateful. Still, the potential...the what-ifs throbbed in her skull. Betty or Dr. Taggart could have been hurt. Officers O'Reilly and Gates—Todd could have been killed trying to protect her and Betty. If not for the quick thinking of Todd and O'Reilly, the day may have ended far more tragically.

How in the world did she fix this and stay alive?

She needed some plan of action. Todd's military training and work with the Colby Agency made him the better choice at figuring out a doable plan of action. Her problem was getting him to go there. He would like nothing better than for her to stay in hiding until this was over. That route wasn't feasible. Deep down he had to know this. Dr. Pierce surely grasped that fact as well—which brought up a whole other issue. How could she expect Pierce to hold her position without a reasonable return-to-work date?

She couldn't.

Pushing the troubling thoughts aside she surveyed Todd's bedroom. She hadn't gotten much of a look at it last night. Flashes of bare skin and flexing muscles filtered through her weary mind along with whispered words and soft sounds. How had she ever believed for even a minute that any other man could make her feel the way he did? There had been others, a few. Not one had been able to touch that place inside her that only Todd Christian had reached.

Again she cleared her head and focused on the mundane details. The layout of his room was much like her own, a large space with elegant furnishings.

The closet door was open, as was the door to the en suite bath. He'd tossed a T-shirt on the bed.

Her throat tightened as her gaze moved over the rumpled bed.

Closet. Stick to the far less dangerous spaces. She shifted her gaze to the closet. His duffel bag had been delivered here which made her wonder again why she'd ended up with a new wardrobe. Maybe it was the privacy issue of going through her things. On the other hand, it might simply be the best way to ensure nothing of sentimental value that belonged to her was damaged in all this running for their lives.

She ran her fingers along the shirts and tees that hung in a neat row in the closet. Jeans and a pair of black trousers were efficiently folded and placed on a shelf. A pair of leather loafers sat on the floor beneath the hanging shirts. The military had made him a little neater than she recalled.

With a deep sigh that made her heart uncomfortable, she turned away from his clothes and wandered to the door of the bathroom. A bottle of aftershave sat on the counter alongside a comb and a razor. The aftershave was the same one he'd always worn. Subtle hints of leather and sandalwood with the tiniest trace of citrus. She didn't have to look in the shower to know there would be a matching bodywash. The gentle fragrance of the toiletries he chose was so understated that his own natural scent was by far the more distinct.

His clothes, his car, even the apartment where he'd lived before had been modest, understated. The man himself had always been what stood out. How was it that a man so unpretentious and kind could have stolen her heart and then walked away without looking back? So many times she had asked herself that question. Had he found someone new? Had he grown bored with her? Had she done or said something that pushed him away? Yet, deep down she somehow understood that his decision was not her fault. He'd left for reasons she did not comprehend. But she hadn't come to that conclusion overnight. It had taken months, perhaps even years to realize that she'd done nothing wrong. Todd Christian had decided to walk away.

End of story.

"Sorry. It took me a minute."

Eva turned to face him. She'd intended to tell him to have a seat so she could look at his shoulder. Instead, she blurted, "Why did you leave without so much as saying goodbye?"

His fingers tightened on the first aid case. Eva vaguely wondered if it would suddenly crack and fall to pieces as her heart had all those years ago.

"What?"

His apparent confusion frustrated her. "You just left one day and never came back." She shrugged. "You didn't say a word or leave a note. I never heard from you again. I'm asking you why. Why did you do something so callous?"

He gave a single, small nod of his head. "Fair question." He waved the first aid case toward the bathroom. "I'll give you the best answer I know how while you work."

Surprised that he'd caved to her demand so easily, she followed him into the bathroom where he closed the toilet lid and sat down. He placed the case on the counter and stared at the wall he faced.

Eva decided to give him a moment while she surveyed the available medical supplies. The case offered the usual home first aid kit supplies with a few extras. In addition to the usual items, bandages, gauze, antibacterial and antihistamine creams, and antiseptic wipes, there were suture kits and butterfly bandages, tweezers and even a small scalpel.

"There's no lidocaine." Not a good thing in her opinion. "You're going to feel this."

"Just do it. I've endured worse."

His words had her wondering about the small scar on his cheek and the others on his back, but she decided not to distract him from the question she'd already asked. She washed her hands and walked around one muscled leg to reach his shoulder. The position put her square in the *V* of his muscular thighs. Her body reacted with a familiar twinge between her own thighs. How would it be possible not to react to the half-naked, good-looking man who'd saved her life? Particularly one who still owned a considerable chunk of real estate in the vicinity of her heart?

He will never know that sad truth.

Putting those reactions on ignore, she slowly pulled the gauze free of his skin and then tossed it into the sink. The gash was not too deep, not so wide, but the sides were not going to stay together without some assistance. She considered the butterfly bandages but she doubted those would hold the next time they were in a desperate situation. A few stitches would do the trick.

"I cleaned it with bottled water and a little bleach since I didn't have any betadine handy. I didn't see any debris that shouldn't be there, like splinters."

"Good." Eva threaded the eye of the needle with the sutures. She pulled the wound together, getting it as close to pre-gash condition as possible. "You were going to answer my question." She located the spot where she wanted to begin and inserted the needle through the skin.

He grimaced, made a small sound, not quite a grunt.

"Sorry." She secured the first suture and began working back toward the edge. In, out, pull, repeat.

She'd almost reached the final suture when he finally spoke. "I shouldn't have left the way I did. I was a coward."

Of all the answers she'd expected him to give, that was not one of them. Rather than say so, she kept her lips in a tight line and finished sealing the wound with a precise knot to keep the sutures just snug enough to aid in healing without injuring the skin further.

"I spent most of the first eighteen years of my life being tossed from foster home to foster home." He exhaled a big breath. "You were the first person I ever really wanted to please—beyond physically, I mean."

Struggling to keep her hand steady, she set the suturing tools aside and reached for antibacterial ointment. She applied a thin layer and then prepared a proper bandage with gauze and tape. All the while her heart pounded at his confession.

"I'd never wanted to make anyone happy like that before. I wanted to give you everything...to be everything you wanted."

Anger sparked. "I never wanted everything."

He shook his head. "Even if you'd said so at the time, it wouldn't have changed what I wanted."

Her work complete, Eva closed her eyes and dropped her hands to her sides. When she could say the words without her voice trembling, she opened her eyes and asked, "What changed your mind?"

"One morning I woke up and you were still sleeping." He turned his face up to hers, his blue eyes begging for forgiveness or understanding. "I stared at you for so long, wondering how I would ever be the kind of man you deserved. I had no pattern to follow. How could I be the kind of man you could depend on when I wasn't sure I could depend on myself?"

On some level she wanted to understand his reasoning, but she couldn't. How selfless of him to throw away all her hopes and dreams to ensure he didn't hurt her. Ha! Outrage flamed deep in her soul, raging instantly out of control. "Wow. You really gave up everything to save me, didn't you? And all this time I thought you were a selfish ass for leaving without a word."

He looked away. "I needed to grow up. To learn to trust myself before I could let you put all your trust in me."

Incredible. "What a shame your timing was about six months too late." Eva moved away from him, threw the supplies back into the case. "I'm so glad we had this talk. I totally get why you left now."

He pushed to his feet, moved in on her and stared at her in the mirror when she wouldn't look at him. "It was the hardest thing I've ever done. Leaving you tore me apart."

Eva glared back at him. It would be so easy to believe him. To fall back into loving him, just like before.

"So you went off to the military and let them make a man out of you, is that it?"

"Pretty much. That and time."

"Well, I'm glad I was a part of your learning curve." She scooted away from him and headed for the door.

She was halfway across his room before he caught up with her. His fingers curled around her arm and pulled her to a stop.

"What?" she demanded. The sooner she was out of here, the better. She should never have gone down that path with him. Now he knew that a part of her still pined after him. How pathetic was that?

TODD HAD MADE a mess of his explanation. Every damned word had come out wrong. Rather than explain himself, he'd excused himself. Not what he'd intended. "I was wrong. What I did was wrong. There is no excuse."

She glared up at him and the hurt in her beautiful green eyes made his chest ache. "Glad you've seen the error of your ways. Now, if you'll excuse me, I'd like to get some sleep."

He released her but he wasn't ready to let her go. "I thought you wanted to talk about a plan for getting Robles."

She hesitated at the door. "I already know what to do." She turned to face him. "I tell the police I'd like to help set a trap for him. The sooner the better. It works in the movies all the time."

He moved toward her, choosing his words carefully. "This isn't the movies. Real life rarely works that way."

"I've run out of ideas and I refuse to be a party to

another day like this one or like yesterday. I want to finish this thing I set in motion when I killed that son of a bitch."

When she would have turned to walk out the door, he reached over her and closed it. "I won't let you do that."

She turned and glared up at him. "You can't stop me."

He moved in a step nearer, trapping her against the door. "Watch me." He cupped her face in his hands and leaned in close. "I will not let you do this."

She tried to back away, but the door stopped her. "Is this your way of making up for the past? You'll keep me safe and assuage your guilt?" She shook her head. "Like you said, this isn't the movies, this is real life. You can't repair the heart you shattered all those years ago by being the hero today. I can't forgive you for what you did, Todd. If that's what you're expecting, you've overestimated your worthiness."

Her words were like daggers twisting in his chest. "You hate me, is that it?"

She blinked. "Maybe."

"You hate me so much—" he braced his forearms on the door and leaned into her, putting his face right up to hers "—that you came over and over in my arms last night."

She stared at his lips a moment and he longed to taste her. "That was sex," she argued. "Nothing more."

"Sex?" He traced her cheek with his nose. "Just sex?"

"Yes."

The feel of her lips moving against his jaw made him so damn hard he could barely breathe. "Then you won't mind if we do it again, just to be sure it was only physical." He brought his mouth around to hers. She gasped. "It doesn't mean anything." He nipped her bottom lip. "Just sex."

She stilled, lifted her eyes to his. "I've already experienced all your parlor tricks, Christian. I doubt you can show me anything new. I'd suggest you save your strength for helping me take down Miguel Robles."

Parlor tricks, eh? "Give me a minute to change your mind."

When she would have argued, he dropped to his knees. He reached for the waistband of her lounge pants and slid the soft fabric down her thighs, letting them fall to the floor. No panties. His body reacted with a rush of need that rocked him and had his cock pushing against his fly. He kissed her belly button, traced over her belly with his tongue. She pressed against the closed door as if to escape the exquisite torture, her hands braced on either side of it.

He lifted her right leg and settled the crook of her knee onto his left shoulder. Let her try to escape. He was only getting started. She gasped as he bent his head toward the tender flesh between her thighs. He kissed every part of her, slid his tongue along that delicious channel. She whimpered softly. Still she kept her hands plastered against the door. He delved deeper, using his mouth to draw on that place that caused her to cry out. He dipped a finger inside her, savored the moist, sweet heat and then tested her with another.

Her fingers suddenly dove into his hair as if to hold him back. He stilled and then she gasped, surrendering as her body started an instinctive, rhythmic undulating. He used his fingers, his tongue, his lips to explore all of her most intimate places, to bring her to orgasm. She cried out with the pleasure. He kissed her belly, moved up her torso, letting her leg slip down, her foot land on the floor, as he tasted his way to her breasts. He wanted to memorize every inch of her. He savored her breasts with his mouth while he used his fingers to draw her toward climax again. Hot, firm nipples peaked for his attention while those sweet feminine muscles tightened around him. He pressed the pad of his thumb harder against her clitoris. She fought to restrain her cries, but he could feel how hard and fast she was coming undone all over again. Her fingers found his fly and struggled to unfasten his pants. She managed to push his jeans down, releasing his aching cock, but he refused to give her what she wanted just yet. She whimpered with need, rubbed him wantonly with her hands.

When she reached that edge...so very close to exploding with pleasure yet again, he turned her around so fast she lost her breath. He pushed between her thighs, reached around her small waist with one hand and down to that wet, pulsing place to guide himself into her. She screamed with pleasure as he pushed deep inside her. He kept one hand focused on that hot, pulsing nub and the other on her breasts, kneading each one in turn, tweaking those perfect hard nipples. He pressed her against the door as he thrust in and out. This position took him so deep, stretching her to the very limits and she cried out for more.

One more hard, deep thrust and they came together. With her back pressed against his chest and his cock deep inside her, he carried her to the bed. When he would have pulled out of her, she arched her bottom, keeping him deep inside that hot, wet place as they started that sweet, slow rocking motion all over again.

Chapter Twelve

Saturday, May 12, 8:00 a.m.

Eva couldn't blame the wine this time.

Todd had broken through all her defenses, lowered every wall she had so carefully erected over the past ten years to protect her battered heart. Bared her every vulnerability, revealed her rawest emotions. By the time they'd both collapsed, utterly exhausted, she couldn't have argued about the best course of action to take against Robles any more than she could have crossed the hall to her own bed.

When she'd awakened, he'd already been downstairs. She was glad. She'd needed the past forty minutes to gather her scattered composure. This morning she intended to get straight down to business. She had a life she wanted to get back to. She wanted this ugly situation cleared up before her sister returned to Chicago. She needed distance from Todd before she lost her heart and soul to him all over again.

A quick shower had washed his scent from her skin but nothing could scrub those hours from her memory or the sweet ache from her muscles. The way he touched her, as if he knew every part of her and understood how to reach her deepest desires. He had explored every inch of her and she had done the same, relearning his lean, muscled body. Tasting him, touching places that had haunted her dreams for so very long.

She wasn't the only one who had been pushed beyond all carefully lain boundaries—she had given as good as she got. She had made him groan with need, watched his fingers clench in the sheets, made him beg for more. He'd whispered her name over and over. They'd climaxed together so many times, she felt weak with pleasure even now, overwhelmed with the need to touch him again and again.

Todd Christian was a drug she would never be able to resist.

With that undeniable knowledge tucked away for later contemplation, she left her room and headed for the stairs. The smell of bacon lingered in the air as she descended the staircase. Her stomach rumbled and she suddenly realized she was starving. More often than not she grabbed a cup of yogurt and a piece of fruit for breakfast. After what she'd been through the past few days, she had every right to splurge with a self-indulgent breakfast.

Todd looked up from the stove as she walked into the room. His grin was sexy as hell and made her heart skip a beat. "Good morning."

"Good morning." She headed straight for the coffee pot and poured a cup. The rich aroma had her immediately lifting the cup to her lips. Bold flavor burst on her taste buds and she made a satisfied sound. "So good."

"I hope you still like pancakes."

She turned to him, the warm cup cradled in both hands. "The ones with nuts and whole wheat flour?"

"That's the ones." He paddled three pancakes onto a plate and slathered a pat of butter on top, then piled on the bacon. "Since we discovered this recipe, I've never made pancakes any other way."

She wondered how many other women he'd made them for after a long night of hot sex. *None of your business, Eva.*

She claimed a stool while he prepared his own plate and poured them both a glass of orange juice. This could be her last breakfast. After what happened yesterday, it was clear Robles didn't intend to back off. She should claim whatever pleasure available. She blocked more images from last night and focused on the aromas making her mouth water this morning.

"Wow." She dismissed the foolish and wholly unfounded worry about other women. "I can't believe you remembered how I like my pancakes."

He reached around her and poured on the syrup. "You're the only person I've ever made pancakes for."

She smiled, ridiculously pleased by his comment as she lifted a forkful of deliciousness to her mouth. Another of those happy moans vibrated inside her. The pancakes were so good. She grabbed a slice of crisp bacon and devoured it before reaching for her juice. "I might just die right here."

He laughed. "Then I'd have to face the wrath of Lena."

Eva put her hand over her mouth to prevent spewing orange juice. "True."

He fell silent for a minute but she sensed he had more to say. Had he learned something new about her case?

She set her fork aside and turned to him. "Did

something else happen?" *Please, don't let anyone else be dead because of her.*

Realization dawned in his eyes. "No. No, nothing else has happened." He dropped his fork onto the counter. "I was thinking about your mom and how sorry I am that I didn't get a chance to apologize to her for what happened. She must have hated me after... after I left."

Eva picked at her pancakes. "No. She didn't hate you. She adored you."

Surprise replaced the sadness she'd seen in his expression only moments ago. "Are you sure about that? I mean, Lena made it pretty clear how she felt."

She would not—could not—tell him all her mother said. "Lena is Lena, but trust me when I say my mother adored you until the day she died."

"Thank you." He reached out and gave her hand a squeeze. "I appreciate you telling me."

Eva blinked, then looked again. The shine of emotion was heavy in his eyes. She turned away. Maybe slaving over a hot stove had made him teary-eyed. "It's true. She loved you." She clamped her teeth together, could have bitten off her tongue. She hadn't meant to use the *L* word, though her mother made her feelings about Todd clear on numerous occasions. He was the son she never had.

He drew his hand from hers as if her blurted words had stung him almost as badly as they had her. It was definitely time for a change of subject.

"So you joined the army." Her voice sounded too high-pitched and she cursed herself for even speaking again.

He shifted his attention back to his plate. "I did. My

specialty was communications at first." He shrugged. "Apparently there was a shortage in the field since I expected to be an eleven bang-bang—an infantry soldier."

"You were an officer?" He'd just graduated with his degree in science. For hours on end he would talk about how he wanted to be a teacher. A few teachers were the only people who had ever made him feel as if he could be more than what he'd come from.

"No." He shook his head. "They offered me the opportunity but I didn't want to be an officer. I wanted to do what all the other enlisted soldiers had to do."

"Really?" Surprised, she munched on another slice of bacon. "Did you travel the world?"

"Not so much at first." He reached for his coffee. "A couple years after my enlistment, I was recruited by Special Forces. Everything changed then."

She laughed in hopes of lightening the moment. "I suppose you went on all sorts of exciting top secret assignments in Special Forces."

"Now and then." He poked at the pile of pancakes on his plate.

"Is that where you got the scars?" She touched her cheek in the same spot where the scar was on his. It was such a small one, but there were several larger ones on his back. Not a single one detracted from his good looks. She bit her lips together for fear she'd throw in that part, too.

"Shrapnel. I was one of the lucky ones."

Shrapnel meant a blast…a bomb. He could have been killed—probably numerous times. The realization made her angry. Why had he worked so hard in college to achieve his degree—not to mention he'd been accepted into a master's program—just to throw it all away? "What happened to the teaching career you talked about?"

He stared at his plate once more and lifted one shoulder in a halfhearted shrug. "I guess that was another one of those things I figured I didn't deserve."

Why had she never once noticed that deep-seated worry about his self-worth when they were together? Had she loved him so much that she couldn't see the pain? The idea made her sad. But she'd been so young…

"What about Kevin? Have the two of you kept in touch?"

He smiled, and the beauty of it took her breath away. "He graduated law school last year. He just got married. I was his best man."

"That's great." How many times had she planned *their* wedding before he ran away?

The rest of the meal was eaten in silence. Eva had said more than enough. So had he. She couldn't decide which was worse: all the things she'd told him, or the things she allowed herself to do with him.

Or maybe it was all that he hadn't told her when it mattered most.

With every fiber of her being she understood one thing with complete certainty: when this was over—assuming she survived—she would be heartbroken once more because he would leave again.

Some people just never learned.

EVA INSISTED ON cleaning up. Todd tried to help but she shooed him away. "You cooked. I'll clean."

He held up his hands and backed away from the sink. "Have it your way."

A break would do him good. He'd been on edge all morning. Well, no, maybe it started last night after hours of incredible lovemaking. He'd lain awake for hours just watching her sleep. No one had ever made him feel as important and as helpless at the same time as Eva did. She made him yearn to be more...to give her more.

"I'll be in the office." He hitched a thumb toward the hall. "We can have that talk about Robles and where we go from here when you're done."

Her eyebrows reared upward. "Seriously? You're not going to find a way to put me off again or to change the subject?"

His last attempt to distract her had taken an unexpected turn and he'd ended up on his knees. Who was he kidding? He'd dreamed of savoring all of Eva from the moment he saw her again. For years he'd kept thoughts of her—the memories—locked away in a place in his heart that refused to let go of her. He'd ignored those memories for years, unable to touch them. Then he'd returned to Chicago and he'd seen her by complete accident for the first time in more than eight years. She hadn't seen him so he'd followed her and his entire being had ached with the need to touch her...to know her again. If he was honest with himself, he would admit that he'd been trying hard to work up the nerve to talk to her for more than a year. He'd followed her enough times that he felt like a stalker.

Gotta get your head straight, man.

Right now he had a job to do. One of the most important of his life; he had to keep Eva safe. As he walked toward the office he called Michaels to see if there was any news on the agency's investigation into Robles.

Michaels said, "I was about to call you."

Not a good sign. "I take it you've found someone willing to talk."

The agency had concentrated on finding evidence of the gang leader's crimes while Todd focused on protecting Eva. Victoria wanted to do what the police had not been able to—find someone willing to testify against Robles.

"We have and that source warned that Robles is about to make a direct move against Eva. Since her sister is her only family, I've contacted a colleague in DC to put eyes on her. That's a considerable reach for Robles, but at this point he's likely feeling desperate to avenge his brother. More than a week has passed and he hasn't managed to follow through with his declaration of vengeance."

"Never a good thing for the minions to see." Todd agreed completely. Robles was no doubt damned desperate by now. He'd probably exterminated every member of his gang who'd failed to bring Eva to him.

"If our source will testify against Robles, we may have a starting place for Gang Intelligence to build a real, prosecutable case. Until now, they haven't had a source willing to speak out against Robles. But his credibility is in question now. Every day he fails to honor his brother, his followers grow more restless."

"Maybe the world will get lucky and they'll start killing each other." As crazy as it sounded, it happened. Someone inside could decide Robles was too weak to continue to be their leader. It was a long shot but a guy could hope.

"Until then we keep Eva and her sister safe and we continue pursuing potential sources."

They discussed the various avenues for further infiltrating the True Disciples as well as Victoria's urgent requests to her higher-level resources. If anyone could find a way to Robles, it was Victoria.

"Thanks for the update." Todd was grateful for every step that brought them closer to ending the danger to Eva. "Keep us posted."

He ended the call and put his cell away. Now if he could convince Eva to be patient a little longer—

"What update?"

He did an about-face and produced a smile. Eva was the only person who had ever been able to sneak up on him. He'd decided back when they were together that it was because she was such a part of him. They were one. His senses wouldn't alert him to her presence any more than they would warn his right arm that his left was nearby. They began and ended together.

Evidently his instincts hadn't realized that wasn't the case anymore.

Whispers and glimpses of last night's urgent lovemaking echoed through him. Maybe in some ways it was still the same, which was a blessing and a curse at the same time.

"We have a source who may be willing to testify against Robles."

Her eyes widened with anticipation. "Would that be enough to get him off the streets?"

"Depending on what information he has and how much of it he can back up, it's possible. If we're really lucky charges could be brought and the judge would deny bail." He resisted the urge to reach out and touch her in reassurance. "It's a starting place."

He decided not to tell her about Michaels's other concerns. Michaels was on it. Lena would have protection ASAP if it wasn't in place already.

Eva moved into the room, her arms folded over her breasts in a protective manner. "Do you believe he can be stopped this way? I don't understand why that hasn't happened already if it's so simple."

His hands twitched with the need to pull her close and hold her as he explained what Michaels had told him. "He's swiftly losing credibility. Power and fear are the two main ingredients of a dictator's reign and that's what gang leaders like Robles are. He has hundreds of followers and they do as he tells them for various reasons. Some idolize him. Others are too afraid to do otherwise. The life—meaning their membership in the gang—is all they've ever known."

"Afraid?" She frowned. "Why would coldhearted killers be afraid of anything?"

"Those who have second-guessed the life are in too deep to turn back now. Leaving isn't an option. They'd be hunted and killed as would the people they care about. For others, they might be fearless when it comes to fighting, maiming and murdering, but they're terrified of not having the unity they find in the gang. In some cases, it's the only family they've ever known. If their leader fails, someone worse or someone who might not want them could take over. For those guys, protecting the life is all that matters."

"Either way it seems like the empire Robles has

built might be on shaky ground." Hope glimmered in her eyes.

Todd was grateful the news had given her something to hang on to. Maybe it would be enough to keep her smart about how to proceed. "Every day that you're breathing, his credibility weakens. Someone else could step up and go for a takeover."

"How can I help make it happen faster?" She turned her palms up in question. "I could go on the news. Speak out about what a coward he is."

Todd managed a stiff laugh that came out more like a cough. "I think we'll hold off on that avenue for a bit."

"This is good news, though." She hugged herself again, rubbed her hands up and down her arms as if she were chilled. "I should call Lena. Let her know I'm okay. We haven't spoken since early yesterday." A frown furrowed her brow. "She hasn't answered that text I sent from your phone last night letting her know I was okay after what happened at the church."

He dug his phone from his back pocket and offered it to her. "She hasn't. Why don't you give her a call? I'll have a new phone brought to you, if you'd like."

She accepted the phone. "I'm guessing that means we're staying in today."

Before he could answer, his cell rang. Eva jumped and almost dropped it.

She passed it to him. "Geez, that scared the hell out of me."

Todd didn't recognize the local number. "Christian."

"Christian, this is Detective Marsh. We have a problem."

"I'm listening." Todd moved to a desk and awakened a computer monitor just to put some distance between him and Eva without being too obvious about it.

"Someone broke into Lena Bowman's townhouse last night. They tore the place apart and left a vic in the bedroom. We're going to need Eva to come over here and make an identification."

Todd's heart stumbled. "Can you give me a few more specific details?"

"The vic is female. We can't be sure whether or not it's her sister. The general height and weight, hair color are right, but there's too much facial damage to be certain."

Fear snaked around his chest and tightened like a vise. Lena was out of town. Couldn't be her. Still, his gut churned with worry. "We'll be right there."

With great effort he slid the phone back into his pocket without allowing his hand to shake. The worry and no small amount of fear crushed against him. "We have to go to Lena's apartment." He started for the door, taking Eva by the arm and pulling her along as he went.

"Why?"

He kept his gaze forward. Making eye contact right now he feared would show her what he didn't want her to see—not yet anyway. "Someone broke in and ransacked the place."

"Okay," she said, the word thin.

He wouldn't mention the rest until they were there. Having her get hysterical while he needed to watch for a tail could get them both in trouble.

As if she sensed there was something more he wasn't saying, she didn't ask anything else as they loaded into the black Camaro. The next forty-five minutes were some of the longest in his life. Eva tried four times to call her sister. Each time the call went to voice mail. His tension rocketed higher. Thankfully, Eva didn't start asking questions.

By the time they reached Lena's townhouse on East Elm Street, Eva was quietly falling apart piece by piece. Her hands were trembling and she stared out the window. He roared right up to the police perimeter and two uniforms shouted orders for him to move and that this was a crime scene. Like the strands of yellow tape weren't sufficient evidence it was a crime scene. Pedestrians and neighbors stood on the sidewalk across the street and behind the tape. A couple of news vans were already on the scene but they had been held back a full block.

"Detective Marsh is expecting us," Todd said to the officer who marched up to him.

A sharp whistle sounded from the townhouse steps. Marsh motioned at the officer. "Let 'em through."

Todd put his hand to Eva's back and guided her to the steps. Her shoulders were square and her stride was firm, but he felt her body trembling. Marsh waited on the sidewalk to walk up with them. Lena's place was the upper of the two units.

"I'm sorry I had to call you over here, Ms. Bowman," Marsh said as they walked through the front door.

"Can you give us a minute?" Todd asked when they stood in the entry hall with the front door closed, blocking out the prying eyes on the street.

Marsh gave a knowing nod. "Sure. I'll wait in the living room."

Todd turned to Eva and he would give anything in the world not to have to tell her the part he'd been holding back.

As if she suddenly understood what he was about to say, Eva shook her head. "She isn't here. Lena's in DC. You know that."

"I know." He wished his heart would stop pounding so hard and that his hands would stop their damned shaking. "There's a woman, Eva. She was murdered in the bedroom."

Eva fought to keep her expression clean of emotion but her lips trembled and she made this hiccupping sound that ripped his thundering heart right out of his chest even as she shook her head adamantly once more. "She's not here."

He tried to take her hand but she dodged the move. "You're right," he said, the two words uttered out of sheer desperation. "Marsh thought maybe it was one of her neighbors. He hoped you might be able to help them with the identification."

More of those painful sounds wrenched from her throat. "Liar."

"Come on." He closed his hand around hers before she could snatch it away from him this time. "Let's do what we can to help Marsh and then we can get out of here."

She nodded, the movement jerky.

He held on to her small, trembling hand and prayed like he had never prayed before as they went into the living room to catch up with Marsh. The furniture had been turned upside down. Drawers and their contents were strewn over the room. The kitchen and dining room were the same. Broken china and silverware flung across every surface. Chairs were overturned.

They passed the first of two bedrooms, which was Lena's office. Like the other rooms, it had been ransacked, furniture overturned. Files and papers were scattered across the hardwood as if a hurricane had blown through the space.

In the final bedroom—Lena's room—the dresser drawers were tossed in every direction. Framed photographs of the sisters that once sat on the dresser had been crushed on the floor. Lingerie was tossed from one side of the room to the other. The bed covers were torn from the mattress.

Bare feet were visible beyond the end of the bed.

Eva yanked free of his hold and ran to where the victim lay on the floor. She dropped to her knees. His entire body vibrating with fear and tension, Todd crossed the room and crouched beside her. The woman had long brown hair...like Lena. The height and weight were right, as Marsh had said. She wore yoga pants and a bra-like top. Her face was beaten beyond recognition.

Damn these bastards.

For ten full seconds Eva stared at the woman, tears flooding down her cheeks. Todd held his breath and prayed some more.

"It's not her."

Relief rushed through his veins even as regret that someone else's sister or daughter or wife had been murdered tugged at his gut. "You're sure?"

"Look closely," Marsh urged.

"Her hair is too long. Her fingers are thicker than Lena's and her fingernails are too short." Eva drew in a shaky breath. "Lena gets her nails done every week." She gestured to the woman's bare midriff. "Lena has a birthmark on her right side. It looks like a little white cloud." She looked up at Marsh, a shaky smile on her lips even as the tears continued to flow. "She always hated it."

"Okay." Marsh nodded. "Does your sister have a friend or a neighbor with long brown hair?" He looked to the victim. "One who fits what you see here." He shook his head then and looked away.

Eva moved her head side to side. "Lena has so many friends. I'm sorry. I don't know."

Todd helped her to her feet and asked the detective, "We done here?" She'd been through enough. Whatever else Marsh wanted to know he would need to ask Lena.

He nodded. "For now." To Eva he said, "I really am sorry we had to put you through this, Ms. Bowman, but we didn't have a lot of choice. Every minute we waste with red tape is a minute we can't get back. Waiting for the medical examiner to come and remove the body before we let you have a look down at the morgue would have eaten up hours."

Eva took a deep breath. "I understand. I'll let my sister know what's happened."

Marsh had one of his officers bring the Camaro right up in front of the townhouse. Todd ushered Eva into the car as quickly as possible.

Somewhere amid the crowd, Robles's men would be watching.

Chapter Thirteen

Colby Safe House, Noon

Eva paced the living room. Ian Michaels had delivered her new phone. She had finally reached Lena's boss who called a point of contact in DC that confirmed Lena had an early morning interview. According to the contact in DC, she should be finishing up soon and be available to return Eva's call. Lena's boss assured Eva that it was common for a reporter to shut off his or her cell phone during an important interview. She understood that part—Lena had told her as much on numerous occasions—but the knowledge did nothing to alleviate Eva's mounting concern. She couldn't possibly relax until she heard her sister's voice.

Another woman was dead. Eva couldn't pretend that the woman's life or Mrs. Cackowski's mattered less than her own. She possessed the ability to stop the bloodshed, and putting off that necessary step was unequivocally wrong.

She summoned her courage, folded her arms across her chest and said as much. "I want to meet the person the Colby Agency found who might be willing to speak out against Miguel Robles." She met Todd's startled gaze with lead in her own. "He might be able to help us end this now."

"First," he countered, "leaving this house is growing increasingly dangerous. It's my job to protect you and I take that job very seriously."

When she would have argued, he held up a hand and continued, "Second, allowing you to even know the name of the man who's talking to the agency much less speak with him could shut him down. Even if for some strange reason he agreed to meet with you, some small thing you say or do might change his mind. We can't risk rocking that particular boat right now. He's far too potentially valuable to the investigation."

"You promised we'd talk about what I *can* do." She checked her new cell phone, willing it to ring and growing all the more frustrated when it didn't. "I can't stay hidden forever. I thought you understood my feelings on the matter. So let's stop going over what I can't do and discuss something I can."

Maybe it was wrong to lay a guilt trip on him but she was desperate. If she didn't hear from Lena soon she might just lose it. It was either that or fall apart and she'd done that once already today. Going there again wasn't an option. She needed to be strong and focused. Two people were dead and another was in the hospital because of her. Eva had to do something besides hide and wait.

He opened his mouth to answer and her cell rang. The number for the television station where Lena worked flashed on the screen. A new stab of worry sliced deep into Eva's heart as she accepted the call. "Hello."

"Eva, this is Scott Mason from Channel 7."

Lena's boss. Eva's fingers tightened on the phone. "Did you hear from Lena?"

"Not exactly." He hesitated and Eva's heart fractured. "I spoke to the cameraman who was supposed to be at the interview with her this morning. He said Lena cancelled the interview because she got word that her sister had been in an accident. She left DC around eight this morning. No one has heard from her since."

Eva's world tilted and the crack in her heart widened. "Thank you, Mr. Mason." He was still speaking when Eva ended the call. She couldn't listen to more of his regrets and offers of comfort. She turned to Todd. "Lena came back to Chicago." Outrage roared through her. "I have to find her. Now."

"Give me five minutes. Let me make some calls."

Rather than debate him, Eva sank into the nearest chair. She wanted to believe that this was some sort of misunderstanding. Maybe a friend who'd heard about the explosion at the church had gotten her wires crossed. Maybe the cameraman misunderstood what Lena said when she cancelled the interview. Even as she turned over all the possibilities, every instinct warned that it wasn't a mistake. Lena had been lured back here by that monster Miguel Robles and now she was in trouble. A new surge of fear and pain extinguished the outrage. Her sister could die…she could be dead already.

Todd ended his call and slid the phone back into his pocket. "I've got the agency verifying that Lena boarded a plane headed for Chicago. It'll take a bit of time, but we'll know one way or the other soon enough. Until then, let's keep in mind that Lena is a very savvy investigative journalist. She wouldn't be fooled easily."

Eva dredged up her fleeing courage. She agreed with his statement; it was a valid point, to a degree. "If that's true, then why hasn't she answered my calls or called me back?"

"Her cell battery may need to be charged. She might be on her way to the agency offices as we speak." He crouched in front of her and searched her eyes a moment, his so certain of his words. "Lena is a fighter. If Robles lured her into a trap, he's in for a hell of a surprise."

Eva managed a faint smile. She would love nothing better than to cling to that scenario, but deep in her heart she knew there was only one explanation for why they hadn't heard from Lena. Every ounce of warmth leeched out of her body. "She hasn't called me because she can't call me. And you're right, she is a fighter, but there are some battles even the strongest person can't win. I'm not going to pretend the situation isn't exactly what it is."

He dropped his head for a moment before meeting her eyes once more. "Until we know for certain she's with Robles, we should stay calm and hope for the best."

Eva wanted to laugh at the suggestion but she couldn't form the sound.

Her cell rang.

Eva stared at the device clenched in her right hand. Lena's face and name flashed on the screen. Her heart thumped hard against her ribs. "Lena."

"Eva."

Lena's voice sounded raw and edged with uncertainty. Eva went numb. "Where are you?"

"They want me to tell you where I am so you can come to me."

The undeniable nuance of fear in her sister's voice stole Eva's breath.

"Put it on Speaker," Todd whispered.

Her hand trembling, Eva touched the speaker image on the screen with one icy finger and said, "I can come right now. Just tell me where."

"He told me to tell you that you can't tell anyone, Eva, and no matter what else happens," she said, her words stilted as if she were taking great care with each one, "don't come!" Lena shouted the final two words.

More shouting and scuffling echoed from the speaker. Eva's heart flailed in her chest. "Lena!"

Todd reached for the phone but Eva twisted away from him. "Lena!"

"Your sister is not a very smart woman," a male voice said.

Eva instantly recognized the voice. *Miguel Robles.* Had to be. This was the same voice that had taunted her about the Chavez woman's shooting. "Tell me where she is. I'll come right now."

"I will send you instructions at six thirty this evening," Robles said. "Keep your phone close. If you deviate from my precise instructions, your sister will die."

"I can come now!"

The connection severed.

Eva pushed to her feet, brushed past Todd and stood in the center of the room. She had to think. She turned all the way around. Where was her charger?

She needed to make sure her phone battery stayed fully charged. The bastard told her to keep her phone close.

Todd was on his cell, his voice low and quiet. Eva ignored him. It didn't matter to whom he was speaking or what he thought she should do; she was doing exactly what Robles told her to do. She would not risk Lena's life under any circumstance. Whatever Robles asked her to do, she would do it. Defeat and certainty settled deep into her bones.

This moment had been coming all week. Fighting it any longer was futile.

"Michaels has a friend at NSA."

Eva dragged her thoughts from the haze of worry and struggled to focus on the man staring at her with such immense concern. "How will that help us?" A numbness had taken over. She felt as though she were under water. She could see and hear but it was all distorted and so far away. The moment felt surreal…as if it were happening to someone else and Eva was only watching.

"NSA can track any cell phone. They can determine in minutes what it takes others days to figure out. That call from Lena's phone will give us what we need. We find the phone and we'll find her. The way I see it, we have a little better than five hours to find her before Robles makes a move."

"I will not take any chances with my sister's life." Eva lifted her chin in defiance of whatever he might have in mind. "I hired you. I can fire you. Unless we do this my way."

"I agree completely." He reached for Eva's free hand. "But for the next five hours I need you to trust me. I've carried out a lot of high-risk rescues. I know what I'm doing."

Eva searched for calm. He had been in Special Forces and the Colby Agency was the best in the business of private investigations and security. "What's your plan?"

He visibly relaxed. "First we find the location the call was made from. Robles was careful. He kept the call short. He feels confident we won't be able to trace him. And he's right, we can't. But there are people who can."

Eva had heard about the NSA's ability to track the cell phones of suspected terrorists but that was the extent of her knowledge on the subject. "How can we be certain the location is accurate?"

"Lena uses a smartphone. At this very minute her phone is attempting to locate cell towers and Wi-Fi hot spots. NSA can narrow her location down to a city block or less within the hour. We will find her and then we'll get her out—safe."

For a moment Eva wanted to argue with him. This was her sister—the only family she had in this world. Eva would do anything to make sure she stayed safe just as Lena would do anything for her. She'd told Eva not to come. Her sister would without hesitation willingly die for her.

But this wasn't about Lena. This was about Eva and if anyone else was going to die today, it would be her.

West 47th Street, 5:40 p.m.

ROBLES CHOSE THE home field advantage. The Back of the Yards neighborhood was one of Chicago's most notorious where more residents than not felt the city had abandoned them, leaving gangs to take over. Century-old houses and aging apartment buildings butted up to derelict warehouses and industrial buildings that once infused life into the economy that was now dying. The handful of determined business owners hanging on to their small shops and slivers of new development and refurbishment continued to provide a glimmer of hope for change, but little actually changed.

Robles wasn't the only one at home along the most dangerous streets of the Windy City. Todd had done some time here. From age fifteen to sixteen he'd lived with a foster family on the fringes of this neglected, gang-infested territory. The mom-and-pop shops had been his favorite haunts, the rail tracks and the box-cars his playground.

The commercial equipment rental company that Robles and his men had taken over for the evening's event extended a full city block. Compressors, back-hoes and excavators lined the parking lot behind the security fence. Warehouses and the main office formed a boundary on three sides, leaving only the front with its ten-foot-high fence to afford a visual onto the property. Directly across the street was the rail yard, and behind the rental compound was a street lined with trees and more of those early twentieth-century bungalows built by immigrants and stock-yard workers.

Way too many people lived around the target to go in without backup from Chicago PD. Eva hadn't taken the news well. He'd had a hell of a time talk-ing her out of walking away from his protection. Her concerns about involving the police were understandable but hardly reasonable. Ultimately, they'd reached a standoff and he'd called Marsh. Eva had told Todd in no uncertain terms how she felt about his decision.

If this operation went to hell and her sister was hurt or worse, it was on him.

"We have eyes all around the property," Sergeant Carter assured them now. "We've quietly evacuated residents for two blocks in either direction."

"We're making sure none of the evacuees uses a cell phone until this is over in an effort to ensure no one alerts Robles's people," Marsh added. "We're keeping the folks entertained over at St. Joseph's on Hermitage."

Eva shook her head, her doubts about how this would go down clear. "If any of his men spot a cop—"

"Don't worry, Ms. Bowman," Carter said, "we've got this. We've even got unmarked units monitoring traffic all around our position."

To Todd's surprise Eva didn't say another word. Instead, she walked around the corner of the double boxcar and stared through the bushes and trees separating the rail yard from the street. If her sister was with her cell phone as they believed, she was likely no more than twenty, twenty-five yards in front of where Eva stood. Todd tried to think of something reassuring to say as he followed that same path.

"He's going to call or text me with instructions and they'll go in." She shook her head and hugged her arms more tightly around herself. "This plan is too risky. I'm not willing to risk Lena's life this way."

"Do you really believe Robles will let Lena go if you surrender yourself?" They'd been over this same territory twice already and her answer was always the same.

"It's a risk I have to take."

Todd glanced back toward the huddle of cops. He hadn't planned to share the other op already in motion with her until they had eyes on Lena. At this point he would do just about anything to give Eva some sense of relief.

"Marsh and the others don't know that we have a two-man team working their way inside." Her shoulders stiffened as he spoke, but she kept her attention straight ahead. "They were already here," he went on, "and in place before Chicago PD developed their game plan and moved in."

For the first time since he told Eva the Colby Agency had coordinated with Chicago PD after Robles's call, she looked him in the eye. A faint glimmer of hope stirred in hers. "Can they see what's happening inside?"

"They have eyes in the main office. So far they haven't seen Lena but they've watched two men going in and out of an inner office. We believe Lena and Robles are in that office. His disciples are scattered all over the property. All heavily armed."

"I don't understand why he would put himself in this position." Her gaze shifted back across the street. "He must have known there was a chance I would go to the police. How does he expect to escape when all hell breaks loose?" She shook her head. "It feels like a setup. Her phone might very well be here, but Robles and Lena could be anywhere."

Todd glanced at Marsh and Carter who had separated from the main huddle and appeared to be in deep conversation. "We're prepared for that move as well. Michaels is standing by to take us wherever we need to go."

His phone vibrated. Todd pulled it from his hip pocket. The name *Jim Colby*, Victoria's son and head of field operations at the agency, appeared on the screen. Todd's gut clenched as he answered the phone. This couldn't be good news. "What's happening inside?"

"Robles's troops are leaving."

As if on cue the large gate across the street slid open and a line of pimped-out automobiles rolled onto the street. Dread congealed in Todd's gut. "All of them?"

"Every damned one our scouts can see from their vantage points have picked up their weapons and walked out."

"What about the ones you can't see?" Todd resisted the urge to race across the street and yank one of the bastards out of a car and beat the truth out of him. The whole damned parade moved nice and slow as if they wanted those watching to get a good look at the show.

"We're working on getting eyes into that room from a ceiling vent."

"Hello."

Todd turned at the sound of Eva's voice. Her eyes were wide with fear as she listened to the caller. Todd checked the time. Robles was early by fifteen minutes.

"Hold on," he said to Jim.

Eva drew the phone from her ear and stared at the screen, her hand shaking.

"What did he say?"

"He said further instructions are coming by text and that he's sending me a photo of Lena."

The call to Eva's cell had drawn Marsh and Carter. They both looked to Todd. "I'm putting you on speaker, Jim." He set his phone to Speaker and moved closer to Eva to watch for the message from Robles.

The text appeared on her screen.

Your sister is waiting across the street from where you are standing. You have five minutes before she dies.

A photo appeared on the screen.

Lena was gagged, blindfolded and tied to an office chair with a package strapped around her chest. On the package was a clock counting down the seconds. *Bomb.*

Chapter Fourteen

"We need the bomb squad! Now! Do not let her move!"

Eva heard Todd's words but her brain refused to assimilate the meaning behind them. She stared at the photo of Lena. Tears had dragged streaks of mascara past the blindfold and down her cheeks to melt into the gag tied around her mouth.

Bomb.

A bomb was strapped to her sister's body.

Todd, Sergeant Carter and several police officers rushed across the street. Detective Marsh gripped Eva by the arm. "Let's move back behind the rail cars."

Eva stared at him for two or three seconds and then she looked back across the street to the men now disappearing into the center building of the equipment rental company.

Lena was in there.

Bomb.

Eva jerked out of the detective's grip and ran. She sprinted across the street.

A horn blared. She lunged forward and the car whipped left, barely avoiding hitting her. Adrenaline fired through her veins. Her heart soared into her throat but she didn't slow. She had to get to her sister.

She reached the building the others had gone into before Marsh caught up with her. She wrenched open the door and rushed inside with him shouting for her to stop.

Can't stop. Gotta get to Lena!

Cops stood seemingly frozen all around the room on this side of a long service counter. Behind the counter, a door stood open. All eyes were on that door.

Sergeant Carter suddenly appeared in the doorway. "Everyone out of the building! Now!"

While the others hurried to obey the sergeant's order, Eva sprinted for the counter. She dodged Marsh as he reached for her again. She rounded the end of the counter and reached the door to find Carter blocking her path to the office and to Lena.

"You need to go with the others," he ordered.

"Get out of my way," she demanded, fear and anger making her shake so hard her teeth nearly chattered.

For one long moment the man stared at her. Whether he sympathized with her plight or simply didn't want to waste time arguing, he stepped aside.

Eva moved around him and into the office. Her heart sank to her feet as she watched a man clad completely in black and whom she didn't recognize remove the gag from her sister's mouth. The blindfold was already gone.

Lena's fear-filled gaze collided with hers. "Get out of here, Eva!" she cried.

Eva moved forward but the man attending to Lena stopped her with an upraised hand. "Don't touch her. We don't know what might trigger the detonator."

Todd was on the phone explaining what the bomb

looked like, she assumed to someone from the bomb squad.

She swallowed hard. Help couldn't possibly make it in time.

Eva eased as close as she dared to her sister. "I'm so sorry." Hot tears spilled down her cheeks as she watched the readout on the clock go from 2:00 to 1:59.

Please don't let his happen.

Another man dressed in black burst into the room. "Wire snips!" He handed the tool to Todd. She realized then that the two men in black were probably the two from the Colby Agency who had infiltrated the building.

Lena smiled up at Eva, her lips trembling with the effort. "I love you, little sister, and I appreciate that you're sorry but you need to go. If we both die, he wins."

Eva dropped to her knees next to Lena and dared to take her hand. "Then let him win."

Todd glanced at her for one second before reaching into the mass of colored wires and snipping one.

1:29

He moved to another as the voice on the phone instructed, she presumed. "Please leave, Eva," he murmured as he reached for the tangle of wires again.

"Sorry." She drew in a shaky breath. "Can't do it." Nothing could make her leave the two people she loved most in the world.

Todd swore and snipped the second wire.

1:18...1:17

"This is not working," he muttered.

Eva thought of all the wonderful times she and her sister had shared. Of how much she loved and missed their parents...and she thought of Todd and how she had missed him...how she loved him so much her heart wanted to burst even now—particularly now. He was prepared to give his life for Lena. He was a hero. He'd always been one, she'd just been too hurt to see it.

In that terrifying moment one truth crystalized for Eva. She should have gone after him. All this time she had been angry and crushed because he'd left and not once had she considered going after him. She had been well aware of how difficult his childhood was. She should have recognized that he might have trouble committing and tracked him down and demanded answers. Pride had kept her from taking that step.

"If my cameraman was here," Lena said as more tears slipped down her blackened cheeks, "this would make a hell of a breaking news story." Lena laughed but the sound held no humor.

Eva nodded. "You can tell Channel 7 viewers the whole story on the late news tonight."

Lena gifted her with another of those shaky smiles. "Absolutely."

Carter rushed back into the room with a larger tool. Using what appeared to be large pruning shears or maybe bolt cutters, he and the man standing next to Lena attempted to cut through the thick nylon straps holding her and the bomb bound to the chair.

0:59

Fear tightened its ruthless grip on Eva. *Hurry!*

Lena squeezed her hand and whispered, "Please go."

Eva shook her head and held her sister's hand even tighter. "No way."

"Hold on a minute," Todd said to the man on the phone. "Something isn't right."

The bottom dropped out of Eva's stomach. *Oh no. What now?*

0:42

Carter and the other man Eva believed to be from the Colby Agency carefully cut through another of the straps as Todd explained something about the bomb that Eva couldn't hope to comprehend.

Her heart fluttered so wildly she felt light-headed as the men cut away a third strap. *Please, please hurry.*

Todd suddenly tossed his phone aside. It slid across the tile floor as he grabbed the remainder of the wires and yanked them free of the box.

0:19

Eva held her breath.

Lena's face paled to a ghostly white.

Todd gripped the box and pulled. The face of the box as well as the clock came loose in his hands.

Inside the black box strapped to Lena's chest there was nothing.

It was empty.

"Son of a bitch," Todd muttered.

The last strap fell away from Lena. Eva scrambled to her feet as the man in black whose name she didn't know helped Lena out of the chair. Lena's knees gave way and he scooped her into his arms.

"Get everyone out!" Todd commanded.

Before Eva could ask what was happening now, the double doors of a large cabinet on the other side of the room burst open. What the hell?

Eva saw the weapon first, then the man. The scream

that filled the air was hers; she couldn't seem to stop the sound.

He leveled the barrel of the weapon on her. "Die, bitch!"

The blast exploded, shaking the air in the room.

Todd's body slammed into her where she stood frozen to the spot.

They crashed onto the floor. Eva grunted as the breath burst from her lungs.

Lena's mouth opened in a scream.

Time lapsed into slow motion...drawing out the sound of her sister's scream. Other voices shouted but Eva couldn't make out the seemingly distorted words.

The man with the gun charged forward, his face contorted with hatred, his weapon still in his hand.

The eerie quiet was ruptured by one, two, three more gunshots.

Then there was silence again.

Eva dragged in a breath, the sound shattering the dreamlike slow motion.

Todd moved off her. "You okay?"

His voice sounded strangely far away.

Eva tried to nod but her head bobbled. She felt disconnected and tattered.

The muffled sound of Lena crying came from somewhere.

There was blood...so much blood.

"He's down," Sergeant Carter said.

"We need an ambulance," someone else said, one of the men wearing black maybe.

Eva looked first at Lena. No blood. She was okay. The man who'd been holding her had stood her on her feet and was now providing directions for the ambulance.

Eva stared at her bloody T-shirt. Where was all the blood coming from? Had she been shot? She was reasonably sure not, but considering the sluggish way her senses were reacting she wasn't certain of anything.

The man who'd come out of that cabinet intending to shoot her lay on the floor a few feet away, his eyes open, a bullet hole in the center of his forehead.

Todd reached down to her.

She stared at the wide hand and fingers that had touched her body and soul. The blood smeared on his palm showed her what she hadn't wanted to see.

She hadn't been shot...it was Todd. Blood had soaked into his shirt. The bullet appeared to have hit his left upper arm in the area of the deltoid muscle.

Hers shaking, she took his hand and got to her feet. "Oh my God. You're..."

He grinned. "It's nothing. Besides, I know an excellent nurse."

The Edge, 9:00 p.m.

TODD FLINCHED.

Dr. Marissa Frasier smiled. "Good thing that was the last one." She finished the final suture and stepped back from the exam table.

"Thanks, Doc." Todd moved his arm, wincing at the pain.

Frasier peeled off her gloves and tossed them into the trash receptacle. "The nurse will be in shortly and she'll bandage that for you. Thank you, Mr. Christian, for keeping Eva safe. She means a great deal to all of us."

Todd gave the lady a nod. When she'd left the room he exhaled a big breath. He'd never felt more tired in his life. He closed his eyes. Those few minutes with that clock ticking down had been the longest and most terrifying of his life. If Eva or Lena had...

No. He couldn't think about that. It was over. They were both fine. He was fine. The nightmare was over.

The door opened and he looked up, his heart lifting in expectation.

"Looks like you're good to go," Lena said.

"No worse for the wear," he returned, tension rifling through him. He'd expected Eva to walk through that door or maybe one of the other nurses. Lena was about the last person he'd figured he would see again tonight. Didn't she have a hot breaking story to report?

She folded her arms over her chest and stared at him for a long moment. He braced for all hell to break loose.

"You broke my sister's heart when you left."

He couldn't deny the charge. "I won't offer you an excuse because I don't have one. I was a coward who didn't deserve her."

She looked surprised at his confession "A coward for sure. And a jerk as well as a—"

He held up a hand. "I was all those things, yes. I've apologized to Eva."

Lena threw her head back and laughed. When she finally regained her composure, she said, "I love my sister more than anything else in this world. You hurt her again and I will make you wish you had never come back to Chicago."

He nodded. "Got it."

She turned and stepped toward the door. Her hand on the handle, she hesitated a second or two before turning back to him. "Thank you." She stared at the floor before meeting his gaze once more. "It's a rare man who would willingly give his life while trying to save another. Whatever you were ten years ago, you're a good man now. I saw that today."

A smile spread across his lips. "Thank you. Hearing you say that means a lot."

She pointed a finger at him. "But I'll still kick your ass if you hurt her."

With that she left the room. Kim came in next and bandaged his freshly sutured wound while going over the care instructions the doctor had left.

"There you go, Mr. Christian." She handed him his discharge papers. "You're all done." She sighed. "It's a little crazy tonight so we had to put Eva to work. She told me to tell you that if you didn't want to wait she would understand."

Todd hopped off the table. "I'll wait."

Kim flashed him a grin and said, "I thought you might." With that, she hurried out the door to move on to the next patient.

He'd waited a long time to have Eva back in his life. What was a few more hours?

West Grace Street Apartments, Midnight

EVA CHECKED HER door one last time. Locked. She pressed her forehead to the cool surface and thought of Mrs. Cackowski's door across the hall. However longer Eva lived in this building, on this floor, she

would never be able to pass that door without thinking of the sweet lady. Eva hoped Miguel Robles died
screaming for what he'd done. With Lena's help the
police had identified the murdered woman found in
her town house. She had worked at a coffee shop down
the street from where Lena lived. Robles's people had
likely chosen her because she and Lena had similar
features. *Bastards*.

Another innocent victim slain for no other reason
except to terrify Eva.

But Miguel Robles wasn't getting away with his
heinous deeds anymore. The police had found him
with the help of their new informant, thanks to the
Colby Agency. Robles had been so certain that his
chosen assassin would kill both Eva and Lena, he had
personally and boldly tortured Lena with promises
that both she and Eva would die today—all as he held
her hostage. With the informant's testimony as well
as Lena's, Robles was done. He would spend the rest
of his life in prison.

"I'm starving."

Eva turned away from the door and smiled at her
hero. "If you'll give me a moment to change, I'll prepare you the most amazing meal you've ever eaten."

It was the least she could do after he'd saved her
life. Her heart squeezed. He'd taken the bullet meant
for her. He'd kept her safe and protected her through
this entire nightmare. Now he had matching bandages,
one on his right shoulder, the other on his left upper
arm. Poor guy.

At his skeptical look, she said, "I've become quite
the chef since college."

Propped against her kitchen counter, his gorgeous

chest bare, he grinned. "Been keeping secrets, have you?"

He'd tossed his shirt at the hospital. She'd been so damn glad the bullet hadn't caused any real damage she wouldn't have cared if he'd walked out of there naked. Every female in the vicinity had swooned as he walked by as it was. She'd had to help out with the Saturday night rush for a couple of hours and Todd had stationed himself where he could watch. Every time she glanced at him she saw the hunger in his eyes, but she was pretty sure it had nothing to do with food. Her entire being tingled with anticipation.

"I have," she confessed. "A woman should always have at least a few secrets." She headed for the bathroom. "Relax. I'll only be a minute."

Shutting herself away in the room that now felt like a closet compared to the bathroom she'd had at the Colby safe house, she stared at herself in the mirror for a long moment. "What're you doing, Eva?"

She'd insisted on bringing Todd home with her. He shouldn't be alone. He had been shot after all. But that had been an excuse. This wasn't about taking care of him for the night or even showing her gratitude for his protection. This was far more.

She wasn't ready to let him go. When Kim had told her that he intended to wait while Eva helped out, her heart had started to beat so fast she could hardly stay focused on her work. He was here and there were things she needed to say. Before Lena left the hospital tonight she had made Eva promise that she would tell Todd the truth. Apparently her big sister had recognized that truth just watching the two of them together.

You're still in love with him.

Eva had denied Lena's accusation. She'd spent the better part of the past decade pretending she hated him. She peeled off her scrub top and shimmied out of the bottom and tossed both aside. She'd changed out of her bloody clothes at the hospital to help out. Sometimes sudden bursts of incoming patients happened like that, especially on the weekends.

Eva drew in a reaffirming breath. Lena was right. Eva did love Todd. She hoped her sister was right about the other as well. Lena was convinced that Todd still loved Eva. Eva wasn't so sure. Yes, Todd had stepped in front of a bullet for her, but that had been his job.

She thought of the way he touched her. The way he had apologized for leaving, admitting that he'd been afraid he didn't deserve her.

Maybe he did still care for her. Her mother had sworn he would be back.

"Stop." Eva shook her head. She was setting herself up for major heartbreak. Time to give it a rest. She would know soon enough how he felt. Frankly she was surprised Lena hadn't scared him off with her warning. If Eva hadn't been so busy with patients, she would have headed off that awkward scene.

He'd taken Lena's scolding and still waited for Eva. That was something. She ran a brush through her hair before going to her closet where she shuffled through the offerings until she found another tee and a pair of lounge pants. What she really needed was a shower, but Todd was hungry and she didn't want to make him wait.

A knock at her door was followed by, "Hey, I found what I really wanted."

"Oh yeah?" she asked as he opened the door. Holding the tee and pants to her body as if she needed to hide the fact that she was standing there in panties and a bra, she beamed a smile she hoped covered for the worrisome thoughts nagging at her. "Can't wait for a decent meal, eh?"

He held up the chocolate frosting as he took a step toward her. "I decided I wanted to go straight to dessert."

Her skin felt on fire. "You're an injured man." She tossed the clothes aside. This was one aspect of their relationship where she had nothing to hide from him. "I'm not sure you're up for dessert."

He licked his lips and her nipples stung. "I think I can hold my own."

She reached behind her and unfastened her bra, letting it fall forward, revealing her breasts before falling into a wisp of lace on the floor. "There are things we need to talk about."

Another step disappeared between them. Her breath caught. No other man had ever made her wet by just walking toward her. How could she possibly ever deny how much she loved this man? She loved every perfectly sculpted inch of him. His gorgeous body, scars and all. That handsome face. Blue, blue eyes and lips so kissable her mouth ached to taste them. That thick hair she loved running her fingers through.

"What kind of things?" he asked.

And that voice. So deep, it wrapped around her and made her want to close her eyes and fall into the sound.

He stood right in front of her now, waiting for her

answer to his question. "Like," she stammered, "what *this* is?"

The way he looked at her—as if he intended to devour her rather than the chocolate—she knew she was in trouble.

"This," he murmured in that steamy, sexy voice as he moved closer and closer, forcing her to step back until he'd backed her all the way to the bed, "is me wanting you so badly I can barely breathe."

He moved in another step and she dropped onto the bed, scooted out of his reach. He tossed the chocolate onto the covers and climbed onto the bed on all fours, crawling slowly toward her.

"This is us taking back what I let slip away before." He moved over her, lowered his mouth to hers and kissed her so softly she whimpered with the sweetness of it. "I ran away before because I was afraid." His lips hovered just centimeters above hers. "I swear to you I'm not afraid anymore. I'm here to stay, if you'll have me."

She reached up and nipped at his lips. "I might need a little more convincing."

He grinned, his lips brushing hers. "Happy to oblige."

He sat back on his heels and reached for the frosting. He tore open the package and dipped his finger into the luscious chocolate. Slowly, he traced a path down her throat and around her breasts, tipping each nipple with the sweet stuff before dipping down to her belly button. He leaned down and traced that path with his tongue. It was all she could do to bear the exquisite torture. She shivered and moaned, reminding herself to breathe as her fingers fisted in the covers.

He moved slowly, savoring the chocolate as he went. Then he made a new path, this one right down to the waistband of her lacy panties. He dragged the strappy lace down her legs and off before crawling back up her body until he reached her belly button. As he teased her belly button with his mouth, he stroked her inner thighs with his fingers, tortured her clitoris, pushing her beyond her limits.

By the time he reached for his fly she was writhing with need. "Hurry," she whispered.

She helped him push his jeans down his lean hips and then guide himself into her. With her legs locked around his, she closed her eyes and melted with the feel of him filling her body so completely.

He kissed her cheek, tracing a path to her ear as he held his body too damn still. "I love you, Eva," he whispered.

She stared into his eyes, trailing her fingers down his sinewy torso and wrapped her arms around his waist. "I love you, Todd."

The rest of what they had to say, they said with their bodies.

Chapter Fifteen

Sunday, May 13, 9:00 a.m.

Victoria sipped her hot tea and smiled. Her husband was doing what he always did on Sunday morning: reading the newspaper while his second cup of coffee cooled. She and Lucas Camp had been friends for most of their lives, husband and wife for a good number of years now.

When she studied him like this, she wondered how it was possible to love him more each day, but she did. Ten or so years ago they had decided to retire. They'd even moved to the warmer climate of Texas and pretended to relax for a while. But that hadn't worked out so well. The Colby Agency was too much a part of the fabric of their lives. Cold, windy Chicago was as well. Their children and grandchildren were here. The worst tragedies of their lives as well as the happiest days of their lives had all played out right here. After only a few months away they had made a mutual decision to return and to never again leave their beloved home.

The two of them would go into the office Monday through Friday until they drew their last breaths.

Lucas still consulted on cases with his old team at the CIA. He and Thomas Casey, the former director of Lucas's shadow unit, still had lunch once a month. It was hard to let go of a life's work, and the powers that be still needed old-school spies like Lucas and Thomas.

Victoria felt immensely grateful that she and Lucas spent most of their time helping others. Life could be so difficult sometimes. They were both committed to seeing that her son Jim and Lucas's son Slade followed in their footsteps. The Colby Agency had become a cornerstone of Chicago; that legacy must be carried on.

Victoria smiled. "I'm very pleased with Jamie's ability to work without supervision. She's learning quickly to anticipate the necessary steps in a case."

Lucas folded the newspaper and set it aside. "It's refreshing to see such ambition in a young lady her age."

Victoria set her teacup aside. "I hope Luke is as excited about following in his father's and his grandparents' shoes as his older sister."

Lucas laughed. "Give the boy time. Girls mature much faster than boys."

Victoria had to laugh. "This is very true."

The sparkle of mischief in her husband's gray eyes made her smile. "But our women love us anyway."

"We do, indeed." She could not imagine her life without this man. They were two of a kind. "Tell me, did you discover anything useful in your search into Dr. Pierce's past?"

Dr. Devon Pierce, former renowned surgeon and the genius behind the Edge facility, had a ghost from his past haunting his newly found success. He'd ignored it for some time but when he and Victoria had been discussing Eva Bowman's troubles, Pierce had confessed to having a problem of his own.

Lucas raised his cup to his lips, savoring the bold flavor of his favorite blend. When he'd placed the cup in its saucer once more, he considered her question a moment longer. "Pierce's background is littered with tragedy."

Victoria was aware of his personal tragedy. He and his wife had been visiting her family in Binghamton, New York, for the holidays when an awful car accident left her gravely injured. Pierce had been severely injured himself and the local hospital simply wasn't equipped to handle their needs. With no time to wait for his wife to be airlifted to another hospital and no surgeon available to help her, Pierce had tried to save her himself. She died on the operating table.

Eventually he had returned to work as the head of surgery at Chicago's prestigious Rush University Medical Center. Within a year he had resigned to focus solely on reinventing the Emergency Department. Six years later his creation, the Edge, was the prototype for new facilities all over the country.

As much as Victoria respected Devon Pierce, she felt sympathy for him as well. He had not allowed himself to have a real life since his wife died. Work was his only companion. He continued to live alone in the massive mansion in Lake Bluff he'd built for her. Victoria and Lucas had been to his home once, before he lost his wife. They'd hosted a fund-raiser for a new wing at Rush. The Georgian-style mansion had been more like a castle than a home.

How sad that such a brilliant and caring man refused to open his heart again.

"You didn't find anything that might have fostered trouble in his career since developing the Edge?"

Lucas propped his elbows on the table and clasped his hands in front of him. "Not yet, but, my dear, you know as well as I do that you don't rise to the top in anything without leaving a few skeletons in your closet."

Her husband was full of sage proverbs this morning. "Then we must find the one doing the rattling."

Lucas gave her a nod. "You have the perfect investigator for the job."

"Isabella Lytle," Victoria agreed.

"Shall we schedule breakfast with Bella in the morning to discuss the case?"

Victoria reached across the table for her cell phone. "I'll send her a text now."

Once Dr. Pierce's troubles were resolved, perhaps he would finally let go of the past and live the life he continued to ignore in the present.

As if he'd sensed her thought, Lucas laid his hand on hers. "Don't worry, my dear, the Colby Agency never fails a client."

That was one truth she intended to spend the rest of her life backing up.

* * * * *

UNDERCOVER SCOUT

JENNA KERNAN

For Jim, always.

Chapter One

Detective Ava Hood watched her prime suspect, Dr. Kee Redhorse, through her field glasses and scowled. You couldn't tell about a person by looking. Dr. Redhorse was a great example of that. Charming, well liked by his tribe, above reproach and the very last person you would suspect. But as it turned out, Ava suspected everyone. And no one was this squeaky clean.

Redhorse was a trusted member of the Turquoise Canyon people. A physician, newly board certified and quite possibly a monster.

She sat in her Chevy Malibu, parked nose out, between the battered yellow bulldozer that created the temporary road and a ten-foot pile of gravel. From her position she could see the FEMA housing trailers that included her sister's and the one assigned to Dr. Richard Day and Dr. Kee Redhorse. She noted in her log that Kee left his assigned FEMA trailer on Sunday to go for a walk at 8:08 a.m., October 15.

Ava didn't trust the tribal police on this rez mostly because Dr. Redhorse had a brother on the force, Jake Redhorse. Plenty of opportunities to look the other way. She knew if she wanted to get to the bottom of her investigation she had to do it herself and she didn't have time for official channels. She accepted the potential risks and didn't care for the cost. State evidence be damned. Justice would be served, one way or another.

Her niece was missing—quite possibly a victim of the series of kidnappings that had recently hit the reservation.

All young women. All to be used as surrogates in a baby trafficking ring run by the Russian mob.

And all of them patients at the clinic shortly before their disappearance. That connection had been made only three weeks ago, ten days before her niece had been taken.

She adjusted her field glasses in her hands and studied her subject. Redhorse was dressed in faded jeans and a college T-shirt, over which he yanked a well-worn, gray hooded sweatshirt as he descended the steps. He looked more approachable in casual clothing, losing some of that air of professionalism that clung to him during his shifts at the tribe's clinic. She tried to ignore the way the clothing hung on his perfect frame and failed.

"No one is that perfect, Ava," she muttered to herself. She knew that much.

Today, he wore scratched and scuffed Timberland boots and a ball cap. He was the sort of man that you noticed right off because of his easy smile and dark, intelligent eyes. Ava noticed him because she thought he was guilty. And if she reacted to him as a man, well, she would ignore it.

How much had he gotten away with in his life because of his good looks and natural appeal? She hated charmers because that was how her grandmother described Ava's father—the father she had never known. *A real charmer.*

She had been watching both doctors from the reservation clinic, Hector Hauser and Kee Redhorse, since last Saturday night. She'd come the minute she'd heard from Sara that one of the missing girls, Kacey Doka, had reappeared after escaping her captors. She'd hoped to speak to Kacey but she and Colt Redhorse had vanished four days ago and she had suspected the Justice Department had them. She'd taken a leave of absence from her own tribe's police force, the Saguaro Flats Apache. She only had a few weeks left in the position. She'd already accepted a new job here on the Turquoise Canyon police force, but the job didn't start until the first of November. That was too long to wait to start her investigation. Time was of the essence and she had to start ASAP. Every good cop knew a missing person's trail got significantly colder after the first forty-eight hours. Her sixteen-year-old niece, Louisa, had been gone for fourteen days and the police here had found nothing.

No, she couldn't trust the Turquoise Canyon tribal force to handle the investigation on their own—especially if one of their officers was blocking evidence.

As far as her force knew, she was here only to comfort her sister, Sara, and help Sara out with her daughters, which was true. But they didn't know she also planned to track down Louisa. That she'd do so alone just made sense. No one else to endanger or to let her down.

Ava had managed to break into both Redhorse's and Hauser's temporary FEMA trailers and install a tracking program on their personal computers. The simple program gave her access to their bank records, email, calendars, browser history and social media accounts. She'd done criminal record checks on each and all their closest associates. The only hit was Kee Redhorse's father, Colton, who was serving a sentence in federal prison for armed robbery. And his brother Ty, who had a juvie record, which was closed. Ava wondered about that one since the dates corresponded exactly to Colton Redhorse's last heist. Even though there had been no other convictions, Ty was currently under investigation by tribal police for kidnapping Kacey Doka—the girlfriend of his youngest brother, Colt. Not enough evidence had been found to tag him to the crime yet, but there was still a big question mark over his head.

And Colt? His record was clean. After Kacey had escaped her captors and fingered Ty as the driver, Ava had confirmed that Kacey and Colt had entered witness protection until the crime ring could be stopped.

"Something that's taking too long in my book," Ava muttered to herself.

Today was day eight of her investigation and she was running out of time. Soon she'd have to ask for help, return home or resign her job and stay. She thought about resigning from Saguaro Flats force altogether before coming here to Turquoise Canyon, but there were perks to being a cop—even one on leave. She still had access to police databases, which was imperative to her success. Quitting the police force would cause her to lose effectiveness.

She knew the FBI was involved with the investigation because she'd received an alert on her reservation from Turquoise Canyon Tribal Police that they had requested assistance last week after it was discovered that one of their missing persons, Kacey Doka, was not a runaway but a victim of kidnapping who'd identified several other missing girls held captive with her. The Bureau's focus would be on capture and conviction of those responsible. Hers was on recovery by any means.

Ava had already spoken to Kacey's kidnapper. The Russian was paralyzed from the waist down, still in the hospital at Darabee and on suicide watch. Ava got nothing from him as he still elected to pretend he did not speak English. She did get a photo of his tattoos and was running a check on them through the available database. Gang affiliations were often written on the skin and his said Russian organized crime. But they'd need connections here.

First, she'd figure out who and they'd lead her to where the missing were kept. That was the plan.

She'd learned all she could from her surveillance of Kee

and Hauser and from their personal computers and found nothing to implicate either physician.

She needed to get inside that clinic.

Ava drove along the rutted gravel road, hastily laid before the trailers had been hauled in by the dozens. The dam collapse that touched off the move out of the tribe's tribal seat happened just a little over three weeks ago. The evacuees from lowland areas along the river were moved to temporary shelters out of the potential flood area. The FEMA trailers had arrived and her sister had been among the first to receive one because she had young children.

She parked before her sister's FEMA trailer and ignored the barking as she opened the door. Woody, the big brown family dog, jumped up to say hello. She was surprised to see him, as he had been staying with her sister's mother-in-law, who lived outside the reach of potential flooding. Woody had been added to the family at Louisa's insistence and seeing him made Ava's throat tighten. She gave him a quick scratch behind the ears and pushed him off until he dropped to all fours. His tail swung back and forth, thick and hairless at the base from too much chewing. A shepherd/pit bull mix, he had a head the size and shape of a shovel.

Ava checked her watch. Redhorse should be back by here in about ten minutes. Woody poked around the trailer and returned with a faded, worn, green tennis ball. Ava accepted the offering and tossed the ball. She kept her attention on the end of the street until Redhorse returned.

He was only a few hundred yards away with a newspaper tucked under his arm when he noticed her. She could tell by the hesitation in his stride.

She continued to toss the ball as Redhorse approached.

This was how he found them. Ava throwing a slippery tennis ball to an oversize puppy.

Kee Redhorse's black hair was trimmed short. His skin

was tawny-brown with bronze undertones. He had a broad forehead, a blade of a nose that hooked downward over a generous mouth and pinholes in each earlobe for earrings, which he did not wear. Handsome by any standard, she thought.

He hadn't shaved this morning. She found that the dark stubble only added to his appeal. The hair growing beneath his lower lip brought her attention to his mouth. It was a sensual mouth. His lips parted and he inhaled, making his nostrils flare. Then that winning smile appeared. She felt a twitch in her stomach.

Suspect, she reminded herself.

Woody spotted Redhorse and trotted over to say hello. The man offered his hand. It was a nice hand with tight medium brown skin and a sprinkling of dark hair on the back, and the hand itself was broad and square with long elegant fingers. Ava blew away her frustration at her body's reaction to the doctor.

"He's friendly," said Ava and forced a wide smile as she descended the steps and stood with her hands in her back pockets. She'd dressed for success today, in jeans that left room for her ankle holster but hugged everything else and a blouse that was feminine without broadcasting her cup size. Woody sniffed Redhorse's hand and the wet ball fell to the ground.

Ava made a grab for the ball but Woody was too quick and snatched it up again. The tug-of-war ensued with the dog crouched, growling as he shook his shovel of a head, tail thumping. Ava wasn't much of a frolicker but she did her best.

Redhorse laughed. "He's not giving up."

"He loves to play," she said.

Woody won. The canine dropped the ball at Redhorse's feet.

Traitor, she thought.

"He wants you to throw it," she said keeping her smile until he turned to retrieve the ball.

He did and it was a really good throw. She gauged his physical strength and was glad she had both her service weapon and her training.

Woody returned, chewing as he trotted. He folded to the ground to begin gnawing in earnest, the ball between his paws. She could swear the canine was smiling.

Ava put a hand on her hip and sighed.

"Guess I finally wore him out," she said and gave Redhorse another smile, making eye contact. He seemed to be looking right through her. Heat sizzled inside her and her stomach tensed. She knew he was single, dated occasionally but never for long and had been engaged to an Anglo in med school. Circumstances of the breakup were unclear.

Redhorse cleared his throat and looked back to the dog. Ava took a deep breath and pinched her lips together as she fought the troubling physical zip of awareness for him. It had never happened to her with a suspect before.

He cast her an effortless smile and the tug grew stronger. She was going to have to arrest him or sleep with him.

Yeah, right. She didn't have the justification for either action.

Their eyes met and her heart gave an irritating flutter again. She wished she had enough evidence to read him his rights. She bet handcuffs would wipe that smile off his face.

Her grandmother would approve, she thought. Also possibly a felon. She scowled.

Redhorse was a suspect, not a prospect.

Woody stared up at her, his ball forgotten.

She pointed. "That's Woody."

Her gaze dropped to the sensual curve of his upper lip. *You're staring at his mouth.*

He switched to Tonto Apache. "Hello. I am Roadrun-

ner born of Wolf, the oldest son of Colton and May Redhorse." Then he switched back to English as he completed
his introduction and extended his free hand. "I'm Doctor
Kee Redhorse."

Trotting out the title, she thought. She didn't trust him
and did not accept his hand. She was already attracted to
the man. Touching him would only make the nagging stab
of desire worse. Instead, Ava lifted her hands out before
her, palms up.

"Wet," she said, with dog slobber.

He held his smile as his arm dropped to his side. Was
he disappointed?

"I live just up that way," he said, motioning the way
he had come. "For now anyway. Until we move back to
Piñon Flats."

She knew that. Likely knew more about him than his
own family.

Since the dam collapsed upriver of this reservation,
most of the residents of the community of Piñon Flats had
been relocated here to high ground in Turquoise Canyon
while the temporary rubble dam was reinforced by FEMA.
Their permanent houses were still intact, but the dam had
already been destroyed in an act of eco-extremism. Neither the tribe elders nor FEMA wanted to put anyone else
at risk.

"I heard that will be any day," she said.

He nodded and grinned.

"How is it I have never seen you before?" he asked and
switched to Tonto. "I know that I would remember you."

That smile made her insides roll and her stomach flutter.
It was like swimming against a strong current. Those teeth,
that jawline, that elegant nose. Oh, boy, was she in over
her head. She hoped he wasn't guilty because…what? He
was handsome? She was smitten? She needed to get a grip.

It wasn't her job to hope he was guilty or innocent. It

was her job to find Louisa. If he had her or was responsible for her disappearance, then that was that.

Ava, you need to lock this down.

"I didn't get your name," said Kee.

"I'm Ava Hood." She didn't use her legal name, her father's name. Never had, though her surname, Yokota, did crop up on things like her diplomas and legal documents.

"You didn't grow up on the rez, Ava. I'd have noticed you." His smile was so dazzling she needed sunglasses. Suddenly his charm and charisma seemed a threat. It made it easier to resist.

"I am Snake born of Spider," she said in perfect Tonto Apache in the traditional form of greeting. One always began with the tribe, moved to clans and then relations. Only after these important ties were given, did one mention their own name. "My parents are Eldon and Lydia Hood from Saguaro Flats reservation." Though her father was Eldon Yokota, she had given the correct first name.

"You speak very well," he said in English.

The compliment seemed an insult. Besides, she had little choice as her grandmother had no other language but Tonto and she had lived with her until she was eight.

"I know that rez. Small, right?"

"Very."

"What brings you up here?"

"Visiting my sister. She married a man up here."

"What's his name?"

"Diamond Tah."

Kee's smile slipped. "Oh." He nodded and then met her gaze, his smile gone and his eyes serious. "I knew him very well. I used to listen to him play the flute at gatherings. So your sister is—"

"Sara Tah."

Ava's sister was newly widowed. Her husband had died one night on his way to the bathroom from a brain aneu-

rysm. He'd been forty-two. That should have been enough
tragedy for one year, but it turned out to be only the start.

His gaze flicked away again. Was that guilt? Or did he
know that her sister was in far worse shape since her husband's death than Ava had imagined. The drinking had
gotten worse and there had been calls to protective services. It was reason enough for Ava to visit.

Ava waited for him to speak. What would a man who
she suspected had a hand in the kidnappings say at this
moment?

"I'm very sorry," he said.

Appropriate, she thought.

"For what?"

He looked surprised, as if this was obvious, but she
wanted to hear him say it. "Sara lost her husband recently
and now...well, Louisa is missing. I know she's been...
struggling. It's a terrible tragedy."

He did not do or say anything that might reveal that he
could be the reason for Louisa's disappearance.

"We are still hopeful."

"Of course." He shifted uncomfortably. "How is Sara
doing?"

Did he know about her sister's drinking?

She went on the defensive. It was her fallback position,
and protecting her sister came naturally as breathing. The
truth was that her sister had lost weight, and didn't eat. The
entire situation made Ava's chest hurt. "It's a hard time."

He nodded. "And the girls?"

She wanted to press a finger into his broad chest and
tell him that he didn't have the right to ask about them.
Not ever.

"They're frightened, mostly. The twins are afraid to
leave for school or take the bus. So I'm driving them, for
now."

Margarita and Alexandra were five, and Olivia, only

three. These were the children Sara had with Diamond. She'd brought Louisa to the marriage after her first marriage had failed.

Redhorse had treated each one of her sister's kids. Most damning, he'd treated Louisa on September 30, on her last visit to the tribe's clinic, just two days before her disappearance.

"I understand that," he said. "Good of you to be with her at this time. Are you her younger sister?"

"Why do you ask?"

He cast her a shy smile. "You look young."

"I am the younger sister but not by much. I'm twenty-eight."

He looked shocked. She got that a lot but not looking her age had advantages. People often underestimated her.

She watched him. He didn't shift or rub his neck. His gaze did not cut away as if he were anxious to put her behind him. He only held the appropriate look of sadness and concern.

He smiled. "Nice folks."

"They sure are. I'd do anything for my sister and her kids." She waited through the awkward pause. Still, he radiated nothing but concern.

"Is that why you bumped into me? You wanted to ask me about them?"

He was smart. She'd give him that but that only made him more dangerous if he was guilty.

"Is there something you'd like to get off your chest?" she asked.

"Off my…me? No," he said and looked puzzled.

She waited as he cocked his head to study her, brow wrinkling.

"Well, it's a pleasure to meet you, Ava. May I call you Ava?"

She nodded.

"And please call me Kee."

She preferred to call him prime suspect.

"What do you do down there on your rez, Ava?"

"Why do you ask?"

"I'm not sure. You have a certain directness to you."

The pause seemed especially long. He stared at her and she noted the golden flecks in his deep brown eyes.

"So what do you do down there on the flats?" he asked again.

"I used to work for the casino. Dealer. High rollers, mostly. But I'm taking a break." Actually that was her sister's bio but she wasn't going to tell him she was ROTC, had done four years of active duty in Germany and had just finished her four additional years on reserve while completing police training, and recently earned her gold shield. Given how her sister had completely withdrawn from society after her husband's death and buried herself in a bottle, she doubted that Sara would have the opportunity to blow her cover.

The small talk continued. He told her what she already knew, that their clinic had only seven employees. Two physicians. One administrator, Betty Mills, and five nurses, one of whom—Lori Mott Redhorse—was well on her way to becoming a midwife. Lori was also Kee's sister-in-law and the one who'd first made the connection between the clinic and the six missing women from his tribe.

Ava had already spoken with Lori and believed she was one of the good guys. The woman seemed interested in finding the missing teenagers and willing to do all she could to help the investigation. Not the actions of someone guilty of a crime.

"I thought there were three physicians," Ava said when she caught an inaccuracy in Redhorse's story.

"Oh, yes. That's right. Dr. Day is on loan from FEMA. That's my roommate, temporarily, until we get the all-clear to move back home." Since Ava had searched the trailer, she was aware of the roommate situation. But Dr. Day hadn't been around long enough to be a suspect, so she'd focused entirely on Dr. Kee Redhorse.

"I didn't know that FEMA provided doctors."

"Oh, yeah. And they have emergency medical response teams. Our clinic is currently set up in two of their mobile medical units. Crowded, but we are getting the job done. It's been good to have another set of hands during the crisis. We've been super busy but we'll lose Day soon."

She quirked a brow. "That so?"

He casually slipped a hand into his back pocket. She watched his hands, wondering if he had a weapon. Kee kept talking.

"Once we get back to the clinic in Piñon Flats and out of those trailers, I'm sure they'll recall him. Too bad, he's a nice guy."

There was something implied in his tone. She took a guess. "But not a good doctor?"

The side of his mouth quirked. His tell, she decided, that little gesture that said she had made the right guess. "He's adequate."

"But not Native."

Kee made a sound that might have been a laugh. "Oh, I don't mind that. But he is from Minnesota. So he thinks it's too hot up here."

"He'd hate Saguaro Flats."

Now Kee did laugh. The sound buzzed over her skin and the hairs on her neck lifted at the pure musical joy in that deep male rumble of delight. She was reconsidering her strategy. Ava had not anticipated liking her suspect.

"His specialty is emergency medicine. He's less interested in ongoing treatment of chronic conditions and I think he's had his fill of diabetes and high blood pressure."

"I see."

Woody discovered an abandoned soda bottle, which he trotted over to Ava with. Her attempts to retrieve it from his mouth resulted in another game of chase.

"He can have it," said Ava, recognizing defeat first. She turned back to her questioning. "How do you like working at the clinic?"

He shifted his weight from one leg to the other. "Oh, I like it, but I really prefer emergency medicine, too. Plus I'm only here part-time. Just finishing up my residency. Dr. Hauser, he's our head physician, he arranged for me to split my time between here and Darabee Hospital."

Ava crinkled up her face. "Sounds busy."

Kee shrugged, a good-natured expression on his face. "It is. Doesn't leave much time for a social life—or even a chance to catch up with the people in my own family. And since the dam collapse the clinic hours have been crazy. But I love the work and with my loans…" He held a hand to his throat and pretended to be strangling. "Gotta get a position in a hospital. Plan is to leave for a few years to get the best salary possible. I hope to come back someday."

That didn't mesh with a man making oodles of money from the Russian mob unless he knew that his tribal police force had made connections between the missing girls and his clinic. Then crying poverty was smart. His little brother was on the force. Had Officer Jake Redhorse given Kee some insider info?

"Medical school is expensive," she said, hoping she sounded sympathetic. Her computer-hacking had exposed he was in up to his eyeballs in debt and had a really good motive for wanting to make a boatload of fast cash.

"I've had some assistance from the tribe. Dr. Hauser helped me qualify for a grant that covered some of it."

She made a mental note to check on that.

"Sounds like a great guy." *Or a dangerous criminal*, she thought.

"Yeah. He is. Hector is the one who encouraged me to practice medicine. I had a leg-length discrepancy as a kid." He shrugged. "He took an interest."

She thought of the photo she'd seen in his room in the FEMA trailer. He'd been younger, with a single crutch under one thin arm.

"I had lots of surgeries down in Phoenix." He held his arms wide. "Now I'm the shortest male in my family."

He wasn't short, by any means. She marked him at nearly six feet.

"Why is that?" she asked.

"Well, they can't add to the shorter leg. You know, make you taller. So they make corrections by reducing the size of the longer limb."

She flinched as she imagined someone sawing through her lower leg bone.

"Yeah, exactly. Lost three inches. But they even up within an eighth of an inch." He bent slightly at the waist and presented his straight legs for her examination. They were fine muscular legs. She could see that even through the denim of his jeans. "Hector arranged for all that and the therapy. Pulled strings and it was all taken care of."

So Hector was a string puller and Kee was forever in his debt. How far would Kee go to pay him back?

"It was a hard time. My dad was...gone."

In prison, she thought.

"We didn't have much money."

"Your head physician sounds like a wonderful man." Her smile felt tight and unnatural. Kee didn't seem to notice.

"He used to operate out of a room at tribal headquarters when I was a kid. Gave me all my shots there. But you should see the facility now. We have an urgent care center, triage, three exam rooms, reception, radiology and a woman's health center with three birthing rooms, plus additional ob-gyn exam rooms."

"That's impressive. Paid through gaming?" she asked. It wasn't, she knew, because she'd seen their budget, via her sister's login on the tribe's website. Some areas of the tribe's website were public while others were pass-word-protected to ensure only tribal members could access them. The page holding the minutes from tribal government meetings was one of these pages.

Kee shrugged. "Our administrator handles all that."

Betty Mills, Ava knew. Recently divorced. Mother of three grown boys and driving an Audi leased by the clinic.

Woody tore the bottle in two and Ava threw the ball so she could retrieve the jagged pieces.

"I better check on my sister and the girls." Sara was probably still in bed and likely hungover. The girls were being raised by a game console, as far as Ava could tell. She could at least get them all out of bed and feed them a healthy breakfast.

Anything to keep them all afloat until Louisa and the other missing children could be found.

"Oh," he looked disappointed. "Of course. Umm, Ava? Will you be here a few days?"

"I plan to be. Yes."

"Would you like to have a drink sometime this week?" His face was red when he finished, which she was cha-grined to find she found absolutely adorable. Her heart was not behaving, hammered as if this was something other than a stakeout. Her department had another word for it…*entrapment*.

She didn't care. All rules were off when you messed with hers.

So, here it was, the opportunity she had been hoping for. But that was before she realized she would be attracted to the good doctor. She hesitated, biting her bottom lip as she tapped the two sides of the ruined plastic bottle together before her in a nervous tattoo.

Dating Kee would give her access to him, to Hauser and to the clinic and she needed to know what was going on in there.

"Ava?" His dark brow lifted. "Are you seeing someone?"

She shook her head. "Oh, no. Not currently." It was unfortunate that not one of the men in her past made her silly heart pitter-patter like this one, here. "I just need to work around the kids' schedules and my sister. And I don't really drink."

Because it meant a possible loss of control and Ava did not go there.

"Oh. Coincidence," he said. "Neither do I. And I understand about your family. You're here for them. Family first, my dad always said."

How reassuring. An adage from a con.

As far as she could tell Kee and Jake were the only ones that visited dear old dad and not often. But at least they had a dad.

"My sister gets home from work at five fifteen. I've been getting the kids dinner and I'm free after that."

"Oh, great."

"When?" she asked.

"How about Tuesday? Dinner at the casino?"

Ava was known here as Sara's sister and a member of the Saguaro Flats tribe. But like many detectives, she kept her profession secret mainly so as not to make people uncomfortable but also to allow her to more easily do her job. Anyone who would have asked was told that she worked in her tribe's adult education program, her usual cover.

"That sounds fun." Ava held her smile.

"I'll pick you up around six?"

"Seven."

"Sure," Kee agreed.

She drew a pen from her back pocket. "Give me your hand."

He did. His palm slid across hers, warm and dry. The tingle of awareness began at her fingers and rippled up her arm. Whatever attraction was between them was as strong as it was unwanted. She stared up at him, meeting his welcoming brown eyes. Then she used her teeth to remove the cap to the pen and she wrote her cell phone number on the back of his hand. Her task done, she was both anxious and reluctant to let him go. She did and stepped back, sitting on the step of her sister's trailer.

"Now, don't scrub up before you copy that," she teased lightly.

He studied the back of his hand and grinned. "I won't."

His smile made her insides tumble as if she were spinning. She had no trouble returning his grin and that worried her.

"See you Tuesday, Dr. Redhorse."

"Kee, please."

"I'll try to remember that."

Ava smiled against the chill that swept through her. If he was behind this, she'd see he never got within sight of another girl for as long as he lived.

Chapter Two

Monday afternoon the tribe's urgent care center had gone from crazy to ridiculous. Since the dam collapse in September there was no more normal. Kee had hoped that with the arrival of FEMA things would get better. But the EMTs had just brought him another patient. He knew this one. Not unusual on such a small reservation. But this one was the son of his high school friend Robert Corrales.

Robert had the boy when they were in tenth grade and Robbie Junior was now twelve years old. But he wouldn't make thirteen if Kee didn't stop the bleeding.

Lori Mott assisted and he was happy for the extra hands. *Redhorse*, his mind corrected. She was no longer a Mott, since she had married his younger brother Jake, less than a month ago. Kee kept forgetting to call her Lori Redhorse. His brother had married the nurse so fast, he still hadn't gotten accustomed to the change.

Kee assessed the damage. The EMTs had done a fair job stopping the bleeding on his arm. But his head wound wasn't the same story. The plate-glass window had opened a gash on Robbie's forehead that was giving Kee trouble. Lori kept pressure on that wound, allowing him the time he needed to clamp the artery Robbie had sliced open in his right forearm. Either one was hemorrhaging fast enough to kill him. The boy was pale from shock and blood loss, his lips had gone blue and his skin had taken on the ghastly pallor of a corpse.

"Got it," he said. "I'll finish that after I stitch his head."

"The EMT said he didn't think he could make it to Darabee," said Lori.

"He was right." Kee quickly stitched the gash that ran in a jagged line from the boy's hairline to above the outer edge of his eyebrow.

Lori shook her head as she assessed the lacerations. "I'll get another Ringer's lactate. You want plasma?"

"No. This should do."

Lori left him to use the computer terminal at the intake station in the FEMA trailer that now served as their urgent care facility. When she came back with the fluids he had the gash closed.

"As soon as he's stable, arrange transport to Darabee," said Kee.

Darabee was only twenty miles away but with the river road under construction and the switchbacks leading down the mountain the ride was thirty to forty minutes from Piñon Forks, and from Turquoise Ridge, where the clinic had been temporarily placed, it was more like an hour.

Lori finished inserting the IV and nodded. "You got it. His dad is waiting."

"He needs a vascular surgeon if he's going to keep that hand."

"Betty is calling over. They'll have one." She smiled at him. His sister-in-law, he realized. Jake was a lucky man. He was so happy the two had finally worked out their differences.

"Good work, Kee."

Kee stripped off his gloves as Dr. Hector Hauser stepped into the curtained examining area.

"Need a hand?" he asked.

"We got it," said Kee.

Lori pulled the blood pressure cuff off the wall and slipped it around Robbie's thin arm.

Hauser looked around at the amount of blood and bloody gauze and gave a low whistle. He checked the boy's pupils and his pulse.

"Weak," he said and then checked the IV bag suspended on the stainless-steel rack.

Day poked his head into the room. "Need a hand?"

Before he could answer, Hauser waved him off. "We got it."

Kee gave Day an apologetic shrug. Day's mouth was a grim line as he sighed and returned the way he had come.

"I'll speak to the dad," said Hauser.

"You know his expertise is emergency medicine. Right?" Kee lifted his chin toward the exam area Day occupied. "He's taken the FEMA emergency medical specialist training. And he's board certified."

"Well, if the trailer collapses, I'll be sure to call him."

Hauser returned a few minutes later with Robbie's younger brother, Teddy, who had a gash on his lower leg.

"Parents didn't even see this one," said Hector. "Cut himself getting to his brother." He switched to Tonto. "You are a hero, son. Got his big brother help in time."

Teddy gave him a confused stare. Hector's smile dropped. "Did you understand that?"

Teddy shook his head.

Hector sighed. It was a crusade of his, that children learn their language. He held Teddy's hand and steered the boy out of the curtained area and right into the boys' parents.

Robert Corrales turned to Kee but peered past him to his older boy. "Is Robbie going to be okay?"

"He'll need some surgery at Darabee. But, yes, he's going to make it."

Robert threw himself at Kee, forcing Kee to take a

step back as Robert hugged him. His wife joined in and Kee was pressed like chicken salad between two slices of bread. Weeping and *thank-you*s blurred together. Lori took Teddy into the exam area beside Robbie's to wait for Dr. Hauser, and the parents crossed through the curtain to their oldest child.

It was another twenty minutes more before Kee was satisfied that Robbie was ready for transport. Robert accompanied his son and his wife remained with Teddy.

Once his patient was off, Kee waited for Hector to finish stitching up Teddy's lower leg. Kee was aiming for the momentary pause between one patient and the next to speak to Hector about his decision to resign from the clinic. Kee had agonized about leaving at such a time, but his mother had decided to foster the three teenage Doka girls. A wonderful act on her part, but unfortunately, a decision that would leave Kee without a place to live once they returned to Piñon Flats. The young fosterlings would need the space. Kee had moved in with his mother to help decrease his monthly expenses, and it was unrealistic of him to expect to afford a place of his own on his current salary. Not with the massive medical school debt hanging over his head.

Dr. Hauser had been only slightly older than he was now when Kee had first met him in the tribe's health clinic. He had not known at the time that meeting Hector would change his life. Kee wanted nothing more than to stay on his reservation and tend the sick and injured on Turquoise Canyon. But you did not always get what you wanted. And he had financial obligations that could no longer be put off.

Hector glanced up at Kee over the thick black rims of his transition lenses. His hairline had receded to the point where he had more forehead than hair. What was left was trimmed short so you could see the single gold medicine shield earring he wore in his right earlobe. Kee frowned as he noticed the diagonal earlobe crease, knowing that it was a possible indicator of coronary artery disease.

Hauser lifted his brow, making his forehead a field of furrows. "What's up?" he asked.

"I need a minute."

"Sure. Hand me that gauze." He pointed with a thick finger, his light russet skin a sharp contrast against the white of his lab coat. The dam collapse, which had necessitated them moving into the temporary FEMA trailers, had tripled their workload. Kee had never expected any sort of terrorism to touch his little corner of Arizona. But he thought that the extra load might be too much for Hector, judging from the puffy circles beneath his eyes.

Kee handed over the gauze and Dr. Hauser stripped off the outer covering, then expertly wrapped the boy's leg in a herringbone pattern that would prevent slipping.

"There, now," he said to the boy. "All done."

The boy still had tear tracks on his cheeks but he was quiet now that the Novocain was working and the blood had been mopped up. Hauser turned to the boy's mother. "Give him some Tylenol when you get him home. Two 80 mg tablets, three times a day, for today only, and keep this dry. Bring him back in ten days and I'll take out the stitches."

The boy swung his legs off the table and glanced at Hauser.

"Go on. You can walk on it. But no running or swimming or scratching!" He held out his hand to shake. Teddy hesitated but took Hector's hand. "Good work today, Teddy. You should be proud. You take care of your brother and look after your mom."

Teddy nodded his acceptance of this duty and slid to the floor. It was what Kee's dad had said to him before the sentencing. Ironic, since his father had never done so. He was a living example of what happened when you made your own rules.

The pair headed out of the curtained exam room. Hauser followed to the hall.

"Give me a minute, Lori," he called.

Lori Redhorse waved in acknowledgment, taking charge of the boy and his mother, ushering them out.

Dr. Day popped his head out of the exam area beside Hauser's.

"Mrs. Cruz says she wants to see you," he said to Hauser.

"Well, of course she does. She's been seeing me since she was born." He muttered something, and Kee caught the word *worthless*. "In a minute." Hauser glanced at Kee, motioning with his head. Kee followed. They paused halfway between Day's examining area and the reception table, where Lori sat at the computer.

Hauser's mouth turned down, making him look like one of the largemouth bass Kee loved to catch. Hauser shook his head. "That ambulance arrived. He—" Hauser jerked his head toward Dr. Day's examining area "—didn't even step out to check on it. He must have heard it. You sure did."

Kee shrugged, having no explanation.

"I swear he needs more looking after than the babies in our NICU. What kind of doctors do they have at FEMA anyway?" He tugged at the black stethoscope looped around his thick neck.

"Give him a chance."

"Nobody wants to see him. Besides, this is my clinic. Up until now that is. The tribal council has no right to meddle here."

The dam collapse gave them every right, Kee thought, but said nothing.

Requests like Mrs. Cruz's had been happening a lot

lately but Kee could not figure why so many patients were being so difficult. The clinic was short-staffed and the tribe had managed to get FEMA to provide them with an extra hand. Richard Day seemed nice enough, but he sure was not a hit with patients.

"So…" said Hauser, changing the subject. "How was the interview?"

Kee was a finalist for a position at St. Martin's Medical Center in Phoenix. It was internal medicine and he preferred emergency medicine and he also preferred to live here with his tribe instead of out there. But beggars could not be choosers. He'd been shocked at how fast the loans came due once he finished the last of his educational requirements. Now he stared up from a seemingly bottomless pit of debt. It would take years and years to get clear of them and return to the tribe. Reaching his dreams had come at a high cost. The ironic part was that his ambition was to help his tribe members the way Hauser had once helped him. Now, instead, he'd be miles away treating strangers.

"They've offered me a position," said Kee.

"Not surprised. But I hope you'll consider ours, as well."

Kee's brows lifted. He hadn't known that was a possibility and had assumed there would be no place for him. With his residency completed, he needed a job.

"What about Dr. Day?"

"He's temporary. Once we get back to the clinic at Piñon Flats, we'll be able to handle the load with two doctors. Maybe add a physician's assistant."

They'd had this discussion before. When he got his residency in Darabee, just off the rez, Hauser had managed to keep Kee here part-time and count the hours toward his residency requirements.

"My mother is fostering the Doka girls," said Kee.

"I heard that. She brought them in for a checkup. Malnourished and need some dental work, but nothing your mom can't handle."

"The point is, eventually I'll need a place to live." Sharing a FEMA trailer with Dr. Day worked for now, giving him easy access to the temporary clinic. But they expected to be back in their permanent facility this week.

"I see. The Doka girls have taken your bedroom, I imagine."

Kee nodded. "Dr. Hauser, I need to start repayment on my loans. I can't afford to work here part-time." *And I don't know how much longer I can survive with only work, work and more work, with only a few hours of sleep in between.*

He'd been living with his mom, but he'd had so little time to spend with her, he barely knew how the transition with the Doka girls was going. And he hadn't seen his brothers Colt or Ty since a week ago Saturday when they'd driven off on Ty's motorcycle after he and Jake had tried and failed to get Colt to seek help for his PTSD. Jake had told him that Colt had been seen and released. Kee worried about Colt living up in the woods at the family's mining claim since he'd come home from Afghanistan. Jake said Colt took off every time he went up there. Only Ty had succeeded in reaching him.

"Listen, is this about your living situation or your loans?"

"Both."

"Easy. My grant to hire you was approved."

Kee fiddled with the head of his stethoscope. "I need a permanent posting."

"Five years sound permanent enough?"

Kee didn't keep the surprise from his voice. "Five?"

"Yes, includes housing. In the new housing in Piñon Flats. We're building especially for the tribal employees. Doctors get priority. Should take about three months, so you can move in by Christmas. We'll all be in the same area near the clinic. Three bedrooms, garage and screened deck. You get an auto allowance of $500 a month. Plus forgiveness of your loans for working in a rural facility if you stay the full five years."

"And the salary?"

After Dr. Hauser's response, Kee's hands dropped to his sides. He blinked in shock.

"Plus a five percent cost of living raise each year," Hauser added.

Kee had been embarrassed to accept the Big Money his brother Ty had offered. Big Money was the sum total of each tribe member's royalties from the casino held in trust and released when each member reached their majority. Ty's money amounted to eighteen thousand and had kept Kee's head just above water, covering his living expenses during medical school in Phoenix. Without it, Kee could not have completed his education. With the salary Hauser had just offered, he could pay his brother back and fix his mother's car.

Hauser was still talking. "So about the auto stipend— get rid of that wreck you drive."

The 2004 midnight blue RAM pickup truck had been used when he bought it. The only reason it was still running was because Ty fixed it for free.

"Besides," Hauser continued. "I'm used to you. I don't like breaking in new physicians." He thumbed toward the corridor and Dr. Day.

"Why didn't you tell me this before today?" Kee had been interviewing from Flagstaff to Tucson and was heartsick at having to leave the rez, especially now. People were moving and building and naturally getting hurt in the process. Accidents due to drinking were way up and there was a troubling spike in heroin overdoses.

"I only got word today. Email's in my computer. It's

just been approved by our oversight board. So, you need time to think about it?"

"Forgiveness of all my loans? I have five."

"All."

"Private and government?"

"All means all," said Hauser.

Kee felt the weight of his burden lifting off his shoulders and he almost felt like dancing. He laughed.

"Well, then yes." Kee grinned. "I could work with that."

Hauser extended his hand and they shook. His mentor reeled him in and wrapped an arm around Kee's shoulders.

"Good, good. I've been thinking. I've been here doing this thirty-five years. When the time comes to turn over the reins, I'd like that someone to be you."

Kee was speechless.

Hauser let him go and spoke in Tonto. "You are like a second son to me."

Kee felt the hitch in his throat and didn't think he could speak.

"You know Turquoise Canyon," said Hauser. "You are a part of this place. You belong here with your people." He switched back to English. "Besides, I'll be damned if I'll lose you to some big city hospital when you are needed right here."

"I'm honored to follow your example, sir."

"Well, it's settled, then. I'll get you the paperwork. Get it back when you can."

Kee felt humbled. This man was all he ever wanted to become and earning his respect...well, Kee was brimming with joy. All the hard work and effort was paying off. Hauser had called him a second son. Kee thought he might cry.

"Now we have to find you a nice girl, hmm?"

Kee flushed. That was an odd thing to say. "Time still for that."

"No time like the present. Pay off the loans. Find a wife and have a few children. You'll be all set. Settled. A man the community can trust."

That was a strange way of saying it, thought Kee. He thought he'd build trust by having a sterling reputation and all the necessary credentials. Unlike his father and Ty, Kee had steered clear of trouble and taken the road that involved hard work and sacrifice.

"My wife has a niece you should meet. She's beautiful, traditional and lives in Koun'nde," he said naming one of their three settlements.

"Well, we'll see."

Hauser clapped him on the shoulder. "Good man." Then he turned to go, waving a hand in farewell. "Patients waiting."

The female voice came from behind them. "Dr. Hauser?"

Kee knew that voice. It was the clinic administrator, Betty Mills.

Hauser turned and smiled at the woman who kept the place running. Betty was in her middle years, with onyx eyes and hair to match. She dressed better than anyone Kee knew, with never a hair out of place. Her makeup was thick and meticulous from the liner to the bright unnatural pink of her lips. High heels and the jangling gold bracelets she always wore on her left arm announced her on each approach. Betty loved her bling. Even the chain that held her reading glasses on the bright purple blouse was gold with clear crystal beads.

"There's my boss," said Hauser to Kee and winked. "What's up, Betty?"

"Waiting room is full and so we've set up lawn chairs outside. They're full now, too. You both need to pick up the pace." She snapped her fingers, the long acrylic nails painted purple to match her outfit.

Hauser winked at Kee and then scuttled down the corridor to the exam area where Dr. Day waited.

Betty gave Kee a critical stare. "I'll tell Lori you're ready for the next one."

Down the corridor, Dr. Day stepped out of the examination area rubbing his neck. Hauser frowned after him and then drew the curtains closed behind him.

Hauser had not liked Day since the minute the tribal council had informed him that they had voted to get them extra help. It seemed Hector did not mind being bossed by Betty, but he did not like the tribal council interfering with *his* clinic.

Dr. Day reached Kee and gave him a defeated look. "All I did was ask if he'd speak in English when I'm there."

"I can imagine how that went over," said Kee, feeling sympathy for the doctor who was struggling to fit in with the local culture.

Kee glanced to the receiving station and the young mother carrying a crying toddler in his direction. He smiled and motioned them into the free exam area.

She spoke to him in Tonto Apache and Kee answered in kind. He could not believe how lucky he was to be able to stay here in the place he loved with the people he knew. A house. A car and a salary that was more money than he could even imagine. It seemed nearly too good to be true.

Chapter Three

Tuesday morning at the temporary clinic was crazy, made more so by the fact that Dr. Day did not appear at his usual time. Kee covered the women's health clinic, now in the adjoining trailer, and Hauser took the urgent care center. Kee called Day several times but got no answer.

Hauser popped into Kee's exam area.

"Anything?" he asked.

"No answer on his phone."

"FEMA sent us a dud."

Kee didn't think Hauser was giving Day a chance. He almost seemed to be undercutting his efforts. Kee didn't understand it because he'd never seen Hauser act like this.

Hauser waved a dismissive hand. "Social skills of a tortoise and just as much personality."

Kee was now officially really worried. He knew Day had set out with his Subaru at seven, his mountain bike strapped onto the vehicle's bike rack, and that he was always back by just after eight thirty, which was why he was usually late for their 9 a.m. opening. Still, he was never *this* late. Something felt off but he told himself to be patient.

Kee glanced at his watch. Day had been missing for hours.

When they reached noon and Kee still had no word, he called his brother Jake Redhorse.

"When did you see him last?" asked Jake.

"This morning. He was going for a ride before work."

"On a horse?" asked Jake.

"He rides his bike. Mountain biking."

"Okay, yup. I've seen him. Looks like a giant canary escaping a coal mine?"

Kee thought of the bright yellow exercise gear Dr. Day wore when biking and smiled.

"Yeah, that's him."

"I'll put the word out, but I'm down at the worksite on the river. I'll call FEMA. Meanwhile, you got a neighbor who could see if his car is there? Maybe check the house?"

Kee thought of Ava Hood. She lived just down the street.

"Yeah. I have someone."

Kee gave Jake the details on Day's vehicle.

"Let me know if the neighbor finds him."

"Will do."

Kee disconnected and held the phone to his chest a moment. He was going to call Ava. He hoped that she was at her sister's trailer, right down the road from his. He had already put Ava's number in his contacts. He blew out a breath and made the call.

He explained the situation. "Could you check if his car is in the drive?"

"Hold on. I'm walking out the door now."

He heard a door open and close.

"He ever do this before?" she asked.

"He bikes every morning. And he's late every morning. But not like this."

"Does he have someone here, somewhere he might be?"

"He might have a girlfriend down on the flats somewhere and a brother in some kind of law enforcement. DEA or ICE? I can't remember. Alphabet soup, you know? But I saw him this morning and it's a work day."

"Almost there," said Ava. "Yeah. Okay. No Subaru. No other vehicle. You want me to look inside?"

"Door is locked."

"I'm looking in the front door window now. Big hook on the wall in the entrance."

"For his bike," said Kee.

"It's empty. I'm knocking." He heard the pounding knock and the silence that followed. "No one here, Kee."

Kee pressed his free hand to his forehead. "So he's still out there."

"Call Chief Tinnin. Report him missing. Do you know the route he takes?"

Kee squeezed his eyes shut thinking. "He has several."

"What are they?"

He relayed the routes he knew and she said she'd drive them. Kee called Jake again. His brother assured him he'd report that Day was unaccounted for. Kee went back to work with a cold knot in his stomach. He just felt something was wrong.

He was just finishing a round of immunizations on an eighteen-month-old when the phone rang. He snatched it out of his pocket right there in the exam room. It was Ava. A glance at the clock showed that it was three in the afternoon. Kee punched the receive button and lifted the phone to his ear.

"I found Day's car," Ava said.

He pressed his hand to his forehead. "Where?"

She told him.

"That's the trailhead to the ruins," said Kee.

"Hard to know which way he went from there," she said. "Lots of trails through the cliff dwellings. Right?"

"My brother Ty has a dog. She's an excellent tracker."

There was a long pause.

"Ava?"

"Yeah, call him. Meet me here."

"Should I call the police?" he asked.

"Up to you. Would Ty want the police here?" she asked matter-of-factly.

He pressed his lips together. Ava was just a visitor on their rez and yet she knew about Ty. She likely knew about their father, as well. "I'll wait."

"We need something of Day's," said Ava. "Something he recently wore or frequently wears, to help the dog find his scent."

Kee swallowed at this and then raked a hand through his black hair. "I'll stop at the trailer and find something. Meet you there at the trailhead in ten."

AVA LEANED AGAINST her Malibu in the bright golden light of the crisp late afternoon. The blue sky and bird sounds belied her mood. Day had parked in a parking area before the lower ruins. His pale blue Subaru was covered with a fine coating of red dust, so it had been here awhile. It did not make sense that he'd be here all day when he was supposed to be at work.

She checked her service weapon and then returned it to her holster beneath her suede russet-colored jacket. She wore her badge under her shirt. The jacket would cover her service weapon from sight and she just felt more comfortable with the weapon near at hand.

Before Kee's call, Ava had broken into the tribe's clinic, which she knew was due to reopen this week. As she suspected, all their files were digitized and the computers password-protected. Kee's and Hauser's passwords had been easy to discern, but the clinic's was a different story. So much for that plan, she thought. Shifting approaches, she'd placed a hidden camera directly over the administrator's desk. Then she could remotely activate the camera, which had a six-hour battery. But then she had to wait for the clinic to open and for Betty Mills to log in before Ava could gain access to their system.

She wondered how long before their police discovered she was here and how long before her police force learned that she'd very definitely gone off the reservation. What she was doing could cost her her job. Her position gave her authority, respect and the autonomy she'd always longed for. She didn't want to lose all that. But she was willing to chance it because the only thing more important than being a detective was finding Louisa and saving those missing girls.

She wondered if Day's disappearance was related to this case. Suspicious things were happening and they all spun like a tornado around that clinic.

She hoped the worst thing that could've happened to Dr. Day was an accident that had left him lying along the trail somewhere with a twisted ankle and without a phone. But her gut told her that his disappearance could be related to her case.

Kidnapping a federal employee would be a terrible move and very brazen. Even if they thought he was investigating the clinic and closing in on the culprit, which he likely wasn't, it would be better to…push him off a cliff.

The thought made Ava's stomach churn.

Ava stared up at the mountain. Somewhere along that trail were several cliff dwellings. She'd never seen them but her sister, Sara, had told her about them. That also meant that there were cliffs.

Kee pulled up in his old blue pickup. He climbed down and hurried toward her, looking distracted as he greeted her by clasping both elbows and kissing her on the cheek. She was so rattled by the simple brushing of his mouth on her cheek that it wasn't until Kee was already halfway to Day's Subaru that she realized what he intended.

"Don't touch that!" she called.

He paused and turned back. "Why?"

"Umm, what if something happened to him, then

wouldn't this be a crime scene?" That wasn't well-done, she thought.

Kee backed up. "A crime scene?" He looked even more agitated as he looked in through the dusty windows from a safe distance. "Everything looks normal. He didn't lock it."

"You know this trail?" asked Ava, drawing him away from the vehicle.

"Part of it. It's a quarter mile past the pasture to the lower ruins. I only hiked to the upper ruins once." He rubbed his leg and frowned. "Couldn't keep up with my kid brothers."

How hard that must have been, always being the slowest, Ava thought. She touched his cheek with the palm of her hand.

"Well, you can keep up now."

They shared a smile and she resisted the urge to step closer. His hands went to her waist and she moved away, not wanting him to discover her service weapon.

"There's miles of trails up there," he pointed to the ridgeline against the crystal blue sky. "And cliff dwellings, several. I suppose Richard could have tried to bike it."

From the distance she heard a low rumble.

Kee turned toward the road. "That will be Ty. You know about him?"

She had run his record but she didn't say that. Instead she offered a half-truth. "I mentioned meeting you to my sister. And…"

Kee flushed. "She naturally mentioned Ty and…my father, too?"

She nodded, wondering why he looked so ashamed. *He* hadn't robbed a store. Mr. Perfect, she thought again. No missteps except the ones of his family reflecting badly on him. The law didn't judge families; it judged individuals. She did the same. But she knew the pain caused by the poor decisions made by family members. Her mother had been a train wreck and Sara had gotten pregnant in high school. It happened.

"No one is perfect," she said.

"I'm not like my dad." He met her gaze and she thought the expression was not shame but anger. Was he angry at his father for being a con or at her sister for gossiping? "I've never broken a law in my life."

She'd have to see about that.

"In fact, seeing my dad's sentencing, well, it changed me. I'd always been cautious because of my leg. But that made me realize that your reputation, well, it's more breakable than bones."

She thought about how one wrong step and her own reputation would be beyond repair. She had a stellar law enforcement career, but even that wouldn't survive the fallout of her rogue investigation if she was caught. But wasn't Louisa's life worth that?

The distinctive sound of a powerful engine brought all heads about.

"That's his chopper," said Kee.

"Harley?" she asked, raising her voice as the rumble became a roar.

"Indian," he said. "Wait. That's a new bike."

Ty made an entrance. Up until today, Ava had only heard about him. The family black sheep, currently under investigation for his role in the abduction of Kacey Doka. They had statements from both his youngest brother, Colt, and Kacey, but neither could testify as they were in witness protection. The signed statements implicating Ty in Kacey Doka's kidnapping from the clinic should be enough to convict him in tribal court. So why were they letting him run around free?

The roar grew louder and Ava had to shout to be heard.

"Isn't he bringing the dog?" she asked.

Kee nodded and pointed. In rolled Ty Redhorse on a cof-

fee-brown-and-cream Harley Davidson motorcycle laden
with so much chrome she could see reflections of the sky
and road and man all at once.

At first she thought he was riding double, and he was,
after a fashion. The dog sat behind him, paws on his shoulders, with goggles on his massive head. As Ty pulled forward, she could see the shepherd sat in a bucket fixed to
the rear seat and wore some sort of restraining belt.

The engine idled and Ty fixed his stare on them both.
No smile, she realized, and he looked less than pleased to
be here. Ty's hair was shoulder length and cut blunt. He
resembled Kee but for the cleft in his chin. He also sent all
her cop senses into high alert. That challenge in his eyes
as he met her gaze would have made her pull him over if
she had her cruiser.

Badass didn't cover it. And he wore black, of course.

Ava regarded the dog, with its lolling, pink tongue
and—what appeared to be—a wide grin.

"Looks like a wolf," said Ava.

"German shepherd mix," said Kee.

"Mixed with wolf," she said and Kee laughed.

The deep masculine rumble did crazy things to her
insides.

"Ty thinks it's funny because he's riding with his bi…"
Kee changed his mind about what he was going to say and
motioned to Ava. "Shall we?"

Ty rocked the bike onto its kickstand. He greeted Kee
with a bear hug that nearly lifted Kee off his feet. Ty was
taller, broader and more intimidating.

Kee had a cell phone clipped to his clean, fitted jeans
and he wore a blue button-up shirt with a turquoise bolo
and brown lace-up shoes. Ty had a knife clipped to his
leather belt and had a wallet connected to a belt loop by
a stainless-steel chain. He wore black leather chaps over
jeans, high moccasins with the distinctive toe-tab mark-

ing them as Apache footwear and a black muscle shirt that revealed a tribal tattoo circling each arm. What he didn't wear was a helmet.

She watched Ty stroke his dog's pointed ear, momentarily bending it flat before releasing her from the bucket-style pet transporter. The dog came forward to sniff Kee and then turned to Ava. She extended her hand, but the dog stopped short of her and dropped to all fours, lying alert before her.

She glanced first to Kee and then to Ty, who was narrowing his eyes at her.

Kee made introductions but Ty remained where he was. Her skin prickled a warning. She was made. She knew it.

Ty gave her a hard look.

"She a cop?" he asked Kee.

She narrowed her eyes, wondering if it was her appearance or his dog that had tipped him off.

"No," said Kee. "A neighbor."

"You packing?" he asked.

She nodded and showed her sidearm.

Ty's eyes narrowed and Kee gaped.

"You can't carry a weapon here," said Kee.

Ty held her gaze a long while and Kee shifted restlessly. Finally, he broke the silence.

"We brought something of Richard's for Hemi," said Kee. "Let me get it." He retrieved a pair of gray bike riding gloves.

Kee offered them to Ty and Ava noted that his younger brother was a few inches taller than Kee, but likely hadn't been originally. The surgeries had taken three inches from his healthy leg.

Ty took the gloves and offered them to Hemi. The dog stood and was all business when she checked out the neoprene gloves and then lowered her head to the ground, making straight for the Subaru.

She jumped so that she stood on her back legs, with her front paws pressed to the door.

"Good girl," said Ty, in a tone that seemed out of place from such a tough character. It gave her hope that he might be more than he appeared, because he appeared to be a gang member. But he had come at Kee's request and that allowed her to continue to operate covertly.

Ty waved his dog toward the trail.

"Track," he said.

Hemi put her nose to the ground and bounded away straight for the path that cut through the pasture toward the lower ruins.

Ty used Richard's gloves to wipe away the paw prints from the Subaru. Ava's eyes narrowed. Clearly, he suspected foul play and was removing evidence of Hemi's contact with the vehicle. Was he just keeping his involvement secret or did he have something to hide?

They headed up the trail with Hemi darting ahead. She fell in beside Kee.

Kee asked Ty about Colt, how he was doing and if he was still talking. Ty paused to give him a long inscrutable look and then told Kee that he was but failed to mention that Colt was not on the rez. Kee didn't seem to know that and Ty didn't tell him.

Very odd, she thought.

"When you see him last?" asked Ty.

"The Saturday when you took him to Darabee Hospital."

Almost two weeks ago. Kee had let his work erode his connection to family. He was right here on the rez but seemed to have little idea what was happening under his nose.

"Is he getting some help?" asked Kee.

"Yeah. Lots of help."

Help relocating, thought Ava.

She had read in Ty's file that he had driven a '73 Plymouth Barracuda when he allegedly kidnapped Kacey Doka, the only girl to escape her captors. But the car was never found. No car, no physical evidence connecting Kacey Doka to Ty Redhorse. Just the statement by Kacey, who was no longer here to back it up with her physical presence during testimony in tribal court, and the tribe's council had declined the FBI's request for custody of Ty. That in itself was not unusual. Most tribes were exceedingly reluctant to allow outsiders to try their defendants. Considering the history between the Tonto Apache tribes and the federal government, few would blame them.

"What kind of a car does Ty drive?" Ava asked.

"I can't keep up," said Kee. "He changes cars like I change surgical gloves. I think he's working on a '67 Pontiac GTO."

"Fast car. What color? Black?"

"No, gold."

Gang colors, she thought. Yellow and black. Those were the colors worn by the Wolf Posse here.

So Ty was a gang member, and his brother Jake was a member of the tribal police force. Which side was Kee on?

When they reached the trailhead with the marker of regulations and the one of historical information, they paused. It delineated the rules in bullet points including no fires and no firearms.

Hemi flashed by, circling the ruins. The red stone walls still stood rising ten feet in places and in others lay as piles of rock strewn on the ground. The interior chambers of rooms that had collapsed hundreds of years ago were visible and the roof beams hung at odd angles.

Once an ancient people had lived and farmed in this place, leaving behind the remnants of these communal residences. Her people called them the ancient ones, for they were here and gone before the Apache moved into the Southwestern territory.

Funny that many Americans thought that settlement of

this country began in Plymouth in 1622 when at that time this settlement of hunter-farmers was living in an ancient version of a condominium right here.

The upper ruins were even older and of a different people. The Anasazi dwelt in cliffs and the whys of that were still mysterious. A drought? A new enemy? All that was known was what they had left behind.

"How many cliff dwellings up there?" she asked.

"Four, I think. More tucked all over the ridges around here."

Hemi was now on the move toward the winding path that led to the upper ruins.

Ava knew that the tribal museum gave guided tours to these two archeological sites twice a week or by arrangement. She had never seen either, but she had seen ones like it.

They hiked for thirty minutes up a steep trail. She saw tire tracks in the sandy places consistent with a bike tire. Her thigh muscles burned from the strenuous hike. She wondered how anyone could bike such a thing. The sweat on her body dried in the arid air, making her wish she had brought water.

Hemi disappeared and then reappeared, checking on the progress of the slow-moving humans. They found her, at last sitting beside an expensive-looking mountain bike that lay on its side.

"That's not good," said Ty.

"That's his," said Kee, studying the bike with worried eyes. He reached and then stopped himself.

She was glad because she didn't want to talk like a cop in front of Ty.

Ty glanced at Hemi, who lay with her paws outstretched toward the bike.

"Trail ends here," said Ty.

"Definitely?" asked Kee.

Ty glanced at Hemi, her tongue lolling as his dog looked to him for further instructions.

"It ends here or goes where Hemi can't follow."

They all stepped past the bike to look over the cliff. Below were rocks and trees but no obvious sign of Dr. Day.

"Might have fallen," said Ty.

"With his bike way over there?" she asked. That didn't seem right.

"Stopped to take in the view. Lost his footing." Ty shrugged.

Was he trying to sell her on this scenario?

"Either way, he's not here," said Kee. "We should call Jake."

Ty backed away. "If you're calling tribal, I'm gone. They're already trying to hang me for giving Kacey a ride. They'll tie me up in this, too."

A ride? Is that what he called kidnapping? Ava could not keep from gaping.

Kee stared at Ty. "What are you talking about?"

Didn't Kee know?

Ty had been detained for questioning and released. He had not been arrested or charged. Tribal police would keep such matters private particularly if there was an ongoing investigation. She knew of Ty's situation only because her chief had been told of a possible connection to the tribe's gang and a known associate, Ty Redhorse. But the police here had taken steps to be certain Ty's detention remained secret. She knew he was a suspect but Kee did not, which meant that his brother had not told him. Ty did not want Kee to know. Was Ty protecting him or hanging him out to dry?

Ty shook his head. "Just tell them you found the car and followed the trail. That you know he bikes this route and you were checking. But I was never here. Got it?"

Kee's mouth was tight. "You want me to lie to the police?"

"Omit," said Ty.

"It's lying."

"Hey, you do what you want. Just don't call me for help again." He turned to Ava and gave her a two-finger salute. "Officer."

Then he disappeared back down the trail. Hemi followed, venturing out before him.

Kee turned to her immediately. "Why did he call you—"

"What's that?"

Ava spotted a tiny speck of canary yellow visible between the treetops below the cliff upon which they stood.

Exactly the color Kee said Dr. Day had been wearing.

Chapter Four

Ava didn't think Kee had pushed Richard Day, but she kept him in front of her on the descent. When they reached the bottom of the trail it was nearly six at night. The sun had disappeared behind the opposite ridgeline and the colors were gradually fading all around them. Kee tried tribal police but there was no cell service out here. He offered Ava the last of the water he carried and she took a long swallow before returning the empty bottle.

"You know it will be really dark soon. We have thirty minutes," she said.

"Maybe we should go to the police."

Yeah, except she was certain how Detective Jack Bear Den or the chief of police would respond if they knew where her personal leave from her soon-to-be previous job had taken her.

She'd interviewed. Been hired here, and Tinnin himself had briefed her about her first case. This case. The missing women from Turquoise Canyon, but he did not know that the last girl taken was Ava's niece. The niece that she had helped raise. So Ava was not playing by the rules on this investigation. So for now, she couldn't let either of those men see her. Not yet.

"We could find him," she coaxed. "He's maybe ten minutes in that direction. It will be harder in the dark."

Kee hesitated, glancing in the direction of the lot.

She gave one final push. "What if he's alive?"

That set him in motion. She pushed back the admiration. Kee seemed kind and conscientious and really sweet. But appearances could be deceiving.

"Do you know if anyone would want to hurt him?" she asked.

"No. I don't. He's only been here since early October. You think it's him, don't you?"

"You said he was wearing yellow."

Kee looked back along the trail. The sky still held a few bands of orange but that wouldn't last.

"I don't think anyone could survive such a fall." He looked to her. "How can you be so calm?"

Because she'd seen death before, too many times.

"We should hurry," she said, motioning. "Have you seen anyone strange around lately?"

"Outsiders?"

"Yeah. At the clinic or speaking to Day or maybe just in your neighborhood?"

"We only treat tribal members."

Kee drew up short. "It's him."

Ava came alongside him. It was a body, battered and bloody, and wearing yellow spandex that seemed to glow with unnatural brightness in the twilight.

Ava had seen bodies in worse shape. Mostly natural causes, left inside a hot trailer for days before anyone went to check, and then there were the auto accidents. But her reservation was small and relatively quiet and flat. No one fell off anything high and she was not prepared for the damage to Dr. Day.

His body had clearly struck the rock face on the descent and possibly some of the tall pines, judging from the deep lacerations on his torso and thigh. There were branches and debris surrounding him. He lay on his stomach with his arms and legs sprawled as if he were about to use a horizontal Stairmaster.

Kee knelt beside his roommate and checked his carotid pulse, but Ava knew from the brownish stain on Day's cornea and the pooling of blood in the lower half of his face that Day was gone.

Her Apache heritage included all sorts of beliefs that it was dangerous to touch the dead. That ghosts could follow you even if the deceased was a good friend in life. Ava didn't believe that dead bodies and ghosts could haunt her but she dearly hoped that whoever did this would be haunted because she was certain Day had not fallen. He'd been pushed. That was her theory and she was going with it.

She swept the body with her gaze, looking for clues, and found them right there in Day's hand. His nails were torn and bloody and there was skin and hair under them. That was what you'd see if Day had fought his attacker. So whoever pushed him would have scratches on their face or arms. Maybe both.

Ava tried to think of a way to take a sample from his nails.

"I have to call Hector," said Kee.

That was an odd first call, she thought. Why not to Jake, his brother who was on the force?

He looked at Ava with wide, troubled eyes and swallowed, sending his Adam's apple bobbing. "He's our medical examiner."

Of course he was, she thought.

Kee rocked back on his heels and wiped his mouth with his hand, looking truly unsettled. Rattled, she corrected. She knew he had faced death. All physicians did. But this death was harder. He knew the man, so it was personal. Day was young and he had been Kee's colleague plus they'd shared a FEMA trailer. Add to that the damage to the corpse and you had a horror that would not soon be forgotten.

She dropped to a knee beside Kee and draped an arm around his shoulders. Kee clasped her hand with his opposite one.

"Look at his nails," she said and pointed.

"What is that?" He leaned closer.

"Looks like skin."

Kee straightened and stepped quickly away. She watched him pace, both hands locked behind his head. Finally, he came back beside her.

"You think he was pushed. You think he fought his attacker."

"Don't you?"

He nodded gravely.

"Should you take a sample?" she asked.

He shook his head. "The police will do that. I'll make sure they do."

"What about photos?" she asked. The scene might not be so pristine later on and it would be dark. She did not want to use her phone knowing that it would be confiscated as evidence and that would give the police here easy access to who she was. But those photos could be vital.

"Should I take some?" He had his phone out.

"Might help your police."

Kee took a few shots, his mouth squeezed in a look of distaste. She nudged him to photograph Day's hands, face and all other injuries. Finally she suggested a few long shots of the scene.

"Might help with location," she said, knowing it would. He finished and his arm dropped to his side with the glowing phone gripped in his hand. He stood staring at Day as if he could not believe what he was seeing.

She slipped her hand into the crook of his elbow and he jumped.

"You want to see if you have cell service here?" she asked.

He placed his hand over hers and rubbed as if to give her comfort. "Doubtful. But I'll try."

Kee lifted the phone, searching for a signal.

"Nothing."

"Come on," she said. "We'll go tell the police what we found. You can lead them back here."

Kee stood over the body, head bowed as if he were a mourner at a grave.

"I was afraid something like this had happened," he said.

Ava's antenna picked up. It was the sort of thing a person who knew what would happen would say.

"Why is that?" she asked, keeping her tone conversational.

"He was gone too long." Kee glanced back toward the body, arms folded protectively before him. "He was going to get a haircut after work today."

Now, that was the kind of crazy thing people did say when someone was ripped unexpectedly from their life.

She didn't like to admit it, but her opinions as to Kee's involvement were eroding. Ava had an instructor in the academy who told her students to keep a few brain cells open to the possibility that your prime suspect was innocent. Those brain cells were recruiting others and that troubled her. What if she was wrong about Dr. Redhorse? If she were, then she needed to expand her search or target his fellow doctor more closely. It just seemed with his brother Ty's involvement and his brother Colt's disappearance into witness protection without Kee's knowledge that the tribe considered Kee a prime suspect. Ava was unsettled and she did not like the uncertainty growing within her.

They walked back using their phone flashlights to help illuminate the trail. Once at the cars they paused. Ava needed to not be here when the police arrived.

"Listen, I'd like to get home. My sister has a thing at the

school tonight and if I'm there she can cancel the sitter."
An AA meeting that Sara had promised to attend. "The
girls are more anxious since Louisa's disappearance." Ava
shrugged. "So how about this, I'll call the police when I
get cell service and send them back to you. Okay?"

Kee frowned. "I'm sure they'll want to speak to you."

"Yes, I'll be at my sister's. They can come there. Better
if it's after nine. Kids in bed." She shrugged.

"All right. I'll tell them." He clasped her arm and she
felt the strength of his hands as he leaned in. "You be okay
walking back alone?"

"Yes. I'll be fine." She tried and failed not to let his concern affect her. Ava smiled and met his warm gaze, feeling
the unwelcome stirring of attraction thread between them.

"Thank you, for everything."

On impulse, Ava lifted to her toes and planted a kiss
on his cheek.

Kee's mouth dropped open and his hand slipped away.
She'd surprised him. She took the opportunity to make
her escape.

She did call the police, did not give her name, pretending she was upset by events, and sent help in Kee's direction. They had her number, of course, but there was no
need to track it unless they could not find her. If she was
lucky, she had a day or two of anonymity left.

AVA GOT BACK to her sister's place around eight. Woody
greeted her with much enthusiasm and she let him out.
Her sister was sprawled on the couch and did not move as
Ava closed the door. Her snores and the beer cans covering the coffee table told her all she needed to know. Beyond her sister's unconscious body sat the kitchen table
on which lay various plastic containers and a greasy red-
and-white-striped paper bucket from the fast-food chicken
place in Darabee.

She would deal with Sara later; right now she wanted to check on the girls. She continued down the narrow hallway of the trailer to the first, smaller bedroom. Inside, all the girls sat on the lower bunk with their eyes fixed on the television as avatars danced in bright colors across the screen. The twins, Alexandra and Margarita, held the controls while Olivia watched the screen. Margarita glanced up at her return and offered a weak smile before her gaze cut back to the game. Ava nodded to her and returned the smile. Then she shut off the TV. The controls that Alexandra and Margarita held sagged as they groaned in unison.

"You all get some supper?" she asked, stroking Olivia's soft hair.

The chorus of yeses followed.

"Homework?"

Their eyes glanced here and there but did not meet hers.

"Kitchen table. Now. Bring your work."

The groans were unanimous but they dragged their backpacks to the table as Ava cleared away the remains of the take-out meal. The girls drew out their school workbooks and Ava cut up the apples she had purchased. To this she added celery filled with peanut butter and raw broccoli and ranch dressing.

Woody scratched on the front door and Ava let him in. He settled under the table at the girls' feet.

Ava gave Olivia paper and a large pencil so she could doodle while her sisters worked on tracing letters of the alphabet. Margarita was excellent at counting and needed no help. But neither girl could do the matching of Tonto words to pictures of animals.

"Mom doesn't speak to us in Apache," said Margarita.

Ava switched to Tonto Apache and determined that she would use more of their native language from here on. Who they were, their culture and their heritage included their language.

The girls ate everything but the broccoli. Well, it was worth a try.

She told them in Tonto that it was bedtime and they understood that well enough to protest.

"Mom sleeps a lot," said Olivia.

Ava thought of the promise her sister had made to seek help. Yet here Sara was, drunk with such young children in the house. How could she be so irresponsible and give up control like that? It made Ava sad and angry all at once.

She had them in their beds before nine thirty. Since her arrival, the twins shared the top bunk, giving Ava the lower one. Olivia slept in the other bedroom with her mom but had crept in to sleep with Ava on two occasions, so tonight Ava just put her to bed in the lower bunk.

Ava drew the covers up around Margarita and Alexandra, who shared the top one. Then she kissed each girl good-night.

Olivia had the covers drawn up to her chin when Ava stooped to kiss her on the forehead.

"I'm glad you're here," said Margarita.

"Me, too."

"Can you stay?" Alexandra asked her aunt.

"For a while."

Alexandra rolled to her side, giving Ava her back. She didn't blame the girl. Her father had left by dying. Her big sister was taken and her mother was here but still gone. It filled Ava with a bone-deep sadness. She stroked Margarita's shoulder and whispered good-night in Tonto. From the door she flicked off the light but left the hall light on, as they preferred.

Back in the trailer's living room she helped her sister rise from the couch.

"Diamond?" she muttered, her husband's name.

That cut through Ava. She knew how much her sister missed him. But it made her angry, too, because she did not want these girls bounced around like rubber balls. Why couldn't Sara pull herself together?

"It's Ava," she said, drawing her sister's arm around hers.

"Ava? What are you doing here?"

"I've been here a week."

"Where are the girls?"

"In their room. Sara, you promised you'd go to that meeting tonight."

"What meeting?"

Ava sighed and continued toward her sister's room.

She got her sister to the bedroom, where she sat, head bowed. At first, Ava thought Sara had fallen asleep again, but then she saw her shoulders shake and heard the familiar sound of her sister's weeping.

"Louisa," she whispered and covered her face with her hands.

Ava sat on the bed beside her sister and pulled her in. Sara collapsed against her, clinging to her shirt. Ava hugged her tight, cradling her older sister to her chest.

"We're going to get her back, Sara. I swear to God, we are."

Chapter Five

Sara and the girls had fallen asleep when the knock for Ava came on her door. It was a young police officer whom she had not met on her interviews. He identified himself as Officer Daniel Wetselline.

She motioned him in and got him a cup of coffee. He asked her all the questions he should have asked her for a preliminary round interview, scribbling on his pad as he drank his coffee.

Ava wondered how long before someone at tribal realized that Ava Hood was Avangeline Hood Yokota, their new hire from the Saguaro Flat Apache Tribe?

"And you were the one who discovered the body?"

"I found his car based on information provided by Dr. Redhorse. From the cliff I saw something bright yellow. But Dr. Redhorse and I discovered the body together."

Wetselline nodded, showing that this answer agreed with what he had already heard. She'd have to talk to him about that. It was bad practice to let witnesses or suspects know what you thought you already knew.

He finished his coffee and then thanked her for her time. She walked him to the door. He asked her to stop by the station tomorrow to meet with the investigating detective, Jack Bear Den.

She saw him out just before eleven. She closed the door behind him and resisted the urge to sag against the trailer door.

Woody sat before her, staring soulfully up into her eyes, his thick balding tail thumping against the linoleum tile.

"No one took you for a walk today. Did they?"

His eyebrows lifted.

"No, I didn't think so."

Ava slipped into a fleece jacket and took Woody out on a leash. Lots of folks let their dogs roam around the rez, but she'd seen family pets stalked and attacked by wild dogs, so she didn't take chances. Woody wasn't used to the restraint and tugged her along in his hurry to get from one interesting smell to the next.

When they reached Kee's trailer she noticed the light. She paused, thinking of him, home from the crime scene in the trailer he had shared with Richard Day. If he were innocent, it would be a tough night. Her feeling was that he might not know what was happening. She didn't yet know, either. But she believed that whatever it was, it centered on the tribe's health clinic.

She considered knocking on his front door when she noticed the light from the back of the trailer. She and Woody walked along between the trailers. She smelled the sweet scent of a citronella candle. She took another step toward the back, rounding the trailer at the same time she spotted the triple flame in the large candle set in a tin bucket perched on the side table between two folding chairs. Kee sat in one, speaking to someone in the second chair. In the light of the candle's flame she could not make out the identity of the occupant.

She stepped closer and saw that the second man was Dr. Hector Hauser. There they sat, prime suspects, number one and two. Ava had gone as far as she could checking out Kee. The desire to meet Hauser was irresistible.

She held her position, pressing her elbow against her side and feeling the reassuring bulge of her service pistol in her shoulder holster. She unzipped her jacket.

"Hello?" she called.

Both men spun in their chairs.

Woody led her forward into the meager candlelight.

"Who's that?" said Hauser.

Woody was now wagging his tail and tugging at the leash.

"Woody?" said Kee.

"Yes, that's him," she said and allowed him to pull her into the light.

"Ava!" Kee was on his feet and approaching, hands out to greet her. "We were just talking about you."

That, of course, made her ears go back. She didn't want to be the subject of conversation, especially not between these two men.

"Come here," he said. His wide grin made it seem as if he were delighted to see her. "I want you to meet Hector."

Dr. Hauser was now on his feet. She knew him very well, but he had never laid eyes on her. She'd been very careful to be certain of that. But the time for surveillance was past. She needed to stir the pot.

He didn't look like a monster, either.

Hauser's curious eyes raked her with a quick down and up glance as he offered his hand to the dog. He did not offer his hand to her, however, except to lift it in the old style of greeting. She found herself checking his arms and face for any sign of recent injury and found none visible. But he wore a light jacket against the chill. The temperature dropped at night more quickly here than down on the flats.

Kee made formal introductions. That provided Dr. Hauser with enough information that he might be able to discover who she was if he was looking. Ava tried and failed to ignore the cold chill that raced down her spine.

Dr. Hauser greeted her formally in Tonto Apache. She responded in kind and he asked her a few simple questions in Apache.

"You are visiting your sister?" he asked in Tonto.

"Yes, for two weeks."

"Then back to your home?" he asked.

"That is what I intend. Yes."

"Kee tells me you do not yet have a husband."

She held her smile. "This is true."

Hauser turned to Kee and switched to English. "She speaks our language beautifully." He nodded in approval as he turned to her. "Good to see that they teach their children well down on Saguaro."

"Well, I learned at school, but also from my grandmother."

"Very good. Please take my seat. I was just leaving."

"Oh, don't leave on my account. I'm just taking Woody for a walk. I need to get back."

"Isn't your sister at home?" asked Hauser.

"Yes, but..." She wasn't offering information about her sister's condition, but she feared she already had.

"Ah," said Hauser. "I see. Well, she has suffered two great losses. It is understandable, her grief."

He held his smile.

Ava did not think that drinking and grieving were the same thing, but she only murmured her agreement.

Hauser clapped Kee on the shoulder and then turned to Ava.

"Nice to meet you, Ava Hood." He offered a farewell in Tonto and headed off.

"He's very big on learning our language," said Kee.

"I see that."

Why hadn't she seen Hauser's car?

"Did he walk here?" she asked. It was over a mile between Kee's trailer and Hauser's.

"Yes, why?"

She shook her head.

"It's not too far. Hector doesn't sleep well and we all are reeling over what has happened."

Hauser didn't seem to be reeling. He seemed...content. And now he had her name, most of it. Things were about to get interesting.

"Come and sit. Can I get you something? I have vitamin water and tap water." His smile left him and he glanced around as if he'd misplaced something.

Woody went to him and nuzzled his hand. Kee stroked his head absently.

"We got ahold of Day's family. His parents. He wasn't married."

He offered the chair and she sat. He drew his chair up close to hers. His feet were bare and his button-up shirt flapped open. His hair was wet and he smelled like something spicy and enticing. Why was she here again?

She glanced at the three empty beer bottles on the table.

"You drinking?" she asked.

"Yup. Ice tea. You going to turn me in?"

Warning bells rang in her mind. Turn him in? Did he know who she was? He'd given no indication. Ty suspected. Had Ty called Kee? She was certain that Jake Redhorse had not tipped him, because she and Jake had not met on her visits to her soon-to-be new police force. Tribal police didn't expect her until November 1, and by then she planned to have her niece back if she didn't get killed or fired before then. Besides, with what she was doing, it was better all around if she was not affiliated with either force.

"For what?"

"Drinking caffeine past bedtime. I couldn't sleep, so..." He motioned to the yard.

"What about your boss? He drop by often?"

"No, but tonight... Well, just checking in."

Because his roommate had just died or was he checking up? She suspected that either Kee or Hauser or both of them were tied up in the recent disappearances. She wanted it to be Hauser and not Kee.

But for that to all be happening under Kee's nose, it was unlikely, despite his obvious hero worship of Hauser. The man was not a hero. Heroes didn't cheat on their wives, which she'd already found out about. What other secrets was he harboring?

She made a sound in her throat. "It's been a hard day."

"Yet you don't seem rattled."

"I didn't know him."

"But at the car, waiting by yourself and then on the trail with Ty, you were so calm. And at the body." He waved his hand at the sky. "You weren't even fazed? Why is that?"

He was too damn smart.

"Most folks I know would go out of their way not to see what we saw today," he continued. "I know I'll have nightmares. Finding a body, my roommate." He grimaced. "It's a different way of seeing death. What about you, Ava?"

She needed him off this line of questioning. She slipped her hand into his. His brows rose in surprise.

"Hector seems nice."

He shook his head. "Tonight he was on again about how I need to settle down. Fill that big house I'll have with babies." He gave her an assessing stare and now she was the one rattled.

"What house?"

He told her about the perks of working for the clinic. She managed not to look completely stunned. Her clinic had a doctor out of medical school and a tribe member who was a nurse practitioner. The doctors came and went as they moved on and up.

She turned in her seat.

"Is that what you want? A wife and lots of babies."

The way he held her gaze made her insides quicken. His slow smile only increased her breathing rate. "Eventually. But not because I have an extra bedroom. I've seen a lot of unwanted children born. I think every child born should be wanted."

She could not disagree.

She squeezed his hand, trying and failing not to notice the heat generated by his palm pressed to hers. Only afterward did she start thinking of who the unwanted children he was referring to might be. Did he mean the missing girls? The ones from big, troubled families?

"You must have had some opportunities, some women or a woman," she said.

"A few."

His smile was charming and his face, well, it was the kind of face she knew she would never grow tired of. Why did he have to be tied up in this? In other circumstances, he would be just the sort of man she would find appealing because he was so different than the jaded, sarcastic law enforcement officers that filled her world. Maybe it was because Kee got to save people. He wasn't exposed to the kind of human wreckage witnessed by police officers.

"Yet no one has managed to tag and bag the doctor?" she asked.

His smile vanished and he redirected his gaze away from her.

"You know, that's just it. I've been made to feel like an eight-point buck in hunting season. Women down there in Phoenix, well, they were definitely on the hunt." He looked away. "There was one woman. I almost married her."

"Almost?"

He sank back in his chair, legs thrust out in front of him. "Once we got engaged she got very pushy. Wanted to spend money on the wedding and a honeymoon in Fiji, and meanwhile I was eating mac and cheese from a box. I tried to explain that not all doctors make big bucks and none at first but…"

"You broke up with her?"

"She broke up with me. Married a dentist."

"Ouch."

"Better off. I felt hurt but mostly relieved."

"Lots of reasons to want to marry a doctor, I suppose," she said. She ticked them off. "Security, status, bragging rights over all your girlfriends and let's not forget the money."

"Not all doctors earn high salaries."

"Better than cops," she said.

He gave her a puzzled look and she smiled, trying to cover her slip.

"Your brother is a police officer. Right?"

"Oh, yeah."

"What about you, Ava. Those things important to you? Bragging rights and all?"

She met his gaze and saw the humor she had used had not transferred to him. He looked sad and wary.

"First off, I don't need a man to define who I am. Second, I like my independence and third, I don't think I'd like being married to a doctor, especially an emergency medicine doctor."

"Why?"

"You're like cops. You see all the bad stuff and it makes you either cynical or overly cautious."

"I've always been cautious."

"Why is that?"

He shrugged. "Mostly my leg problems. Fragile bones during the time when most young men are crashing into people and things on purpose."

"Sports?"

"Not for me. Plus it stresses me out to break the rules. I've never been pulled over by police. Not even a traffic ticket. I set my cruise control five miles below the limit. I wear my safety belt. Look before I leap and spend way too much time thinking through decisions."

In other words, he was the opposite of Ty, who tested the limits and broke rules consistently, and Jake, who took chances just by virtue of his job.

He pressed a hand to the top of his head and blew out a long breath.

"Sound kind of—"

"Boring?" he asked.

"Unexpected."

"I'm not like my brothers. Colt and Ty went off to defend their country. Jake swore to protect and serve."

"And you swore to do no harm."

He smiled. "Yes."

Ava was beginning to doubt that Kee was the sort of man capable of taking those girls. And if she could clear him she could…

Bad idea, Ava. He could be playing you.

As if on cue, Kee said, "So, what kind of a man do you like?"

Chapter Six

Ava was tempted to say she liked the sort of man that stuck around. She'd never met her father and her grandfather had died when she was two. The closest thing Ava had to a man she could rely on was her drill sergeant and that was just sad.

"Kee, listen, if you're asking because you're interested, I'll tell you right off that I don't have a great track record with men. I tend to bail when they get possessive."

"Why?"

"Independence, again."

"Why is independence more important to you than a committed relationship?"

"Committed?" She laughed. "Well, I haven't seen too many of them." But she had been on her share of domestic disturbance calls.

"Your parents? They still together?"

Wow. Right to the heart of her personal chaos.

"My mom got pregnant young. The boy, my older sister's dad, left the rez right after he found out Mom was pregnant because he was nineteen and she was only sixteen. Mom dropped out and moved back in with my grandparents. She had me three years later..." She turned to face him.

"I can't believe you're twenty-eight. Honestly, you look barely old enough to order a drink."

"Don't I know it. I get proofed a lot."

The smile they shared lingered far too long. Ava broke the contact of their gaze.

"So you lived with your mom and grandmother," he prompted, then waited.

"You sure you want to hear this?"

He nodded. "Go on."

"So after I was born Mom ran off with the boy. Left me with her mother. My grandmother raised us until I was eight."

"Then your mom came back?"

She snorted. There he was, searching for a happy ending.

"Yes, because my grandmother was sick and then she died shortly afterward. My sister and I lived with my mom until... You don't need to hear this. Let's just say I had really good reasons to learn how to take care of myself."

"Your mom still around?"

"Died of liver cancer after contracting hepatitis C."

As a doctor, Kee could make some educated guesses on how her mom got sick. His silence was telling.

"Yeah, she was in court-ordered rehab. She broke the rules and was in prison so off to foster care for us again."

"I'm so sorry."

"Don't be. What doesn't kill you makes you stronger. Right?"

"I'm not sure about that."

"Yeah, well, so anyway, if you're asking about male role models, mine sucked."

"Sounds like neither of our dads got the nod to win father of the year."

"True that."

They sat in silence divided by their thoughts and the flickering candlelight. Why did she feel like she could talk about her family to Kee?

"My dad was a small-time thief," said Kee. "Not a good

one. He had several convictions on the rez. Too many. Then he dragged one of my younger brothers into a big mess. Had him driving the getaway car. He was only seventeen. It was my father's third strike and the tribe turned him over to the district attorney for prosecution. He's still in prison down in Phoenix. Used to visit him when I was in medical school. He has served six of a ten-year sentence. With luck he'll stay in until my sister Abbie is grown. He's not a nice man, Ava. And my brother was arrested with him and narrowly avoided being tried as an adult."

"Ty?"

"Good guess. Yes, that was Ty. They let him join the military and avoid jail time."

She tried to think of the next logical question. Should she ask about Ty, knowing what happened to him? Or about his dad or just commiserate?

"So, I know something about bad role models," said Kee. "My father was an excellent one for what not to do. Don't steal. Don't drag your son into a gang. Don't hit your wife."

"He was physically abusive?"

"Sometimes, when my father was on a tear, we'd all take cover. But not Ty." Kee shook his head. "I don't want to talk about it. I just wanted you to know. I understand being trapped in a difficult situation. My way out was school. Ty joined the Marines. Jake joined the police and Colt..."

"He's your youngest brother?"

"He's living up in the woods like a hermit. He won't talk to anyone but Ty. He was always our lost boy, but when he came back from the US Marines he was different."

Ava couldn't keep the surprise from showing. Colt was no longer up on Turquoise Ridge but instead in witness protection. Didn't Kee even know that?

"Colt was a POW, captured. Every one of his team was tortured and killed. Ty told me that. Colt got a psych discharge. Ty got him to the clinic and I saw him there. We got him as far as Darabee Hospital, but he didn't stay. Checked himself out. He's all messed up because his girl came back."

Kacey Doka. The only one to escape captivity.

"Isn't that a good thing?" Ava asked.

"She came back pregnant with someone else's kid. Just what he needs. And now that baby will grow up without a father, too." Kee was shaking his head.

He was either the best actor in the world or he had no idea what was happening.

"When did you see Colt last?" She just had to ask.

"About a week ago. Saturday last, the seventh. But he won't speak to me."

That was only a few days before Ty allegedly took Kacey to the Russians. It was also before Colt and Kacey agreed to witness protection. This reinforced her belief that neither Ty nor Colt had told Kee. Was it possible he'd had his head down with all the extra work after the dam collapse, the injuries, the clinic's temporary move that he had missed what was happening in his family? Before the FEMA trailers, Kee had lived in his mother's home. Ava was reasonably certain that May Redhorse knew her baby boy was gone. She added this to her list of information to run down.

"Well, that's a lot to deal with." She tried not to show her confusion. "Is your mom still alone?"

"Divorced and remarried. This one is a great guy. Not terribly ambitious but a nice man. Treats her well."

Ava smiled. The man in question was Burt Rope. He had no priors.

"Well, it's late." She sat forward and he followed. "I just came by to see how you were doing. Ask you if you needed anything."

He smiled and laced his fingers with hers and then

brought her hand to his lips. The dry heat of his mouth pressed to her skin, setting off a tingle of awareness and a sharp stab of need.

He drew back but kept hold of her hand. She felt the firm grasp and thought of the weapon that she had holstered just a few inches from the place where her palm pressed to his. She was safe.

"I also wanted to tell you that I'm sorry we missed our dinner tonight," she said.

His smile dropped away and he released her.

"Tuesday! Today. Ava, I'm so sorry. I forgot."

"Weren't you at the police station tonight?" she asked.

"Yes. Did they speak to you?"

She nodded.

"Could we try again? I need it, you know, with all that is going on. Tomorrow will be rough because of the autopsy."

She sat forward, all the lethargy and warm fuzzy gone as she scented prey. How convenient for Hauser to be the MDI. As the Medical Death Investigator he could put whatever he wanted as the cause of death.

"Since Dr. Hauser is doing the autopsy, I'll have to cover the clinic alone," said Kee. "Richard's family doesn't want an autopsy, but you know, accidental deaths...well." His words fell off. Then he drew a long breath and launched in again, one hand on his neck. "So I have to see patients and then get things in order for transport because we will be moving back to Piñon Flats ahead of schedule."

"When?"

"Tomorrow afternoon, sometime."

She needed to get into the clinic and to Betty Mills's computer before they reopened. It would be infinitely harder to infiltrate the permanent clinic than it was the temporary FEMA one. Who could get her inside? She eyed Kee. He could but he wouldn't do it knowingly. Breaking the rules, she thought, not his thing.

"I'm sorry," he said, shaking his head apologetically. "You don't need to hear all this."

"I don't mind." She reached out and clasped his hand. "Do you need help moving to the clinic?"

"They've got people for that."

"I'd love a private tour," she pressed. "You've spoken so highly of the facility."

"Sure."

"What about tomorrow before it opens? It would be quiet."

"Except I'm needed at the FEMA clinic. Last day in the trailers. It will be just me and the nurses. We close at noon, because of the move, but it won't really be noon. You know? We are done when we see the last patient. And then we move everything out of the trailers and back to Piñon Flats. Oh, I hope I'm not too late for dinner. Could we eat late?"

"You just give me thirty minutes' notice."

"Really? That would be great."

"So the clinic in Piñon Flats is closed until Thursday?"

"We thought so. But the women's clinic opens in the morning because they have a baby transferring back from Darabee."

A baby? Ava knew that Lori Redhorse worked in the women's facility. Kee's sister-in-law might get her in.

"When does Richard's family arrive?" Ava asked.

"Not until Thursday. They're going to bring his body back up to Minnesota for burial."

"They must be heartbroken."

"Yes. Tribal council director made the call. Spared me that. But I plan to see them in Darabee. I understand they'll stay there until arrangements can be made."

"Will you be there for the autopsy?"

He cocked his head at her question and paused.

"No, just Dr. Hauser and the guy over there in Darabee Hospital. He's the ME for the county. But since Richard died on tribal lands, Hector will be there, too. Not a normal situation because he is not a member of our tribe."

"I see." That was good news, as the medical examiner for the county would be sure that things were done correctly. Unless Hector got there first and removed evidence. "Anyone from your police force be there?"

He cocked his head and regarded her for a long moment. She realized too late that it wasn't the usual sort of question.

"I don't know."

She drew out her phone and glanced at the time. "I better get home."

Kee released her hand and rose. Woody groaned and stretched, then lifted on all fours, watching them with his tail set on medium wag.

"Let me just snuff this." He blew the flames out with a single breath and she collected Woody's leash in her right hand. He fell in beside her at her left side as they meandered toward her sister's home.

The temporary trailer park was dark, with only the light from Kee's trailer to guide them. That fell away as they continued along the road under the light of a pale quarter moon. The stars seemed especially bright and the sky more a deep blue than black. How many centuries had her people stared up at the night sky? They had named all the constellations, and stars of all varieties appeared often in their art and regalia.

She kept him on her left as they walked. If she needed her pistol, she'd only have to drop the leash and reach inside her jacket. But that did put him side by side with her shoulder holster and weapon. She wondered what he thought about handguns. Most doctors were not gun people, as they spent time pulling bullets out of human bodies.

He took her hand and locked his fingers through hers.

"I'm glad you came visiting," he said.

She wondered if he meant visiting him or her sister. But it didn't matter. The moonlight and the quiet night were weaving a spell. Making her forget who she was and who he was. The darkness shrouded them, giving them the illusion of privacy and the feeling that they were the only two people here.

"So? Dinner tomorrow night?" he asked.

She smiled. "Sure."

"I'll call before I pick you up."

When they reached her sister's FEMA trailer, they drew to a halt and he turned to face her. Kee was leaning in. She looked up at him. The moon cast his face in silvery light, making his sculpted features seem to be carved of some exotic wood. His smile was gentle but his eyes glittered with unmistakable desire. Her heart kicked into high gear.

"I'm going to kiss you good-night," he said.

Warning or promise, she wondered and thought it a little of both. It was just a kiss. What harm could that do?

She lifted on her toes, meeting him halfway. He gripped her shoulders, his hands sweeping down to her elbows. And then his mouth was slanting over hers, soft at first as he explored the fit of their mouths and then harder as he cradled her head and deepened the kiss.

All her senses jumped and quivered. Her skin puckered on her arms as every hair on her skin lifted up in recognition of the powerful chemistry activated by his kiss. Ava was not without experience and that was exactly why she knew that this man, this kiss was different. Very different.

Worst choice imaginable.

But her body wasn't listening. She fell against one broad shoulder, sliding naturally into the hard plains of his chest as she relished the heat and the pressure. And she opened her mouth to let him stroke and suck and tease.

Her words echoed back to her, mocking now.

What harm could one kiss do?

Chapter Seven

Kee felt the explosion of sensation and the building heat at the first contact of his lips to hers. His heart sped. He inhaled the sweet fragrance of her skin and felt the erotic slide of his tongue along hers. He knew the physiological reasons for each one, could describe arousal in clinical terms, but this kiss just flat-out took his words away. He could barely think, let alone speak. All he knew for certain was that he wanted more. So much more. But when his hands slid to her hips and tugged to bring them together, Ava stepped back.

He set his jaw and fixed a smile on his lips to keep her from seeing his disappointment. He'd gone too fast. He knew it and still he could not help himself. What Ava described as independent he saw as wounded. But her wounds could not be bound and healed. Not without patience and time.

He found he wanted to try, to accept that challenge if for no other reason than it might bring her to trust him enough…yes, to sleep with him. He'd admit it to himself. He wanted Ava and he was prepared to work for it just as he had worked for everything else.

"Good night, Ava. I'll see you tomorrow night."

As Kee gave Woody's head another pat, he told himself to turn around to head home. Instead he stood locked in place. He thought of his empty trailer and all that had happened and suddenly felt sad.

She blinked up at him, holding the leash, looking troubled.

"Kee?"

He gave her a smile, waiting, hoping she wasn't going to call off their dinner date.

"Will you be all right over there, you know…alone?"

"Oh, yes. I'll be okay." It wasn't an offer of anything but concern and when he'd tried to draw her against him, she'd called a halt. She was a good girl. Their culture valued modesty in both men and women. He liked that Ava didn't let him get away with too much. So far he liked everything he saw. Kee was already trying to figure out how to get her to stay in the area and he'd only met her two days ago.

His mother said it was like that sometimes. Like falling off a cliff. Kee's head dropped, thinking of Richard again.

Such a day, filled with the ordinary at the clinic and the horror of finding Richard and the wonder of kissing Ava.

She lifted on her toes and dropped a kiss on his cheek. Her mouth was warm and soft and she brought with her the enticing fragrance of earth and flowers.

Ava stepped back and made a hasty retreat, headed for her sister's front door. Kee watched her go. Too good to be true—that had been his initial thought. Every woman he met recently was after something. Mostly when they heard that he was a doctor, their eyes lit up as if they were starving and he was dinner. He didn't get that vibe from Ava. But there was something about her that was off. She was smart, clearly, and obviously beautiful. She had a nice sense of humor and was empathetic. But her reactions to stress were just out of the ordinary. She'd have made a good paramedic with that cool head on her lovely shoulders. Seemed a waste to have her dealing cards for high rollers.

Kee headed home, glad to imagine her lying in her bed alone. It took his mind off Richard lying on a slab. He wondered what she wore to sleep as he relived their kiss. Best darn kiss he'd had in...well, forever. After he broke up with Connie, he'd buried himself in the library and had been so busy during his residency that he didn't have the time or energy for a woman. But he wanted a woman, a wife and a family. The right kind of woman, one who understood him and where he came from. Could Ava understand how much he loved and hated this place?

Could she be the one he could trust with the bad things as well as the good? Could Ava Hood be the woman who could love him for himself?

WEDNESDAY MORNING, BETTY MILLS met Hector Hauser at the temporary clinic before opening.

"I have some information from Saguaro Flats. I told them I was running a background check for employment," she said offering him the sheet. "Tribal registry shows three Ava Hoods down there. But see, this one is eighteen. This one is sixty-two. The other does work for the casino, but she's in her late forties."

Betty registered members of their tribe onto the rolls. She had connections with all of the surrounding tribes and many outside the state. A simple phone call could gain her access to information unavailable to most.

He took the page. "Hood is a common name. But why isn't she turning up?"

"That was what I wondered. So I ran just Ava. I got twenty hits. Five in the correct age range and this one..." She pointed a long acrylic nail at the paper.

Hauser read the entry. "Avangeline H. Yokota." His eyes scanned and then lowered the page to meet her eyes. "Tribal police detective?"

Betty nodded.

"Is that her?"

"I'm trying to find out if anyone knows what Sara Tah's sister does down there in Saguaro Flats. I've made some calls."

"This is bad." Hector swore in Tonto Apache. "We just had Yury here for Day. If Ava dies, as well..."

He and Betty shared a look of understanding. The distinct-looking Russian stood out among the Tonto Apache people and would arouse suspicion if spotted. And Kee had already expressed interested in the beautiful Turquoise Canyon newcomer, which complicated plans even more.

Betty spoke first. "You do the autopsies. Just put down accidental death."

"Damn ME will be there."

"You can handle him. Day was snooping around on the computers. Trying to access my protected files. We had to take precautions."

"But why was he doing that?"

"We'll never know."

"Well, I've changed all passwords and now I get an alert if anyone accesses those files."

"Do I call him again?"

She hesitated, chewing on her knuckle.

"Wait or call the Russians?" he asked.

She dropped her hand from her mouth. "I'd err on the side of caution."

Hector lifted his mobile phone and dialed.

AVA HEADED TO tribal police headquarters in Piñon Flats just after nine on Wednesday. Autopsy was this morning and the clinic was moving today, so she figured tribal must already be set up. She was, unfortunately, right.

She had put off reporting to her soon-to-be new boss. But Day's death had changed things. She needed to be sure that neither Hauser nor Redhorse performed that autopsy. That meant coming in out of the cold. She thought she preferred the cold to the heat she was about to take. Tinnin was smart and it was better to report than let him run her to ground.

Not being affiliated with any police department gave her some leeway and, acting as a private citizen, she was involving no one but herself.

During her interview process, Tinnin had told her that they were focusing their investigation on the tribe's health clinic because all the girls had been seen there. It was the only certain connection they had yet discovered and plenty for Ava to go on. She had not told them that her main reason for applying for the position was not that she wanted a larger force, as she had told them. It was Louisa.

Tribal headquarters was unlocked and had a faint musty odor about it. She headed to the wing containing the police station and was met upon entrance by Carol Dorset, a nice older woman and longtime dispatcher for the tribe. Her face was soft and the pink lipstick she wore had bled into the wrinkles surrounding her mouth but her eyes were sharp and she recognized Ava instantly.

"We were expecting you in November," she said.

"Yes. That's right."

Carol cocked her head and waited for an explanation that Ava was not going to give her.

"We only just got back ourselves," said Carol. "Electric is back on, so tribal government, public works and the health clinic are all allowed in today and the tribal members will be allowed in on Thursday. Businesses open on Friday. Should be more folks at the diner with the construction right down the street."

"Good news," said Ava. "Is the chief busy?"

"Always. I'll tell him you're here."

Carol spoke to the chief by phone and then waved her

on past the dispatch area. Ava crossed the empty squad room to the office beyond.

She found Chief Wallace Tinnin looking out of the plate-glass window at her, his phone pressed to his ear. The door was open so she stepped inside and glanced about. When she'd been here last the sideboard and desk were piled high with folders and paper. Now only the walls were cluttered with the faded photos. His desk held the phone's base and two cardboard boxes. Leaning on the near side were a pair of aluminum crutches he'd needed since breaking his foot during the dam collapse. It seemed he had not yet found time to unpack. He wore no uniform, just jeans and a pistol holstered at his hip. The gold tribal shield was clipped beside it. The desk blocked her view of his legs, but she assumed his foot was still in a cast since his injury during the dam collapse.

He had his hand on top of his graying head capping the loose hair that brushed his shoulders. She judged him to be in his midfifties because of the loose brown skin on his face and the deep crow's feet at his eyes. His lean frame bulged only slightly at the belly extending past his wide belt.

His brows rose at seeing her and he spoke into the phone. "I found her. Speak to you later." He hung up. "You want to tell me what you're doing up here, Detective?"

"You saw Wetselline's report?" she asked.

"Hell, yes, I did. You know what you're doing?"

"My sister is—"

He interrupted. "Sara Tah, mother of Louisa Tah, the last girl to go missing. It was in Wetselline's report. Funny that you never mentioned that in your interview."

She clamped her lips tight and waited.

Tinnin pressed his thumb and the knuckle of his index finger against the bridge of his nose and squeezed his eyes shut. He looked like he had a sinus infection but Ava suspected she was the cause of his headache.

"You up here doing your own investigation. Maybe bending a few rules. Is that it?"

She didn't deny it.

He dropped his hand away from his face. The chief rested both hands on his hips and lowered his chin. "Detective Hood, I know you are new here, but my law enforcement personnel follow procedure."

Ava waited for the other shoe to drop. It only took an eye-blink.

"You're off the case," he said.

"I'm not really on it yet. I'm on leave from my office and I don't start here until next month. This is personal time."

"Detective, this is you coming up here to find the guilty. And the fact that you're not yet a member of my force, and might never be, doesn't keep you from following our laws."

"I'm here to find my niece."

"You could have been working on this case through proper channels," said Tinnin. "Instead of sneaking around up here doing who knows what. Why didn't you come to me?"

Ava lifted her chin. "I thought you might be involved."

He leaned back against the window sill behind him and folded his arms, glowering. "Cross me off your list, did you?"

She nodded.

"Why's that?"

"No motive. No opportunity and no evidence of any connection to my prime suspects."

"It's a small reservation, everyone is connected to everyone else somehow. Even you."

She'd do it all again. And the only way he was stopping her was to put her in his jail.

"I'm making progress."

"That so? By interfering with a murder investigation?"

"I found you Day's car and his body and I made certain that Redhorse didn't contaminate your crime scene." Now would be the time to mention Ty Redhorse. She didn't.

"I've got a call into your supervisor," said Tinnin. "Let him know where you've been spending your vacation time."

The thing was she wasn't sorry. She knew the police were trying to recover the missing, but they were also investigating suspects to arrest and were slowed by making a case while she was unencumbered. If her actions meant that she got a reprimand, then so be it.

"And if you are doing anything illegal you need to stop."

She narrowed her eyes. "What would you do to get your son back?"

He leaned on his desk, hands flat so she could see both the red coral and the turquoise rings on the index and middle fingers of his right hand. They'd make really good brass knuckles, she thought.

"My older son is in the DEA somewhere in Oklahoma. Safe and sound, last I checked. My younger son is sixteen and sometimes I wish someone would take him."

"You don't mean that."

"No, I don't."

He straightened and waited.

"You can't have Hauser do the autopsy," she said.

He rolled his eyes. "I've got a ME in Darabee. He'll be lead. He's FBI but Hauser will think he's a sub. That all right with you, Hood? Or should I say Yokota?"

"I don't use that name."

"Yet it is the one that you used on the paperwork for your background check. Your legal name."

"Look, I'm not going to give you a whole family history, but my dad did not win father of the year. I don't know him. I don't use his name."

"Except when you have to."

"Exactly. If you've got the autopsy covered, then I'll leave you to your unpacking." Ava headed toward the door.

"Just a minute."

She turned to face him. He gave her a hard look.

"You take anything from my crime scene?"

"No, sir."

"Anything else you'd like me to know?"

"Redhorse asked me out."

Tinnin's hand dropped as he stared at her. "Jake?"

"Kee."

He looked to the ceiling of his office as if gathering his patience.

"Dr. Kee Redhorse, my suspect?"

"Yes, sir. Dinner tonight."

"Does he know who you are?"

"Yes."

Tinnin's shoulders relaxed.

"But not that I'm a detective. I also gave my name to Hector Hauser."

"Entrapment."

"No. I don't work for you. Anything I tell you would be from a witness. Anything I dig up is free information for you."

"You work for Saguaro. I've called your chief. He wants you home pronto."

She lowered her head, trying to avoid this. But she couldn't. So she drew back her shoulders. Then she said, "I'll resign."

"You break the law and I'll arrest you."

"No, Chief. You'll thank me because I'm going to bring you the person or persons who did this."

"Going to solve the whole thing all by your lonesome. Is that it?"

Ava pulled a face but did not reply as she withdrew a folded page from her pocket and set it on the worn surface of his battered wooden desk.

"What's this?"

"Dr. Hauser is having instant message sex with his receptionist."

He regarded the paper.

"How did you get this?"

She met his gaze and did not answer.

"How, Ava?"

"Any evidence that comes into your possession is admissible as long as you didn't break the law to get it. So…"

"You're going to lose everything," he warned.

"As long as I get her back."

"Not necessarily going to work out like that. Kacey Doka nearly got herself killed trying a similar stunt when she showed up unprotected at the clinic and nearly ended up recaptured."

"I read that because of her actions, they found two-dozen girls in a camp out in the desert north of my reservation."

"Twenty-three women," he said.

"Sounds to me like she made the right choice."

"We follow the law here and you swore an oath."

She nodded her head. "Protect and serve. That's what I'm doing, Chief."

"What if they go after your sister or her kids?"

Ava stilled. She'd thought of that, of course, and it chilled her blood. It was one thing to endanger her own life, but not those three little girls or her sister. But if she gave up now, Louisa would never come home. She knew it in her heart.

"A tough choice," said Tinnin.

Ava pressed her teeth together, not trusting her voice.

Tinnin frowned and then rested a hand on his hip, regarding her for a long moment.

"There were no prints on the bike," he said.

She could not hide her surprise on that one. "Day's bike?"

He nodded.

"You mean other than Day's?" she asked.

"No. Not even Day's. Wiped clean."

Her heart accelerated at the implication.

"You listing this as homicide?" she asked.

"Open case," he said. "But I've got questions."

"I noticed something odd on your tribe's website." She motioned to his laptop. "May I?"

He turned it toward her and she sat before his desk, opened a browser and loaded the tribe's website. As it loaded she wondered absently how many years it took to wear the varnish off the surface.

When the site appeared she logged in.

"You have to be a member to access this part of the site," he said.

"My sister was checking," said Ava and glanced up to see his sour expression. Then she pointed at the spreadsheet.

He rounded the desk to look at the screen, limping as he advanced.

"Looks like no casino profits are needed for the clinic's operation."

He squinted at the screen and then looked to her.

"Most people don't really look at what's not listed on a budget. But I'm wondering where you get your clinic's operations budget. The equipment in the clinic? Radiology area, women's health clinic, three exam rooms and a fully stocked procedure room on-site."

"I think they operate on grant money and Medicare. State of Arizona chips in, too," said Tinnin, hand now working the muscles at the back of his neck.

Ava shook her head. "Our health clinic takes twenty-two percent of our entire operating budget from the casino profits, in addition to Medicare, and yours runs itself." She smiled. "Lucky you."

Tinnin sat on the edge of the desk and folded his hands on one thigh. "You have my attention."

Chapter Eight

"Your clinic includes…" Ava leaned in and clicked to another screen that showed Dr. Hauser's photo in an article on the tribe's website. Ava placed her finger on the line of text and read to Chief Tinnin from the page, "'a full-service, highly complex laboratory working with state-of-the-art diagnostic equipment providing a spectrum of tests necessary to diagnose and treat many medical problems.' Yada, yada…'drawing blood and…staffed with trained lab personnel.'" She turned to him. "You have only three doctors but you have a full-service lab? Meanwhile, our blood and samples go out daily to a lab for testing. I checked."

Tinnin shrugged.

"Lab like that could run pregnancy tests in-house. Pretty fast, too, I'll bet," said Ava, thinking of the baby ring.

"So who's on your short list?"

"Dr. Redhorse and Dr. Hauser and Ms. Betty Mills. Any of the nurses might be involved along with the lab techs."

"Not Lori Mott. She was the one who discovered the girls had all been seen there shortly before their disappearances."

"And she's married to Kee's brother Jake," said Ava.

"One of our officers."

"Gives her insider info on your investigation."

"No way."

Ava shrugged. "Maybe not. Turning them in doesn't make sense if she's involved, of course."

"We are looking at Kee and Hector very seriously," said Tinnin.

"So if you know Hauser might be involved, why let him do the autopsy on Day?"

Tinnin grinned and scratched beneath his chin.

"Unless…you wanted to use it as bait."

"If he tries to access that body early, I will know. If he meddles with the evidence, I'll know. We already took samples."

"His nails?"

"You noticed that in the dark?"

She nodded.

"Yeah, we have skin samples. Should have something in a few days."

"So we're good?" said Ava.

"Not exactly." He stood. "I spoke to your captain. I've told him that we are withdrawing our offer for employment. He wants you back home tomorrow."

KEE COVERED THE urgent care clinic solo most of Wednesday morning so Dr. Hauser could perform the autopsy on Day. Kee didn't envy him that. Being the ME for their tribe put Hector in the center of much human tragedy. He saw the worst of them, no question.

They were full up since the clinic was closing at noon instead of four so they could move back to Piñon Flats. Betty told him that Dr. Hauser was en route back from the autopsy and would meet them at the clinic. Dr. Hauser had held the position as ME since before Kee was even born. If he did retire, would that be Kee's duty, as well?

He finished the last of the patients at one o'clock, instead of noon. Betty brought him a sandwich to munch as he boxed his personal gear and afterward helped see their equipment into a tractor trailer. Much of their supplies had remained in Piñon Flats and he would be so happy to be back where they had better facilities and more room. The tribe was recovering from the crisis.

When Kee arrived, Betty Mills was already at her post at reception working on a backlog of paperwork.

Hauser was there behind the desk as Kee arrived carrying a box.

Hauser spotted Kee and smiled broadly. "Welcome home!"

Kee returned the smile. "Thanks. It's good to be back."

He didn't say great because Dr. Day was not here. And it didn't feel the same here since the eco-extremists attack that had changed their river forever and now the death of a colleague. Perhaps it was the beginning of a new normal and the worst was behind them. He hoped so, at least.

"How did it go this morning?" Kee asked.

"Nothing unexpected. Bruises I saw were consistent with the fall and his neck was broken. Likely died instantly."

Instantly, after falling all the way to the ground, thought Kee. What must he have been thinking as he careened through space? Kee shuddered.

"Cold?" said Hauser. "What's the A/C set at, Betty?"

"Seventy-five, as always."

"Well, you're just in from the heat. You'll adjust." Hauser gave him a friendly pat on the shoulder.

"So you don't think he fell?" asked Kee.

"Yes. Manner of death was a fall. Cause of death, accidental. My report will say as much."

Kee shifted a moving box to his hip.

"Well, get your office set up. We open tomorrow."

They spent the afternoon settling in but did open for a tribe member who was in active labor. His sister-in-law Lori did all the heavy lifting since she had more experience with delivery than he did. But he assisted and when he checked the wall clock for a time of birth, he realized he'd been working for ten hours straight and that if he was going to pick Ava up for a dinner date, he needed to get out of here.

"I have to go," he said to Lori.

"Hot date?" joked Lori.

"I sure hope so."

Her brows lifted and then she laughed. "Well, good for you. Hell, yeah, and about time. Anyone I know?"

"She's the sister of Sara Tah," said Kee.

Lori's smile wavered at this. No one who heard Sara's name was not reminded of her husband's recent and very untimely death and the daughter who had gone missing at the beginning of the month.

"I know," he said. "She's here to help out. And she's terrific."

"Sara is from Saguaro Flats. Right?"

"Yes."

"So what's her sister do down there among the cactus, swimming pools and Anglos?"

"I'm trying to figure that out."

"Well, have fun."

He made it back to Turquoise Ridge at seven thirty. He called Ava's phone but got no answer. He showered and dressed and called again at eight with the sinking feeling that he was too late for supper.

There was a knock on the trailer door as he was sliding his phone into his front pocket. His dress shirt was open showing a wide swath of medium brown skin and his hair was sticking up with the product he'd tried and not yet tamed.

The knock came again and he jogged the rest of the way, fastening his belt buckle just before he reached the door and pulled it open.

There stood Ava, dressed in an oversize sweater with a

scoop neck that showed smooth tawny skin flushed with a rosy color and draped with a thin gold chain that caught the light. Kee felt his pulse beating in his veins as he lifted his gaze to meet hers.

"I'm so sorry I'm so late. I tried to call."

"I know. I was driving. I called the clinic and spoke to your sister-in-law. She said you just delivered a bouncing baby boy." Ava's generous smile made his body tingle.

"Yes. Well, she and the mother did most of it."

She held out a large brown paper bag and a bottle of ice tea to him. He took the bags and she hiked up the strap to her oversize purse.

"What's this?" he asked regarding the bag.

"Picnic supper. I have potato salad, fry bread, pulled pork, corn and chocolate cream pie."

"Oh, but I wanted to take you out," he said.

"You had a hard day." They were all hard, which was why he slept so well.

"And...this is more private," she said.

He lifted his brows at the implication and she gave him a coy smile. Despite his disappointment at not being about to take her out, his body reacted instantly to her suggestion of privacy. He'd like to have some private time with Ava, after he figured out what was going on.

Her kiss and Ty's discovery that Ava carried a concealed weapon had kept him up last night and the more he thought about it the more he wondered who she was and what she was up to. He didn't know but he planned to find out. And when he did, after he did, perhaps he wouldn't be so enamored. Ava was just too good to be true. He knew it.

"Unless you want to get out of this trailer?" she asked after his hesitance.

He stepped aside and motioned her in.

"No, this is fine. Let me set the table."

She stepped past him. "Mind if I use the bathroom? Too much coffee today."

"Sure." He took the bags and went with them to the kitchen. She followed as far as the dinette, where she draped her purse over a chair back. Then she did go into the bathroom, but upon exiting she crossed to Day's bedroom. His eyes narrowed.

He unpacked their dinner. By the time she got back he had his shirt buttoned, the table set and was working on pouring drinks. She glanced at her bag and then to him. There was something off about her. And what was she doing in Richard's bedroom?

"Are you sure this is all right?" he said.

"Why? Because I brought you a meal?"

"That's part of it." Come to think of it, not one woman in his experience had ever reached in her pocket to pay for anything.

"Kee, I went to community college but I worked my way through. I can only imagine what it cost to go to medical school. You don't need to impress me with a fancy meal."

That was a switch. The women he'd met did not understand that residents worked long hours for not very much money. They heard doctor and made assumptions. Had he finally found a girl who was not drawn to the lure of prestige and money?

Or did she want something else?

She was drawn to something. But he wasn't entirely sure what that something was.

"Well, I owe you a meal," he said.

"If you cook it, I'll eat it," she promised.

"Oh, well, I'm not much of a cook."

"You survived medical school—you must know how to make something."

He laughed. "Spaghetti and meat sauce, Cup O' Noodles, mac and cheese, brownies from a box."

"That's nearly a complete meal."

"Steamed broccoli."

"There you go!"

He laughed.

"Spaghetti is my favorite." She wiggled her eyebrows. "Grilled cheese is second and I love a burger made any way out of anything as long as it had four hooves."

"Refined taste."

"Hey, I ponied up for the ice tea, didn't I?"

They were both laughing now. He liked her, damn it. But he didn't like being tricked or used. Ava wasn't here for dinner. He knew that much.

His smile faded.

"What's wrong?"

"Oh, sorry. I was just thinking how much I am enjoying myself and how much I like you and then I thought of Richard. It's just terrible."

She nodded and laid a hand on his shoulder, rubbing up and down. "I'm sorry this happened. Did Dr. Hauser say what caused Dr. Day's death?"

"Accident, he said."

Ava's eyes narrowed but she said nothing to this.

He turned toward her and took her hand. He tugged to draw her closer but she resisted so he leaned forward and dropped a soft, gentle kiss on her mouth.

It might have been perfect if not for his reservations. She was up to something. But what?

He drew back.

She rounded the table. Kee glanced at her purse hanging from the chair back. It gaped open. Inside he saw a black pistol in a stitched leather holster with a quick draw feature. Clipped to the holster was a gold badge that read *Saguaro Flats Tribal Police Detective*.

He lifted the weapon and badge and held them in two hands. So, Ty had been right all along.

Chapter Nine

Ava held her second pistol in her hand, straight down at her side away from Kee's line of sight. He'd found her empty pistol and badge, both of which he held in his open hands with a look of utter confusion on his face. His mouth gaped and his brow wrinkled. A quicksilver flash of panic washed over her as she realized this was it, the test she hoped he'd pass.

Finally!

Had he handled enough weapons to know what one felt like with an empty clip? She knew he hadn't touched her purse before because it was exactly as she had left it, right down to the twisted strap and zipper not quite done up. That made her resort to leaving it unzipped and hanging half-open.

She met his accusatory stare and waited for what he would do next. His mouth turned down in a tight angry frown and the muscles at his jaw bulged.

She pressed her arms tight to her sides, feeling the Kevlar vest beneath her bulky sweater and the weight of the pistol gripped tight in her hand. Her mouth was dry and her heartbeat raced as she waited for him to reveal himself.

He dropped the holstered weapon and badge to the kitchen table. It thumped to the surface, making the silverware clatter.

"A badge," he said, leveling her with a hard look. "Makes sense."

"Yes," she admitted, as her heart continued to prepare her for whatever came next. But she could breathe now. She relaxed her hand, flicking the safety back on as she kept her eyes trained on Kee. Was he this cool a customer or was he innocent? Every day this took was another day Louisa was trapped in some horrible place. She just had to get her home.

She knew confronting Kee like this was in direct conflict with what the Turquoise Canyon police force wanted her to do. But they knew why she was here and every day that her niece was being held captive against her will was torture. She wasn't going to wait around and play nice.

"Officer. It's what Ty called you. He knew."

She remembered, of course.

"What kind of game are you playing, Detective?"

She lifted one hand in a gesture meant for him to halt as she crept forward. "Step away from the table, Kee."

He did, complying exactly with her order. But he did not look frightened or surprised. He just looked defeated as he stomped to the window and lifted his hands.

"I should have known that you were after something, too. Just not me."

She wished it could be different. Wished she could be the woman he believed her to be. But she had tricked him and that would not be easily forgotten. He was allowed to be angry.

She retrieved her weapon, holster and badge, returning them to the bag and setting them on the chair before her.

"You want to frisk me or maybe kiss me again? How about I wait here while you finish searching Richard's room?"

Ava crept forward, returned the clip to the pistol and holstered her weapon at her hip. Then she slipped the second firearm into her purse. Finally, she pressed her palm to the table as she released a long breath.

"You think I was going to shoot you, Ava? I've spent too many hours stitching up bodies to do that."

"I'm sorry. I had to find out what you would do."

"This was a test? I don't know who or what you think I am, but I think I deserve an explanation."

"I'm here to find my niece."

He folded his arms but did not look the least bit guilty or surprised. "Okay. I don't know what that has to do with me, so keep going."

"Why don't you sit down," she said.

"I'll stay right here, thanks."

She had thought about this at length and had still not decided how much to tell him. Kee had known her name for four days. That was more than enough to figure out who she was and make a move. He hadn't. Yesterday, she'd given her name to Hauser. If he and Hauser were involved with the disappearances, less information was better. If Hauser was working without Kee, then Kee could be an asset. Plus, if he was not involved, he deserved to know.

"Why are you looking for your niece in Richard's room?"

She forced her arms down away from her service pistol and sat herself backward in a kitchen chair. Kee leaned against the counter beside the window across from her, arms now tightly folded in a defensive posture that echoed the tight lines in his handsome face.

"One of the nurses on your staff discovered something in your clinic's medical records. She brought it to your tribal police. Kee, all the missing girls were seen at your clinic."

He blinked at this revelation and then scowled. "Of course they all were. Almost every single member of this tribe has been treated there. You might as well check the tribal registration records. The names are all there, as well."

"No, Kee, it's worse than that." She swallowed and rested both forearms on the chair back. "The girls all attended different schools, from Turquoise Ridge to Koun'nde to Piñon Flats. They didn't all know each other, but they were all treated at the tribe's women's health clinic at least twice over the course of a single month each and disappeared within days of their second visit."

His shoulders relaxed as the angry expression eased to be replaced by worry.

"That's odd."

He didn't ask which nurse, she realized. A guilty man would likely want to know who had leaked information to the police.

"I've spoken to Zella Colelay. You know her?"

"Yes."

"Have you treated her?"

"No. I don't think so."

"Within the last year?"

"What was her condition?"

"She had an infection."

"I didn't treat her."

The medical records said that he did. Lori had given them to tribal police and Ava had spoken at length to Lori Redhorse. But Ava didn't have those records. Not yet.

She couldn't wait to join the Turquoise Canyon police force to get them. That only left Kee.

"Zella was warned by Marta Garcia that someone was following her. When Marta went missing, Zella dropped out of school, hid and escaped capture."

"Did you say capture?"

"Yes."

"I thought these girls were runaways."

"Zella didn't run. She delivered a baby that your brother Jake adopted. You must know that."

"I've seen Jake and Lori and their baby, Fortune. I

didn't know Zella was the birth mother. That seems odd because…"

She finished his sentence. "Because Fortune is white."

Kee nodded. "She seems to be, at least. Jake found her in his truck."

"Yes, I know," said Ava.

"How many girls are missing?"

"Five. That does not include Kacey."

"That's related? Kacey coming back? Her coming home pregnant?"

"How do you know about that?" she asked.

"Colt called me. He was with my brother Jake and having some psychological problems. He's got PTSD since his service in Afghanistan. I got a therapist here to see him, outside actually, because he wouldn't come in the clinic. He wanted to know if Kacey was all right. He said she was in labor and in Darabee Hospital. I checked that information for him and she was there. Delivered a baby girl."

"Where is Colt now?"

"I don't know. Last Tuesday, he was at Darabee Hospital. But he checked himself out. I've been to his cabin. But he only lets Ty see him."

Ava's shoulders tightened. A week ago Ty and Colt might well have been talking. But not anymore. Clearly, Kee did not know that Colt and Kacey had left the rez with the Justice Department or that Ty was under investigation.

"Did you check with Ty?"

"Of course. He says Colt and Kacey are off on some road trip."

"Is that right?" It wasn't.

"I doubt it. Ty often covers for Colt. Besides, who takes a baby on a road trip? My mother seems to know something but she won't say, either. Just said that he'll be gone for a while. Does this have to do with…"

"He's in witness protection. He and Kacey both. That's what Lori told me."

Kee's mouth dropped open. A hand went to his forehead.

"Why didn't Jake tell me?"

"Because he's a law enforcement officer and would be breaking federal law by revealing your brother's status."

"By telling me? I'm his brother." His voice held a sharp edge she had not heard before.

"You are a suspect."

"Wait a second. Where are you getting this? Why not go to the police here?"

"I theorized that someone in the force could be involved in the disappearances."

His brows lifted. "Your badge says Saguaro Flats."

"That's right."

"So you have no authority here."

"Also right."

His eyes narrowed on her. "So how did you get all this information?"

"First from my department. Your chief gave us a courtesy call. When Louisa went missing, I came up here and interviewed with your tribal police. When I was hired, I was briefed in preparation for my appointment as a new detective here. That probably won't happen now."

"Does Ty know who you are?"

"He suspects. Also, you should know that he's under federal investigation for his part in transporting Kacey Doka back into the hands of her captors."

"What?"

"All related." She tried and failed to remain unaffected by the grief now clearly evident in Kee's expression.

Kee reached for the closest chair and sat hard.

"I checked your personal computer. Day wasn't a suspect, so I had no need to check his but after his death, I thought I had better have a look."

"But the police already took it."

"Exactly."

"So you show up here bearing take-out dinner and make me think you want some alone time, just so you can search my place."

"I did that over a week ago. Tonight was just to see your reaction."

"That's just great."

She shrugged. "She's my niece."

A suspect's first reaction would not be self-righteousness, she thought. Ava's chest ached in something that she thought might be sympathy for his hurt and confusion. This was new ground and she did not like the feelings he stirred in her.

"Does your job as a police officer give you permission to hack my computer?"

"No." He had her if he wanted her. He could just pick up the phone and call his tribal police. She waited as their eyes met.

"So you've gone off the reservation, literally. I'm not a cop, but I know you can't obtain evidence like this. You can't break in without permission from our tribal leadership or without a warrant from the police."

She laid it out there, trying to make him understand.

"I'm not trying to build a case here, Kee. I'm trying to find my niece before she disappears forever. What do you think happens to those girls after they give birth?"

He ground his teeth. Her heart hammered as she waited for him to decide.

"I could pick up the phone and call the real police and have you arrested. Right?"

She nodded. "That's correct. You could also press charges."

He rubbed his hand over his broad forehead as if trying to come up with the right move. He held her freedom in the balance.

He dropped his hand and faced her across the table, his face pale and grave. "Give me a reason not to call Chief Tinnin."

"Because then you might never know who did this."

Kee slapped a hand on the table, making the silverware shake. "You're wrong, you know."

"About?"

"About me and about my clinic. We are helping people. I am never alone with a female patient. It's for my protection as much as theirs. We have procedures that are followed to the letter. We sure as hell don't kidnap them or inseminate them. We're doctors."

She held her tongue.

"It's not Hector," said Kee.

"If you'd like to prove that, you're going to need to help me."

"Help you how?"

"Get me those records."

"No."

"I've ruled you out. Hauser is now my focus."

He made a sound of disbelief choked in a laugh. "Hector? He's the founder of our clinic."

"He also may have arranged for six women to be kidnapped."

"I'm not going to betray my friends," said Kee.

"Even if they are feeding your children to these criminals?"

"That could be anyone on the reservation."

"I know each missing girl was seen by your clinic shortly before their disappearances. I know that your name is on the record as treating each one of those girls."

Kee gasped. "That's impossible."

"Not according to my sources."

"I never treated any of them!"

"Either you did or someone from *your* clinic changed the records."

"You have these records?"

"Not yet."

"But you've seen them?"

"I've heard from a credible source."

"Hearsay, you mean. You have nothing. No proof."

"I have a dead body."

"Day's death is unrelated to what you are alleging."

She made a sound deep in the back of her throat.

Kee continued on. "We would never, ever do something like this."

"You sure about that?"

"Absolutely."

"Willing to put your money where your mouth is?"

"What does that mean?" he asked.

"Well, if everything is hunky-dory at your clinic, then you won't mind checking the girls' records. I'll give you the names and you see who treated them and if it's you, we talk some more."

He considered the proposal and then dipped his chin. "All right."

Chapter Ten

"I can't believe I agreed to this. There could be serious consequences for breaking patients' rights."

She cocked her head to stare at him. "That's your concern? Breaking the rules? We are talking about young girls captured and taken."

Kee turned his troubled eyes on her. "Ava, what you say is happening is truly heinous, but my clinic had nothing to do with it. This is the first time I've heard that the disappearances might be tied to our clinic."

Ava shook her head. "If not you, then it's Hauser."

"No. No way. Hector is one of the best men I know. Right down deep inside. He's a good doctor and a loving husband. He's raised a son who is a credit to this tribe."

She folded her arms. "People are not always what they seem. And as for the records, I'll bet you that your name appears on every damn one," she said.

"That's impossible. I rarely work in the women's health clinic."

"That's Hector's baby, so to speak," Ava provided.

"Yes."

She lifted her brows. She was certain that Hector was involved. She just wasn't sure about Kee.

"So what will you do if your name is listed as the treating physician for all appointments for the missing girls?" she asked.

"That won't happen," he said, a determined set to his jaw.

"Humor me."

"If so, well, I'd go to Hector."

"Nope. Wrong answer. Someone pushed Richard off a cliff."

"Not Hector."

"He's dirty." She made a face and waited.

"No. He's our ME. He's…"

"I'll bet that someone thought Day knew something. And I'll also bet that someone is Hector. So you do not want to let him know you think he might be tied up in this."

"I don't. He's not," Kee said, shaking his head in denial, but his eyes looked wide and worried.

"We saw Day's body, Kee. You saw blood and tissue under his fingernails. The kind of thing you see when someone is fighting for their life."

"It's up to the medical examiner to determine if that blood was Day's." Kee's heart sank. Hector was the ME. The hopelessness grew inside him like a parasite.

She didn't let up. "How did Hauser feel about Dr. Day?"

Kee looked away and she had her answer before he spoke.

"He didn't trust him." Kee shrugged. "An outsider."

"Kee, look at me."

Dark troubled eyes met hers and he held himself across the middle as if in physical pain. It was a posture she recognized from the times she had to give family members bad news. Hector was important to Kee. Not just a boss, but a role model, and he was so far up on a pedestal that the fall would be spectacular.

"This is no coincidence. It's not someone else. It's you or Hector or it's you *and* Hector."

"I had your gun. If it were me…"

"Yes, you passed that test. It's why we are having this conversation. My gut tells me that you're a good guy, Kee, if a little too trusting of those you love. Plus I took precautions." She lifted her bulky sweater and showed him her body armor and the pistol holstered at her hip. "This one was empty. I have another in there," she said, motioning to her bag.

"You thought I'd shoot you!" He lifted to his feet and threw his hands in the air. His face felt hot and his fingers tingled. He could not remember ever being this angry. His indignation beat inside him with his pounding heart.

She lifted her chin and set her jaw, waiting.

His voice emerged between clenched teeth. "I don't like being used."

She held her ground against his indignation. "It's a homicide investigation that includes six kidnappings."

He was shaking his head in a slow, steady beat, as if he'd stopped listening. Then he turned away and began pacing back and forth across the narrow kitchen like a criminal in lockup. "Jake's been avoiding me. I've left messages. He wasn't allowed to talk to me. Is that right?"

"I'm sure he was warned not to do so."

"Ty?"

"He's up to his neck. His involvement is contradictory. But I know he is under investigation."

Ava was very confused by Ty Redhorse's behavior. It almost seemed as if he wanted to appear to be in the gang but help the police. It seemed that he had picked his brothers over the gang on at least two occasions.

Kee rose from the chair, stumbled the three steps to the couch and fell back into the cushions. Ava tracked him, her hand going to the warm, familiar grip of her gun. He sat and Ava waited.

"This can't be happening," said Kee.

She almost felt sorry for him. Then she recalled what Lori had told her of Kacey's captivity, months in a basement with a mattress on the floor. Kacey had escaped while in active labor and she'd been very lucky to make it to her rez and to a man capable of defending her. Whatever Colt's mental health issues, he was a protector. Kacey's decision to try to lure the Russians into recapturing her had not led to finding her friends, as she had hoped. But it did lead to the FBI finding another group of imprisoned women. Unfortunately, her decision to leave protection also drew Ty into the middle of a bad situation. Ava suspected that the tribe's gang had sent Ty to recover her because as her boyfriend's brother, Kacey might trust him. What she had not figured out was if Ty was working with the gang to recapture Kacey or with Colt to recover her.

Kee sat with his head in his hands and Ava resisted the urge to go and sit beside him. Comfort him. The urge was so overwhelming she had to fold her arms over her chest and move in the opposite direction. That brought her to the short kitchen counter adjacent to the couch.

At last he lifted his head. His eyes were now bloodshot and he seemed like a man who had just received word of a death in the family. Grief deepened the lines about his mouth and gave his eyes a lost quality.

"Kee?"

"I don't believe this. I don't believe you. Hector is a good man."

"Perhaps in some ways."

"You said it is him or me. I know it's not me. So you want me to believe that the man who changed my life, gave me two straight legs, encouraged me, pushed me and helped me to become a physician—you want me to believe that that man is capable of...of this?" He pinched his eyes shut and gripped the bridge of his nose with a thumb and forefinger.

Ava struggled not to go to him, comfort him. Instead she focused on controlling the tightness in her chest as it moved to her stomach. "Yes."

She lifted her hand to him but he stepped out of her reach. She let her hand drop back to her side. He had every right to be angry and upset. She'd just kicked a hole in his perceptions. It would take time to come to grips with everything she had hit him with. She wondered if he would ever forgive her.

"But why? Why would anyone do such a thing?"

She blew away a breath but failed to control the internal turmoil caused by his upset. "Most crimes fall into three categories: rage, revenge or money."

"He doesn't have a lot of money," Kee argued.

"He has a clinic."

Kee sat back, confusion now furrowing his brow. "What?"

"You said he built it from the ground up. You said you have a facility to rival any like it. How did that happen without money?"

"The tribe…the casino…" He shook his head, bewildered.

"Nope. Tribal budget lists zero operating budget for your clinic. Operational budget comes from federal subsidies and grants."

"That's impossible," he whispered.

"Exactly."

He stared at her as if seeing her for the first time. His arms lay limp at his sides as if all the life had drained out of him. Would he give up or fight?

"You could help me, Kee. You're a good guy. I know you want the truth. You could help us get those girls back home to their families."

"Which girls do you suspect have been taken? Tell me the girl's names."

She listed them in order of disappearance. "Elsie Weaver, November; Marta Garcia, February; Kacey Doka, February; Brenda Espinoza, May; Maggie Kesselman, September; and my niece, Louisa Tah, October second. She's sixteen by the way."

His head sunk. "I know their families. They don't miss them."

"What's that supposed to mean?" she asked.

He gave her a hard stare. "Let's take your sister, Sara. She didn't file a missing person's report. The school did. Noted that Louisa was absent and checked her home. She'd been missing for days."

Now it was Ava's jaw swung open and she staggered back. Her hands clamped over her heart, which squeezed painfully. Her throat burned and she feared for a moment she would cry. Somehow she forced her words past her constricted throat. "How many days?"

"I don't know. Three. Four. The point is, how do you not notice your daughter not coming home?"

Ava had no answer. She felt her insides churn with outrage and disbelief. How could Sara have ignored her own daughter's welfare? She tried to think past the pain. "Maybe that is how they were chosen. Hector picked girls from troubled families."

Kee rose to his feet. "Stop talking about him as if he's guilty."

So, he was going to fight. Fight for the man he trusted and loved. She could work with that.

"Are you a detective at Saguaro Flats?"

"Suspended," she said.

"Because of this?"

She gave a slow nod.

He looked to someplace beyond her, his gaze going out of focus. "My mom is fostering the Doka girls."

She knew that and thought it was both the kind and right thing to do.

"Those are Kacey's sisters."

"That's another thing. Those girls are your family now because Kacey and Colt are married."

He cradled his chin in his palm and braced his elbow in

the cup of his other hand. He looked as if he had a tooth-ache instead of a heartache. If he was innocent, she had just dropped another bomb in the epicenter of his world.

His eyes were watery as he stared at the floor. He did not look like a man caught in a web of lies. He looked like one who had just found that his foundation was made of sand.

He lifted his gaze to meet hers. His fingers brushed over his lips and settled on the opposite side, the pads curling under his jaw.

"All this, Colt, Day's death, Ty's involvement, even the clinic connection with the missing women, all this has been going on right under my nose because I've been too damn buried in work to notice. That's what you are saying."

"I'm sorry, Kee." She stood and came to perch on the arm of the couch opposite him. "Sometimes it's hardest to see what is right in front of you."

His hand dropped, folding protectively over his chest. "I've been killing myself at the clinic. Killing myself to pay the bills. Until yesterday, I was beating myself up be-cause I thought I had to leave here in order to stay afloat, and then a miracle happened that enabled me to stay, to make a difference. I've been so busy burning the candle at both ends trying to make good that I haven't given the missing girls the attention they deserved. Hell, I don't even know what's going on with my own family." He blew out a breath, his frustration evident. "I thought I was a part of something great. You're telling me it's all twisted. Rotten."

"It appears so to me."

"Then I want to know what is happening. What is re-ally happening. Not your theory or whatever. I want solid proof that what you theorize is true."

"I can work with that. Shall we go have a look at Day's room together?"

Chapter Eleven

Ava drove the short distance from Kee's trailer to her sister's. The first thing she noticed was that the lights were out and Sara's car was gone. Had something happened to them?

Ava threw open the door as panic washed through her, and she ran to the door, finding it unlocked. A quick check inside showed that all three girls were asleep in their beds but their mother was not in the trailer. Ava stormed back to the kitchen and caught the glint of an empty liquor bottle on the counter and another in the trash. She reached the kitchen sink and gripped the bottle as the rage thundered inside her.

Had Sara seriously left these girls alone here?

She was reaching for her phone when headlights flashed around the room and then went out. Ava watched Sara exit the car, holding a bag in one hand as she walked toward the entrance. She touched the hood of the car three times on her slow journey. A moment later the doorknob turned ever so slowly. Ava waited. When Sara was halfway to the kitchen, Ava flicked on the light. Sara gasped and jumped. Then she clutched the brown bag to her chest. Ava recognized the size and shape. It was a liquor bottle. The extra large sort, and Sara clutched the neck in one fist and cradled the bottom in the other.

"Ava. What are you doing here?"

Was she serious? Hadn't Sara even seen her car?

"I thought you were on a date."

"You left them alone," said Ava, her voice a growl.

Sara waved a dismissive hand and chuckled. "Just for a few minutes. They're fine."

"Is Louisa fine?"

Sara's smile dropped. She teetered and then sidestepped before regaining her balance.

"What do you mean?" said Sara, still clutching her bottle.

"You didn't even know she was missing."

"Yes, I did."

"When did you see her last?"

"Sunday, I think. Day before the school called."

"And she was out all night?"

Sara's chin fell. The arm holding the liquor dropped to her side as she pressed her opposite hand to her forehead.

"Maybe it was Saturday I saw her."

Ava rocked back against the counter. "Which was it?"

Sara lifted her eyes to meet Ava's and those eyes were bloodshot and filling with tears.

Her words were a wail. "I don't know."

Ava almost went to her. Almost took her in her arms. She took a step in that direction and then she stopped, spun and threw the empty bottle she held into the trash on top of the other with enough force to shatter both. Then she rounded on Sara. "Give me that bottle."

Sara did. Ava dumped the contents down the drain.

GOING TO WORK on Thursday was harder than taking the medical boards. How did one act around a mentor that had overnight become a stranger? Kee's main tactic was avoidance.

Something bad was happening here. Last night they'd discovered a file with print copies of emails Richard had written to his FEMA supervisors regarding Dr. Hauser's refusal to allow him to input his medical data or allow him access to the clinic's records. That in itself was exceedingly odd. But it got worse.

Ava had been right. Kee was listed as the attending physician for each of the missing girls' visits and "his" notes on each visit were included. They looked for all the world as if he had written them. But he knew he had not.

It was as if he had woken up this morning in a parallel universe where everything looked the same but was badly and dangerously different. There was physical pain at learning that the man he so respected and admired had used him. Betrayal mixed with a sense of his own failures to make it hard to think.

Somehow he struggled through the day and left the clinic early that evening. Mills and Hauser were still there and waved him out, promising to lock up. Why did their smiles no longer seem to meet their eyes?

Kee drove to his mother's place for dinner. Housing was tight now in Piñon Flats as the tribe returned to their homes and the FEMA trailers were being reclaimed. His trailer was scheduled for pickup tomorrow, so he had been there to remove his gear. Richard's personal belongings had already been boxed and shipped to his family. Kee supposed he could sleep there tonight but now that he suspected Richard had been murdered, he just didn't feel comfortable there. Instead, he'd be sleeping on his mother's couch until he could make other arrangements.

He needed his own place because of the Doka girls now fostered at his childhood home. Two of them were staying in the room that had once belonged to Colt and Jake. The other girl was sharing his sister Abbie's room.

Where was Ava tonight? Was she working on the Day case or something else? Ava was the first woman he'd taken notice of in years. He didn't know what made him feel more furious, that she'd used him or the recognition that, even knowing what she had done, he still cared what she was doing. He reached for the door, which was never locked, and paused as he noticed his hand was shaking. He squeezed his fingers into a fist and swallowed down the lump in his throat. After several deep breaths, the tightness in his chest eased and he let himself into his mom's entryway.

Ava had used him. Still, he would hand over the medical records that could get him fired or possibly cost him his license to practice medicine.

His mother knew something was wrong with him at first glance. She was perceptive that way. After the girls were all in their rooms for the night, he sat with her at her kitchen table, automatically taking the seat he had used during his growing-up years.

"I heard about Dr. Day," she said, guessing at the reason he was upset and guessing correctly, in part.

"Yes, it's a blow." He looked at his mother and wondered if he knew her at all. "You didn't tell me about Colt being in witness protection."

Her inhalation was sharp. "Did Ty tell you?"

Kee shook his head. "Can't say where I heard."

"I was going to tell you, Kee. Despite what Ty told me."

"What did he say?"

"Not too much. That you could get in trouble or worse, get hurt. But I was going to tell you. It all happened so fast and you haven't been around much since the dam break."

"You could call me, Mom."

She shook her head. "Not the kind of thing I can say on the phone."

"All right. So where's Colt?"

His mom leaned in and lowered her voice to a whisper. "We're not supposed to know. It's witness protection and they just up and take them someplace where they don't know a soul and we can't contact him and he can't call or write. It's how they keep them safe. But Ty followed him. He's always looked out for his baby brother and I feel better knowing."

"Where?"

"Kenai, Alaska. Colt is some kind of commercial fisherman."

"And he's married?"

"Yes. I was at the wedding and so was Ty. The ceremony was at the compound just last week. Don't feel bad. Jake missed it, too."

"But he at least knew about it."

His mother pressed her hands flat on her worn tabletop. "Jake explained everything to me. He said you couldn't be seen there because you were undercover at the clinic."

Kee's brows lifted. *Undercover?* Was that Jake's way of protecting their mom from the truth that he was a suspect in a surrogate baby ring?

"He told you that?" Kee told his mom about Ava and how she had hacked his computer, broken at least a dozen laws and found Richard's body.

"You could have her arrested."

"Seems that way."

"So why don't you turn her in?"

He leaned forward, resting his elbows on his knees and lacing his fingers together. "Because I think she may be right that the disappearances of our girls is somehow connected to our clinic."

"That can't be. Can it?" asked his mother.

Kee cleared his throat. "I don't even know anymore."

"All you kids were treated by Dr. Hauser. I trusted him with each one of you. He treated every illness and stitched you all up more than once. And your legs, well, I can't ever repay him for that. How could he do something like this?"

Kee had no answer.

His mother gasped. "He just gave Abbie her sports physical for volleyball."

Kee felt an instant surge of fury. His pulse pounded in his ears and he clenched his fists. If Dr. Hauser had harmed his sister...

"Maybe your cop lady's just wrong about everything," said his mom.

"I hope so. But I know that Lori thinks so and Ava is certain. She doesn't have the proof yet."

"Our Lori?" asked his mother.

"Yes. Jake's Lori. She found something. Now I've seen it, too. All the girls were seen at our clinic only days before they vanished."

"A coincidence?" asked his mother, but her expression had changed from disbelief to one of worry.

"I sure hope so."

The silence was broken only by the occasional thumping from the bedroom followed by the giggle of girls who were not sleeping.

"It's like a slumber party here every night," said his mom.

"They happy here?"

"Seem to be. They ask about their mother and what's going to happen."

Kee knew that the foster girls' mother had been arrested on drug charges and not for the first time. This time it was more serious because she had been caught with quantities that meant she was either dealing or transporting illegal substances. She likely would do federal time.

"They miss their big sister, Kacey. She practically raised them, with her mother gone and now we know where. Delivering drugs." His mother made a tsking sound. "The youngest, Shirley, still steals food."

"Steals?" he asked.

"She's still not quite sure there will be a next meal."

Kee's heart broke at the news. "So what do you do?"

"Let her steal it, if it makes her feel better. She'll get over it in time. Being hungry is hard and it isn't something you can just get past because someone says so."

Kee had never been that hungry. Even when their father had been in jail or off for weeks at a time, his mother always had a meal on the table. He wondered now how she had managed.

"Abbie and Shirley are becoming best friends, though Winnie is closer to her age."

"I'm glad they have you, Mom."

She flushed and smiled, waving away the compliment as if keeping three more girls fed and safe and loved was no big deal.

"How's your leg?" he asked. His mom had diabetes and was recovering from an open wound on her ankle where she'd nicked the coffee table.

"All healed. They got me wearing special stockings now. But don't change the subject. You said two reasons for not having her arrested and you gave me one. What's the other?"

Now Kee flushed.

"Oh, I see. You like her, despite the fact that she was playing you."

"That's about it."

"You got anything to be ashamed of, son?"

He looked startled and felt about fifteen again. He met her gaze.

"Kee?"

"No, ma'am."

"Well, then she'll figure that out eventually. And you can't blame her for protecting her own. Think what you'd be prepared to do if Abbie went missing."

That thought made his stomach frost and caused a pain in his heart. What had Ava been going through?

"You're right," he answered. "But I think her interest in me centers on her investigation."

"Maybe it did. But now that she's met you, her interests might change."

She rose heavily from her seat, using her arms and the armrests to help hoist her upright. Then she shuffled over to him, stooped to kiss his forehead. "Good night, son. Thank you for giving up your bedroom for the girls."

Kee followed her as far as the living room and watched her slow progress down the hall. His mother had raised all her children, except his little sister, who was still under her roof. Now she also had three foster girls and he wondered if it might be too much.

He settled on the couch, slipping between the folded blanket and sheet on the sagging cushions that had barely survived the raising of four hopping, bouncing boys. He closed his eyes, certain that he would not sleep. He thought of Ava and all she had told him. His mother was right. She had a duty to look for her niece and if that meant lying to him, he could at least understand the whys of it. Even if he didn't like it.

The following morning he was up, washed and dressed as the girls poured into the kitchen for breakfast. He knew that he did not want to be stuck in line for the bathroom behind four girls.

His mother kissed him goodbye and whispered that he should be careful. Because of his early departure, he had time to walk down by the river before the clinic opened and speak to Jake, who was on traffic duty there again.

Most of the residents of Piñon Flats were returning today and some were making several trips with pickups hastily packed. Traffic was heavy. Kee pulled his pickup to the shoulder and stood in the road with Jake, who was acting as a human stop signal in a place that never needed one until today.

"Hey, big brother," said Jake. "How are things?"

He was tempted to tell him exactly how things were but instead he stuck to the purpose of his visit. He wasn't all right. And things had never been worse.

"Do you know Ava Hood?" he asked.

Jake kept his attention on his work but he nodded. "She's our new hire."

A truck rolled past and Jake stopped the next one, motioning for the perpendicular lane of traffic to proceed.

"Have you seen her?"

Jake shook his head. "Never met."

"Did you know she's up here investigating my clinic?"

"Where'd you hear that?"

"From her." Kee quickly told him what Ava had shared.

"I can't really talk about this, Kee. You understand?" Another line of vehicles rolled past, some with their windows down and the driver's elbows resting on the open window frames. Most waved or called a greeting. He stopped the line for the arrival of a huge dump truck and their conversation resumed.

"I gave her access to the records of each girl's visit. The visits all have my name on them."

Jake's arms dropped. "They do?"

"But I didn't see them. I don't understand. He said he wants me to follow his footsteps and take over our clinic one day. Then he implicates me."

"Maybe he was hoping to include you in his illegal activities, too."

"I would never…"

"So when things started to get hot and he had to choose him or you, well…"

Kee grimaced.

"He couldn't use Day's name. He wasn't here long enough to be involved."

Jake's rational made him feel simultaneously better and worse.

"According to Ava, Lori figured out the connection when you were investigating the missing girls. Why did they give you that assignment? You're first year. A rookie."

"I can't talk about cases with you. But I can say that I took on extra responsibilities when Jack Bear Den was handling the eco-extremists attack on the dam case and the evacuation. So I was asked to interview a few families and responded to a few calls that normally would have been his. I'd been out to see most of the families before the girls went missing, on escort with protective services or for disturbance calls. Big families, single-parent families." Jake began waving traffic forward again, his arms sweeping in graceful circles.

"Did your daughter arrive in your care before or after this?"

"Kee, you need to be careful. If you think something is happening at your clinic, you should go to Tinnin or Bear Den."

"Is Ty in trouble?"

"Yes."

"What kind?"

"I can't say."

"Damn it, Jake."

The dump truck made it off the road and into the construction site. Jake waved on the waiting traffic.

He cast Kee a pained look as his hand continued a rhythmic sweep. "He took Kacey…" He shook his head. "She wanted to be taken and they sent Ty."

"Who?"

Jake gave him an exasperated look and his hand waved faster. Kee wasn't sure if he was impatient for the traffic to move or with his big brother.

"The gang?"

"I'm not sure if wanted is the right way of saying it. Ty told Kacey that Colt sent him and Colt *was* there when she arrived."

"But…?"

"Kacey went to our clinic to be captured. You understand? She showed up and was picked up again right on our rez. Evidence leads us to believe Ty was the pickup man and Kacey's statement corroborates. Only reason he's not in jail is that in Colt's statement—" Jake stopped. "I can't talk about this. Point is, we couldn't find the others and Kacey hoped to lead the FBI to the new location where her friends had been taken because they moved them after she escaped."

"So was Ty helping her or helping the gang?"

"That's the question. Maybe both." Jake pushed his cowboy hat back on his head, making him look younger and less intimidating.

"And Ty was the pickup man?" asked Kee.

"Kacey knew him. Colt's big brother. He'd be the logical one for the Wolf Posse to send because she'd trust him. Get in the car with him."

"But she wanted to be captured?" Kee said, echoing Jake's words.

"The Wolf Posse couldn't have known that," said Jake as traffic continued to roll past, referring to the tribe's gang.

"True," Kee said.

More vehicles rolled by. Several called a greeting in Tonto.

"Listen, I'll tell you something else about Ty. The only reason I'm not dead is because he knew that the gang sent two kidnappers after us. To get Fortune, you understand? He was there. He and Hemi…you know Hemi?"

"Hemi also found Richard's body."

"I heard that."

"I didn't know any of this. I'm sorry, Jake, that I wasn't there for you."

Jake looked at Kee. "Are you mixed up in this, Kee?"

"No. I swear."

"I'll help you all I can. Be careful at work. I'm sure that someone killed your coworker."

Jake hugged him and then Kee headed back to his truck more troubled than he had been since his father's sentencing.

Kee had played by every rule and guarded his reputation fiercely, and yet he still found himself implicated. How could something like this happen?

Chapter Twelve

Despite Kee's detour, he made it to the clinic nearly forty-five minutes early. He pulled his truck behind the building, parking in his usual place before tribal headquarters. He liked this spot because it had shade all day from the large pines planted long ago. It did require him to walk across the road that divided the two buildings, behind the women's health wing windows and around the side of the building where he usually entered through the women's clinic entrance, or, if he arrived before the clinic opened, through the break-room-side entrance beyond. As he rounded the corner to the break room, he spotted an unfamiliar black dually pickup with Arizona plates pull up on the sidewalk.

Hector emerged from the clinic's break room door followed by Betty, who carried something in her hands. Kee paused as he wondered what was going on.

Hector and Betty stood not ten feet away from Kee as a white man exited the truck. The man was thin and muscular and wore motorcycle boots, jeans and a green T-shirt. His short brown hair seemed vaguely military in style. His arms were covered from his sleeve to his wrist with blue-black tattoos including circular bands on each bicep depicting a linked chain punctuated by a skull design. A tattooed dagger dripping blood appeared to pass from one side of his clavicle, through his neck, and emerge out the other. He also had a long series of gouges on his right arm that dripped pus.

Hauser was speaking to the man and handed over what Kee recognized as a Z-pak. Zithromax was an antibiotic used to treat bacterial infections like the ones on the man's arms. But this clinic only treated tribe members. There was something off about this and all Ava's suppositions about his clinic rose up in his mind.

The man glanced up, spotted Kee and reached behind him. Kee had the distinct feeling he was going for a gun. Kee called out to Hector. "Need any help?"

Betty spun about and Hauser glanced over his shoulder at Kee and then pressed a hand to the man's forearm, speaking in a tone too low for Kee to hear. Then he smiled at Kee.

"Kee, my boy." Then he turned to Betty. "See to him, will you?"

Betty dropped the gauze roll into Hector's hand before hurrying across the sidewalk to intercept Kee.

"What's going on?" asked Kee.

"The guy was sent over by FEMA. One of the construction workers."

"Why isn't he inside?"

"Because he refused to come in. Claustrophobic or afraid of hospitals. Who knows?" She tossed up her hands and retrieved the key she had on a pink plastic spiral bracelet. She unlocked the women's clinic doors and shooed him inside. "Glad to get away from him. He gives me the creeps."

She followed him inside and breathed a sigh of relief, then locked the door. Then she peered out. "You think Hector will be all right?"

Kee stood beside Betty but he could no longer see the patient. "You want me to go out?"

A moment later the truck roared past. The man turned to fix Kee with a hard look through the clinic windows.

"See, he's loco," said Betty and then turned to him. "You're here awful early."

"Trying to beat the Doka girls to the bathroom."

Betty laughed. "That's right. You've moved back home again. Want me to make some calls? See if I can get you something temporary?"

"That would be great."

She patted his arm, making her gold bracelets chime, and then headed toward her office at the main reception area in the urgent care wing of their clinic.

It wasn't until he was halfway back to the break room that he recalled what Ava had said the evening they found Day's body. That his death was no accident and there was blood and skin under Day's nails.

Hauser said that all the injuries were consistent with a fall. But if Ava was right, then this man, the one with the tattoos, could be the one who pushed Richard off that cliff.

He pondered the wounds he had seen on the stranger's arms. Long gouges. Kee curled his fingers into a claw and imagined raking it down a man's arm. Yes, that was what they'd look like.

Kee stood frozen in the hallway. Should he tell Ava or call his brother Jake?

He lifted his phone and dialed Ava.

"What did he look like?" she asked.

He described the man in as much detail as he could.

"Describe the tattoos again."

He did.

"We have a database for tattoos. Let me make a call and see what I can come up with."

"Ava, if it is Hector and he has your name, that guy might come after you next."

There was silence on the line. Was that her plan all along, to use herself as bait?

"What can I do to help?"

"Treat your patients, Kee, and don't do anything that would alert Hauser that you are suspicious."

That was certainly easier said than done.

"And text me when you are done. I want to meet you somewhere private."

"We have a tribal compound. It's private."

"Okay. Just tell me how to get there."

BETTY SPOKE TO Hector from her seat at the receptionist desk between patients who were waiting beyond the glass partition or scribbling in the boxes on their forms.

"You remember I set a trigger after Kacey Doka showed up, to see if anyone accessed her file or any of the packages we sent over?" she asked.

"Yes." He wasn't as good as Betty at keeping the worry from showing. Since Kacey Doka had escaped they'd been in defense mode. They had two more "packages" ready, but knew they'd both be missed now that tribal police suspected that the runaways were actually abducted. What would happen when they figured out they were pregnant?

"Well, it went off."

Turning her attention back to her receptionist duties, Betty smiled at Mr. Imperius, who slid the clipboard through the slot. "Thank you, Andy. It will be just a few more minutes." She held that smile until Andy turned his back and lumbered back to his chair. She followed him with her eyes. "His color isn't good."

"What about the trigger? Who was it?" asked Hector.

Betty spun to face him and gave him the name.

"Kee Redhorse."

Hector's jaw dropped. "No."

"I've already made the call."

"No. Let's wait a minute. It could be…"

She rested a hand on his and gave a squeeze, bringing his attention back to her. Her dark eyes met his.

"There's no mistake. Avangeline Yokota is a detective,

she found Richard's body and now she's gotten Kee to log in to our system."

"But you can't see anything there. It's just appointments."

"It's enough. Kee knows he didn't treat those girls. I'll call Yury. He'll take care of it."

Hector rocked forward and only just caught himself on his knuckles, cracking the clipboard beneath his fist.

"Like he took care of Day?" whispered Hauser. "They took tissue samples from Day. I couldn't stop them. They have Yury's physical evidence."

"So they'll have a suspect."

"A Russian mobster. He's been in prison. Why would he push Day?"

"It doesn't matter as long as it doesn't come back to us. He's an outsider. Plus he'll never betray his bosses. That would be suicide."

"Kee." Hauser shook his head.

"Who knows what he's been doing?" said Betty. "I know for a fact that he saw me with at least one pregnancy test," said Betty. "Back in February with Marta Garcia, and I am not sure that he bought my story that it was standard for us to take this precaution in young women with certain markers in their medical history. He'll think back on that. If he knows we are involved with the missing girls, he might figure it out. Plus he saw Yury outside this morning."

He laid a hand on her shoulder. "Yury pushing Day. It's made it worse. Now we have a detective sniffing around. Kee saw him, and Louisa is the detective's niece. He might do something to point to us."

"The only one who has seen him with us is Kee."

"This is bad." He started to pace.

"Hector," she hissed. "You have patients. I called Yury again. Don't worry."

"But Kee. He's not involved."

"He is now. She's using him to get to us. You know that."

"But Kee. I've been grooming him."

"Hector, it's your life's work. Your legacy. Remember that."

"Excuse me?" said a female voice at the window counter.

Betty turned to face Lucinda Olive, a warm smile fixed on her face. Lucinda was full-blood Apache, spoke the language perfectly and held her young feverish son in her arms.

"Uriah is feeling like he might be sick."

Betty rose. "Well, that makes two of you."

"What?" said Lucinda.

"Bring him in, dear. Dr. Hauser will see him right away."

AVA CALLED KEE from the parking lot of tribal headquarters, right next to the clinic.

"I've got information on the tattoos you saw and some images. They photograph prisoners and their tattoos. Have you got a minute to come out and see me?"

Kee had patients waiting but he headed for the break room and then stepped out the back to meet Ava, who sat in her Chevy with the laptop booted up. He slipped into the passenger seat.

"I don't want them to know I'm gone."

"I'll be quick. I have them narrowed down."

She placed the laptop between them and began flicking through photos of neck tattoos.

"No," he said to the first and the next three she showed him. On the fourth he pointed. "That's it. It looked like this."

"Exactly like it or similar?"

"Seems the same."

She regained possession of the laptop and clicked away.

"That particular tattoo is favored by Russian mobsters. It means he is a hired killer. It's like a billboard advertising his specialty."

"Doesn't that make him easier to catch?" asked Kee.

"Unfortunately tattoos like this are just indicators, not evidence."

She placed the laptop between them again, showing him several other tattoos.

"I didn't see his hands or...what is that, his back?"

She clicked to the next photo. There, looking out at him with a face filled with sullen rage was a white man with his head shaved, square jaw lifted and neck tattoo clearly visible.

"That's him."

"You sure?"

"A hundred percent."

She glanced at the screen, scanning. "His name is Yury Churkin. He works for Leonard Usov, who is his Avtoritet, or authority, like a captain. They both belong to the Kuznetsov crime family out of Atlanta. Narcotics, money laundering and human trafficking. They run strip clubs and various businesses catering to the hospitality business."

"Hospitality?" asked Kee.

"Prostitution."

"Usov likely runs all the kidnapping rings in this region. Churkin is just muscle. A killer. He was here for Day. I still don't know why. But I need you to get Betty away from her office for a few minutes so I can get my camera and take a look at the footage."

"What footage?"

"I placed a camera above her computer so I can grab her passwords. It's been running all day."

Kee gaped. "You broke in?"

"Actually one of the nurses let me in. It was easy to tape the door so I could get back in after she went back to the nursery."

"That's breaking and entering."

"It sure is. So, can you get me into the clinic later so I can access her computer?"

Kee's jaw hardened. "I'm not sure how to do that. Betty stays pretty close to her desk. Even eats lunch there."

"Do you have any patients in the women's health clinic?"

"Not today. The one newborn has gone home with her family."

"So all patients are in the reception area or exam rooms?"

He nodded.

"What about a fire alarm?"

Kee went pale. "You want me to pull a false alarm?"

"Yes. Or get me inside and I'll pull it."

He blinked at her and then scrubbed his hand over his mouth. He spoke more to himself than to her. "It's against the law."

"So is kidnapping young women."

"You're going with the ends justifying the means. Is that it?" he challenged.

"Whatever gets that alarm pulled," she countered.

He met her gaze and she waited as the seconds ticked and he battled with his conscience. "You saw Churkin. You saw the scratches. You saw Day's body. Kee, this is happening right here at your clinic."

"I could call Jake or the chief."

"It could take them weeks to get what I can in a few minutes."

"Because they'll do it legally."

Her searing gaze never wavered. "They have my niece."

He sighed, knowing he was going to help her even as his inner rule-follower screamed *don't!* "I'll get you in the break room. Then I'll pull the alarm. But only after I am sure there are no patients in the exam rooms and no one will get hurt."

She looked impressed. "Sounds good."

"When?"

"Now."

Chapter Thirteen

Ava slipped into the break room and waited as Kee continued on out into the corridor. Had she convinced him? Did he now see what she saw? It hurt her to know that she had caused him to see just what was happening here, but she was relieved to know that Kee was not involved.

Unless he was playing her and now she was here in the break room with no backup and just her personal service weapon. She thought of the Russian, Yury Churkin. The man was a cold-blooded killer and even with all her training, she would not want to face him. Ava glanced toward the door, considering escape. Why had she trusted Kee? She knew better than to rely on anyone.

She shouldn't let her physical reaction to Kee sway her. Shouldn't let her breath catch or her heart ache. Shouldn't have to battle the urge to stroke his broad chest or notice the way the concern caused a deep line to form between his brows.

Every time she was near him, Ava took the opportunity to breathe in his rich, enticing scent. Kee smelled of mint and some exotic earthy fragrance like teak. There were traces of him here still in the air all about her. She was losing her battle not to touch him every time she got near him.

She hovered by the window, considering escape as the minutes dragged by endlessly.

When the siren sounded she exhaled a long breath and

stared at the ceiling. It was so hard not knowing whom to trust.

He'd done it. The doctor who played all things by the rules had just pulled a false alarm in his clinic. Kee ducked his head into the room and nodded.

"All clear."

She walked quickly down the hall, passing Radiology, and then turned left to the lobby and the reception area. Betty Mills's office. It was locked. The woman had locked the door behind her upon leaving. Smart. That move only made Ava more certain about Mills. Ava stared up at the one smoke detector beyond the glass partition that was not sounding because it was not a detector, but did hold a tiny camera pointing straight down at Betty's keyboard. She had activated it remotely this morning as Betty arrived.

Ava used her locksmith kit to work on the door. It was a simple latch with no deadbolt. Relatively easy to pick, except her heart was hammering and her hand shook. The volunteer fire department was right next to tribal police and would be here any second. She heard the tumblers click at the same time she heard the front door open.

She ducked inside and closed the door, using the wall between the lobby and this office as cover as the fire department crew entered. She heard them moving down the hall and away from her position. She calculated it would take them only a few minutes to check each room for smoke.

Ava was quick as a cat as she leaped up onto Betty's desk. She yanked the detector down and tossed it in her bag. Then she headed out of the office, pressing the lock button before drawing the door softly closed. She followed the route the men would have taken, planning to stay behind them. Down the hall past Hauser's office she went, turning at exam room number one and the supply closet, where she turned right. She made it to the end of the next short hall and faced the procedure room. The men had already passed Radiology and were heading to the women's health clinic when Ava ducked out the door that led to a courtyard and tribal headquarters and right into Chief Wallace Tinnin.

"Just the person I was looking for," said the chief.

Tinnin stood with hands on his crutch grips, his chin dipped and his brows lifted, giving her a look from under the brim of his cowboy hat that one might cast an unmanageable child. She could almost see the storm clouds forming over his head.

"I'm going to need you to come with me."

She followed him across the courtyard and into the side entrance of tribal headquarters. She trailed behind him down the corridor, the extra weight of the smoke detector heavy in her bag. He clicked slowly along on the crutches. So she took the opportunity to open the detector and remove the camera and SIM card. These she slipped into her bra. If he was arresting her, then it wouldn't make any difference. She knew that Chief Tinnin would not use the information on the recorder to break into Betty Mills's computer because he followed the letter of the law and she had not completely ruled out the possibly that he was working with the clinic. But she was leaning toward taking him at face value. Tinnin appeared to be a good man and good cop who was overworked and understaffed.

He opened the door to the squad room and she marched past Carol Dorset, the dispatcher. The woman lifted her penciled eyebrows at Ava and returned to her call, taking down an address in a log.

She walked before the chief past the four desks, only one of which was occupied by Detective Jack Bear Den, who rose as she passed. He spoke to the chief.

"You found her."

"Wasn't hard. Just followed the sounds of sirens."

The two men waited for her to enter the chief's office. Tinnin rounded his ancient desk and motioned to the wooden chair. Bear Den closed the door with a snap and stood behind her.

At least she wasn't in the single interrogation room... yet.

Behind Tinnin on the full bookshelf were rows of empty moving boxes. His desk was clear except for the phone, computer and a rusty spur atop a stack of files. She narrowed her eyes on the object that seemed to belong in a scrap heap.

"You pull that alarm?" asked Tinnin.

"No, sir."

"You know who did?"

She said nothing. Tinnin's mouth tipped down at both corners.

He took off his hat, threw it to the coatrack and missed. He swore and lifted the hat from the floor with his crutch and lowered it to the hook. Then he took a seat.

"We have the autopsy reports."

"Reports? Plural?"

"Yes, ma'am. First is from Hauser." He retrieved a page from a file and set the report before her, turning it to face her. "Says accidental death as a result of a fall."

She lifted her brows. "But what caused the fall?"

"Hauser doesn't speculate. But he also did not note the blood and skin cells under the deceased person's nails. You noted them in the dark, I recall."

"You have samples?" she asked.

"The ME took them before Hauser arrived." Tinnin nodded. "Do you have any?"

"No, sir."

"The FBI is expediting the test results. Nothing yet. I'm listing the death as a homicide, but not making that public knowledge."

It was not the sort of thing a police chief would tell someone if he was involved in a cover-up. Was he collaborating with her?

"I see."

"You wondering why I'm letting you run around loose on my rez?"

"It occurred to me."

"Because you're doing what I can't. I'm sure you'll lose your badge. That's the best outcome. But in the meantime, if you don't get killed, you might just find me something I can use."

She already had. The tissue sample the ME collected was hard evidence that Day had not fallen.

Her phone chimed. She glanced at the screen to the text from Kee.

Where are u?

Did u get it?

She texted back.

Got it and am out. Call u later.

Tinnin watched her with a level gaze, his face revealing nothing. The fact that he did not stop her from reading or sending text messages was another point in his favor.

"Why isn't Ty Redhorse in jail?" she asked.

"On what charge?"

"He drove Kacey Doka to an isolated spot and turned her over to two men, one of whom is still in the hospital paralyzed."

"All true."

"So why isn't he in jail?"

"Because it's unclear if Ty was protecting her or kidnapping her."

"He brought her to her captors."

"Which was her intention when she left protective custody, to lead the FBI to her captors and her friends. Ty alerted his brother Colt, who called us. He and Colt took proactive action to ensure Kacey's escape."

"But then, is Ty working with the gang or with you?"

Tinnin waved away her question. "Ongoing investigation."

That was bullshit. She knew it and so did he. Whatever the reason, he wasn't telling her. And he didn't have to. She was no longer a detective working a case. She'd gone rogue and he owed her nothing. With the situation reversed, she'd have said the exact same thing.

Ava suggested, deciding to trust the chief with what she knew, "Check the tissue samples against Yury Churkin, if you can."

Tinnin opened his desk drawer and Ava braced for what he might draw from within. He hadn't taken her weapon and she planned to use it if she needed to. Detective Bear Den looked ready to do the same.

The drawer was empty. Tinnin swore and looked at the boxes on the floor. "Don't even have a damn pencil."

"Use your cell phone," said Bear Den. "Take a note there."

Tinnin drew out his phone and punched at an app, typing in the name she had offered.

"How did you get that name?" he asked.

She told them about the man that Kee had seen this morning before the clinic opened and watched Tinnin's reaction. Her best guess was that he had not known. If he was in on this, he should have.

"We don't treat outsiders," said Bear Den.

"Well, Hauser just did."

"We need to get Kee in here," said Tinnin to Bear Den.

Ava lifted a hand. "You might not want to march him into police headquarters. Maybe send his brother to talk to him. It would seem less suspicious."

Tinnin and Bear Den had a silent exchange and Bear Den nodded and left.

"Was that a yes?" she asked.

"We'll be discreet. And you be careful. Keep that pistol handy, wear your vest and call me if you see Churkin again."

"Yes, sir."

She rose and the chief gave her a long steady look.

"It's a shame because I really would have enjoyed working with you, Detective."

AFTER COMFORTING SARA, Ava had called Sara's mother-in-law and explained the situation. Sylavania Tah was a widow in her midsixties. She was extremely overweight, and suffered from numerous health issues including high blood pressure, gout and diabetes. But she did love her grandbabies, and Ava knew they would be safe with her.

Ava no longer trusted Sara alone with her kids, but she did want to help her. So on Thursday morning, after Sara had sobered up, Ava had given her sister an ultimatum. She got help or Ava would petition the tribe for custody of her girls. Ava had reminded Sara about their mother's closet drinking and the auto accident when Ava was eleven and Sara fourteen. It had caused their mom to take oxycodone for the pain and the next thing they knew, Mom was using heroin and they were in foster care.

Sara had, at least, been willing to admit she had a problem. Their mom had been in denial until she contracted Hepatitis C.

In the afternoon, Ava took Sara to her first AA meeting. Ava was not optimistic by nature but she hoped Sara could turn it around. When they got back to the trailer, they started packing, tossed all the stashed liquor in the trash and switched Sara to iced coffee. It was going to be a rough couple of days at the Tah household.

She texted Kee and asked him to call her but he sent a text back with a two-word reply.

With Patients

She helped her sister move back into her home. It took three trips from Turquoise Ridge to Piñon Flats, in two cars. Afterward, Ava helped Sara clean up until Sara went to pick up the girls at school.

The following day, Sara went food shopping in the afternoon and Ava picked up her nieces from their former school building, which had reopened today. She started dinner when she began to worry. Sara's usual schedule was to stay sober until the girls were home and then start drinking until she passed out on the sofa. But Sara wasn't home yet.

She dialed Sara's phone and got voice mail. Just before 6:30 p.m. there was a knock at the door. She thought it would be Kee, but instead found Officer Wetselline standing on the step, his face grim.

"What happened?" Ava asked.

"There's been an accident."

Chapter Fourteen

Ava waited until the girls' paternal grandmother arrived at a little past eight. Sara's mother-in-law had packed an overnight bag and was prepared to stay for a day or two but Ava assured her that she'd be back tonight.

"Just preparing. Last time I had them for nearly two weeks."

Ava's mouth gaped. "I had no idea."

Her frightened nieces wanted to know why their mother was not home.

"She's been in an accident," said Ava. "But she's all right."

"Was she sober again?" asked Alexandra, getting the words mixed up. Ava did not think a five-year-old should even have to know the difference between the words *drunk* and *sober*.

"She drove her car into a ditch. I'm going to see her now."

Margarita began to cry and her twin followed suit. Olivia gripped Ava's leg.

"You come back?" asked the three-year-old.

Ava dropped to a knee to hug her. "I will come back."

The grandmother got the girls all back to the table and Ava set out to tribal police headquarters.

When she'd come here she had thought that she was unencumbered. That she was risking her job and possibly making some moves that could land her in jail or worse. She'd accepted all those risks, even given her name to

Hauser, hoping to draw him out. But now she saw her mistake.

She wasn't free and what happened to her *did* matter, because of Sara's children. She had come here to rescue Louisa, only to discover that all of Sara's children needed a rescue. And if Ava was being targeted by Hauser, if he called in his Russian killers or the tribe's gang and something happened to Ava...what then? She would be leaving her nieces with an alcoholic mother and a grandmother who was in very poor health. Worse still, those girls gave her exactly the kind of vulnerability that could be used against her. Worse still, her enemies might attack Sara and her girls directly or try to use them against her.

What had she done?

If she could go back, she would have brought what she learned to Chief Tinnin. But now it was too late for that. The only way out was through and she prayed this did not touch Olivia, Margarita and Alexandra.

Ava called Jack Bear Den from the driveway of her sister's home. He did not diminish her worry but took what she said so seriously that it gave her chills. He agreed to stake out her sister's house until she got back. She waited thirty minutes for him to arrive before departing. She didn't like trusting the safety of her sister's family to anyone else, but the alternative of leaving them unprotected was not an option.

She reached the police station a few minutes before nine and was met by Jake Redhorse. He'd been the first on scene. He brought her to the jail cell, where Ava found Sara sound asleep on a cot, with a bandaged nose and two black eyes.

"I took her to her first AA meeting yesterday."

"Blood alcohol was 0.15. She'll be arraigned in tribal court on Monday morning. No bail until then. Ava, who's got her kids?"

"Grandmother." *And Jack Bear Den*, she thought.

Redhorse nodded. "I've called protective services. They'll be around sometime tomorrow. I don't think Sara can take care of them for a while."

"Their grandmother…"

Redhorse looked away. "How's she doing?"

"She's…ill."

"Not going to be able to handle three kids all under six. Right?"

Ava changed the subject. "What do you think Sara will get? Bail? Release on recognizance?"

Redhorse made a face. "It's not her first offense. And she's driving on a suspended license."

"What?" Ava had no idea.

"She's going to do some time. I'm guessing three months."

Now Ava looked away. "I'll take them."

But first she was going to find their older sister, Louisa.

"Tell Sara I was here. Will you?"

Redhorse nodded and showed her out.

Ava left the jail and headed out. She now had Betty's passwords and she was anxious to try them. She sent Kee a text and he called back.

"Where are you?" he asked.

The concern in his voice was the tipping point. Her throat constricted and the tears came, wetting her cheeks. She wanted to tell him about Sara and how worried she was about the safety of her nieces. She wanted to tell him that she was afraid her investigation would backfire on them and that might just kill her. Instead she told him where she was and asked him for another favor that could cost him his job.

"The break room window?" he asked.

"Yes. Just leave it cracked before you go."

"Now?"

"Yes." She held her breath, waiting for him to decide.

He'd already shared medical records with her and pulled a fire alarm to give her access to Betty's office. The fact that he would do things so contrary to his nature showed either how disturbed he was by what was happening at his workplace or how much he trusted her. Maybe both.

She couldn't get caught. If she was discovered in the building, Hauser's first suspect would be Kee.

"I'll leave it open."

"Thank you. I couldn't do this without you."

"Will I see you later?" he asked.

"Yes."

And he was gone. Ava made mental preparations.

Breaking in was impossibly simple thanks to Kee leaving the break room window unlocked and cracked enough for her to get her fingers underneath. Once inside she retraced her footsteps of earlier in the day and again picked the lock to Mills's door. Without the pressure of time, she managed the lock on the first try. She logged in to Betty's terminal a little after 10 p.m., had Betty's hard drive copied and was out the door before eleven with the flash drive in hand. With luck she'd have the files duplicated and a copy into Tinnin's hands this evening.

She made it to her car and was heading toward her sister's home when her phone chimed with an incoming call from Kee. She pulled over and picked up.

"I just heard about Sara."

"How?"

"Jake phoned me. You all right?"

"Not really. Sara is in jail."

"Where are the girls?"

"With their grandmother."

"Alone?"

"Tribal is keeping watch."

She heard Kee exhale into the speaker in a sound that seemed like relief.

"Where are you?"

"En route to Sara's place."

"I'm coming over."

Her first response was no. It was how she answered most invitations. But she discovered that she wanted Kee there with her tonight so much she ached with need.

Still, she said, "No. It's dangerous. Hauser has my name. He should have figured out who I am by now."

"If you think you are in danger, you shouldn't be there with the girls or alone."

"Tribal police is there."

"And in a few minutes, I will be, as well."

It broke her heart to say the next part. "protective services is coming tomorrow. I'd turn them over for their own safety, but I don't think they can protect them from this. I don't know where else to take them. I've made a terrible mistake."

"Call Chief Tinnin."

"Detective Bear Den is there. But they can't watch over us forever."

"His fiancée is still up here. She's FBI."

"That might work. Temporarily."

"I'm on my way to you."

Her heart gave a lurch of anticipation and squeezed as worry mingled with relief. She could count on Kee. She knew it.

"Don't. It's not safe."

Kee hung up on her. She reeled in the hurt she had no right to feel at this rejection.

AVA CONTINUED TOWARD her sister's place in Piñon Flats. She slowed as she neared the house, and pulled up beside Bear Den's unit and explained that she was ready to call the FBI for help. He called his fiancée and FBI Field Agent Sophia Rivas called her boss, an agent named Luke Forrest.

Bear Den waited out front while Ava met Sylavania at the door and explained what she knew about Sara's situation. Sara's mother-in-law had known that Sara had one DUI within the year. Everyone knew, apparently, because her mug shot had been in the tribal newspaper and, worse still, Sara had been arrested off the rez so she'd faced the Arizona county court system.

"You know I'd be pleased to take them," said Sylavania.

History repeating itself, thought Ava. Their mom had had Sara at fifteen and Ava at eighteen and then left them with their grandmother to run off to Oklahoma with some guy. Her mom hadn't returned until Ava was seven. Then she'd come home to stay with them, hiding her drinking for a while. But after Ava's grandmother died, her mom's drinking had gotten much worse.

This was exactly what Ava had been trying to prevent and here it was happening anyway.

"Wouldn't it be difficult because of your health issues?" Ava asked.

Sylavania drew her mouth into a tight line and looked away. "I'd manage."

Ava admired her spirit. "We'll talk about it tomorrow."

And tomorrow she'd tell Sylavania that the girls were in FBI protective custody. She doubted their grandmother would forgive her.

"Are you sure you don't want me to stay?"

So sure, she thought. The sooner Sylavania got home the sooner she'd be out of the crosshairs.

"I'll call if I need a break. How will that be?"

"Yes, that will work." Sylavania gathered her bag and her keys. "Speak to you tomorrow, sometime."

Sylavania took Ava's hand. "Sara and the girls are so lucky to have you."

Ava felt the stab of guilt. She'd put them in danger in

her bid to find Louisa. Now she had to get help to keep them safe.

Ava saw her out and watched the woman struggle to her car and drop into her seat. The car's springs sagged. That woman had a full heart, but Ava could see the future. She didn't want her nieces in the custody of a grandmother who would not live to see them grown. What she wanted was for her sister to get sober and take responsibility for her children. But that would be up to protective services. In the short-term, Ava meant to see that her search for Louisa did not endanger her other nieces. That meant getting Margarita, Alexandra and Olivia to safety.

Sylavania passed Bear Den as she pulled out, though she doubted the woman noticed his cruiser parked just off the road in a neighbor's drive.

Ava wanted to get to the computer records, but first she'd see her nieces safe. She did not have long to wait. Bear Den was at her door with a woman who identified herself as FBI field agent Sophia Rivas. She was a beautiful woman with an athletic build and a serious no-nonsense expression. Her clothing was practical and Ava saw she preferred a shoulder holster, as well.

They agreed to take the girls to a safe house for the night in exchange for Ava's full cooperation in the morning.

"You should come with us," said Rivas.

"I have some work."

Rivas gave her a hard look. "We could be working together, you know."

She shook her head. She knew the FBI was investigating the connection between the tribe's missing women and the Russian crime family operating out of Atlanta. They'd likely make a case, but it would take months. Months that Louisa did not have.

"You are not the only one working here. Not the only

one who cares and certainly not the only one hurt by these disappearances. It's not an excuse to go vigilante."

"Just take care of the girls."

"That I will do. And you take care of yourself, because you seem incapable of letting anyone else near you. Must be very lonely in that tower where you live."

Ava set her jaw and glared. What right did this woman have to come in here and judge her?

She showed them both back to the girls' room. Olivia did not even wake when Ava took her from her bed and set her in the car seat now in the back of Bear Den's cruiser, but Margarita and Alexandra were both scared and crying when the three girls were driven away in Bear Den's police unit. Ava could see them in the rear car seats and in her mind's eye she could see Sara and herself being driven away that first time when Mom was assigned mandatory drug rehab for the oxycodone. How had she let this happen?

She was still staring after them even though they were out of sight when a dark truck appeared on the road.

Ava switched off the light behind her and ducked down. Was it Churkin?

The truck slowed and Ava drew her weapon. With a flick of one finger she had the safety off.

The truck pulled into Sara's drive. It was not the sort of move a killer would make. Ava hazarded a quick look at the vehicle. It was an older model dark blue RAM pickup.

Kee.

Ava stood on the step as Kee stepped out of the truck. He spotted her just after rounding the hood and smiled.

"I told you not to come over," she said.

He ignored her as he closed the door with a thud.

"And I'm no better at following orders than my patients."

She hesitated, wanting so badly to run to him and throw herself into his arms.

"You're not the only one who can break the rules. And I can make up my own mind about what I choose to do. And I wanted to see you."

Up until pulling that fire alarm, Kee had not been the sort of man to color outside the lines. She liked it but she didn't want him hurt because of her.

He opened his arms to her and she threw herself against him. His arms enfolded her as she squeezed her eyes shut tight, overwhelmed at the joy that came from his strong arms around her.

"It's dangerous," she whispered. "Your being here."

"You don't want to put me in danger?"

"Of course not."

"But you're in danger."

She nodded.

"Then more reason that I'm staying."

He dropped a kiss on her forehead and then her cheek. She lifted her chin, offering her lips. The quicksilver reaction of his mouth brushing hers took her breath away. In a moment she was deepening the kiss as her heart jackhammered in her chest. He placed his hands on her shoulders and then swept them down to her lower back, bringing them together at the hip. Nothing ever felt so right. But there were too many layers of clothing between her and him. She wanted—no, needed—to feel his skin gliding over hers.

She drew back to reach for the buttons on his shirt and stopped herself. They were still standing on the stoop before her sister's house. Ava dropped her hands to her sides.

"You should go."

He never took his hungry eyes off her as he spoke. "I won't, though. So let me in or I'll camp on your front step."

Ava glanced at the street and saw nothing and no one.

She stepped aside and Kee swept past her. She followed him, locking the door behind them.

Chapter Fifteen

The familiar musical melody of his cell phone woke Hector before it could repeat. He was as used to being awakened from a sound sleep to handle medical emergencies as his wife was to sleeping through such calls. She rolled to her side and made a gurgling sound as he answered.

"This is Dr. Hauser," he said, his voice gravelly. He'd been asleep just long enough to feel dim-witted.

"Someone logged on to my terminal," said a familiar female voice.

He knew the voice immediately. It was Betty Mills calling him at home. She never called him at home. Not ever. At this time of night, all emergency calls came from the volunteer fire department. His heart was hammering as he spun to an upright position.

"Say that again?"

"My computer terminal at the clinic. Someone logged on. I just got the alert."

"What time is it?" He glanced at the table and the glowing red numbers on his bedside clock, which read 10:55. He slipped out of the bedroom and down the hall to the kitchen, one hand pressed to his forehead.

"Hector? Are you there?"

"Are you sure?" he asked.

"Yes, I'm sure!"

"What about the passwords?"

"I don't know how. But someone got in. What do we do?"

He couldn't call the police and report a break-in. That was for sure.

"It's that woman. The detective. I knew that fire alarm was something," said Betty. "I'll bet you she did something to my computer. She might be with the police right now. Oh, Hector. Should we run?"

"No. Easy, Betty. Everything is encrypted. Right?"

"Yes. That's right. No one can see the important information."

He heard her breathing in the phone receiver, fast, panting. He got excited thinking of her there in her house, in her nightgown, alone and scared.

"I'll send Churkin after Detective Yokota. He'll take care of it."

"Well, he hasn't. Has he?"

"Let me make a call. Stay home. Do not go to that clinic. It could be a trap."

"Yes, Hector. But I'm scared."

"You want me to come over?"

Ava MOTIONED HIM into the room.

"My computer is decrypting the files from Mills's computer. She had them password-protected but now that I'm in, it should be fairly simple to unlock what's inside."

"How long will that take?" He glanced at the computer on the glass table.

"It will chime when it's done." She cast him a smile that she hoped let him know what she was thinking.

Ava seemed closer to finding Louisa than ever before. Her younger nieces were safe and Kee was here with her. She felt optimistic for the first time since her arrival.

"Did you call Bear Den?" asked Kee, glancing about the empty living room.

She filled him in. Her sister's smaller girls were all

safe and someone from his tribal police was watching this house. Sara was beyond her help at the moment. Perhaps this was the kick in the behind that Sara needed to get serious about recovery. She hoped so. In the meantime, those little ones would need protecting and raising. She just didn't think their grandmother was the right one for the job.

"So we wait for your computer and see what we've got."

She smiled, liking the way he said *we*. It was ironic how her feelings had done such a 180. First she'd tried to find proof of his guilt. Now she just wanted to keep him from getting hurt. No, that wasn't all, she admitted to herself. She wanted more than his safety. But first he'd have to forgive her deceit.

Her smile faltered. "There's no *we*, Kee. I did this. It's all me and if anyone asks you, you have no idea who pulled that fire alarm."

"Did Tinnin ask you?"

"Of course. I denied it and didn't mention you. I won't, either. When this all falls apart, and it will, I want you clear. Your tribe will need you more than ever once I take down Hauser and Mills."

"Do you think anyone here will believe that I didn't know? That I wasn't involved? My innocence will play as stupidity."

She thought he might be right.

"All I know for sure is that I want this solved as badly as you do now. I don't like being used or lied to. And I am sickened by what is happening. It was so hard to see Hauser today and think that he's wearing some kind of a mask. That he could be capable of this. I still have hope that you're wrong. That someone else has done this."

"We should know soon." She could not meet his gaze when next she spoke. "Kee, I'm sorry I didn't see sooner what kind of a man you are. I regret deceiving you."

"It's part of your job. Isn't it?" he asked, his voice tight and controlled.

"It is and usually I'm fine with that. But not this time. You deserved better."

She'd only known him for a week, yet already she was beginning to trust him. It was new ground for Ava. She'd been with men before. But never one she had real feelings for because that would be too dangerous. She'd never wanted to give a man that kind of power. But now she wondered what she had missed by holding back that part of herself.

She could no longer deny that Kee wasn't like other men. He possessed a strong moral compass and seemed genuinely *good*. Growing up, she'd seen time and time again the fallout of loving the wrong man. Look at her own mother's actions. But nothing about Kee screamed *wrong man!*

She offered her hand and he took it, coming in close as he wrapped her up in his arms. She slipped into his arms and pressed against him. Kee's smile changed to something hungry as his lips parted.

"Ava?"

"Kiss me," she said.

His fingers tangled in her hair as he swooped down to take her mouth in a kiss that left her no doubt that he had crossed the point of restraint along with her. They were alone. Safe for the moment, and there was no one she needed to protect or care for.

His tongue thrust with hungry strokes, strong as the rest of him and tempting her with the promise of what he intended to do to her. She wanted it, wanted it all.

The heat and the thrill of his body pressing to hers made her pulse quicken and her breasts ache with need. She lifted one of his hands from her hip to her breast and relished the feel of his fingers splayed and kneading her wanton flesh. The strangled cry that escaped her brought an echoing growl of need from his throat.

He released her to unzip her jacket, pausing at the sight of her shoulder holster. She shucked out of the jacket, removed the holster, blouse and body armor, shoes and slacks, leaving her dressed in only a cotton T-shirt, bra and underwear. He grasped the bottom of her white T-shirt. Their eyes met and the mutual desire sparked as he swept the garment up and over her head. She tugged his shirt from the fitted jeans and slid her hands up his bare back. His skin was warm and taut. The sensitive nerves on the pads of her fingers relayed each curve and hollow as he unbuttoned the cuffs of his shirt and the collar, reaching over his head to grab the back of the cotton shirt and tug it free. It fell upon hers as she reached for his belt. She had it off as he used the heel of one cowboy boot to catch the heel of the other and step free. Then he hopped to that foot to drag off the remaining boot. He lost an inch at the removal of his footwear, which brought her head just under his chin. Perfect for kissing, she decided as his mouth slashed across hers, stoking the fire of need in her belly.

She felt his hand slide over the back of her bra and lifted her hands to the center of her chest to the clasp that held her undergarment. With its release she felt free and unfettered as he stepped back to look at her.

"I'll never forget this sight for as long as I live," he said. "Ava, you are the most beautiful woman I have ever seen."

She flushed at the compliment as she devoured the sight of him. His chest was well-defined and his stomach armored with tempting ripples of muscle punctuated by the enticing hollow of his navel. She drew one finger down the center of his chest and watched his nipples bud and his skin turn to gooseflesh. She stopped only when she reached the waistband of his jeans. The hard, defined ridge made her ache to touch him. She did, rubbing her hand over his erection sheathed in denim.

"I've been thinking about this. Imagining," she said.

His brows lifted. "Me, too."

He stepped closer, his mouth on hers and then on her

neck, tasting and nipping. His tongue swirled in delicious circles down the most sensitive spots. When he reached her breast she arched back, giving him access as she leaned against his mouth. The tug and draw sent shards of pleasure through her, stirring a deep, insistent, pulsing need.

He stripped her out of her underwear. She moved only to step clear as she sank to her knees before him. He lowered her to the rug and snatched a couch pillow from the sofa that he tucked under her hips, lifting her and giving him better access to everything.

Kee sank between her legs and Ava bit her lower lip as the sensation built, climbing and cresting until she crashed over the edge of her release.

She cried out and lifted up to meet his mouth and that clever, darting tongue. Oh, how she loved a man who knew his way about. She reached for him, drawing him upward, and he kissed his way back over her hips and stomach and neck.

"That was amazing," she whispered.

He grinned, pleased with himself, and she stroked his cheek as she reached, finding him hard with want.

He was a passionate lover, so different from the careful man. Kee showed her a vulnerability that was completely unexpected. He reached into his front pocket.

She thought back to how she would have reacted only a week ago if he had made such a move. He withdrew a blue foil packet and offered it to her. His caution was only for her, making sure he wore protection before he saw to his needs. Ava tore the packet with her teeth and then reached for the rivet of his jeans.

THE LAPTOP CHIMED a tune and Kee made a sound as he came awake, his arm tightening about her.

"What?" He opened his eyes to the unfamiliar living room. It took a moment to remember where he was.

Ava lay curled beside him on her sister's couch, naked

with only the crocheted afghan to cover her hips. One knee was draped over his thigh and her hand tightened on his opposite shoulder as the chime sounded again. How long had they been asleep?

He thought back on their lovemaking. She was so sweet. He had expected passion. Ava was passionate about everything and fierce and hot-blooded. But the sweetness had been an unexpected gift.

She pushed her hair out of her face and smiled up at him, her chin now resting on top of her closed fist. Their eyes met and he saw no regret, just the tousled hair and sleepy face of the woman he thought was very quickly wheedling into his heart.

The chime rang again and Ava stiffened.

"My computer. It's finished decoding." She swept to her seat in a graceful spin that brought the afghan away with her as she crossed the room to the glass dining room table.

Kee reached for his briefs and jeans, slipping into them before following her. She sat clutching the crocheted blanket to her chest as she peered at the glowing laptop. Kee retrieved his phone and saw it was now officially tomorrow. Ten after one on Saturday, one week since he had met Ava. That seemed completely impossible, but it was so.

He tried and failed to ignore the tug of need that pulsed within. He rested a hand on her shoulder and she covered it with hers as she glanced back at him. Their eyes met and he knew he could not handle Ava Hood any more than he could handle this situation. He was in over his head.

He was suddenly afraid of what she would find there. He'd broken the law for her and he knew he'd do whatever she asked. Not just because he needed to know, but because he needed to prove Hector was innocent. Kee was convinced that someone was using his mentor or blackmailing him. Hector just could not have done what Ava thought. He wasn't capable of doing something so very wrong. Once they discovered the truth of his innocence, Ava would look elsewhere for her criminals.

Ava went back to the computer, copying the flash drive onto two other similar ones. Then she began opening documents and spreadsheets rapid-fire as if shooting an automatic weapon.

"Look!" She pointed at the screen and the Excel spreadsheet. "A list of possible candidates. Girls' names, visits, pregnancy test results and pickup dates."

Kee's stomach twisted as his fears crystallized like shards of glass in his stomach.

"Louisa!" Ava exclaimed. "There she is."

So Betty was involved. Kee made the next step alone. Betty could not have managed such a thing without the help of a physician at the minimum. Hector could run a simple test, of course. Like a pregnancy test. As for inseminating "candidates," as Ava called them, yes, Hector was physically capable. And if he followed the law, he would have a female in the room with him. That should have been one of the nurses, but it might have been Betty. It likely was Betty, he decided and frowned.

Kee sank to the seat beside hers, shoulders sagging with the weight of this discovery.

Ava didn't notice him as she continued to read aloud.

"This might be the birth parents but she's just used numbers to identify them. Betty is very organized." Her fingers flashed on the keys, bringing Kee's world apart. "What I don't see is who picked up the girls and where they were taken. But it's enough. I need to call Tinnin and FBI Agent Forrest. I don't want Hauser and Mills to flee before they can make an arrest." She curled her fingers before the keyboard and blew away a breath. "I was right." She lifted her gaze to him and the smile that curled her lips vanished by slow degrees. "Kee? What's wrong?"

Chapter Sixteen

Kee didn't know where to begin. He stood and snatched up his shirt from the floor. He was on the sofa tugging on his socks and boots a moment later.

"Kee, tell me what's happening."

She held the blanket around her shoulders as she came to sit beside him and reached toward him. He leaned away, avoiding her touch.

"You didn't think Hauser did this," she said.

He drew the legs of his jeans down over the boots and stood.

"Of course I didn't. Now I've betrayed the greatest man I ever knew. Or a man I thought I knew. I don't know what to think."

"He's a monster."

"He's the reason I'm not still limping around this rez. I was so unredeemable my own father chose Ty to drive him instead of me. And the Wolf Posse? I didn't make the smart choice and avoid joining the gang. I tried when I was thirteen. They didn't want me. You know who did? Hector Hauser. He believed in me. Now what do I have?"

"I'm sorry, Kee. But he isn't the man you thought he was."

"He's got a wife and three grown daughters."

"And a mistress. Betty and Hector have been having a longtime affair." She hadn't known the woman involved when she first uncovered the messages, but now she knew. Without a doubt.

His shock showed in his flaring nostrils and sharp intake of breath. He recovered, his brow furrowing. "How do you know that?"

She took his hand. He allowed it but it was like holding a store manikin. His body was stiff and unyielding. He did not clasp her hand or meet her gaze. "Nobody is all bad, Kee. Bad guys have some really good reasons for what they do."

"So call Tinnin. Call the FBI. If this is true, we need to stop it now."

AVA SAT IN the squad room of the Turquoise Canyon police station. The FBI had done their best to get Tinnin to agree to extradite Hauser and Mills from the rez to the FBI field office in Tucson. Tinnin had refused. It was up to the tribal council to make such decisions. Only they had the authority to request that a suspect be tried by the federal court system but rarely did so. This was sovereign land. So while the FBI had jurisdiction to investigate crime, they had no right to demand that either suspect be surrendered to them. Hauser might be many things but he was still Apache and Tinnin would not permit Hauser or Mills to lose sovereign rights without the tribal executive council's approval.

So the FBI had set up here, quickly and with shocking efficiency. Tinnin and Bear Den had both looked over the files that she had provided and agreed to enlist the help of the FBI. Arrest warrants were issued and search warrants obtained.

In the wee hours of the night, Hector Hauser and his wife, Beatrice, were taken into custody. Betty Mills was arrested and all three were transported to the tribe's ceremonial grounds and a temporary, mobile detention unit.

The FBI techs were in the health clinic much of the night and obtained legally what Ava had glimpsed illegally. They discovered the name of "a package," which they determined to be the next girl scheduled to disappear. No time or date had been entered in Mills's carefully maintained logs. The victim's name was Heather Cosay. What they did not find was a location for Louisa or the other girls. It seemed Dr. Hauser and Betty Mills's responsibilities ended after the scheduling of the pickup.

Kee had been grim-faced during the night as he watched the man he had respected arrive in handcuffs. Ava had tried to comfort him but Kee's misery was still palpable. She had nodded off in her chair beside Kee when Forrest arrived to wake her. "Where's Kee?" she asked.

"At the clinic delivering a baby," said Forrest.

Forrest wore a gray suit that still had crisp seams down the legs, despite the fact that he'd been working all night. His white shirt had not fared so well but the charcoal-colored tie covered the worst of the wrinkles. He was clearly Native, with deep brown eyes and short black hair. He was fit and muscular, with an angular face that said he worked more than he ate, and seemed to be in his late thirties.

"Hauser has admitted to seeing the girls as needed for neonatal care at the Darabee location."

"Where Kacey Doka was held?"

"Yes. But after the raid, the Russians holding them decided to use a different physician. Compartmentalize in case Hauser was under surveillance."

Ava rolled her lips between her teeth and felt her heart sink. Had it all been for nothing?

"We don't know where Louisa is," said Ava.

"No. I'm sorry. But this information will go a long way in making this case."

She'd given away her career on a gamble for Louisa, and lost.

Ava glanced at the large clock on the wall. It was Saturday morning, just before seven. The clinic was closed.

"Do you think Hauser would take a deal?" she asked.

Forrest rested the knuckles of one hand on the table to her left. "What kind of a deal?"

"He'll call for the pickup for Heather Cosay. The pickup man will not know what girl to expect. I could be that girl. I could be Heather Cosay."

Forrest gave her an assessing look and pursed his lips. "I'm not sure you can look that young."

"With the right clothing, makeup and hairstyle, I could do it."

"Pass for eighteen?"

Ava was nearly twenty-eight. It was a stretch but everyone said she didn't look her age. She still got proofed every time she went into a bar.

"It would be Mills to take that deal. She's the one who arranges transport," said Forrest.

"She turns witness and makes your case," said Ava, "plus we get the missing women back."

Forrest made a sound that more resembled a growl than a laugh. "Or you get killed."

"We don't have a lot of time here."

"You know what you are doing? Because the way Wallace spins it you're a little bit crazy and your sister is in jail, leaving three little girls with no one but their granny to see to them. Have you thought of that? Really thought?"

"There should be four little girls," Ava countered. "Louisa is missing and crazy is exactly what you need right now."

"I'll bring it to my boss. But don't get your hopes up. If we offer up a decoy girl, it will likely be one of our agents."

"You got someone who speaks Tonto Apache? Someone who can pass for nineteen and who can be briefed and ready in…" She glanced at the wall clock. "In three hours?"

Chapter Seventeen

Kee Redhorse had been with Ava most of the night, but a woman in labor had drawn him away so he had not been there in those all-important few minutes when she somehow convinced the Federal Bureau of Investigation to use her as a body double for the woman who was scheduled to be captured next.

He found out upon arrival at the tribal gathering grounds from Detective Bear Den and by then Ava was already gone.

When Bear Den told him what Ava was doing, he'd lost his mind.

Had he actually taken a swing at a detective?

Bear Den had dodged and had him in an armlock, which he held until Kee had stopped cursing in Tonto. Then he'd turned him loose.

Bear Den told him that Ava had been in the clinic and that his sister-in-law Lori had assisted the FBI in taking a photo of Ava at their reception area in the same manner Betty would for any new patient's file. This was important because it was the type of digital image Betty Mills routinely sent to the kidnappers to help them ID their target. They had used Heather Cosay's real photo as a guide for Ava's hair and makeup.

She'd been prepped to take the young woman's place.

"Where is she now?" Kee was so angry it was hard to think, let alone speak.

"You can't go to her."

"Hell I can't."

Kee knew better than to challenge Bear Den.

The wall clock in the squad room read 10:23 a.m. on Saturday morning.

"If she dies, I blame you," said Kee.

"If you move your truck in the next hour, I arrest you," he replied.

His gut told him she was in danger.

"It's our best chance to find them. The missing. If she can convince the Russians that she's Heather, they'll bring her to the others."

"You don't know that!" Kee threw his arms up. "They could take her anywhere. They could kill her on the spot. Ava looks young, but eighteen? And she acts like a cop. We need to stop her."

"She won't be alone," said Bear Den. "Tinnin is already on-site and FBI has surveillance in place. They will know where she is every second."

"I can't stand it if anything happens to her," said Kee.

"I know the feeling." Bear Den blew out a blast of air. Kee had thought he'd told Ava his feelings for her without words on Friday night, but the moment the opportunity to find her niece arose she'd taken the chance.

"She didn't even tell me," he said.

He did not figure into her decisions in the least, so clearly his feelings for her were one-sided.

"There wasn't time."

Kee's snort told Bear Den what he thought of that excuse.

"She's got guts. You have to admire that," said the detective.

Kee said nothing. His hurt and anger were still too raw.

"You care that much," said Bear Den, "makes me wonder why."

Kee shook his head. How did he explain caring for a woman so much it hurt and then having her not even seem to notice you were gone.

"She's worth it, I think," said Bear Den.

"What is?" asked Kee.

"Loving Ava."

Kee stood couldn't speak past the lump in his throat. Kee left him at the station. He heard Bear Den pick up his radio and call for Kee to have an escort. Before Kee reached his old truck there was a squad car behind him. He clenched his jaw until it ached and the burning in his eyes ceased. Then he turned over the motor and waited for his vision to clear. He did not wipe at the tears that rolled down his face as he drove. He parked and flicked off the motor. Then he tugged his shirttails from his trousers and used them to wipe his face.

He drove past his mother's place and noticed that her minivan was missing. Likely his mother, her husband, sister and the three foster girls were still at church. Jake would not be joining them because he'd be working the biggest case since the eco-extremists attack. Colt would not be coming because he was in witness protection. There was one person he could go to who might know what was happening. Whether Ty would tell him about it was another matter. Ty had always kept secrets. Kee just prayed Ty had nothing to do with Heather Cosay.

As he exited the truck, the squad car parked across the road in the turnaround. Halfway to the garage, Hemi trotted out from the cover of the carport to greet Kee. For reasons he did not wish to examine, he dropped to one knee and hugged the dog, burying his face in the thick coat at her neck.

When he lifted his head it was to see that Ty's motorcycle was already there in the carport and his brother was making his way in Kee's direction.

"What's wrong?" Ty asked.

Kee told him. He didn't hold back a thing, even though he knew Ty had connections to the tribe's gang. He trusted Ty and would always trust him, even with Ava's life.

"This is bad," Ty said, giving his head a slow shake from side to side.

Kee's anxiety doubled.

"What is?"

"I didn't know about Day until afterward. But when we found his bike, I went to Faras. He told me they sent someone for Day."

Faras Pike was the head of the tribe's gang. Kee knew him but avoided him when possible. That was something Ty had never been able to do.

"They? Who's they? The Wolf Posse?"

"No. Not our guys. The ones the posse is working with. Moving drugs, mostly. At least that's the part of the organization that I know about. Keeping the cars ready to roll, that's my gig. They're sending him again."

"Who?"

"The same one they sent after Day."

Kee didn't know if this was a trick or a trap. He didn't know what to do.

"Why would Faras tell you?"

"I'm a driver. A good one."

Driver? That's what he'd been doing for their dad when they got caught but Ty had crashed the getaway car.

"You helped the killer get away?"

Ty shook his head. "Didn't need me for Day. No heat."

"Who are they after today?" The answer came to him at the same moment as he finished the question. "No." He was gasping now, trying to get the words past the panic. "They couldn't have known who she was. No one did."

"Someone might have figured it out."

"He's after Heather," said Kee.

"Heather? Heather who?"

"The next surrogate."

Ty laced his fingers behind his neck and paced away and then back. "No. No. No. This is really bad." He gripped Kee hard by both shoulders and gave him a little shake. "They don't send this guy on pickups. You understand?"

"Are they sending him for Ava?"

Ty's look was bereft. "I don't know. But he's here for someone. She's my first guess."

"Why did Faras call you? Why would he even tell you?"

Ty leveled him with a hard stare. "Because I'm the driver assigned to get him off the rez if something goes wrong."

Kee glanced back at the empty street. Yury Churkin was coming for Ava.

"Call him off!" shouted Kee.

"I can't do that. And when they call me it will be too late. She'll be dead."

Kee reached for his phone, dialing Ava as Ty's phone rang. The two brothers stared at one another for an instant before Ty answered the call.

AVA STEPPED OUT of the shower and onto the white terry-cloth bath mat on the pink tiled floor. This house had been built in the 1950s and all the tiles were pink trimmed with black. The sink and tub were also pink. Only the toilet, switched out for a more water-efficient model, was white.

Ava worried that the lack of sleep and resulting puffiness under her eyes would make it difficult for anyone to believe that she was ten years younger than her actual age. She'd said she could do it and she intended to make this work.

Mills had told the FBI that she routinely sent the kidnappers the target's address and the patient photo from the clinic. Mills had helped the FBI send the photo of Ava impersonating Heather to the correct address. Now Ava stared at Heather's real photo, which showed a pretty young face with too much eye makeup, hair in pigtails and a mouth covered in bright pink lipstick. So that was the look Ava would emulate again, just as she did for the photo that would soon be in her kidnapper's hands. Ava would use Heather's photo as a guide to apply her makeup.

Thankfully, they were of similar height, weight and build. The Russian captors never saw the girls until pickup.

She toweled off and headed to the bedroom, where she combed out the tangles, parted and tugged her shoulder-length hair into pigtails. Ava took special care to use the fastenings that included a tracker. She would have trackers on her phone, in her sneakers and in her hair.

After she had her hair arranged, she dressed in Louisa's things. The denim shorts were way too short for her liking, with the pockets sticking out below the frayed hem at each leg. The baby doll T-shirt was thin and showed her skin and the color of her bra right through the fabric.

"How do girls wear this stuff?" she asked her reflection.

Ava applied her makeup and then regarded herself in the full-length mirror affixed to the back of Louisa's bedroom door. A stranger stared back at her with eyes ringed with black eyeliner, glossy pink lips and legs that went on and on until they met the running shoes. She was glad to be wearing shoes in which she could run. She wore no body armor and felt positively naked without her service weapon. Ava shifted from side to side but could not feel the tracker that she had slipped in between the insole and sole of her right shoe.

She glanced at her cell phone. Agent Forrest would call her when contact had been made and the kidnappers were en route. Then she would be transported to Heather's current residence to wait. For now she had nothing to do but prepare. She marked the time on her phone as she wondered if Agent Forrest had succeeded yet in collecting the real Heather and her boyfriend, Lenny.

She knew that Heather lived with her boyfriend, since her father had found out about the boy and had tossed her out a month ago. According to Mills, Heather had been seen at the clinic on Friday for the ruse of anemia, had tested positive for pregnancy and did not yet suspect she was with child. Lenny was also to be taken into custody for his own safety and because he had affiliations with the Wolf Posse.

Mills had confessed that she had notified the pickup team on Friday that a "package" was ready despite Hauser's worry that there was too much heat. But the Russians were insistent and Mills feared for their safety if she did not comply.

The FBI would receive a text on Mills's prepaid phone sometime today requesting pickup details. Mills had cooperated, describing her normal routine with agents as part of her deal to avoid prosecution, which included texting back an address, photo and any other information such as a car make and model and license if pertinent. Mills had sent this intel on a burner phone provided by their associates. At nine this morning, Ava's photo had been sent. In the image she had worn Louisa's style of makeup as they'd created a photo at the health clinic, where all patient photos were taken and added to the files during intake. This digital image was exactly the sort that Mills would have sent in prior pickups.

Ava was ready.

There was something wrong. She felt a presence now that had been absent before. She cocked her head but heard nothing. But her body tensed. Someone was in the house.

Her mind flew through the possibilities. The FBI would not enter her house unannounced. Kee wouldn't, either.

She hesitated, confused. Was it one of the agents? Had something happened?

"Hello?" she called. "Sylavania? Is that you?"

Ava was halfway across the living room when she found Woody in the hall before her door. He had been out in the backyard and his appearance meant someone had let him in. A chill ran up her arms.

A man stepped into view. He was big, white, with a balding head and eyes the color of storm clouds. Numerous gang-style tattoos encircled his upper arms marred by long, healing scabs on each forearm. Her eyes widened as she spotted the dagger tattoo at his throat.

Yury Churkin.

She recognized him instantly.

She knew him. But did he know her?

He looked as surprised to see her as she was to see him. He lifted his pistol, pointing it at her gut. Woody left her to greet the new arrival, tail wagging. Yury ignored the canine, focusing on Ava instead.

"What are you doing here?" he asked.

Ava could not have spoken if she tried. Her heart was pounding so fast she could barely hear and all her muscles went tight. Her breath came in rapid pants through her open mouth, bringing the sickly sweet fragrance of bubblegum from the lipstick into her lungs.

He outweighed her by more than a hundred pounds.

Ava backed down the hall and he advanced in slow pursuit.

What was happening? Why was he here?

"What's your name?" he asked.

"H-Heather," she stammered. "Heather Cosay."

He didn't recognize her, then. Not yet anyway.

Her mouth was so dry. Had he come to kill Detective

Hood and somehow stumbled on the woman next to be taken? As long as he thought she was Heather, he might not kill her. But the instant they figured out who she really was, she was dead.

"Where's the detective?"

"I don't know. She left a few minutes ago."

"Why are you here?" he asked again, his voice raised as he advanced. Woody trotted along with him, tail wagging. Churkin ignored him.

Ava tried to figure it out, what Churkin would think. If Heather was here in Ava's sister's house, that would mean she knew that Heather was going to be taken. Didn't it?

"She's picking up her nieces. I'm supposed to babysit so she can take her sister to mass."

Churkin spoke in Russian, what she assumed was a curse or a string of them. Would he buy the coincidence? Staying alive was her first priority but it did strike her that she still might be taken to Louisa and as long as she had the trackers, they could follow her.

He advanced. She judged the distance to the bedroom door and found it too far.

"Who are you? What do you want?" she said. The fear was genuine, no reason to act.

He said nothing. She ran and he caught her by one pigtail. It was one of the reasons officers wore their long hair pinned up. Hair made too easy a handle. He dragged her backward. In a moment he had her in a choke hold as one hand ran up her hip and to her backside, where he plucked the phone from her rear pocket.

Ava thrashed as her attacker threw her over a shoulder.

"Let me go."

He was taking her down the hall to the bedroom. Oh, God, was he going to rape her?

Churkin threw her on the bed. She rolled to escape off the other side but he gripped her ankle, dragging her back to the middle of the bed with one hand. The other held her phone, which was now ringing. She knew the ringtone because she'd set it. Kee was phoning.

Her attacker set the ringing phone on the bedside table. Where was his gun? She kicked out at him, missing his face by inches. He growled and tugged her toward him with the ankle he clasped and slapped her across the face with his free hand. Stunned, she fell back to the bed and stared up at the crack that traveled like a staircase across Sara's ceiling.

He flipped one side of the coverlet over her and wrapped her so quickly Ava had little time to grab a breath before she was surrounded by the covering. A fly caught in the spider's web. She had the tracker in her hair and one in her shoe. But there was no surveillance in her sister's house. They had not needed it and had set up only in Heather's residence. How had he gotten past the FBI waiting out front?

Her phone stopped ringing. He lifted her over his shoulder and carried her again. The house phone began to ring. The FBI? She tracked their progress by the sound. Woody's collar jangled as he followed them out of Sara's bedroom and down the hallway runner. Churkin's shoes clicked on the tile and then thudded on the living room carpet and finally gave a soft tapping on the kitchen linoleum. He was going out the rear door and all the agents were out front. Did he know that they were there?

The hot exterior air told her they were in the backyard, but her head was still covered. She could see nothing. Behind her, the door clicked shut. She listened for Woody's collar but heard nothing.

Could anyone see her? Was there anyone in the backyard that ran to the crumpling fence that butted against the neighbor's yard this Sunday morning? Most of Sara's neighbors would be in church or still in bed.

She marked the distance, guessing that they were traveling between the neighbor's homes that sat on the street behind her sister's place. When he dropped her in the trunk, she thought she might have a chance. All trunks in newer-model cars had release levers that glowed in the dark. But then he uncovered her lower legs. A moment later she felt the bite of a plastic zip tie cinched around her ankles. The door closed a moment later and she found herself in total darkness.

She'd known this might happen when she'd given Hauser her name. Known that he could use it to discover who she really was. She'd recognized, too, that her attempts to get Louisa back might bring trouble to her sister and youngest nieces. She'd thought she could protect them. When she realized she couldn't she'd called in help. Her sister and nieces were safe. As she lay there, thinking, half-naked and wrapped like a human burrito in the sweltering trunk of a killer's car, she hoped she'd have the chance to do what she came for and find Louisa.

This was the hired killer they'd sent for Day. Would they send an assassin to capture Heather? This was wrong. All wrong. But some part of her still wanted this to work, to find Louisa and bring her home.

Why hadn't Mills told them that Churkin knew who she was? She could see Betty laughing inside with the knowledge that the killer was stalking Ava, even as she seemed to cooperate. Mills had broken the terms of her plea deal. Of course, Ava would have to survive to tell anyone.

Chapter Eighteen

The fear swept down on Kee like a thundercloud. Inside, the lightning crashed through his nervous system as his mind and body seemed to break apart. Agent Forrest confirmed his fears. Ava was missing from her sister's home.

"I don't understand," said Kee to Agent Forrest. He had the phone on speaker as Ty drove. "She's not at her sister's."

"Looks like she was abducted from this location using the coverlet from her sister's bed," said Forrest.

"But you're following her?" asked Kee.

"Yes. We have a team en route to her location."

"Where?"

"Toward Antelope Lake."

Ty shook his head.

"Keep me updated." Kee hung up. "What does that mean?" he asked Ty.

"First of all, the Russian would have killed Ava on-site the moment he made contact, and he would have left her body there because driving around with a body is dangerous."

"But he didn't do that."

"Which I don't understand. He took her. That makes no sense."

Kee rubbed his hands nervously. "Does Yury pick up the captives?"

"I don't know anything about that. I just know that this

Russian is a professional killer. They bring him in when Hauser has trouble."

"He's done this before?"

Ty nodded and mentioned the shooting that had gone unsolved. Kee knew her. Had treated her. Been unable to save her.

"What did she do?"

Ty shrugged. "Overheard something. Stumbled on something or just asked the wrong question to the wrong person. All I know is that she's dead and Faras told me it was 'The Russian.'"

"Would Faras know about the pickup of Heather Cosay?"

"Of course he'd know, but I can't call and ask him. Now can I?"

"I think I know the Russian's name. I saw him. Saw Hauser treat him. The name is Yury Churkin. Big, tatted up with scratches on both forearms."

Ty scowled. "Sounds right."

"Would Churkin know what she looked like?"

"Who, Ava?"

"Yes. Does Churkin have the photo of Ava posing as Heather?"

"Again. It's possible."

"But she's not dead. Yury went to Sara's house to kill Ava and instead he found the young woman he thinks is Heather Cosay. Bear Den told me that the FBI would send Heather's details but would use Ava's photo. Maybe the Russian saw that photo, too."

Ty gaped. "It explains why they didn't find her body."

Kee sat back in the bucket seat. "She's alive. If she convinced him she's Heather, then he would have taken her."

"Even though it's not his job?" asked Ty.

"Maybe. Anyway, it's a theory."

"We need to find the holding facility. FBI will find it. She's being tracked," said Kee.

"Not for long. If, and that is a big *if*, the FBI gets to her before they strip her clean, they have a chance. If the Feds miss her, and they probably will, she'll be in the holding facility."

"Where is that?"

Ty pressed his lips tight and cast Kee an apologetic look.

"You don't know. Do you?" Kee asked.

"Not my area. Cars and transport, remember?" said Ty. "Only reason I know about the girls at all is because of what happened to Jake and then to Colt and Kacey."

He meant their younger brothers. Jake had found a baby born by a woman who'd evaded capture, and Kacey, then pregnant, had escaped capture and run home to the rez and her ex-boyfriend, their little brother Colt.

"I know who does know the holding location," said Ty.

"Who?"

"Hauser. He has to. Kacey said he's the one who preps, checks them and delivers the babies."

"He's locked up in the tribal jail," said Kee.

"Then that's our first stop."

AVA SHIFTED IN the stifling comforter. The blanket and the hot air in the hot trunk smothered her so she stewed in her own sweat. Her skin was slick and her hair wet.

She hoped that the FBI was now tracking her. Enough time had passed for them to have recognized that she was missing and begin the trace. She just had to be patient. She just had to trust…

It wasn't her strongest suit. Trusting. In fact, she could count on one hand the number of people she did trust. And that list unfortunately did not include the FBI. It included one man, Kee Redhorse. But Kee did not have the experience to find her.

As her fear rose up in her throat, it was to Kee that she

called out. Kee Redhorse who she summoned. Despite what
her rational mind told her, her heart whispered his name.

The vibrations in the car changed. She recognized the
difference. They had left the paved road and were now
traveling over dirt and gravel. She tried to think of where
he might be taking her. The time they traveled and the
sound of the tires on the highway helped her calculate
the distance and made her believe they were still on the
reservation. The Turquoise Canyon reservation climbed
up Turquoise Ridge. But there was no way over the ridge
that involved a car. And all roads off the reservation ran
along the paved highway that followed the river to the
east and west.

The car slowed, turned, rolled on and on as sweat
poured off her body. She was dizzy from the heat when the
car finally pulled to a stop. Dust seeped into the trunk and
she gagged, choking. The front door opened and slammed.
She heard the trunk latch release. And still she could not
breathe until he pulled her, blanket and all, from the trunk.
Cool air reached her and she breathed deep. She felt wrung
out as a dishrag as he tossed her over his shoulder and carried her a short distance. She could see nothing but the
blurry image of the coverlet before her eyes. She knew
when he brought her inside because of the change of light.
And she felt the hardwood planking as he dropped her to
the floor.

She braced to fight, fearing she would lose. Churkin
was big, rested and had made the journey in the air-con-
ditioned cab of the car. And fighting was dangerous because, if she lost, he might wonder how a sixteen-year-old
girl came to have the hand-to-hand combat experience of
an army sergeant.

She just needed to stay alive until the FBI found her.
They were coming. They had to be.

What happened next happened so fast she could barely

manage to kick and claw at her attackers. Two men unwrapped her and with shocking speed tore every stitch of clothing from her body.

Churkin said something in Russian to the other man and he stooped to tug the clips and ties from her hair.

No. No. No. The trackers. They'd taken every one of them. Without them, she was lost. As lost as a stone thrown in a lake. She had a good look at the second man as they tossed her a garment. She lifted the offering in one hand and glanced from the drab fabric to Churkin.

"Put on," he ordered.

She did. Sliding her arms into the sleeveless wrap dress and tying the knot of the thin fastenings at her hip. There was no belt. Nothing for her to use as a weapon. Once dressed, she faced the men again.

They were not paying any attention to her. Instead, they spoke in Russian rapidly back and forth. She imagined Churkin was describing the mix-up that had occurred. After all, he'd been sent to eliminate Avangeline Yokota and had instead found the pickup target. She considered the second man. Was he the one assigned to capture Heather Cosay?

Ava cast a quick glance around the cabin. This was clearly some miner's shed. She recognized the rock tailings on the wooden kitchen table. Turquoise Canyon reservation got its name from the ridgeline that was riddled with the veins of precious turquoise. Many of the residents here had claims that were set up in the ridge and were extremely private. The cabin was dusty except for the place where she had been tossed and stripped. Gray blankets covered the two front windows, the sunlight poking through the moth-eaten holes in bright beams.

Churkin and his partner stood between her and the door. But there was the windows as exit and the blankets would protect her from the glass.

Why was it so hot in here? She glanced to the kitchen

that consisted of a counter supported by two-by-fours, a sink that likely worked by gravity from a barrel of water on the roof and adjacent to the sink sat a small wood-burning stove on a pad of bricks. Judging from the heat and the red glow visible through the slots in the front grate, the stove was burning, which was odd as the day and the cabin were hot.

Churkin's partner collected her belongings, and used part of her sister's comforter to open the stove. Then he proceeded to feed in one sneaker and then the next. It would be only moments until the trackers were destroyed, she realized.

Ava glanced back to the window, considering. She had wanted Churkin to bring her to the missing women. But now, without the FBI tracking her, it would be doubtful she could escape, let alone rescue the others. In other words, she would be in no better position than the other captives with one very important difference. She was not pregnant. A fact that would become apparent with time.

In other words, she was on her own. She guessed this cabin was likely isolated. The complete confidence of the men told her that screaming would bring no help. But she knew the out-of-doors and she was strong and fast. They had given her no shoes. That would be a handicap. And she might still be injured by glass in the fall. She saw no other choice. She glanced to her captors. One was on one knee before the stove, using a stick to feed her shorts and underwear into the woodstove. Churkin stood with arms folded, watching the proceedings. She surmised he would stay until she was transferred to the custody of the second man. Then perhaps he would go back after his target.

Ava took a deep breath and ran toward the covered window. She jumped, ducking her head and leading with her shoulder, curling her legs up as she struck the blanket and window at once. The blanket enveloped her as the glass exploded outward.

Chapter Nineteen

Kee and Ty met Chief Tinnin at the nearly empty police station at 11:53 a.m. Tinnin told Ty to stay put in the squad room and walked Kee toward the interrogation room.

"This place still looks closed," said Kee.

"Everyone is out looking for Ava. Except Forrest. He's in with Hauser." Tinnin swung along on his crutches and one good leg that did not entirely straighten. Kee knew he'd been a bronc buster in the rodeo. His father had told him that Tinnin had been the best on the rez and had even been on TV at Madison Square Garden. Broken bones hadn't stopped him, but when he'd wrecked his knees he had to give it up.

"You know that Hauser isn't going to give us this for nothing?" said Tinnin.

Kee didn't care. They needed to find Ava.

"Which means I have to offer a deal. Which means that bastard won't do time."

"That can't happen," said Kee.

Tinnin grimaced. "But it might. You leave this to me."

Tinnin stopped outside the interrogation room and paused a long moment. Tinnin raked a hand through his graying hair, letting it rest on the back of his tanned brown neck. "Wait here."

Kee paced up and down the hall outside the interrogation room, pausing at the one-way mirror on occasion.

Tinnin sat beside Forrest across from Hauser with no table between them and almost knee to knee as if they were all old friends. What was taking so long?

Finally, Tinnin rose and Kee met him at the door. Twenty precious minutes had passed.

"He's agreed to help." Tinnin leaned heavily on his crutches, taking his weight on his armpits and using a free hand to scrub his knuckles over the stubble on his cheek. "The deal all but guarantees that he'd serve no more than five years in jail and avoid federal charges. I don't like it. But I took it." Kee knew that their tribal court system operated apart from state and federal authority. The tribe rarely requested that the state take over prosecution of one of their tribe. But Kee thought Hauser would be a good exception to their practice.

Tinnin straightened. "Since the raid on the facility in Darabee, the Russians have instigated some precautions. According to Hauser, old procedure was to transport the 'package,' is what he called them." Tinnin's mouth twisted in distaste. "They'd take our children. Some are only four-teen. Anyway, he said they take the captives to the facility where Hauser would do a preliminary exam before 'stor-age.' Again, his term."

"What do they do now?" asked Kee.

"The girls are transported to a small facility on-site. It's a miner's cabin up on Turquoise Ridge. There they are stripped to eliminate any possible tracking devices and only then are they transported to the new holding facil-ity. Apparently there are two holding facilities on our rez."

"You know their locations?" asked Kee.

"Hauser does. But he says the Russians will kill him for betraying them. He's right about that. They'll get to him in jail or prison. So he wants protection. Forrest is talk-ing to him about relocation. Hauser wants his wife and son along but that might be a problem. His wife doesn't want any part of him now. I was the one who notified her of the charges. She's not coming here to see him and she sure isn't going with him if he gets witness protection because she don't want nothing from him except a divorce."

"How long do they keep a captive in the prep area?" asked Kee.

"Not long. I would suspect less than an hour. The whole point is to move the girl quickly out to the facility but still ensure that she is not being tracked by federal authorities. Hauser thought they were just being paranoid. Turns out they were right."

Agent Luke Forrest emerged from the interrogation room, his face grim.

"I offered the deal," said Forrest. "And I have the address."

AVA LANDED HARD on the uneven ground beneath the cabin window. She kicked and flailed, escaping the wool blanket that had acted as window covering. Then she rolled to her feet. She did not pause as she ran along the cabin wall, clearing the corner as the first gunshot sounded.

Behind her came the sound of two Russians arguing and the bang of the front door crashing.

Ava glanced about, taking in her surroundings. Behind the cabin was a propane tank. The cabin itself was raised and resting on the stumps of several logs in a wooded area. Through the trunks of the trees she could see the rock face and evidence of mining. A weapon, she thought. The shovel. A pick. It was a poor defense against her captors but better than nothing. Her best hope was to evade recapture.

She did not run to the mining site for the same reason, though she wanted to. It was the direction that the Russians would think she had taken. Instead, she scrambled under the cabin and emerged from the front. Two cars were parked side by side. A quick check showed there were keys in neither.

She had run out of options. Her only chance was to run.

Someone shouted from behind her, the words unrecognizable. Russian. She glanced back to see Churkin, meeting his gaze as he ran at her. He did not draw his weapon but relied on his speed, running her down like a cheetah after a gazelle. His tackle was brutal. The landing even more so.

His partner arrived a moment later. He used plastic restraints similar to the ones Ava had used on several suspects. They zip-tied her hands and feet. She was then carried to the second car and dropped into the trunk. Before slamming the door closed, Churkin spit on her. The warm spittle trailed down her face and neck as the car springs sagged and car doors slammed. The engine engaged and she was moving again.

KEE AND TY stood in the squad room waiting for Tinnin to return. He arrived with Agent Forrest. When Tinnin caught sight of Ty, he glowered.

"You better scat, Ty," said Tinnin.

"My brother asked for my help."

"Only reason you're not in custody now is because the tribal council voted to keep you on the rez until your hearing. And you leave this rez and all bets are off."

Kee broke in. "What hearing?"

"Later," said Ty to Kee and then rested a hand on Kee's shoulder. "I'll be around."

Ty's hand slid away and he sauntered toward the door.

"Leave the rez and you're the FBI's problem," warned Tinnin.

It struck Kee as he watched his brother vanish down the hall that Ty had always been there to support them physically. All through the bad times when Kee's legs were uneven and through the three surgeries required to correct the difference. Ty had protected and defended him. But now Ty was in trouble and who was there to help him?

Ty disappeared down the hallway and out of sight. A moment later, Kee heard his motorcycle engine roar.

Kee turned to Tinnin. "What hearing?"

"Can we focus on Ava?" asked the police chief. The holding facility was off the rez in the resort community of Antelope Lake. Easy access for Hauser to see to the girls and already in the direction of Phoenix, where the expecting biological parents would receive their newborn. Whether they knew the circumstances surrounding their surrogates was doubtful, but Kee thought that finding them was the next step after finding the missing women.

"Hauser says this is the first stop. He'll run another pregnancy test and do a general physical. Since the raid on the Darabee house after Kacey Doka's escape, they have someone else for deliveries. Compartmentalized the operation, in other words," said Tinnin.

"This is our last shot at getting Ava or the others," added Forrest. "Hauser's contacts await his check to verify pregnancy and then transport to the final location for holding until delivery. He never sees them after that."

"As soon as they get her secured at Antelope Lake, they're going to give Hauser a call," said Tinnin. "That's their system. If he doesn't answer they'll know something is up."

Kee's heart sank.

"We could beat them there. Even better, we could intercept them before they reach the facility," said Kee.

"I have an alternative suggestion," said Agent Forrest.

"What?" asked Kee. He was growing more desperate. Ready to try anything that might get Ava back. How could the FBI have allowed her to endanger herself this way?

If he could only see her safe. He had to. Had to tell her... tell her... Oh, no. This was terrible. Kee gasped as the truth struck him like a blacksmith's hammer ringing on an anvil.

"What is it?" asked Tinnin.

"I love her," said Kee.

"Then you best go get her, son," said Tinnin.

"Dr. Hauser has been grooming Kee to take over the facility for years. He handpicked him when he was a boy. According to Hauser, the Russians know of Kee. When he receives the call, he could bring Kee along. With approval, of course. It's possible that they'll allow Kee into the facility."

Kee shook his head. "How about the FBI just charges the facility with automatic weapons?"

Forrest looked at the ground between them. "Because if Hauser is to be believed, none of the girls inside will be taken alive. They do not want witnesses to be able to identify them or their organization. First sign of attack and they shoot the hostages."

"I'll do it," said Kee.

Tinnin gaped. "Do you even know how to shoot a gun?"

Kee's only answer was to lift his chin.

"How are you going to infiltrate a secure facility guarded by Russian muscle?" asked Tinnin.

"I can because Ava's in there. And I'm going to get her out."

Forrest nodded. "Only Hauser gets in. And maybe Kee."

"Hauser is *my* suspect. I'm not letting him out of custody," said Tinnin.

Kee broke out in a cold sweat. He knew that without Hauser, he would not get into that facility and without Tinnin, they couldn't have Hauser. The FBI technically had jurisdiction over all crimes committed on federal lands and tribal lands fell into that broad category. But to Kee's knowledge, the FBI had never taken over an investigation on sovereign land unless invited by tribal authorities.

He glanced from Tinnin to Forrest as the two faced off and Ava's life hung in the balance.

AVA THOUGHT THE setback of having her wrists, now behind her back, secured to her ankles was something from which she could not recover. Her attempt to escape had brought her into a worse spot. Seeing Louisa while a captive herself was a dismal prospect, especially if Louisa greeted her, as she expected the girl would. It would be a tell that would likely lead to Ava's immediate execution.

She no longer held hopes that the FBI would find her. Possibly they had found the empty cabin and the burned remains of her clothing. But little else. And there would be nothing to use to track her. Unlike much of the outside world, here on the mountain, in Turquoise Canyon Rez, there were no cameras recording license plates and the faces of drivers. There was only one stoplight and that was at tribal headquarters.

Somehow she had avoided serious injury in her leap out the window but had bruised her shoulder on landing. Her main complaint now was her hands and feet, which she could no longer feel, the pins and needles having ceased long ago.

The infuriating part of her capture—well, there were many, but the one that rankled right now—was knowing that she had likely been driven right past the construction site beside the river right under the nose of a tribal police unit parked there.

This trunk was hot but not dangerously so. She thought that was due to the fact that they were traveling so fast and the day was waning. Her attempts to open the latch holding the trunk shut had failed and made her think that the mechanism had been disabled.

She could hear the blinker clicking. The car slowed and the road beneath her needed repair judging from the number of potholes they crossed.

When the car stopped her heart began to gallop and her skin went clammy. She'd never felt so helpless in her life and that included the times she had been taken away by protective services and all the times she could not wake her mother from her drug-induced slumber on the sofa.

This was worse. Way, way worse. She was prepared to die. But she wasn't prepared for the terror that preceded it.

She went rigid, listening as she heard a noise, a motor that she could not identify. The car rolled slowly forward and the motor sound came again. The car door opened and closed. The driver groaned as if stretching. Then he called something to someone yet unseen. She did not hear a reply but when the trunk popped open there were two men peering down at her. They were white and one had a cigarette clamped between thin, pitiless lips. She tried to memorize those faces, longing for the opportunity to identify them.

They spoke but the only thing she understood was a name pronounced with a thick Russian accent. *Heather Cozzay.* Heather Cosay.

So, her cover was still intact. The new man, the one with the cigarette, dragged her out of the trunk, scraping her thigh over the latch controls. She glanced beyond them to her surroundings.

She saw the ceiling beams some ten feet above her. And just beyond her captors a motor boat, perhaps sixteen feet, sat upon a trailer. Her first thought was that she was in a two-or three-car garage. The boat might mean she was on one of the reservoirs. There were four large lakes in the dam system between Goodwin Lake and Antelope Lake. She could not tell the time because they were inside, under bare, fluorescent lights.

The driver flipped open a knife and spun her face down, then released her wrists from her ankles and her ankles from each other. Her bare feet struck the side of the trunk so hard she winced.

She staggered as her legs gave way. The man holding her hoisted her up with a grip that spoke of cruelty.

"Stand up, girlie," he ordered.

She did, somehow, not feeling the ground beneath. Her feet were numb from the lost blood supply. She had to

look down to see that her feet actually touched the con-
crete floor beside the car's dusty tire. The driver flanked
her and she was quick-marched through a garage and into
an entry of a house that was more upscale than Ava expected. As she was tugged through the kitchen, she saw
speckled brown granite countertops littered with bags and
boxes of junk food and a white farmhouse sink full with
dirty dishes. A haze of cigarette smoke hung like a low-
pressure front over the counter peninsula. Clearly the help
had the week off.

What would Heather say in this situation? the voice in
her head asked as she noted the full ashtray beside an open
laptop on the counter before a stool, a series of text messages displayed on the screen.

"Where are you taking me? Who are you?"

They gave no answer as they pulled her through the
living room. With the curtains drawn and the lights out,
she could see little as they continued down the hall. The
stench of cigarette smoke followed them.

She held her terror in check as they stopped before a
closed bedroom door. The man with the cigarette released
her arm to grasp the combination lock fixed through the
latch secured to the door. There was a click and he pulled
the lock open and drew it away.

When they pushed her into the room, she lifted her
hands over her face, shielding her identity from anyone
who might be in the bedroom already.

The door clicked shut behind her and Ava rolled to her
seat to look back at the door. On the opposite side the pad-
lock clicked.

"Aunt Ava?"

Ava turned to see Louisa huddled on a bare queen-size
mattress on the floor. Louisa's dark hair hung limp around
her pale face. Her knees were drawn up to her chest and

her feet were bare. She wore the same sort of wrap dress that Ava now wore.

Louisa scrambled over the mattress to grasp her aunt, clinging like a frightened lost child reunited with her mother. Ava held her niece tight. At least she knew that Louisa was alive. Now if she could just get them out of here.

She looked about the room, taking in her surroundings as she scanned for some way to escape, some tool or weapon. There was nothing in the room except the mattress and the overhead light that was on to illuminate the room. The window curtains were drawn and bars had been fixed to the inside of the frames. There was an open door to the left, through which Ava could see a bathroom sink.

Louisa was sobbing now and Ava rocked her, stroking her head and making soft shushing sounds. But the tears bubbled up in Louisa's throat as the sobs shook her. All the horror and isolation erupting in one terrible display as the fear broke loose of all barriers.

"Where are the others?" she asked.

Louisa lifted her head to meet Ava's stare, her eyes red-rimmed and swimming with tears.

"What others?"

CHIEF TINNIN ARRANGED a conference call with the four available members of the tribal council: Hazel Trans, Linda Herrera, Henry Curtis and Executive Director Zach Gill. The women were in favor of letting Hauser take the deal. They wanted all efforts to focus on the recovery of the missing girls and quickly overcame Henry Curtis's objections that Hauser should face judgment. Forrest had his mole and so when the call came in for Hauser to come check the new girl, he took the call and told them that he had broken his hand and so would be coming with a fellow physician, Dr. Kee Redhorse, as driver and assistant.

Kee, Special Agent Forrest, Chief Tinnin and Detective Bear Den all waited around the speakerphone in the silence that followed.

"Dis is your man?" said Alexie, Hauser's contact.

"Yes."

"I call you back. I have to check with Usov."

The line went dead.

"Did he say Usov?" asked Forrest.

Tinnin nodded. "Yes."

"That might be Leonard Usov. He's a…"

Kee interrupted. "Ava mentioned him! Showed me Churkin's photo and said that Churkin works for Leonard Usov. Said he was an…an…" What was that damn word?

"Avtoritet?" asked Forrest.

"Yes."

"We know Churkin works for Usov. Likely this Alexie fellow does, as well. Usov is connected to the Kuznetsov crime family."

"Atlanta," said Kee. He had very good recall. Had to in order to make it through medical school.

Forrest's brows lifted. "Right again."

Kee wished his brother Ty could come with him. But that would bring him off the rez. Ty was playing a very adult version of the game of tag; his brother was safe only if he kept one foot on home base.

The call came at 5:45 p.m. Ava had been missing for seven hours and Kee was losing his mind, bit by tiny bit, as he imagined what they would do to her if they even suspected that she was a police detective. What if Louisa recognized her and, inadvertently, identified her?

Kee waited in the squad room until Chief Tinnin appeared.

"Hauser got the go-ahead to bring the new doctor. But he's only allowed to the newest facility."

"They have more than one?" asked Kee.

"Apparently."

"How many?" asked Kee.

"No idea. Hauser either doesn't know or he's not saying. I think he knows but is trying to keep some bargaining chips. You ask me, he should give us all of them or no deal. But I'm not the one dangling witness protection in front of him."

"Is Ava with all the missing from our tribe?" asked Kee.

Tinnin shrugged and scratched at the hair at his temple. "Waiting on Forrest. He'll have something, I expect. You know I used to think I understood this place. That I was a part of it. But today I just don't understand anymore. How could one of our own, a physician and a man I called a friend for most of my life, do something like this to our children?"

Kee pressed one hand tight against his mouth. He had no answers.

Tinnin continued on. "He gave my boy all his shots. Came to my house in the middle of the night to treat my wife when she had shingles. So what I really want to know is who was that in my house?"

"He fooled us all," said Kee.

"I thought I was a better judge of character than that."

Kee felt that same sense of betrayal. "I always imagined him as the father I would have chosen."

Forrest led Hauser out of the interrogation room. The men turned to watch Hauser being led past the picture windows lining the wall. His head hung as he walked down the hallway in handcuffs en route to his cell.

Kee rose. "I want to speak to him."

Tinnin lifted a brow. "Don't believe anything he tells you."

Kee nodded and rose. For reasons that he knew in his head were not physical, his leg hurt him as he walked down the hallway, as if even the surgery that corrected the length of his legs had been poisoned by this deceit.

Hector was sitting in one of two small cells that punctuated the end of the hallway just beyond the squad room. He remembered seeing Ty in this cell and his father in the one opposite.

"Kee, my boy!" Hector grinned and rose from his seat to stand with his hands in a relaxed grip on the bars. He might have been greeting him at the clinic on any given day. He did not look stressed or remorseful.

Meanwhile, Kee felt like a bag of sand stacked in a wall against a rising flood. The pressure and the sorrow pushed at him from both inside and out until he thought he might give way.

"Dr. Hauser, how could you do this to our children?"

Hauser flexed his fingers. "They aren't children. They're sexually mature women and not the sort of women we need more of. I can assure you."

Kee thought of Louisa, Ava's niece, and Kacey Doka, his youngest brother's new wife. Not the sort... A fire of rage flicked on in his belly, burning away the sourness and the ache until nothing was left but a hard, solid lump of fury.

"How could you?" This time, his outrage rang in his voice.

"For all of us. They're nothing. No one. Gosh, Kee, they can't even speak their own language. Not a single one of them. Did you know that? I didn't pick anyone important. No one like your lovely sister, Abbie. How is she feeling after that stomach flu?"

"No," said Kee. "You don't get to talk about my sister. You don't get to think about her and you certainly don't get to divert the conversation."

"You were always so smart. So much smarter than your brothers. But not smart enough to see. I wanted to tell you so many times. I was so proud of you and so excited to bring you that lab to run blood work. That was Marta

Garcia. She brought us all the equipment to run the blood work on-site. Do you know how many lives she will save? And what was the point of her life? To marry that boy she was running around with and have more babies who don't speak Tonto Apache? Who don't contribute to the ongoing lifeblood of our tribe? Her boyfriend was only a quarter Apache, himself. And her, as well. Their children wouldn't even qualify for the tribal roles. Did you think about that?"

Kee's fury began to freeze into something new. Something icy and more dangerous. He saw Hauser as far worse than a man who had committed despicable acts, because he was remorseless. He didn't feel shame or sorrow or pity.

The only emotion Kee could detect was pride. The corners of Hauser's mouth lifted in a pleasant smile.

"You understand?" He released the bars to turn his palms up as if offering a perfectly reasonable argument. "They were contaminants. Just like a pathogen. Removing them for profit was a logical way to strengthen our tribe. Trimming away the deadwood and simultaneously bringing us all the health care we need."

"You sold them."

"Yes!" His voice held elation. "Yes, I did. Precisely. I'm so glad you understand. I've wanted to tell you on so many occasions because you know as well as I do the importance of your work here. We've spoken about it often. And the way you jumped at the chance to stay here with your people. It's so admirable. I couldn't be prouder."

Kee felt sick to his stomach. The salary, the auto stipend and the housing. Which girl's life would pay for all that?

He stared at Hauser as his complete belief in his mentor crumbled like the castle of sand that it had always been.

It was like seeing someone through some diabolical lens. Only he realized this was not a distortion of Hector Hauser. This was the real man, the one that Kee had never actually seen until this moment. But he had been there all along.

"Really. What are we to do?" asked Hauser. "Our population has a life expectancy twenty to thirty years *less* than the non-Native counterparts. And don't tell me that's all because of a bad diet and substandard education. It's the absence of decent health care."

"I don't agree with you. Just to be clear. Selling young women as surrogates… It's reprehensible."

Hauser looked as if Kee had slapped him. His arms slid back inside the cell.

"I thought you would understand. They're nothing. Unimportant. With their futures already determined. It's the tribe that matters. Our Apache culture. We have to survive. I've done all I could think of to make that happen. Educating you. Helping the most qualified rise to leadership positions. I've encouraged every single member of our tribe who showed promise, male or female. But this deal I've made with the FBI, it's bad for us. I'll be leaving you, my boy." He looked down the hallway. "I hope they don't send me somewhere cold. Or east!" He shivered. "I've never been past the Mississippi, even for medical conferences. Do you think they'll let me continue to practice medicine?"

Kee doubted it, but who could tell.

The man he had idolized was a psychopath, Kee thought. No remorse. No empathy. Just a strong sense of entitlement and self-preservation.

Kee backed away. He had his answers. Dr. Hauser played God. And if Kee were honest with himself, he'd admit that the power to cheat death, the skill to repair broken bodies and the knowledge to heal the sick could mix into a heady cocktail. The command and the respect that he had accepted as his due could lead a man to delusions of greatness. Kee could see it, the small step from mortal to divine. The fact that Kee could see it so clearly frightened him almost as much as Dr. Hauser.

"Tell me when they want me to bring you, Kee. And be assured that I would never give you up. You're like a second son to me. We'll get them back, if that's the price, and I'll be retired like some used-up old racehorse. But you'll be here. I pass my torch to you and you will carry it forward. Won't you, my boy?"

"That's enough, Hector."

Kee startled at the sound of the familiar voice. Chief Tinnin stood in the corridor before the cell, leaning indolently against one of the walls. His timely arrival had prevented Kee from answering. Kee suspected that wasn't accidental. The chief would not want him to say or do anything that might cause Hauser to betray Kee. Expecting his protégé to continue his work was a powerful incentive to see that Kee survived.

He lifted a hand and motioned to Kee. "Time's up."

Kee was happy to exit, relieved in fact. But he did not think he'd ever forget Hauser's twinkling eyes and delighted expression.

"He's insane," whispered Kee to Tinnin.

Tinnin righted his crutches and fell in beside Kee.

"He's not. He knew exactly what he was doing. Granted, he didn't think he'd get caught. But if he's crazy, he can't stand trial."

"If he's in witness protection, he won't be tried, either."

Tinnin's mouth twisted into a snarl. "Hell of a choice. Either I let him go and maybe get our captives back or I lock him up and maybe never see any one of them again. Glad it's not my choice."

"There's another possibility," said Kee.

"What's that?"

"They send us and none of us come back."

Chapter Twenty

The night had passed with Kee getting very little sleep as preparations continued for the rescue and recovery mission. He did not like the word *recovery* because he knew what it meant. Recovery was what you did to a body. It told him exactly how dangerous the FBI considered this mission. He glanced at the clock that showed it was just after 5 a.m. now. He folded his arms across his chest and closed his eyes, trying to rest. Trying to prepare.

Every minute of preparation was another minute that Ava was a captive. When Agent Luke Forrest came to get him just after six, Kee was already wrung out and exhausted.

"We're ready for you," said Forrest.

The operation was explained to him quickly but in great detail. The support force would stay out of sight until Kee made a visual identification of at least one of the girls. Then they would take the house, at which time Kee was to get on the ground and stay there until the house was secure. He was given two pieces of safety equipment, a small communication device that allowed the FBI to hear everything and a small body camera in the bolo that Kee would be wearing as he entered the house.

What they did not give him worried him almost as much as what they did give him. They did not give him body armor or a weapon.

"Departure in twenty minutes. You have to be ready," said Forrest.

"I will be."

Kee carried the medical bag that had been provided by the FBI for this mission. Hauser would be carrying his usual bag and usual supplies.

His mobile rang and he saw it was Ty. Kee took the call.

"You ready for this?" asked Ty.

"No." Kee did not ask how Ty knew they were preparing an operation or where he was.

"Well, I'd be worried if you were. They give you a weapon?"

"Other than my reflex hammer? No."

"You want one?"

"I'd probably just shoot myself in my bad leg. I'm not a warrior like you, Ty."

"You're not like me. But you *are* a warrior."

Kee loosened the bolo at his throat and then remembered the camera and wondered if it was on. "Ty, I never even completed the warrior training."

While the people of his tribe celebrated the sunrise ceremony for the girls, the boys underwent a rigorous form of physical training, religious education, ceremony and vision quest. Ty had completed all with ease. But Kee, still in a cast, had been able to only watch the physical training that included wrestling and defense tactics. He understood things in principle but he had never spent three days alone in the White Mountains with only a knife, as Ty and the other boys had done. He had been deemed unable to complete the arduous journey from boy to man. And no matter how much education and how many letters he managed to tack on after his name he always felt lacking for this failure.

"You don't learn things just by doing them. You remember how to do a single leg takedown?"

Kee nodded. "In theory."

"You'll do fine. I'll be close."

"What? They're letting you come along?"

KEE HEARD TY exhale into his phone's receiver, making a sound of pure incredulity. "No. But I'll be there just the same."

"Does Tinnin know?"

Kee looked to the closed door. They'd be coming for him in a moment.

"Don't trust Hauser," his brother insisted.

"I won't."

The knock on the door made Kee jump. He opened the door to find Agent Forrest in the hall. Kee held the phone to his side, Ty still on the other end of the call, he hoped.

"Hauser just received word from the Russians. We now have the address and our teams are moving into position. Kee, we need to go." He turned and walked away.

Kee lifted the phone to his ear. "Gotta go. You'll explain things to Mom? I mean, if it comes to that."

"It won't come to that. Still time to drop out."

He didn't say it with any sort of judgment. But Kee knew the underlying message. Ty did not think he was prepared for this.

"I'm going to get Ava."

AVA SAT WITH Louisa on the single mattress. Beyond the locked door, Ava heard the occasional bang of cupboard doors closing.

"That means they are making our meal." Louisa hugged her knees to her chest and rocked slowly back and forth in a gesture Ava recognized as self-comforting.

Ava judged the time based on the amount of light that came through the closed curtains and bars that barricaded the windows, deciding it was Monday morning. According to Louisa, the guards came twice a day to deliver food.

The meals were exceedingly healthy and included pills that Louisa believed to be some sort of One A Day but Ava recognized as neonatal vitamins and iron tablets.

They spoke to them in Russian, which Louisa was beginning to understand. She explained to Ava that they were expected to clean their own bathroom. The towels and their dresses were changed once a week.

The conditions here were much better than the ones described by Kacey Doka. Kacey had spent several months locked in the basement of a house with several other girls sleeping on mattresses with only a thin blanket. Their bathroom facilities had consisted of a toilet and sink.

Louisa now understood how Ava had come to be a fellow captive. She knew that Ava had been mistaken for Heather Cosay and that her survival depended on Louisa making them believe that Ava was Heather. But Ava worried about how long it would take Churkin to report that his target, Ava Hood, had vanished on the same day and at the same time as they had taken Heather. If they put the pieces together before the FBI found her, Ava knew what would happen.

She thought about Kee and wondered if he had missed her yet. She thought of all the things she should have said to him and regretted the time she had kept him in the dark. She had not known him then. But now she did and all regrets centered around Kee Redhorse. Things she would do differently and things she'd never said. Most of all she thought of the time with him that she'd squandered.

"How long until they find us, Heather?" asked Louisa.

She had her fingers in her mouth again after already tearing her cuticles to bloody ribbons. Each fingernail was a short, blunt ragged stub. Ava laid a hand on Louisa's wrist and Louisa dropped her arms back to her knees, slowly returning to the less harmful rocking.

In the time they had been locked together here, Louisa

had told Ava some disturbing things about Sara. According to Louisa, Sara drank much more and much more often than even Ava had suspected. Louisa had been driving the family car since she was thirteen because her mother was often too drunk to do so. All of this information only made Ava more determined to survive this situation. Her nieces needed her, far more than she had suspected.

Her first indication that something different was happening was when the voices switched to English. Louisa tensed.

"That's the doctor," said Louisa.

"What doctor?"

"Dr. Hauser. He's been here already to check me. He must be here to check you. Aunt Ava, he'll know. They check your urine. He'll know that you're not pregnant." Louisa was clutching Ava's arm and tugging at her as if in an attempt to flee or hide.

Neither was possible. If this were Dr. Hauser, he would recognize Ava instantly. Ava watched the door, knowing that when it opened her life would end.

Her heart accelerated, beating in a useless staccato in her chest. Her ears buzzed and her skin tingled. Blood pumped, readying her muscles to fight. Time seemed to stretch out to eternity as footfalls in the hall grew nearer and nearer. The key slipped into the lock and the tumblers turned with a deafening clack. She heard the combination lock's dial spin and the bolt release. A moment later the door opened and in stepped Alexie, one of her two captors. He moved aside and she saw the man behind him, expecting either her second captor, Stenka, or Dr. Hauser. Instead she blinked in amazement, meeting the gaze of Dr. Kee Redhorse.

KEE READ THE shock in Ava's expression. Did she think she was betrayed? He stared at her big beautiful dark eyes as relief flooded him and he prayed she would not blow his cover. Her mouth dropped open and then snapped shut. Her eyes flicked from him to Dr. Hauser standing at his side.

On arrival, Hauser had introduced Kee to Alexie and Stenka. The men had given him the once-over and checked his bag but they had not frisked him as the FBI had anticipated. Once Stenka handed over his bag, Kee looped the strap over one shoulder and across his chest. Then Alexie had escorted them down the hall that Kee assumed led to the bedrooms. Kee followed and Hauser trailed behind. He glanced back, wondering if Hauser would run or give him up. But he had just cast Kee a wide, pleasant smile and continued along.

Kee didn't understand it. They had lost sight of their backup. Hauser had a very good chance of escaping. Why didn't he take it? Was his deal for relocation really a better option?

Alexie had opened the door and preceded them inside. He now stood with one hand upon his Taser, facing Louisa and Ava.

"They don't use weapons around the girls," said Hauser. "Too much chance of harming the fetus."

Kee nodded his understanding; he thought the charge of a Taser would certainly not be good for a fetus.

How far behind them were the agents? They had had a problem, one that he did not know if the agents had anticipated. The house where he and Hector had met Alexie, and where the FBI might have expected to find the missing girls, had been only their first stop. Kee and Hauser had then been rapidly transported through the house to the dock behind it, loaded into a speedboat and jetted to the opposite side of Antelope Lake back toward Red Rock Dam and below the Turquoise Canyon reservation land. There Kee and Hauser left the boat to be escorted up the dock to a lake house. In other words, he thought he was on his own.

All the men paused inside the living area that faced the lake. Their escorts watched the water, Kee suspected, for signs of pursuit.

"So," said Hauser, lifting his splinted hand that was supposed to be broken. "We'll just check the one today, I think."

With that he turned and walked toward the hall. At Kee's hesitation, Alexie pointed after Hauser.

"Exam room is there." His accent made the word *is* sound like he said, "ez." He motioned Kee away. "I bring her."

Hauser stepped into the room across the hall. Kee followed, glancing around. In the center of the room sat the short exam table complete with stirrups. The only other piece of furniture was a card table upon which lay the normal equipment used for a pelvic exam, set out on a white towel. Not sterile, Kee decided. It didn't matter, because he was not going to be performing an exam on Ava and neither was Hauser. Kee looked at the medical equipment again with a new eye as he searched for a weapon. If it came to a fight, which side would his mentor choose?

Alexie appeared a moment later, hustling Ava along by the upper arm. Her hands were now fixed before her with a half-inch-thick white zip tie. He did not wait for Ava to climb onto the table but hoisted her up. She scanned the room, taking in her surroundings in a glance. Then she met his gaze and lifted a brow.

"So, give her the check out." His thick Russian accent turned the word *give* into *geeve* and made his *k*'s hard. He probably meant checkup or examination but Kee did not ask for clarification. Alexie left Ava, passing Kee and then coming to a stop just behind him. He folded his arms and glared.

Kee hesitated. Was Alexie going to remain right there, blocking the doorway, standing between them and the hallway?

Where was the FBI? Wherever their staging area, as they had called it, he was afraid it was on the opposite side of the lake. Plus anyone coming by boat would be easily spotted by the second man in the living area. From his position at the kitchen counter, the guard could see both the front and back entrances to the lake house.

The FBI had given him one weapon: pepper spray.

He was out of time. But there was no sound of the front door collapsing or a shout of warning from the kitchen.

Kee looked to Ava and noted that her fingers curled around one of the stirrups, gripping it with white knuckles in both bound hands. Kee stepped between her and Alexie and rummaged in his bag as he retrieved the pepper spray.

Hauser was speaking to Alexie. "I'm going to need a place to wash my hands. I also need rubbing alcohol, which I do not see here."

From somewhere beyond the house, Kee heard a familiar roar and recognized the sound of a Harley Davidson motorcycle.

Stenka shouted from the kitchen.

"There is a motorcycle guy in the drive. Looks Indian."

Ty, thought Kee. His brother had found them before the FBI. It was backup.

Alexie turned toward the hall, reaching for his gun. "Go check it out."

Kee lifted the pepper spray bottle in his sweating hand and pointed it at Alexie. But at that moment the Russian turned and his hand shot out, slapping the aerosol from Kee.

Alexie drew his pistol with surprising speed.

"No!" shouted Hauser.

Hauser lifted both hands and stepped between Kee and

Alexie as the latter fired. Hauser doubled over, clutching his middle.

Something in Kee's mind snapped. He stopped thinking and acted. The Russian outweighed him by at least fifty pounds but when Alexie aimed, Kee sidestepped, grasped his wrist and directed the second bullet down to the hardwood flooring. Then he ducked and pivoted, performing the moves he had watched each young man practice again and again in the training he had never been able to complete. Ty had been right. He knew these moves and how to do them. An instant later, Kee had Alexie's hand behind his back and pulled until he heard the cartilage crunch and the joint pop. Alexie's shout of pain was punctuated by the clatter of his pistol striking the ground.

Ava was off the table in the blink of an eye and struck the goon a hard blow to the back of the head. This caused him to roar as he leaped to his feet, shoving Ava so hard into the examination table that both Ava and the table skittered backward, impacting the wall beneath the barred window.

From the outer room came the crash of a window shattering and then the pop of gunfire.

The Russian took a step toward Ava, reaching to retrieve his gun. This time Kee dropped to one strong leg and swept the other from his opponent's back to front, striking him just behind the knees. The mobster's legs buckled and he fell on his back.

Ava recovered Alexie's weapon and shot the Russian three times in the chest. Then she was out the door and struggling with the combination lock that imprisoned Louisa across the hall. Another shot broke the lock open. But the door remained bolted. Kee turned to Hauser, finding dark blood welling between the fingers he clutched to his abdomen.

He looped an arm around Hauser and tried to drag him to his feet. Hauser's eyes popped open.

"No, no. Leave me be. Send help if you can."

Kee lowered him back to his seat and nodded solemnly. "I will."

Hauser smiled and a bright red line of viscous blood dripped from his lips down his chin.

"Proud of you, son."

Kee knew there was nothing in his bag that would stop internal hemorrhage.

He followed Ava as Alexie sat up and shook his head. Kee ran for the door just as his attacker came to his feet. Kee got the door closed an instant before the gangster collided with the solid wooden panel. The vibrations of the impact traveled from Kee's fingertips to his chest. Ava threw the deadbolt, trapping the Russian inside with Hauser. It was only a moment before the pounding began.

"You shot him," said Kee.

"Body armor," she said. "That door won't hold." She raised the pistol and aimed at the door.

"Kee!" The shout came from the kitchen.

He recognized Ty's voice.

"Down here!"

Ty rounded the corner, his opposite hand on his bleeding shoulder. He skidded to a halt, facing Ava's raised pistol.

Chapter Twenty-One

Kee stepped between them, hand raised to Ava.

"How many?" asked Ty.

"One," answered Ava. "In there." She motioned with her head and kept her gun raised. "The other?"

"Down. Kitchen," said Ty.

"His gun?" she asked.

"Threw it out the window."

"Are you armed," she asked.

"I don't carry guns," said Ty.

Ava kept the pistol before her and ready as Alexie thudded against the door beside her.

"Louisa," said Kee. Without thought he bent his knee, lifted his leg, the leg that he had favored since well before the multiple surgeries evened his limbs, and, with all his might, kicked the door imprisoning Louisa.

"No," shouted Ty. But as the screws holding the latch gave way and the wood frame splintered, his objections died. The latch pulled away from its anchors and the door crashed inward.

Kee glanced back at Ty to see him blinking back at him with his mouth gaping.

Ava reached her hand to Louisa. "Come!"

They ran toward the center of the house. Another crash sounded behind the opposite bedroom door. Kee knew that Alexie would break the solid wooden frame eventually.

Ava and Louisa raced past Ty and toward the kitchen. But Ty called to them.

"Boat! It can hold us all."

"Keys?" asked Ava.

"Not sure."

Ava turned toward the back of the house, dragging Louisa out of sight.

Kee heard a door slide on its track as he cleared the hall and raced past Ty. He glanced toward the kitchen. Stenka lay, facedown and motionless, amid the shards of glass that littered the kitchen floor. Beside him sat the remains of a large terra-cotta pot in jagged ruin surrounded by the dirt, rock and ejected cactus. Ava ducked down beside the living room wall and fired, pinning Alexie as the others raced toward the boat. Alexie returned fire and Ava continued the exchange until the clip emptied. Then she followed the retreating group.

Kee thundered across the deck after Louisa, his medical bag thumping against his side with each stride. By the time he reached the stairs, Louisa had reached the dock that stretched out over the placid blue lake water toward the boat. Ava appeared on the stairs. He ushered her past him and then followed. Ty, already in the boat, spotted the all-important detail, ignition key on a floating keychain in the ignition.

"Keys!" he called back over his shoulder.

Ava ordered Louisa into the boat, shouting instructions as she released the bowline. Kee darted down the stairs to the lake and onto the dock, where he released the stern line as Ty hopped into the captain's seat. It was a small, single outboard engine boat of perhaps twenty feet in length, painted white with blue trim. The four seats bisected the center of the compartment and were situated back-to-back, with the rear seats facing the engine. Louisa sat on the floor, pressed against the far side of the fiberglass hull, both arms outstretched and braced against the empty seat before her.

Ava jumped onto the bow, scrambled over the windshield and into the seat beside Ty at the same time Kee jumped into the boat next to Louisa.

"You're bleeding," said Ava to Ty. "Let me drive."

"You know how?" he asked as he turned over the engine.

"Yes."

He stepped back, switching places, and plunked down in the empty front seat vacated by Ava.

Kee took in the amount of blood soaking Ty's shirt, really seeing it for the first time. Ty's shirt was torn and he held his hand pressed to his shoulder.

"What happened?" asked Kee.

Ava engaged the throttle and they rocketed away from the deck.

"Cut my shoulder on the glass coming through the window."

"Didn't you throw the cactus first?" Kee had to shout to be heard over the engine.

"Happened when I hit the floor. Rolled on it? Don't know." He glanced back the way they had come. Ty pointed. "Gun!"

Kee looked but Ava did not. Instead she turned the wheel sharply, tossing both Kee and Ty to the deck. If either had been standing, they'd be swimming right now.

Louisa closed her eyes and held tight. Kee could not hear the gunfire. But he saw something spark off the engine and spotted the hole in the stern where a bullet had torn through the fiberglass hull.

Ava swerved again, tossing them in the opposite direction as they put distance between them and their attacker. Only when they were at the opposite shore and speeding back down the long narrow lake did Kee lift his head. He could see a man on a dock, Alexie, far away and growing smaller. He watched him turn back toward the house and raise his arm, pointing the pistol. The last thing Kee saw was the FBI swarming down the dock as the Russian's body jerked and fell backward into the lake.

Kee turned to his kit, retrieving scissors to cut away

the sleeve of Ty's shirt and get a look at the gash. It was six inches long, jagged and shallow, the bleeding coming from injured capillaries.

Ava straightened her course and shouted back for a phone. Ty slipped one from his pocket, unlocked it and turned it over.

Kee cleaned the laceration under the silent, watchful stare of Louisa. He used Steri-Strips to close the wound. He had the gauze pads in place and was winding an Ace bandage in a figure eight around Ty's shoulder and chest to keep his handiwork in place when it hit him.

"We wouldn't have made it without you," said Kee to his brother.

Ty smiled.

"How did you find us?" Kee asked.

Ty's smile turned grim. "FBI has their sources. I have mine."

"What did it cost you?" said Kee. The Wolf Posse did not give away information for free. He knew that much.

Ty shrugged and then flinched. "A little more than it cost to get Jake his baby."

Kee blinked in shock. He'd helped Jake and Colt and now Kee. And it had cost him. Just what exactly, Kee didn't know.

"Faras?" asked Kee. He knew the head of the Wolf Posse well, as they had been classmates. Two sides of the same coin. Kee had been smart and physically weak. Faras had been smart and athletic. Faras had been recruited. They had not wanted Kee. He'd been angry about it at the time because he never got the free sneakers or money that they'd given Faras.

Ty nodded. "Faras wants me back."

"You weren't back before?" asked Kee.

Ty gave a shake of his head. "Just fixed the cars. Then, after Jake, I had to agree to drive the Russian, if he needed me. Which he didn't. Now..."

Kee's heart sank. It wasn't fair. Ty was a good man.

But once you were in the Wolf Posse, it was almost impossible to get out.

Kee's being looked over had been a blessing.

Ava called from the front of the boat. "Does he need medical treatment?"

They answered simultaneously and oppositely.

"Yes," said Kee.

"No," said Ty.

Ava called back. "Forrest wants me to put in at the marina at the north end."

Kee saw the panic on Ty's face. He had not been afraid to throw himself through a plate-glass window or shoot a Russian mobster but the idea of facing Forrest drained the color from his face.

And then Kee remembered Forrest's promise to arrest Ty and charge him with kidnapping if he set foot off the reservation.

"South end!" shouted Kee.

"What?"

"We have to get as close as we can to Red Rock Dam." He moved to stand beside her as she looked up at him.

"Why?"

"It's only a few miles from my reservation. Just up past the dam and it's our sovereign land."

Ava's eyes widened and she glanced back at Ty, his shirt torn and his shoulder bandaged. Then her attention shifted to Louisa, who huddled on the floor of the boat, knees clutched to her chest with a glazed expression like a combat veteran.

"I'll see to Louisa. But you have to get Ty away from Forrest."

Ava hesitated, hands tight on the steering wheel, the phone pressed between her left hand and the wheel.

"Ava, please."

She turned the wheel.

"I'll tell Forrest where we were and that Hauser is shot."

"They're already there. I saw them shoot Alexie."

Ava set her jaw. "That means they will see us go by."

They buzzed over the water and past the house where they had kept Louisa and Ava, where several agents stood on the dock.

Ava lifted the phone.

"Yes, that's us." She lifted the phone and spoke to Kee. "We've been spotted going the wrong way." Then she spoke back into the phone. "All right. Yes. Just got turned around. Heading back." She disconnected and tossed the phone on the seat beside her as she continued on.

Ty sat in the seat nearest Louisa. The phone winked on with an unknown number. Kee was certain it was Forrest but neither he nor Ava moved to pick it up.

It was twenty long minutes before they reached the river that led to the dam. The force of the water made maneuvering more difficult, but Ava still managed another mile. Kee had rummaged in the boat storage and found a fishing knife and first-aid kit but no water.

They put in on the eastern end of the lake, which was still some thirty miles through rough wooded territory to the rez. There were no roads on that side of the river until you reached their reservation. That might play in Ty's favor.

"See you for supper at Ma's," said Ty.

Kee hugged him on his good side. "Thank you for everything."

Ty removed his boots and went over the side and sloshed through the water to the shore, carrying his boots in one hand. Ava put them in reverse and then turned them back on course. Kee watched his brother climb the bank. He was heading toward the woods when he lost sight of him.

"Think he'll make it?" he asked Ava.

Her reply was a baleful look. She did not. But then, she did not know his brother.

Chapter Twenty-Two

Ava's return to the reservation was less triumphant than she'd imagined. Louisa had been transported to Darabee Hospital, where she was recovering from dehydration, the trauma of her captivity and the discovery that she was pregnant. Ava had left Louisa only to call to check on Olivia, Margarita and Alexandra, who were staying with Chief Tinnin's family for their protection and until other arrangements could be made. Sara was still in tribal jail after her DUI, and chances of her being released did not look good. Fortunately, Chief Tinnin's wife was a lovely woman who had raised up one son and had one left at home. This boy, now sixteen, had apparently come in contact with the woman who had made initial scouting missions to the dam above their reservation for the eco-extremists prior to the attack. His description of the woman had helped bring her to justice.

Dr. Hauser had not survived the gunshot wound to his abdomen and had gotten off easily, in Ava's mind. Betty Mills had broken her plea deal by failing to reveal that Yury Churkin had been sent to kill Ava and so would stand trial. Chief Tinnin believed it highly likely that the tribal council would turn her over to federal authorities.

Yury Churkin had not been apprehended and Ty Red-horse had not returned to the rez. Because Churkin was still at large, Ava had round-the-clock protection from either Officer Jake Redhorse, Officer Dan Wetselline or Sergeant Harold Shay.

Most troubling of all were the missing. Ava had thought that all the Turquoise Reservation kidnap victims would be in one facility. But Marta Garcia, Brenda Espinoza and Maggie Kesselman were still among the missing.

That troubled her far more than the voice mail message from her boss telling her that she needed to report to Human Resources for her severance interview.

There had been no word on Ty from anyone. She had reported everything that had happened and both the tribal police and the FBI were searching for Ty Redhorse. It was a footrace with both sides competing for the rabbit. She hoped he made it home because federal prison did not seem a just reward for Ty's efforts to rescue his brother. On the kidnapping charge, she had limited information but reserved judgment against him.

Kee had not spoken to her since her return to tribal police a few days ago.

Ava reported to Chief Tinnin at 9 a.m. on Wednesday morning, as he requested. She expected to be escorted off the reservation but she was not going anywhere as long as her nieces were destined for foster care. She had not come here to assume her sister's place as mother to her children, but it was clear someone needed to do so and she was the logical choice. Ava still held hopes that Sara's current situation would bring her to her senses. Her sister's grief at her husband's passing had changed her.

Ava walked the now-familiar route through the tribal headquarters to the police station. She was greeted by Carol Dorset. The veteran dispatcher for the tribe was rubbing lotion into an arthritic knuckle on her index finger. Her hair was pulled back in a simple clip and her lipstick today was a frosted pink.

She smiled brightly, showing the sort of even rows of teeth never created by nature. "He's expecting you."

Ava showed herself across the squad room, past Officer Wetselline, who was on the phone but nodded as she headed by.

Tinnin had the phone cradled between his chin and shoulder, and was absently spinning the rowel of his spur with one hand as he listened to the caller. When he spotted her, he lowered the spur to the desk and then waved her in. She took one of the battered wooden chairs before his cluttered desk.

"All right. Yes, ma'am. I'll send someone out." He returned the handset to the cradle and called to Wetselline. "Go check on Mrs. Alba out on Dustin Road. Her daughter, down in Tucson, can't reach her on the phone."

Wetselline, now on the computer, gave a two-finger salute and headed out.

Tinnin turned his attention on her.

"How is Louisa?"

"She's talking now and she's seen a counselor. I think she'll be all right in time."

"That's good news." Tinnin used his index finger to push the spur to a spot just under the desk lamp. "I heard from Agent Forrest regarding Yury Churkin. They picked him up in Flagstaff. He's in federal custody."

"Great news," she said.

"Yeah. I asked for notification if they get a match between his DNA and the sample from Day's body." Tinnin met her gaze. "That also means you don't need tribal protection any longer."

"Also good news."

The chief tapped his fingers on his desk.

"Anything else?" she asked.

"I hear you got fired."

She nodded slowly. Tinnin had many good qualities,

but like many law enforcement officers, tact was not one of them.

"Yes. I'll be heading down to my rez to turn in my badge and gear just as soon as I can."

"So you're a trained police officer who made detective and who will not be getting a glowing reference from your former employer."

"That's about it."

"Well, I wouldn't put you in a squad car, either. Too much chance of getting sued."

She sat back, arms folded. She didn't need to hear she'd screwed up. She knew it and in her mind it was worth the price. She'd do it again.

"Not sorry, are you?"

"Not a bit."

Tinnin's mouth quirked. "Well, such decisions carry a price. Glad to see you're willing to pay it. I do hate a whiner. So, to the reason I asked you to come in. You see that woman out there?" He lifted his chin toward the dispatch station.

Ava spun and looked at Carol Dorset, headset in place, speaking on the phone to a caller.

"Yes."

"They built this building around her. Carol came in when they added a telephone up here. She was the dispatcher when we didn't even have a title for that job. Her father was our first officer back in the 1920s. Worked under the State Parks Department and he hired me in 1978. Anyway, she's closer to eighty than seventy and she says she just can't sit for eight hours anymore. She's fixing to up and leave me, just like that, after only fifty-three years."

He had her attention.

"So it seems to me that you are overqualified for dispatch but unlikely to get anything better. Also, you might be feeling the need to be here for your nieces. Now, my wife is a good woman, but that three-year-old is likely to kill her."

Ava smiled. Olivia was a challenge.

"Might be able to convince her to babysit after school until you get home from work, though."

"Olivia isn't old enough for school yet."

"But she's getting older every day. Two years will go by just like that." He snapped his fingers. "And as my sons are not likely to bring us grandchildren for a few years. Or, they had better not. My wife needs a project. Olivia is all that." The next part he said under his breath. "Might just keep her from dragging home another stray dog. We have five now and they shed all over everything."

Ava laughed. The girls would love dogs.

"So what do you say?"

"What's the pay?"

He told her and she was glad she was sitting down. "I'd need a raise."

"I'll speak to the tribal council. Might want to join the volunteer fire department, too. They get called on some of our cases."

"You're trying to get a detective at a dispatch salary?"

Tinnin smiled. "I see you will not disappoint me. So, will you take it?"

She thought of Kee and frowned. Seeing him would be painful.

"What's the holdup?" asked Tinnin.

"I'm not sure Kee Redhorse would like me here permanently."

"Why's that?"

"He hasn't been to see me since we were interviewed by the FBI."

Tinnin sat back in his chair and stared, his head cocked to one side. "And you take that as a sign of disinterest. That about it?"

"Yes, sir."

"Well, let me enlighten you. Kee Redhorse is now the only trained physician on the reservation since that shit Hauser has been fitted for a pine box. Don't expect many mourners at the funeral. Feel sorry for the widow. Always do."

Ava drew him back on point. "Kee Redhorse?"

"Oh, yeah. Kee. He's been working twenty-four seven at the clinic. Delivering babies at three in the morning. Treating falls and sickness and everything in between. I heard from Jake that he fell asleep in a birthing room and they had to wake him up for that motor vehicle accident with multiple vics. Long story short, your boy hasn't had time to take a piss, let alone see his girl. And you are his girl, aren't you?"

Ava pressed her hands to her face. She should have known. Even if Kée did plan to never see her again, he would certainly have told her face-to-face. He was just that kind of man. The sort that did things the right way and gave everything and everyone his best. He was the man she knew she could rely on to help her and support her decisions, but she just didn't know if his feelings for her tipped all the way to love. She didn't know which frightened her more: discovering he would have nothing to do with her or discovering that she had misread the situation. There was still hope. Hope that her love might be shared and there was still the possibility that he would tell her that he did not want what she wanted...to spend the rest of her life loving him.

"I've seen you in action," said Tinnin. "So don't you try and convince me you don't have the spine to go and tell that boy you love him."

She lowered her hands and met his intent stare.

"Is it that obvious?"

"To one who has been there, it sure is. I carried my wife's engagement ring around with me for two months."

"How did you get the courage to finally ask her?"

He flushed. "Let's just say she frisked me and found the box."

Ava laughed. He rose and she got to her feet, too.

"So you got a job. You got your sister's house for the foreseeable future. Seems like only one thing's missing." He motioned toward the door. "Go get him."

Chapter Twenty-Three

Kee dragged himself home at midnight Wednesday night, after another sixteen-hour day. He had still not heard from Ty and that troubled him. If the FBI had him, Tinnin would have been notified and Kee had asked the chief to let him know if he heard anything. The chief had word out to the force to look for him and he knew that his brother Jake had left the reservation land to search for him using Hemi, Ty's dog. What did Hemi think, tracking her master?

Jake said it was as if Ty had disappeared and that meant federal custody to Kee.

The house was quiet and he was greeted by only his mother's tabby cat upon entrance. The feline sat in the dark, green eyes glowing and tail wrapped around her front feet. She rose and sauntered out the door without a backward glance. Kee locked up behind her. In the bathroom, he found an explosion of makeup and hair things as the Doka girls continued to expand their territory. He felt like a stranger in his childhood home. He showered with pink soap and shampoo from a pink bottle containing shea butter and coconut. He had to keep one hand on the tile wall in the shower to keep from swaying with fatigue and when he left the bath, with a towel wrapped around his middle, he was followed by the fragrance of coconut. He barely remembered hitting the sofa and woke to the sounds of his mother in the kitchen and the loud, somewhat frantic conversations of the Doka girls preparing to make the bus.

"Long walk," said his mother. She'd made the same threat to each of them, and Colt, Jake and Ty had missed the bus on more than one occasion, discovering their mom did not make idle threats. Abbie had never missed, and he had not, either. He very much doubted that his mother would let young girls walk to school after the disappearances. Things had changed here, and not for the better.

He rolled to his back. Had there been signs that he had missed? Had he been so tied up in his residency and with treating his patients that he had let this happen right under his nose?

His mother appeared in the doorway. "Clinic called."

Kee threw his arm across his eyes and groaned. They didn't officially open for three hours but there had to be something up.

"Auto accident?" he guessed.

"Baby coming," said his mother. "Not urgent but hurry up anyways. Lori is holding down the fort until you get there."

Kee retrieved his phone and saw a missed call from the clinic and no messages.

"Coffee?" asked his mother.

Kee swung his feet to the carpet and nodded. "Do I have time for breakfast?"

"Depends on that baby, I suppose." She reversed course and returned with a piping hot piece of fry bread sprinkled with cinnamon and sugar and his coffee. "Don't even tell me that my fry bread is unhealthy. You're losing weight again. So eat."

He did. When he finished he found the cat staring at him again. She looked disappointed.

"Maybe you should call Ava," he said to himself.

He grabbed his phone and truck keys, then kissed his mother's cheek before heading out.

When he reached the women's health center he checked their one patient who was in active labor. He was there in time to see the baby boy come into the world and sign the paperwork, but his sister-in-law didn't really need his help. She really needed to finish her midwife training. She was so good at this.

When he left the delivery room it was to find Ava waiting in the hall.

"Ava! I was just thinking about you."

Her smile was crooked and only on half her mouth. "Likewise."

"Ah, come on into the break room." He led the way. With each step he grew more and more nervous because he knew he had to tell her. He had to tell the woman who had told him she preferred her solitude and valued her privacy that he wanted her to give up both for him.

Once inside the break room, Kee found himself breathing fast. Judging from the dizziness, he thought his blood pressure was spiking.

"So, how are you?" he asked by way of a clumsy icebreaker.

"Fired." She explained about losing her position and how Louisa was doing and that her sister was now locked up. He'd heard about her sister. It was a one-car accident, thank goodness.

"I'm sorry about your sister."

"Me, too. I'm taking the girls."

His heart sunk. "Taking them where?" He couldn't leave the clinic now. Not with Dr. Hauser's death. It would take time to bring another professional here, especially with the scandal hanging over them.

"Oh, I mean I'm taking custody of them."

He blew away a long breath and nodded, hands on hips.

"I think that's a good call. You can be the stability they have lacked. And I know you love them like crazy."

"Yes, I hope so."

The awkward silence closed in on him. Ava glanced toward the door. He couldn't let her leave without telling her how he felt.

"Ava, do you need some help with the girls?"

Was that really what he was asking, if she needed help? As if she'd let him live with them, marry her and be a father because it was good for the girls.

"What?" She looked confused.

Kee wiped his forehead. Knowing he was going to have to say it and take the risk. He was going to have to lay his heart out. He knew her and knew he could trust her. She wasn't interested in his position or any possible status that wedding a doctor would bring. She knew enough to know that his salary, whatever it would be, might be less than what she would've earned had she not lost her position.

"I wanted to ask you something, Ava. But I don't want it to sound as if you'd take it because you have to. You don't. I know that."

"Ask me what, Kee?"

"You don't have a job right now. So if you need help."

She lifted her hand before his face in the universal sign for stop.

"Are you offering me money?" She lifted her hand and then dropped it limply to her side as she stared up at the ceiling tiles and the fluorescent lights. "Oh, man. I completely misread you, us... I don't know." She met his gaze. All the hope drained out as her dark eyes hardened into something cold as frozen ground. "I have a job. I'm your new dispatcher. And I can raise those girls without your money."

Kee tucked his elbows in tight and rubbed the back of his neck.

"Ava, I wasn't offering money."

She flapped her arms. "What, then? You selling your truck?"

"I want to marry you."

Her pretty mouth dropped open and she gasped. Then it snapped shut and she scowled. Something in his chest blazed to life and then turned to ash. Was that his heart?

Ava met his gaze and he thought he saw something like sorrow in her eyes. The seconds dragged by with the centuries as he waited for her answer.

"I do not need you, Kee," she said.

And there it was. The rejection he had feared. How could he convince her that her self-reliance could exist inside a relationship? How could he convince her to love him?

Kee had made many rational arguments in his lifetime but there was just no way to make Ava love him with words.

"But," she said, "I also know that my life would be so much richer, not richer, *sweeter* with you by my side. I do not need you. But I want you. I want to share your days and nights and love you. And I want you to love me even when we both know I am less than perfect."

"Perfect is boring. Is that a yes?"

She slipped her arms around him. "That is an unqualified yes."

Sweet relief washed over him and he lifted his head to emit a hoot of pure joy. The laughter that bubbled from his throat had a painful quality and he realized there were tears in his eyes.

"Oh, Kee." She pressed her forehead to his.

He wrapped her up in his arms and kissed her. When he finally let her slide to the floor and drew back they were both panting and the glimmer in her eyes had changed from joyful to needy.

The desire ricocheted through him as the shock splashed

against mental images that he wanted to see with his own two eyes.

"All right, then. If either of us needs CPR afterward, we're in the right spot."

"Want to go back to my place?" she asked.

He glanced at his watch. Clinic didn't officially open for ninety minutes and Ava's sister's place was right down the road. He lifted his brows as all the weariness and the anxiety drained away, leaving nothing but anticipation.

"I'm still on call," he said.

"Oh, you're on call for me from this moment on, buster." Her wicked smile curled upward and the mischief glittering in her eyes promised that this woman would never bore and never cling.

"That's Dr. Buster, to you."

She laughed. "Whatever."

Ava wanted him for all the right reasons and her independence just made her willingness to be his wife all the sweeter.

"Right this way," she said, looping one finger with his and leading him out the door to her awaiting car. He followed and knew he would follow Ava anywhere.

* * * * *

LET'S TALK
Romance

For exclusive extracts, competitions
and special offers, find us online:

- facebook.com/millsandboon
- @millsandboonuk
- @millsandboon

Or get in touch on 0844 844 1351*

For all the latest titles coming soon, visit
millsandboon.co.uk/nextmonth